WAS OUR DOWNFALL.

Where the MOUNTAINS meet the SEA

A.R. BRECK

Where the
MOUNTAINS
meet the
SEA

CONTENT WARNING

Where the Mountains Meet the Sea contains mature themes that may be triggering to some readers. Please proceed with caution.

DISCLAIMER

This book is based off true events. Names, ages, and locations have been changed for confidentiality purposes.

And so it is, that you must go, where tall trees grow and rivers flow.
And I in turn, will go my way, where seagulls soar over a sunlit bay.
Perhaps, someday, we'll meet again, and talk of happy times.
Where salty breezes sway tall trees… and the mountains meet the sea.
- Westworld

Dedication.
To H. Your strength is inspiring.
I love you.

PLAYLIST

Home Sweet Home by Mötley Crüe
More Than a Feeling by Boston
Blowin' in the Wind by Bob Dylan
Let it Be by The Beatles
Knockin' On Heaven's Door by Bob Dylan
Moonlight Sonata by Ludwig van Beethoven
Imagine by John Lennon
I Don't Want to Miss a Thing by Aerosmith
Highway to Hell by AC/DC
Penny Lane by The Beatles
Piano Man by Billy Joel
Can't Fight This Feeling by REO Speedwagon
Für Elise by Ludwig van Beethoven
Hey Jude by The Beatles
Stairway to Heaven by Led Zeppelin
Canon in D by Johann Pachelbel
The Flower Duet by Katherine Jenkins
Keep on Loving You by REO Speedwagon
Unchained Melody by The Righteous Brothers
Time After Time by Cyndi Lauper
Fade Into You by Mazzy Star
Don't Dream It's Over by Sixpence None the Richer
The Sound of Silence by Simon and Garfunkel
One by Metallica
Take Me Home, County Roads by John Denver
Lithium by Nirvana
Lick It Up by Kiss
Beth by Kiss
I Got a Name by Jim Croce

Friend of the Devil by Grateful Dead
Wish You Were Here by Pink Floyd
Amazed by Lonestar
Freak by Silverchair
Badfish by Sublime
Wonderful Tonight by Eric Clapton
You're Still The One by Shania Twain
Wonderwall by Oasis
Love Song by Tesla
When You Say Nothing At All by Alison Krauss
Love Hurts by Nazareth
Forever and For Always by Shania Twain
Landslide by Fleetwood Mac
Linger by The Cranberries
Colorblind by Counting Crows
No One's Gonna Love You by Band of Horses
Hallelujah by Jeff Buckley
The Funeral by Band of Horses
Is There A Ghost by Band of Horses

PART
One

CHAPTER ONE

Roman

1983

There!

I leap forward, my feet slicing through the cold water of the lake. My toes melt into the grainy sand, and I curl them, feeling the roughness scrape against the soles of my feet. The small, green, plastic pail swings in my hands and knocks against my knees. The thump echoes on the quiet beach, startling the school of tadpoles swimming around my ankles.

"Ugh!" I grunt, slapping the water with the palm of my hand. The water splashes up and hits my stomach. "Stupid tadpoles." I sit back against the chipped dock, the backs of my legs warming from the heated wood. My toes kick in the water, barely breaking through the surface. The tadpoles have scattered, long gone and leaving me only with the clear blue waters of Shallow Lake.

I tilt my head up, pushing my damp brown hair from my eyes as I look at the sun. It feels hotter down at the beach, like the sun and water decided to make it almost impossible to sit here on the sand without dipping into the water.

But that's a Wisconsin summer for you.

I watch the neighbor's pontoon glide through the water, and Mr. Sorenson waves to me with his free hand, his other gripping the steering wheel. His tan fisherman's hat creates a shadow over his eyes.

Once he's out of sight around the bend, I watch the water ripple all the way to the shore, the small waves rocking the dock back and forth.

I'm bored.

My friends, Clyde, Flynn, and Lonnie are all on summer vacation. Usually, I'd be with them. We like to go to the park down the road, Tip Town. It's over on the other side of the lake and our parents let us stay there all day until the streetlights turn on. With them gone, I've got nothing to do.

I look over my shoulder at my house. The big white cabin-styled home with a two-story wrap-around porch on the second level. It's one of the biggest cabins on the lake.

A lot of people around here only stay here during the summer months, but we're one of the few families that stay here year-round.

My dad, he's the lead singer of The Ripsons. They're one of the most popular rock bands in the world right now. My dad has toured with Led Zeppelin, Black Sabbath, and AC/DC. He's touring with them now, actually, leaving my mom here by herself to watch me and my baby sister.

Momma and I have gone with him on tour before, but she always tells my dad that a tour bus is no place for a kid. I don't mind it. It's kind of fun, actually. But Momma seems to think I'm too young for whatever happens on the road.

I like the music my dad plays. I love going to his concerts and letting the drums pound against my stomach. It's so loud sometimes that it really feels like they're playing *inside* me. My ears always ring after a concert, and I have to shout afterward so I can hear my own voice.

My dad, he always looks so famous standing on the stage. I watch as everyone reaches for him, like he's the President of the United States. It's funny to think that's the same dad who tucks me in at night and who lets me climb on his back when we swim in the water.

He even lets me pretend to play on his spare drum set in the basement. I'd like to play the guitar like my dad, but my fingers aren't big enough to pull on the chords to play a tune.

Someday, I'll be a rock star just like he is.

I watch the tadpoles come back. The water is still again, no ripples in the current besides my toes trailing along the surface. I dip my foot under the water, and they swim curiously around my ankle. One of them brushes against my skin.

I wipe my forehead with a smile.

The humidity is making my hair stick to my skin, and I want to slip into the water with the tadpoles to have a swim. They'd flee the moment I entered the water, though.

I'm so bored.

"Roman!" I glance up the hill, seeing my mom calling for me from the deck. She places her pointer finger along the line of her eyebrows, shading her eyes from the bright sun. "Roman! Meet me up front, please." She turns around and walks back inside. Her long brown hair hangs in a curly ponytail at the back of her head and swishes with every step she takes.

Her jean shorts are frayed with her striped shirt tucked beneath the waistband. She's much like my dad in the rock style department, although hers is watered down. She tries to be a good mother to me, but I can tell when she gets nervous, biting her nails on the nights my dad has a show. She wants to be with him, but I'm getting too old to be on the road all the time, so she needs to stay home with me.

Isn't that funny? I'm too young to be on the road, and I'm also too old to be on the road.

Life is funny.

My dad is much more rock, with the bell-bottom ripped jeans, the leather jackets, his long brown hair, and his metal chains. He's a rock legend, even here in our little town of Shallow Lake, Wisconsin.

I pull my feet out of the lukewarm water, making wet footprints as I stand on the dock. I walk across the beach, which is only a few feet of dried sand before it turns to grass. I do a small jump, slapping my hand on the clothesline that hangs from one side of the yard to the other. Walking up the hill, I go around the side of the house and to the front yard. Across the street is a corn field—nothing but corn for as far as I can see from all the way to the top of the hill and over the other side. Sometimes I wonder what's on the other side of that hill, but another part of me doesn't want to know. A small part of me likes the mystery.

My eyes widen when I see a huge moving truck and people out front at the next-door neighbor's house. I didn't hear all the commotion when I was out back, but I guess the tadpoles stole my attention.

The black cement burns the soles of my feet as they hit the pavement. My mom walks out the front door, the screen slapping against the frame behind her.

She's shoeless herself as she walks over to me, her feet gliding through the green grass.

"I saw the new neighbors pulled up a while ago. Thought we should go introduce ourselves. What do you say?" she asks, brushing her brown bangs away from her forehead.

I shrug. "Sure."

I don't really want to go say hi to the new neighbors. I was friends with the boy that used to live there. But their parents got a divorce and he had to move to Iowa. The small brown house next door has been vacant for the past month.

My mom places a hand on my bare shoulder, giving it a light squeeze. "Then you can come inside afterward. Your shoulders are turning pink. I can put on some more sunscreen." She ruffles my hair a bit, and my cheeks pinken.

She sure likes to embarrass me. I'm seven, almost eight, yet she still treats me like a baby sometimes.

We walk across the yard, and there's a bunch of people trudging in and out of the back of the truck, moving furniture into the house. A woman steps out of the trailer holding a box, her eyes widening when she sees us standing there.

"Oh!" She sets the box down on the edge of the trailer and slides off. "Charlie! Get over here! We have some guests." The woman brushes her hands over her flowy dress as she smiles at us. Her smile is bright, her blonde hair wavy as it brushes over her shoulders. A man steps out of the house, shoving the door open and propping it with a brown box. His bell-bottom jeans are too hot for this humid day and his white button-up shirt sits halfway unbuttoned down his chest.

My parents talk about people like these. What does she call them?

Oh, yeah.

Hippies.

"Hi, we live next door. I'm Goldie, and this here is Roman." My mom ruffles my hair again, and I want to look up at her and glare. She's taught me manners, though, so all I do is smile at the new neighbors.

The hippies.

"Oh! So lovely to meet you. My name is Jane, and this here is Charlie," the woman says, wrapping her arms around her husband's arm. "We have a little girl, too, just about your age. Where'd she go, Charlie?" She turns around, looking toward the house I know inside and out. "Luna!" Her voice is soft, unnatural in a way that shouldn't be used for yelling. Maybe for singing or humming a lullaby like my mom used to do for me at night. But yelling? *No.*

It's feels like the school of fish from down in the lake made their way into my belly and are bumping into every wall of my insides as a little girl walks outside.

My entire body freezes. My entire mind, and maybe a part of my soul, too.

Her skin is as pale as freshly fallen snow, and her hair is black like a night sky without any stars. Kind of weird-looking, if I were to be honest, but I can't take my eyes off her. Her face is round, with a dainty nose and eyes too big for her face. Her black hair matches her dad, who has stick straight hair just as dark as hers. But her eyes.

Her eyes.

They don't match her dad or her mom. Her dad has blue eyes, and her mom has a weird hazel.

Luna has gray.

No color against the whites of her eyes or the black pupils in the center. Only a pale gray.

She's wearing a blue dress that flows to her shins, with two bright yellow suns crocheted onto the sides.

I stare at her, this unusual creature that came out of nowhere. I've never seen anyone like her.

And I don't think I'll ever meet anyone like her again.

"Luna, these are the new neighbors. Roman, and his mom, Goldie," Jane says, smiling at her daughter. Her entire face brightens with her smile, like there's nothing wrong in the world.

"Hi." Luna gives me a small wave, and I stand like a big dummy in front of her. I can barely form the words on my tongue as I look at her. Her voice sounds like when my dad plays a soft song in the evenings, only plucking the strings on his acoustic guitar.

It makes the world around me freeze.

Luna stands a few inches taller than me, but that doesn't really surprise me. All the girls are weirdly tall in my grade, towering over my short frame.

"Hi." I puff my bare chest out, suddenly feeling uncomfortable in my red swim shorts and nothing else.

"You know," my mom starts, getting the tone in her voice that she usually gets when she wants to be best friends with someone, "I have a daughter, too. Her name is Nora. How old are you, Luna? You look to be about Nora's age."

"I just turned six," she says, the *x* in six coming out more like a *th*.

My mom's hands clap together. "Oh, lovely! That's the same age as Nora. Are you going into first grade this year?"

Luna nods, and I suddenly feel useless standing here as the new girl takes over my old friend's house. It feels like she's taking over my sister, too.

I clench my fists, so I don't shove her onto the grass beneath her.

"You'll be in the same grade as Nora then. Roman, here, is going into second grade. But I'm sure he'd still love to play with you. Wouldn't you, Roman? You can introduce her to Nora." My mom looks down at me, the *be nice* smile on her face.

"I guess," I grumble, kicking a small rock with my bare toe. It rolls over on its opposite side and stops.

Luna stares at me, a curious look on her face.

The parents stare at us, waiting for one of us to make a move.

Waiting for me, actually.

"Come on." I grumble, nodding my head. It feels like now I'm not only going to be dealing with my baby sister, but now I have to deal with the neighbor girl, too.

I listen to her bare feet slide through the grass as she walks behind me. Cutting through my yard, I walk toward the front door. It's only early afternoon, and the sun is at its highest point in the sky. We walk up the couple of steps onto the deck and up to the front door. I pull on the screen, the hinges squeaking with its movement.

"Wow, you have a big house," she says, her big eyes wide and wondrous as she looks around my kitchen. The gray seems to grow, swallowing up her pupils and making her look even more unusual.

My house has two levels. The upper level has a kitchen and dining room, which lead to the living room. A glass sliding door off the living room goes out back to the deck which overlooks the backyard and lake. Inside and down the hall leads to my parents' room, mine, and my sister's. Downstairs has a couple of extra rooms for guests, a living area, and a band room where my dad and his bandmates practice.

I shrug, feeling like it's not all that big, but then again, she's moving into one

24

of the smaller homes on the lake.

Nora sits on the living room floor with her Barbie dolls that she's been obsessed with. "Nora, this is the new neighbor, Luna."

Nora looks up, one hand on a small yellow brush as she combs through Barbie's hair. "Hi. Do you want to play dolls with me?"

I swallow down my groan. I am *not* playing dolls.

Luna's gray eyes swing to mine. "What are you going to do?"

I think about the tadpoles that I've been trying to catch for a week. I'm not going to do anything besides just catch them and let them go. But they're fast, and I'm getting closer with each try.

"I'm going back down to the lake."

Luna looks over her shoulder, glancing out the window and out onto the blue waters. The sunshine casts a glow through the window, lighting up her pale skin. She really is pale. Mostly compared to me. The moment the ice thaws in the spring, I'm usually outside until the first snowfall the next fall. This girl looks like she hasn't been outside a day in her life.

"Where did you come from?" I ask before the thought even clicks in my head.

"Illinois," she sighs, like there's a long story in just those eight letters. She turns her eyes toward mine. "I'd like to go down to the water. Do you want to come, Nora?" Her eyes swing to my sister.

Nora frowns. "Maybe later."

"Can I play with you later?" Luna asks her.

"Yeah." A smile stretches across Nora's lips before she looks back down and continues brushing the Barbie's hair.

Warmth hits my palms, and my fingers get tugged. My eyes widen as I look down, seeing Luna's hand in mine. Her fingers aren't laced against mine, just a simple handhold like my mom would do. But for some reason, it feels like so much more.

"Show me the lake?" Luna asks.

I nod, feeling the tadpoles in my belly again.

We leave hand in hand. Walking down the stairs, through the basement, and out the back door. The air is thick and heavy as we head toward the water and sweat is already dotting along my hairline once my feet hit the sand.

"Ouch!" Luna's hand flies out of mine as she brings them down to the soles of her feet. She hops back and forth, the hot sand burning her as she jumps from foot to foot all the way down to the water. She looks weird. "That sand is hot! Doesn't it hurt?"

My feet burn, but it's welcome against my skin. I've lived here for as long as I can remember. The heat reminds me of home. The slight fishy and beachy smell is refreshing to me instead of gross.

"Not really." I walk toward her until my feet slide into wet sand beneath the water. I curl my toes around the rocks underneath the sand, feeling as they scrape against the skin between my toes.

"You're kind of weird." She bends over and dips the tips of her fingers into the water. The hem of her dress gets wet, the blue fabric darkening to an almost black.

"I'm not weird. You're weird." I scowl at her, cupping my hand and splashing her a little. Only a little, though, because I know my mom will make my life hell if I drench the new neighbor.

But when she brings both hands to her chest, palms out, and pushes a wave of water toward me, I can only think of one thing. I dive under the water, eyes open as I watch her legs move in slow motion in an attempt to run away from me. I wrap my fingers around her skinny ankle and pull her underneath the water. She slips beneath like a piece of paper, folding and bending under the water with her pale, thin limbs.

I cut through the water until I reach the surface, laughing and rubbing the water from my face. Luna reaches the surface a second later, coughing and laughing. Her black hair looks silky as it lays down her back. I want to touch it and see if it feels as soft as it looks, but instead I turn around and go to the dock. Pressing my palms against the chipped wood, I push myself up and sit on the edge, leaving my feet to wade in the water.

Luna follows my motions, walking through the water and over to me in her sopping wet dress. She has a harder time, hopping a few times until she finally lifts herself up and sits close to me.

Really close to me.

Her wet leg brushes against my wet leg, prickling goosebumps against my flesh. I keep my head facing the lake floor but shift my eyes to hers, wondering why she would choose to sit so close to me. I don't even know her.

"My friend used to live in your house," I say, because I'm still angry about the entire situation. I never wanted my friend to move. But my mom says that's what happens when people get a divorce.

Luna looks over at me, her gray eyes trailing across my face. "I didn't want to move here."

"Why did you?" I frown at her, wishing for a moment that she could go back to where she came from.

"My dad got a job here, I guess. Something with cheese."

I nod. Wisconsin has a lot of cheese.

The silence stretches taut, the invisible string between us growing thin, the tiny threads shredding until there is barely anything left. Just as it's about to snap, whatever weird tension is building, I leap into the water and walk up to shore.

The only other time I feel that uncomfortable thickness in my chest is when my parents are yelling at me about something I did wrong.

I know Luna isn't about to yell at me, so I don't want to find out whatever it is that comes after that.

"You can go inside and play with Nora if you want," I suggest. "I'm going to catch some tadpoles."

"I like to catch tadpoles." Her voice is curious and excited as she slides off the dock and into the water. The splash is tiny, like she slipped underneath without disrupting the calm waters. She follows me up to the beach. I keep my back to her as I walk toward my pail, picking it up and walking around to the other side of the dock.

She follows.

"It's not really a girl game." I stare into the water, even though I know our most recent disturbance of the water means they are far away from here.

I just want her to go away. She's making me feel funny.

I can feel the heat of her anger burning me in the back.

"Why not? I've caught tadpoles before! I bet I can do it better than you."

I turn around and look at her. Her hands are on her hips, gripping her wet dress in her fingertips as she glares at me in outrage.

I lift my arm, pail swinging in my fingers. "Show me then. Catch a tadpole." I taunt her with my tone. Nora has never been able to even come close to catching a tadpole. It's hard for *me* to catch one.

This gangly girl in a wet dress doesn't stand a chance.

But she does.

She doesn't catch one. She catches two, and I watch her in shock until her mom calls her in for dinner. She releases the tadpoles into the water and leaves me with a smirk on her face that I bet sticks with her all the way to her house.

"I want to play with Luna," Nora says over lunch, taking another bite of her turkey sandwich.

"Go ahead." I push the potato chips around my plate. Playing with Luna is the last thing I want to do. My friends should all be coming back from their summer vacations in a couple of days, and I've been bored without them. I've been staying in my house, too much of a chicken to run into Luna again. I need my friends to help me deal with her. Until they get home, I'm going to stay inside. My toes are aching to walk on the hot sand and slip into the lake, and the weather has been perfect, but the stupid feeling of fish in my belly keep me away.

I've been watching from my living room window as Luna walks back and forth on the beach. She walks from her house to the edge of our property line, and back again. She stays close enough to the shoreline and on the wet sand, that each step she makes creates a tiny footprint. Then a wave comes, swallowing her prints and bringing them back into the water. But then she turns around and starts up her footprints across the beach all over again.

I've been watching her do this. For days.

She's bored, and every so often, I can see her looking up at my house, like she wants me to come play.

"Poor girl has been bored out there by herself, Roman. Maybe you and Nora can take her to the park," my mom says over by the sink. Her elbows are propped on the edge of the counter, her pink rubber gloves full of suds as she scrubs the dishes with her yellow sponge.

"Nora can go." My toes hang on the edge of the seat in front of me. I rock it back and forth, and it knocks against the table, shaking my glass filled with Kool-Aid.

"Knock it off, Roman." My feet thump to the floor. "You can bring Nora and Luna to the park today. I don't know why you insist on staying inside. It's summer, you should get out and enjoy it."

28

"I don't want to play with her," I grumble.

I can hear the slapping sound of my mom peeling off her gloves before she's in front of me, her curled hair in a high ponytail that's swaying as she stares at me. "What's your issue with her, Roman?"

"I don't have an issue. I just don't want to play with girls."

She laughs at me.

"I'd love to record you saying that, Roman. It won't always be this way."

My face scrunches up, my muscles groaning in protest. I don't want to like girls. I just want to play with my friends.

She walks back over to the sink. "When you're done eating, you can take your sister and Luna to the park to play."

I groan.

"No more groaning."

I swallow down the protest and stick the sandwich in my mouth. The bread sticks to the roof of my mouth and it's hard to swallow down.

Nora is the first to finish. With only breadcrumbs left on her plate, she picks it up and brings it to Mom. "I'm going to go change," she says, excitement making her bounce in place.

I guzzle down my red juice once the sandwich makes it down my throat. It feels like a brick as it hits my stomach. I sigh when I know I've wasted enough time and pick up my plate, bringing it to my mom.

Turning around, I start walking toward the front door. I'll go barefoot, in only my shorts and striped shirt. It's only a short walk down the road.

Nora comes running out a second later in a red polka-dot dress.

"Have fun, you two!" my mom shouts. Nora is already outside, running down the hill to Luna's door.

I follow her, staying behind a little and watch as Nora's small fist pounds on Luna's dark wooden door. The stained-glass on top shines in the sun, reflecting the blues, reds, and yellows against Nora's dress.

The door swings open, and there stands Luna. Her black hair looks even darker in the shadows of her home, if that's possible. A wave of sweet scents come barreling out of her house, and my nose tickles with the need to sneeze.

"Want to go to the park?" Nora asks, completely oblivious to everything in the world.

Luna stares at me, her gray eyes burning into my chest. My hand itches to rub the funny feeling out of my insides.

She's in another dress, this one yellow like the sun. It seems like every time I see her, she's in some sort of dress. She always walks along the beach in a dress, and I watch as a wave catches on the hem, darkening the fabric. It drips and gets full of sand, but she never seems to care as she continues walking back and forth along the lake.

Luna spins around, her long hair flying over her shoulder as she shouts, "Mom!'

Her mom comes out a moment later in a colorful dress. Mismatched patterns look sewn together in a long, flowing fabric that falls to her toes. She has a smile on her face when she sees us in the doorway.

"Roman! I haven't seen you in a couple of days. And this must be Nora. Your mom has told me so much about you!" Her smile lights up her face, her cheeks beaming a rosy pink. She smells like the sweet smell, and I rub my nose to stop the burning.

"They want to go to the park," she says, her voice soft and melodic, and I frown when she stops talking.

"The park? That would be fun. Are you going to the one down the street?" I nod at her.

Jane runs her fingers through Luna's hair. I wonder how soft it feels. It slides right through her fingers like water, not snarly and messy at all like Nora's gets after an hour of playing.

"If Harper goes with you, then I'm fine with it."

Luna frowns.

"Who's Harper?" I ask.

"My sister," Luna grumbles.

"I'll go ask her." Her mom walks off, the dress floating behind her as her bare feet pad across the orange carpet. Luna steps out of the house, looking at me with her sharp gray eyes piercing my brown ones.

"You haven't been outside." She sounds hurt, like we had plans and I stood her up.

I shrug. "I didn't feel like going outside."

"Yes, you did." Nora giggles, coming up beside Luna. "He looked outside every day. He watched you by the water."

Luna stares at me, and she blinks in what feels like slow motion as a flush covers my cheeks. I'm embarrassed, and I want to give Nora a snakebite on her forearm for being a tattletale.

We get stuck in a bubble as we watch each other. A slight breeze picks up and blows her black hair across her face. It's long, almost too long as it nearly reaches her waist.

The door opens, breaking our weird silent bubble with an awkward pop. Luna swipes the hair from her face, looking over her shoulder to the open door.

I glance up, seeing an older version of Luna staring at us. I swallow down the sudden lump in my throat at the sight of Harper. Her blackish hair has a slight wave to it, where Luna's is pencil straight. Harper also has blue eyes, bright blue eyes that glimmer when she steps into the sun. She looks to be around eleven. She has on blue bell-bottom jeans that flare wide at the bottoms, and a tank top. She also has a strip of some type of hand-woven rope wrapped around her head.

Just like the hippies my parents told me about.

"Hi, I'm Harper." Her voice is just as melodic as Luna's, maybe a touch raspier.

"I'm Roman, and this is my sister, Nora."

"Hi!" Nora exclaims, the shout coming from her making us all startle.

"Ready?" Harper asks Luna. Luna stares at me, and I look between the two of them.

Then I look back at Harper.

"Ready."

I gravitate toward her, this girl that's older and more experienced than me, even if it's only by a few years. It's like she's almost a woman, even though I know internally that's far from the case. She is tall, taller than Luna and taller than me.

I walk next to her, feeling the most grown up I've ever felt as I bring this new crew to the park. I'm the man of the group. It's funny, five minutes ago I didn't even want to go. Suddenly, I can't think of anything I'd rather be doing.

Nora stands on my other side, with Luna standing next to her. Nora talks to her about playing, things they want to do later, and maybe having a sleepover this coming weekend. Suddenly, Luna stops, walks behind us, and butts right in between Harper and me.

Corn fields for days line our right side. It reminds me of that movie, *The Wizard of Oz*. I always feel like there should be a tornado in those cornfields, even if tornados are relatively rare here in Wisconsin.

We're all barefoot, walking on the side of the empty road. Pebbles dig into our feet, but it doesn't bother me. I'm used to hot, rocky pavement. I only wear shoes to school or if I'm going somewhere important, otherwise I'm usually barefoot.

Harper looks at Luna with a funny, scrunched up look on her face, chuckling a bit to herself as she continues walking. I stare at Luna, and she stares at me as we continue around the bend.

Once the park, Tip Town, comes into view, Nora takes off into a sprint, running through the small rocks as she makes a beeline for the slide. Harper follows her, heading toward the monkey bars. She climbs up to sit on top of them and looks around. It seems like she's sitting on top of the world. Queen of the castle or something.

Queen of Tip Town.

"Stop that," Luna snaps, pulling on my arm.

I look down at her slender fingers gripping my skin, her nails so deeply embedded in me, my skin turns white. It hurts, but my shock overpowers everything else.

"What?" My eyes narrow at her words.

She drops her fingers. Crescent shaped nail prints are left in my skin. "Stop looking at her like that."

"Like what?"

"Like you think she's pretty. You can't like her." Her voice is small, sharp, but still soft and melodic.

My eyes blink quickly at her words. I don't like her.

I don't like girls. Girls are gross.

"I don't like her." My tone is almost angry as I growl the words at her.

She looks hurt, a little angry, too. "I can tell you do. But you can't, because you're supposed to be my friend. Not hers."

My mouth opens like a fish and I grapple at her words. *Wait, what?*

"You're my friend. You're mine." She kicks a little dust at me, then turns around and speeds off toward the swings.

You're my friend.

You're mine.

The words ring in my ears long after the dust settles.

CHAPTER TWO

Luna

I'm on the top of a cliff. I'm not sure why I'm here, or where I am exactly, but I stand over the cliff and watch the angry waves below me, roaring against the rocks below. They echo all the way up, making the crashing noisy. So noisy I feel like I'm inches from the waves. My toes curl around the side of the cliff. One wrong move and I'd plummet over the side. I take a step back because it feels like I'm too close.

Sand grates against my bare feet. It feels like a different type of sand, a little chalky, dusty. It starts raining sand, and it blows me toward the edge. There's nothing to grab on to, the wind too strong I can't even force myself to the ground. I open my mouth to scream, but my mouth fills with sand. I cough and cough against the grainy thickness filling my tongue. The wind and sand push me closer to the edge even as I try my hardest to back away from it. It rains harder, the sand making the visibility impossible.

I reach the edge once again, my bare feet scraping on the sharp corners.

And then I plummet.

I jackknife from my bed, the fall feeling so real, like I was falling in real life. The entire dream felt real, from the cliff, to the sand, to the scrape on my foot.

My foot throbs now, and I grab my foot, feeling along the sole to make sure it's not bleeding.

It's not.

I hear the water lull against the beach outside, and I shiver, wanting now more than ever to escape the water. My sheer curtains blow in the wind, and I so desperately want to go climb in between my mom and dad and snuggle with them in their own bed.

Mom says I'm too old to sleep with them, though. And nightmares are something I seem to have frequently.

But I've never had a dream like this before.

So, I stay in my bed, crying silently with my patterned quilt drying my tears.

Knock, knock.

I whimper, a scream stuck in my throat.

"Luna?" A whisper blows through my window like the wind, wrapping around my neck and trailing into my ears and belly. "It's me, Roman."

My shaky hands pull the comforter off my body. I pad across my orange carpet and to my window. His figure is barely visible in the night, but I can still see him through my sheer curtains. He has a frown on his face as he stares at me, his dark outline filled with concern.

I pull the curtain back, seeing him standing there in pajama pants, a t-shirt, and nothing else. "What're you doing here?"

"I could hear you crying all the way from my house. Where are your parents?"

"Sleeping," I grumble, wiping my eyes. My tears fight to break free, but I don't want to cry in front of Roman.

"They didn't wake up? You sounded like you were hurt." He steps forward, standing against the cracked open window. "Are you okay? What happened?"

"I just had a bad dream." I take a step back, suddenly feeling like a baby. Turning around, I walk back toward my bed. I already feel like a baby, mostly because yesterday I freaked out on him and told him he can't like my sister.

I see how he looked at her. That's how *everyone* looks at her. Like she's the most beautiful person on the planet, and I'm nothing but the leftover pieces in the cereal box. The stale ones. No one wants the leftovers.

I don't even know what came over me. I just know he needs to be my friend. It's like nothing else matters in the world. From the first moment that I saw him,

I knew that we were going to be best friends. My heart warmed and my belly ached. It sounds really weird, but I know this is where I'm supposed to be.

He might be a dumb jerk sometimes, but I just want him to like me. It's like we were supposed to meet or something.

I was so angry at my dad for taking a job in Wisconsin to make cheese, or sell cheese, or whatever he does. Before here, we lived in Illinoi; and before Illinois, we lived in Kansas. We never stay anywhere for long. It's like every time I start to settle in somewhere, make friends, and feel like I'm starting to be at home, my parents up and leave. They always say it's because of a job, but I think it's just the fact that my parents get bored easily.

When we came to Wisconsin, it was right when my friends started being my *best* friends. Every move we make across the country gets harder. It gets harder for me to find friends, and now, living in Wisconsin, I see Roman in front of me and there isn't anything more that I want than to be the best friend he's ever had.

Forever.

I turn around when I hear a squeak coming from my window, watching as Roman pushes the window up, swinging his leg inside. He presses his bare foot against my carpet as he ducks and slips into my room. "What was your dream about?" he asks, taking a step closer to me. He stares at me quizzically, like he isn't sure what to think of me.

It's hot in here, and my matching pajama set feels like wool as it scratches against my skin. We don't have air conditioning in our new house and have been using fans to get us by during the day. In Wisconsin, the summer air is filled with a dewy moisture that sticks to your skin, and at night, that dewy moisture turns cool, but it never quite goes away. The bugs come out, smelling the sweet scent of sweat on your skin. The mosquitoes leave big welts on my arms and legs, finding their way through the cracks in the old screens on the windows and buzzing a tiny humming noise around the shells of my ears.

I shrug at him, wiping the trail of sweat that drips down the back of my neck. "It was kind of weird."

His eyes brighten at this. "I like weird. Tell me."

I sit on the edge of my mattress, my toes pressing into my orange carpet as I scoot further onto the bed. Roman walks toward me, grabbing one of the two pink pillows from my bed. He drops it on the floor and plops down, lying on his back. His arms fold with his hands going beneath his head. With his eyes on mine, he crosses one ankle over the other and asks again, "Tell me."

I fold over onto my side, my heart suddenly beating quicker than it ever has before. I almost wonder if I'm sick or something. "I was on a tall hill, like a mountain. The ocean swirled below me like the water in the bath when it goes down the drain. It looked angry. It was super windy, too, like a tornado, but it was full of sand. It was in my hair and in my mouth and it hurt as it hit my skin. It pushed me over the edge."

"And then what happened?" Roman asks, his voice enthralled. Like he's listening to an action book or something,

I look up at him, noticing I've been picking at some loose threads on my quilt. "I woke up."

He blinks at me, his eyes worried but also curious. He blinks again, his vision clearing, and a fierceness lights up his eyes, the dark brown glowing around the edges. "I wouldn't let you fall."

I frown. "You weren't even there."

"I'll be there next time."

I want to burst out laughing. How could he be there? He can't come into my dreams. It doesn't make sense to me, but I don't want to ruin the moment, so instead I smile at him and roll onto my back. "Okay, Roman."

I can hear him settle down, and I tilt my gaze to his. "What're you doing?"

His brows furrow. "Going to sleep?" He poses it as a question, like I'm being stupid for even asking.

"On my floor?"

He shrugs, his shoulder brushing his ear with his movements. "I need to be here next time you're on the mountain. To keep you from falling off the cliff."

"Won't your mom get mad if she wakes up and you aren't there? My parents would call the police." It's true. My parents are pretty lax, but they've always been extra cautious about my safety, like one blink and I'll disappear.

"I'll just go back into my room before she wakes up. She stayed up late waiting for my dad to call."

"Where's your dad? At my old house, my friend's dad was in the army. Is that where your dad is? Is he in the army?" Her mom was always waiting for his phone call, and I always saw her meet the postman at her mailbox so she could see right away if she got a letter from him. Sometimes he didn't send letters when he said he would. That always made her sad, but my friend told me it's because people in the war are busy all the time.

He shakes his head, his hair noisy as it brushes against the pillow. "No. My dad's a rock star." He puffs up his chest at this. "I'm going to be a rock star someday. My dad teaches me how to play the guitar when he's home from tour. He says I'll play better than him when I grow up."

I tilt my head toward the ceiling, imagining Roman with an oversized guitar underneath his arm, propped on his thighs as he learns the different tunes.

"I'm going to be a ballerina. I want to dance in front of thousands of people and have everyone come watch me."

Roman doesn't say anything for many moments, and I wonder if he's gone to sleep when he says, "You'll be a ballerina, and I'll be a rock star. And someday, we can go to where your dream was."

I imagine twirling in my ballet slippers on the cliff of the mountain, overlooking the angry waves as they crash against the cliff. Roman can play a soft acoustic tune on his guitar while I dance on the rocky, jagged ground. The sand won't slap at my skin angrily as I dance. The sun will shine, and the waters will be calm, and the world will settle as we dance and play my nightmares away. "Where the mountains meet the sea." I murmur.

"What?" he asks, his voice growing raspy of tiredness.

"Where the mountains meet the sea. We'll go to where the mountains meet the sea."

"Where the mountains meet the sea," he echoes. "I like that."

I roll over and give him my back, smiling as I burrow my face into my pink pillow. I can hear rustling across the room, and I imagine him turning over and getting comfortable himself.

I forget about my nightmare and how scared I was. I forget about needing my parents tonight. I don't need them, not when I have Roman to protect me. I hope he can protect me forever. I hope we can be best friends for the rest of our lives.

And secretly, I'm hoping that one day he'll marry me.

CHAPTER THREE

Luna

The sun tickles my skin, the rays embedding deep within me as I lay on the beach. I'll burn, I know it. I'm not one to get tan. Having that golden shade that Roman seems to constantly have seems to be impossible. I go from pale, to burnt, and back to pale. My mom thinks it's odd. She says her entire family tans well, and I'm the only one that can't seem to catch the rays and gain some color from them.

It's like my body rejects the sun. It'd rather me be a pale, ghostly white. I don't know why I look the way I do, with my weird gray eyes and my pale skin. My hair couldn't get any darker even if I dipped it into a pool of black ink.

I dig my toes into the hot sand, burrowing beneath the dry grains until my toes curl around the cold ones deep into the earth. I dig until the sand is wet, keeping my toes there, letting them cool from the hot day. My hair lays in a mess of strands around my head, probably dirty and grainy from the beach. Strands stick to my forehead, and I pick them away, only for them to stick back to my skin.

I'm alone today, and if I were to be honest, a little crabby.

I start school next week. The summer has been fun. Playing with Nora. Playing with Roman. Playing in the water and going to the park. Nights spent with Roman sneaking in my window to sleep on my floor. I've forgotten about school altogether until this last week when my mom told me that I've grown out of most of my clothes from last year and we needed to go get a few things from the store before school starts.

Then it hit me, I'm going to an entirely new school. *Again.*

The worst part is that Roman is a year older than me. He will be going into second grade, and I'm only going into first. At least I'll have Nora with me. She's become my best friend faster than any of my friends in Illinois and Kansas put together.

But there's something about Roman. He's more than a best friend. It's like he's a part of me. The lace on my ballet slipper. The chord on his guitar. A piece that's needed to make the other whole, and that's what Roman is for me.

I think I'm the same for him, too.

Except, now his friends are back from their summer vacations. The past month Roman has been playing with his friends more and more. He doesn't ask if I want to play with him. I don't know why, because I like to catch frogs and tadpoles, or do anything else that Roman likes to do. But he doesn't want to play with me when they're around. So, I've ended up spending a lot of these last few weeks with Nora. She's excited to start school, telling me that she hopes we're in the same class.

I brush my arms out against the sand, creating a sand angel. The grains are warm against my skin, the insides of my eyelids yellow and glowing from the bright sun above.

Roman's mom brought him and Nora to pick up Roman's friends. That means another day of me all alone. I might as well spend it in the sun, since my mom tells me the nice days are limited. She says the winters here will be worse than any other one we've ever had, being this north in the country. Roman was there when she said that, stuffing his face with a freshly baked chocolate chip cookie. The chocolate was still gooey and stretched from his fingers to his lips as he mumbled, "But we can go ice skating on the lake. That's really fun."

I've never ice skated before, but maybe it'll be fun.

One of the things I am looking forward to is dance. I started doing a general dance class back in Illinois. Jazz, pop, contemporary, ballet—I've done it all. But my mom says I was the best at ballet, and that was my favorite too. So next week, once we start school, I'll also be starting strictly ballet classes at the only studio in town.

I don't open my eyes when I hear voices from up the hill. Multiple voices, and one of them is distinctively Roman's. He has a northerner accent that I didn't know existed, stretching his *O*'s with most of his words.

"Luna! I'm back!" Nora's voice jumps, her feet pounding down the hill, bouncing her words.

I tilt my head up at this, my hair burrowing in the sand as I watch her run toward me. Her curly hair bounces with her steps, creating a messy wave trailing behind her body. Still up at the house is Roman and his three friends. I've seen them only one other time. Otherwise, Roman usually goes to their houses, or they meet up at the park to play.

I roll over and get up, brushing the sand from my dress and patting it from my hair. I'm suddenly embarrassed, and I'm not quite sure why. "Luna!" Nora says, digging her heels into the ground when she reaches me. She's out of breath, and I see she has something clutched in her hand.

"What is it?" I ask.

"My mom stopped at the store and got me a jump rope. I've always wanted one! You want to go try it in the front yard?"

Her hand grips the wooden handles, the rough, pale rope between them heavy and thick. I glance up at the boys who stand by the back door of the house, shaded underneath the wooden deck above them. Roman and a blond friend look over their shoulder at me, quickly turning back around when they notice me staring.

I frown.

"Yeah, let's go," I say, walking toward my property line. I don't want to go anywhere near these boys today. Not if they're going to whisper about me.

Nora follows behind me, telling me all about how we can walk to school together on the first day of school. Our elementary school is right next to Tip Town, so we'll have to walk every day. Nora's mom says there are only a few busses around, and they only go to the edges of town. Because we live in the center, our mornings and afternoons will be spent walking to and from school.

We reach the front yard, walking down the driveway and ending in the street. No one drives down this road besides the locals. I step aside and let Nora jump first. She looks nervous as she grips the handles, but there's an excitement building in her eyes. The thick rope drags and slaps against the black pavement as she swings it a few times. Then she jumps, her pink, flower-patterned overalls swaying as she hops into the air. She gets over it once, twice, and then trips. Frowning, she tries again, only getting it around her body twice before she fumbles again.

"Let me try," I say, holding my hands out to take the rope. She hands it to me, stepping aside so I can take my turn. The wooden handles are hot from Nora gripping them, a little damp, too. My green dress is not right for jump roping, but I give it a try anyway. I swing it against the ground a few times before I jump.

And jump.

And jump.

My toes press into the ground, and I hop effortlessly and weightlessly over the rope as it slaps against the pavement. I smile at Nora, and she watches enthralled. "How do you do that? I want to do that!" she whines.

"It's easy, you just jump!" My black hair swishes against my back, all the way to my waist. I get into a rhythm, a silent beat in my head with the slap of the rope alternated from my toes hitting the ground.

Suddenly, a loud buzzing noise zips past me. All four guys on their bikes whizz by, way too close, soda cans smashed on their back tires, creating a grating buzz as their tires rub against the metal. The gust of wind from their momentum coupled with the loud noise throws me off my feet. The rope wraps around my ankle and I stumble off the road. I fall to my butt, rolling down the small hill and into the corn field. A tall husk wraps around me and encases my body in its tough exterior. It's suddenly dark, the sun shrouded and keeping me in the shadows.

A hand shoots out, yanking me from the thickness of the corn field and pulling me back into the road.

Roman.

He looks angry and worried.

"Are you okay?" He looks me over, from the top of my black hair to the bottom of my dirty bare toes.

I nod at him.

He turns around, walking to his three friends that stand beside their bikes. He stomps up to the blond, giving him the biggest shove he possibly can. I've never seen Roman angry before, but boy is he angry right now.

"What did you do, Lonnie?!" Roman shouts.

Lonnie scowls at Roman. "You wanted to scare them just as much as we did."

"You went too close to her. She could've gotten hurt!"

A dark-haired boy wrinkles up his nose. "Look at her. She's not hurt. Why are you so angry? Do you *like* her?" he asks, the taunting words coming off his tongue sounding as if I'm a dried-up toad that got hit by a car last week.

Roman glances over at me, his eyes wide in shock. "No! I don't like her, Flynn. Gross."

Gross.

It suddenly feels like my nightmare when I swallowed sand. It's difficult to swallow, my tongue feeling swollen and my eyes growing wet. Everyone around me grows blurry.

"Here," I garble, passing the jump rope back to Nora.

Gross.

"Wait, Luna," Nora's voice is panicked.

I shake my head, walking around her and running home. The wind brushes my face and trails my tears along my temples.

"Luna!" Roman shouts at me.

I don't answer him. I don't turn around. I only stare at my small brown house as Roman's five letter word plays like a skipping record in my head.

Gross, gross, gross, gross.

"I'm telling Mom!" Nora shouts at Roman. That's the last thing I hear before I shut my front door. I leave everyone outside, but somehow, Roman's voice grating out the word *gross* has already curled around my heart.

My knees dig into my rough carpet as I kneel by my window, staring out at the lake. It's a little breezy this evening, the water crashing against the shore louder than normal. My sheer curtains billow in the wind around me. If I were to look over my shoulder, I bet they would look like a cape on my back. Like I'm flying in the sky.

My elbows press into my windowsill, my chin sitting in my palms.

I've been in my room since I ran inside earlier. My parents came to check on me, wanting me to come eat dinner with them. I didn't want to. I didn't want to talk, and I'm not hungry in the slightest. My mom could tell something was wrong, but I didn't feel like talking about it.

My best friend thinks I'm gross.

I don't want to cry over him, but it hurt me when he said those words. I would never say anything bad about him, but he was so quick to call me a name to his friends.

The sun has set over the lake, the reflection of the moon distorted, moving against the water. I watch it wiggle and dance, shimmering and effortless, with my heart heavy and possibly a bit empty.

A shadow creeps along my house, and I can tell who it is before I see him. I'm about to shut my windows but my arms won't let me. I stare until he appears, standing on the outside of my house, as I stay kneeling on the inside. Roman looks sad, remorseful, and like I'm the one that said gross instead of him.

How can he be sad?

"What do you want?" I grumble, flicking my eyes back to the water. I don't want Roman's fake friendship. If he wants to be my friend, okay. But if he's going to pretend and then be a bully to me the next day, I don't want to be friends with him at all.

"I'm sorry," he groans, and my eyes can't help but slide up to his. Underneath his eyes, they look red, almost bruised as he stares at me. His mouth is pulled down in a frown. "I'm so sorry, Luna. My friends are stupid."

I blink at him.

"I'm stupid. I never should have agreed to ride my bike or let them ride their bikes right next to you. That was really dumb. You could've gotten hurt."

I blink again.

He blinks back at me. "What am I missing?"

"You called me gross!" I shout at him, my anger from the day flowing out of me like the waves at the beach. "You called me *gross*!" I repeat, slapping my windowsill as tears fill my eyes this time. "How could you do that?"

His frown pulls even lower. "I didn't mean it."

"But you said it," I sniffle.

His hands shoot through my window, gripping onto my forearms. "I didn't mean it. It's not what you think."

I rip my arms from his hold. "What did you mean then? Your friends asked if you like me, and you said I'm *gross*."

"They meant if I *liked you, liked you*. Like more than a friend."

46

Silence.

I'm too embarrassed to say that the words still sting. The venom from his words still burns in my veins, even though I'm starting to understand what he meant.

He likes me as a friend.

Just not like that.

"Am I so gross to you that you couldn't see me as more than a friend?"

His face scrunches. Then falters, his eyes blinking a few times. His long eyelashes shutter against his tanned cheeks, and his jaw goes slack.

"Do *you?*" he asks, his chin jutting forward.

Do I tell him yes, I do like him more than a friend? That the love I see in my parents is how I hope to love him someday? That I could possibly love him more than the love I see my parents share? That hanging out with him for only these short couple of months has given me these feelings that I've never felt before? Boys have always been booger-ridden, butt-picking, dirty stinkers that ick me out more than anything else. But with Roman?

With Roman, *everything is different.*

Or do I lie?

"You're just my friend, obviously." I roll my eyes, even if my stomach guts in the process.

He smiles, his lips a little uneven as he bends over, placing his hand on the windowsill. His leg swings inside, and then the other. Then he's in front of me, and even though my stomach is turning in an agony I've never felt before, I smile, and he wraps me into his arms in the first hug I've ever had from him.

My body jolts on the inside even though I know I'm still on the outside. His body is hot, like he's got a fever or something. A complete contradiction to my own body, with my toes that are permanent ice cubes.

"Sorry if I made you sad, Luna," he sighs into my hair, his voice muffled beneath my tresses. The puff out from each breath he takes tickles my ears.

"It's okay." My voice comes out choked, and it feels like he's holding my heart in a strong grip. His smell has become so familiar, too. A combination of sunscreen and sand. It's so perfect, and it makes me sad.

I step out of his hold, turn around and walk to my bed. Crawling beneath my covers, I wipe my eyes on my pink pillowcase before turning around to face him.

"What's the matter?"

I give him a piece of honesty, even if it's not all of me. "I'm scared about school. I don't know anybody."

He plops down onto the floor, and I toss him his usual pillow. He gets comfy, propping his hands beneath his head, elbow on the pillow so he can still see me. "You don't have to worry. I'll protect you in school."

"Even from your own friends?" I lift my eyebrows. It doesn't seem like anything will come between him and his friends.

He narrows his eyes. "They won't do anything."

I shrug, not totally sure if I should believe him or not.

"You'll be fine, Luna." His hand pulls out from behind his head, and he shoves both beneath his pillow to prop himself up further.

I roll over so my back faces him, nodding into my pillow. I can't help the nerves in my belly, though. It happens every time I start at a new school. I can't help it.

"Luna!" my mom shouts from down the hall. "It's time to go! Harper is outside waiting for you!"

I rub at my stomach, the nerves having only gotten stronger over the past week. This morning they are so bad I even feel like I might get sick.

"Luna!" my mom shouts again.

"Coming!" I grab my Looney Tunes backpack and straighten my velvet green skirt and white top. The teeth from my white barrette in my black hair stabs at my skin, and I want to cry.

I hate first days.

My white socks have lace on the edges, and they're shoved into a brand-new pair of shoes that aren't even broken in yet. I'll have a sore on my heels by the end of the day.

I miss summer. My flowy dresses and my bare feet. They've grown strong running on the rough, hot pavement to the park everyday this summer. Now I'm dressed as a doll and feel ridiculous, but my parents wanted me to look presentable on my first day.

It smells like scrambled eggs and toast as I walk down the hall. My dad sits at the kitchen table with a pair of his oversized glasses perched on his nose. A cup of coffee sits on the table, steam rising from the dark liquid. I don't know how he can drink that stuff all the time. He let me try it once, it tasted like dirt.

My dad lowers his newspaper from his face, folding it over in the middle as he looks at me. "Well, don't you look beautiful this morning. Are you ready for your first day?"

I adjust the straps on my backpack, feeling the jiggly feeling in my stomach again. "I'm nervous."

A frown lowers the corners of his lips. He presses the newspaper against the table, and it crinkles against his hand. He stands up, walking around our small round table and stops in front of me. His bare hands are hot as he grips my shoulders, probably from his coffee cup, his fingers digging into my tense skin as he gives me a squeeze. "What? What would you be nervous about? You'll do great!"

"Are we going to stay here a while?" I ignore his question and go to one of my own. I don't want to get comfortable here if he plans to pack us up in a year and move to an entirely new place where I'll have to start all over. *Again.*

His frown pulls lower, his lips almost hitting his chin as he takes a step back. He smells like coffee and marijuana.

My parents smoke pot, and they say there's nothing wrong with it. It's always been a way of living for them.

"Well, I imagine we'll be here a while. Why?" He sits back down and picks up his coffee cup, taking a slurpy sip. He winces when the hot liquid touches his tongue.

I take a deep breath. "We keep moving everywhere. I want to just stay somewhere. I'm tired of having to make new friends every couple of years."

His face softens, the small wrinkles that have formed on his skin the last few years smooth out as he looks at me sadly. "Sometimes grownups have to move when a job opportunity comes up for them. So, I'm not saying it's not going to happen again, but I will say that I'll do my best to keep us here. Do you like it here?"

I nod.

He smiles as he picks up his paper. "I thought so. Don't worry about the future, Luna. Don't worry at all. Just go and have some fun. And have a great day at school."

My mom bustles out of her bedroom at that moment, her long hair trailing behind her back, and another one of her flowing dresses fluttering behind her. It always looks like a soft wave follows her.

"Come on, Luna. You're going to be late."

I smile at my dad when he makes a funny face behind my mom's back. Snickering, I head to the door when she calls my name. "Luna!"

I turn around and watch as she grabs a piece of toast, and an apple from the fruit bowl on the counter. "I know you'll be eating breakfast at school, but you should still try and eat something at home."

I grab them from her with a smile, the nerves making eating impossible at this point.

She brushes my black hair from my face and bends down to give me a kiss on the cheek. Her lipstick makes her lips stick to me, and she licks her thumb before swiping away the smear of pink on my skin. I frown.

"Have a great day. Don't forget you start ballet tonight. We still have to go buy you a new pair of slippers after school."

That puts a genuine smile on my face. I can't wait to get back into dance. I stopped last spring when we started looking for a new place to live, and I've been so ready to get back into it. "Okay!" I rush out the door before she can stop me for anything else and stop in my tracks right when I see the sight in front of me.

The toe of my shoes presses into the grass as I screech to a halt, and the week roots split from the ground with the force.

"Whoa," Roman says from in front of me. He takes a step toward me to make sure I'm okay, but second-guesses his movements and stops in place. "Are you all right?"

"What're you doing here?" I ask, then feel immediately bad when Nora frowns next to him. Roman doesn't flinch, though; he only continues to stare at me.

"My mom asked Harper if she would be okay bringing us to school, since she's heading that way anyway."

My eyebrows lift and I look over at Harper who's picking at her nails. She can sense the heat of my stare and looks up at me. "Can we go yet?"

Nora walks up to me, her rainbow backpack shiny and new. "Nice backpack," I say, because it is.

"Thanks." She lifts her lunchbox. "I've got a matching lunchbox." It's metal and square and looks awesome.

"Cool."

We all start walking to school, down the dirt road and along the cornfield. The tassels of the cornstalks blow in the wind and crunch as the dried leaves crack against each other. The air is cool this morning, the slight bite of fall making its appearance early. Or maybe it isn't early, and this is just how Wisconsin does things. I don't know.

Roman ends up beside me, with Nora on my other side. Harper stays a few paces ahead of us. She's wearing a jean jumper today and her pants are wide bell-bottoms that flare at the bottoms of her legs. She's tall, but Daddy says I'm going to be taller than she is when I grow up.

"You still scared?" Roman asks.

I turn to glare at him.

"What're you scared about?" Nora turns to look at me with a frown.

I want to grab one of the corn husks and whack him in the face with it.

"I'm not scared."

I give him my back, because I don't want him to see that I'm lying. I really am scared, but he's a jerk for saying it in front of other people. I nibble on the piece of toast that's now cold and soggy, handing the apple off to Nora. She bites into it easily, the juices wetting the corners of her lips and some of it hits my arms.

"Gross," I mumble, my nose wrinkling up in disgust as I wipe off the small droplets.

"Sorry." Nora wipes her glistening mouth with the back of her hand.

Our school is up ahead, and right across the street is the middle school that Harper will be attending. The grass is damp from the dew, and a bit of a fog still lingers in the air. If I listen hard enough, I might even be able to hear the loon that sings a beautiful tune every morning from across the lake.

It doesn't take long for us to walk down the quiet road. The sun is up, though it's not very bright out yet, and soon enough, our feet crunch through the small rocks at the park as we make our way across the street.

Big yellow busses park against the sidewalk by the school, opening their accordion doors, and I watch as a flood of kids in all colors of the rainbow fly down the stairs and into the school.

The nervous feeling tickles my belly again.

A warm hand folds over mine and gives it a tight squeeze. My eyes shoot over and lock with Roman's. His dark brown eyes swirl with a warmth and protectiveness that shouldn't be there at our age. He shouldn't have this nobleness about him. Sometimes it's like he's an old soul. At least, that's what my mom calls it. She tells me that I have an old soul all the time. "You're an old soul, Luna," is what she would say. "I have a feeling you've lived many lives." Then she'd take another hit of her joint before passing it to my dad.

"Don't be scared. I'll see you at lunch and recess." He slides his hand out of mine, but not before giving it one more squeeze.

"You okay, Luna?" Harper walks over to me, her backpack slung over one arm. She's so cool. She knows less people than I do. At least I already have two friends. She doesn't know a single person, yet she looks like she's ready to go inside and conquer the entire school.

I nod at her, feeling less certain than I look, I'm sure.

"I'm going to head inside. Go to the park after school, okay? I'll meet you there and we can walk home together."

I nod at her again, feeling like helium is filling up my brain. My head feels full, and all I can hear around me are the sounds of a bunch of kids who are all great friends and I only know two people.

Harper gives me one last wave before hopping off across the street. Then it's only us three.

"Ready?" Roman asks, his shoulder bumping mine.

"Yeah."

"Let's go."

CHAPTER FOUR

Roman

"Everyone is talking about your neighbor, Roman," Flynn says as he scribbles on his Seven Summer list. We really were lucky this year; I have Clyde, Flynn, and Lonnie in class with me. We have Ms. Bierbaum as our teacher. She's about one hundred years old, and my mom had her as a teacher when she was a kid. That's how old she is. Mom says she's a crotchety old hag. I'm not sure what that means, but if it's true, she's going to have a fun time with the four of us this year.

We were all assigned to get in a group and fill out our Seven Summer list. The seven best things we did over the summer. My summer was actually pretty boring, and I'm having a hard time listing enough things to fill the list.

And even worse, I want to list Luna as one of those things on my list.

I look up at Flynn, feeling like he's digging into my thoughts or something. The pencil in my hand is brand new and sharp as a knife. I press it into my thumb until I have a tiny brown dot in the center. I bring it up and rub it across the eraser, frowning at the rough and unmovable pink surface.

Mom bought the crappy pencils this year.

"What are they saying?" I don't need him to tell me, because it's all I've been hearing all day. We went out for recess and I searched her out. She and Nora were already playing with Nora's friends. Luna paused in her laughter when she saw me, her face frozen with her cheeks rounded and rosy in the fall breeze. Her silver eyes glimmering in the sun as her black hair tumbled over her shoulder and down to her small waist. She's the most unique person I've ever met, and I've met a lot of weirdos on tour with my dad.

But Luna... Luna is unlike anyone I've ever met before and I don't think I'll meet anyone like her again. It's not just her looks, although those are one of a kind. The way she laughs at my jokes that aren't funny, or the way she isn't afraid to play in the dirt or with frogs and tadpoles like Nora is. Nora can't stand the slimy texture of the wet frogs or the way their little legs bend and extend so quickly. Luna doesn't care, though, not at all.

So, I shouldn't be surprised that the moment she got to school, every person would be just as enamored with her as I have been all summer. But I am surprised, and if I were being honest, I'm jealous too. I want to go back to the summer when it was just us two. The days I couldn't hang out with my friends, and Nora would be too tired and would go inside, and it would just be me and Luna. Those were my favorite times. When the sun would go down and the fireflies would twinkle through the tall weeds near the water. How she could blend in with the night when we'd play past dark, her dark hair melding in with the darkness, except her pale skin made her stand out like milk poured onto the night sky.

"Duncan thinks she's pretty," Lonnie says, flipping his paper upside down so he can doodle on the back.

"Duncan is stupid," I spit the words before I can swallow them down. They ripped from my chest like a vicious hiccup, and all my friends swing their eyes to mine.

"Whoa," Clyde says, pushing his brown hair from his face.

I stand up from my chair. "I have to sharpen my pencil." I walk away before they have a chance to say anything else. Walking across the room, I push the tip of my pencil into the small hole of the sharpener and start cranking the handle. The metal squeaks as it rolls around, and small shavings fall from the bottom and into the small trash bin that's placed beneath. I take longer than I should, and when I pull the pencil out, I see it's so sharp it's unusable. The moment the tip hits paper, it's going to crack.

I shove my pencil down to my side and walk back to the table. My friends are all staring at me. "Your pencil didn't need to be sharpened," Lonnie says.

I wrinkle my nose at him.

"You like her, don't you? You like Luna?" Clyde says from beside me.

I shake my head, but my mouth can't form the words this time.

"Don't lie about it. I could tell from the moment she fell into the cornfield last week. You were so mad when we questioned you about it."

"I don't," I growl through my teeth, tired of my friends bringing up this stupid question. The worst part is I can feel my cheeks growing red and the tips of my ears begin to burn. "Quit asking."

"Whatever, Roman."

I don't respond, keeping quiet and hoping that my friends will change the subject. I don't want to like her, and I don't want Duncan to like her, either. But ever since last week when Luna asked if I liked her, I haven't been able to get it out of my mind. It's like she was bummed when I said I didn't like have feelings for her like that. Though now, it's like she's planted a small seed in my head, and it's been watered every day. Now I have this root that won't stop thinking about her.

I want to be next to her.

I want to play with her.

I want to protect her.

I want *her*.

Once the final bell rings for class, I'm out of my seat and waving bye to my friends before they can ask if I want to hang out. We usually spend our days at the park until the cold freezes the metal bars of the swing set. But today, my mind is only on one thing.

Luna.

I speed walk out of school, barely passing a glance at the traffic as I walk across the street. I see a wave of black hair up ahead, along with my sister's short curls, and the sandy brown head of Duncan talking to them.

My fists clench, and my feet punch the ground harder as I make my way across the street.

This isn't happening. Not now. Not ever.

"Roman!" My sister spots me first, running up and giving me a hug. I wrap my arm around her loosely, my eyes not able to drop from Luna's. She looks at me, her face tinged pink like she hasn't been able to stop smiling all day.

"Hi, Roman!" she says.

"Hi." My eyes swing from Luna's, to Duncan's, and back to Luna's. "What're you doing?"

"Duncan is in my class and was just walking me to the park."

Duncan looks over at me, a smile on his face that makes him look like he was just crowned king. "Hi, Roman."

"I could've walked you to the park. You didn't wait for me," I grumble to Luna. She frowns at me, her gray eyes darkening into silver pools.

She doesn't say anything, only watches me quizzically.

"Oh, it's okay. I was heading to the park anyway," Duncan says, his voice innocent and dumb. Duncan is dumb. Dumb Duncan.

I turn my head to face his. Reaching my hand out, I grab onto his forearm and pull him toward the swings on the other side of the playground. Luna watches me curiously, and a little nervously. "Roman?" she asks, a tremor in her tone.

I ignore her as I pull Duncan far, far away from Luna.

"Roman! What're you doing?" Duncan asks, ripping his arm from mine.

"Stay away from her," I say once we're a safe enough distance away from her. "Stay away from Luna."

He backs up a step, his feet kicking rocks as the fierceness in my tone takes him aback. I'm not an angry kid. I'm usually the playful one. The one that gets along with everyone. But not with this. Not with Luna.

"What?" His eyes widen into large circular dinner plates taking over the expanse of his face.

"Stay away from Luna. She won't like you."

He frowns at this, which slowly drips into a scowl. "How do you know? Can you read her mind or something?"

I grip his arm again, this time squeezing until I know he can feel the pain. He flinches.

"Stay away from her, Duncan. Or else I'll tell everyone you wet the bed almost every night at summer camp the other year."

The color drains from his face, leaving him a ghostly shade of white. "You wouldn't."

I nod my head. "She's not yours to like, Duncan."

I turn away from him after that, walking through the heavy rock piles. It always makes walking slower, and I have to pick up my feet a little extra to make the next step. It makes my anger a little more aggravating.

"What did you do?" Luna asks, her eyes on Duncan as he turns the other way. He doesn't give us a backward glance as he heads toward his house on the other side of the lake.

"Nothing," I grunt, kicking the rocks and watching the dust plume around my shoes.

"It didn't look like nothing. You looked mad."

I look at up at her. My mouth opens to tell her something, I don't know what, when Harper walks up to us. "Hey, guys."

Luna spins toward her sister. "Hi."

"How was your first day?" Harper wraps her arms around Luna's shoulders.

"Good. I met some new friends."

Harper smiles. "Me too. Ready to head home? You have ballet tonight, right?"

I frown. "You start ballet tonight?" I wanted to hang out with her. Go down to the dock and sit with her, just the two of us down by the water, for one of the last nice days of the year.

I just want to be around her.

"Yeah." Genuine excitement lights up her face.

I smile with her. I smile for her. But on the inside, a part of me feels lost.

"What're you doing?" Nora asks from her bike. I don't answer, so she rings her bell that sits on her handlebars, then rings it again, and one more time.

I stand up, startling her to the point her bike nearly tumbles onto its side. I take a huge step forward and plant my hands on the handlebars, keeping her upright. "Quit being annoying."

"Quit ignoring me! I asked what you're doing. You look like someone kicked your dog; except we don't have a dog so it can't be that. What else is it?"

"Nothing," I lie.

It is something, though.

Luna rode off a while ago in her mom's Oldsmobile. I was only able to catch a glance at her, but her long, wild hair was pulled up to the top of her head in a tight bun. She waved at me as she passed.

I'm in a bad mood now, and I'm not sure why.

Although I do, and I just don't want to admit it.

"Tell Mom I'm going to meet the guys at the park."

"Can I come?" she asks, her near fall all but forgotten. She circles around our driveway again, getting up onto her feet so she can peddle faster.

"Not today, Nora."

"I'm bored, though," she whines. "Luna went to ballet. I don't have anything to do."

I know.

"You wanna catch frogs with us? The big, slimy ones with the huge black eyes? Maybe his tongue will come out and wrap around your fingers."

"Ewwwww." Her faces curls in disgust. "Never mind. I don't want to hang out with you guys."

"I'll be back before it's dark," I say, my hands wrapping around my handlebars and lifting my bike upright. I slide onto my seat and fly down the road. The lights from the homes brighten the road up on the left side of me, keeping the cornfields on my right darkened from the lowering sun. I stay on the left side. The shadows in the cornfield always creep me out.

The park appears around the corner, and I see my friends in the distance. I'm about to turn their way when my bike gets a mind of its own. Or maybe it's not my bike at all. I end up taking a right toward town where all the small shops and businesses are crammed together on two streets. My bike drops down from the curb as I cross the street. I pop a wheelie to get up onto the curb on the other side of the street and end up in front of the only dance studio in town. My foot drops to the ground, sliding across the sidewalk and makes a loud *kshhhhh* noise as the sole of my shoe slides across the sandy pavement.

I slip off my bike and lean it up against the light post on the corner. A yellow lab stares at me from a nearby bench. I walk over to him and give him a pat on the head. "Hey, Billy." I scratch behind his blond ear and smile when he tilts his head to the side in pleasure.

Billy is Mr. Sorenson's dog. Billy usually hangs out here in the evenings while Mr. Sorenson goes into the bait shop across the street to prepare for his early morning fishing trip. He's one of the people on the lake who spends most of his days on the water, and his boat is the first one on the lake in the morning. He's always trying to catch the best fish.

Billy doesn't even need to be tied up. He just walks over and lays on the bench. Everyone in town knows Billy and Mr. Sorenson. I think Billy even likes this spot because sometimes he gets treats from the locals.

After a few more pets, I shake my hand free of his loose, blond hair and walk toward the dance studio. The windows are large, and I can see the entire space from out front. I've never been here before, never been inside. But I'm assuming this is where Luna went, since this is the only studio in town.

I notice her mom sitting on a bench attached to the wall that extends from one side of the room to the next. She has a smile on her face that shines as bright as her colorful dress. I follow her gaze, my eyes landing on Luna.

Wow.

Her hair is tied up into a tight bun on the top of her head. I've never seen her hair up, almost like she's allergic to ponytails. It's always down in a long mess that floats to her waist. Not today. Today it's tight, slicked, and shiny on top of her head.

A pale pink leotard suctions against her body. My eyes fall down her long, long legs to her feet, which are wrapped in those weird-looking slippers with the flat toe. A silky ribbon wraps around her feet and ends on the back of her calf in a small bow.

She looks taller than she is. She looks like so much more, standing there in a baby pink outfit. Her pale skin nearly blends in with her leotard. She doesn't do much as she wanders around the room. Bending a bit here and there and stretching across a long bar that extends along the wall from one side to the other.

She hops up on the tips of her toes, and my cheeks grow warm as her arms extend up, the line of her body flawless and straight.

She's perfect.

My throat feels full, like I just swallowed an oversized piece of bread. I clear my throat a few times hoping the feeling will go away, but as I continue watching her, it only grows bigger. My heart feels like it's about to break from my chest and run inside the studio all on its own. It wants to clutch onto her, and I don't understand this feeling.

I've never felt this feeling before.

She spins around, floating into the air like a feather before landing on her feet. Her body is turned in my direction, and her eyes float up and connect with mine. I stare at her, feeling like a creep watching her with my hands at my sides. She stares at me too, her gray eyes lighting a fire in her irises that burns me. It burns my skin, and it burns my heart.

With a blink of her eyes, she turns around and continues dancing, breaking the spell her silver eyes put me under. I reach up to the back of my neck and wipe away the sweat that shouldn't even be here this evening. The sun has started to set and there's a fall chill in the air.

I wander back to my bike, seeing the empty bench where Billy lay just a short while ago. I lift my bike from against the light pole and hop on, peddling home as quickly as I can. I don't even think about my friends that are at the park probably waiting for me.

I can only think of the strange, gray-eyed ballerina who left a burn mark in the pit of my being.

I lie in my bed, the heels of my feet scratching against my blue sheets. My solar system quilt set suctions me against the bed and makes me hot. It's a claustrophobic feeling. Although, I don't think it's the blanket that's making me feel like this. After watching Luna earlier, I came home for a late dinner and a quick phone call from my dad. I barely remember a word that was spoken, my eyes still playing the image of Luna's dark hair in the bun, rolled tight on the top of her head. Her gray eyes. Her long legs. The small shoes that wrapped around her feet like they were meant to be there. After a quick bath, now I'm in bed. Wondering why this feeling hasn't left my chest. I'm a little frustrated at the fact that I can't get her out of my head.

Tap, tap.

I would think it's a moth flitting against my window, until I hear it again in the same tempo.

Tap, tap.

I toss my sheets back and slide out of bed. I sleep on the second level, so I don't know how anyone could be tapping on my window unless they were on the deck. It's the middle of the night, too. That thought alone makes me want to go get my mom before finding out who it is myself.

That doesn't stop my body from wandering over to the window, though. I pull my dark curtains back, and there she is.

Luna.

Dressed in a matching pant and button-up shirt set, she stands there with a sad look on her face. Her head nods, gesturing for me to come outside.

My eyebrows furrow, worry and curiosity getting the best of me. I nod, walking out of my room and tiptoeing across the carpet. My floors are creaky, and I make sure to step on the firm spots to not wake up my mom. Once I reach the back door, I flick the lock up and pull open the heavy door. Luna stands against the edge of the deck, her front pressed against the railing as she looks out at the lake. Her hair blows in the night wind gently, blending in with the night sky.

The cool wood creaks as I take a step outside, walking up to her.

"Are you okay?"

She lets out a shuddering breath, a heavy frown on her face. Her eyes are a little glossy. "I had another nightmare."

I turn toward her at the same time she turns toward me. "What was it about?"

"The same thing." Her gray eyes burn brightly in the night, a yellow hue lighting up the edges. "I'm on a mountain. The waves are so angry. It's almost like they are mad at me. And this soft sand, almost like dust, it chokes me. It gets in my hair and my eyes as it rains around me. Then a huge gust of wind comes, and I fall over the edge."

"And?"

"And I wake up." A tear leaks from the corner of her eye, and I don't think twice as I lift a hand and brush it away. It's wet as I rub it between my thumb and forefinger. I let it seep into me, my skin absorbing her tear as my own.

She looks so scared and concerned. I want to make her feel better, but it's a little risky to be talking to someone in the middle of the night out on my deck. I would go fall asleep on her floor like I have all summer, but with it being the school year now, my mom wakes me up really early in the morning. I'd be in big trouble if she came to my room and I wasn't there.

"Want to go down to the lake?" I suggest.

She looks at me sideways, like I'm crazy or something. "You want me to go down to the lake after I just had a nightmare that I drowned?"

"I wouldn't let you drown, Luna," I say the words with such sincerity that her snark drops, and wonder fills her cheeks, blossoming them with a light pink hue against her stark white skin.

"Okay, just for a minute. I better get back home before someone finds out I'm gone."

I nod, and we walk across my deck and down onto the wet grass. It's cold, and my feet are instantly freezing. The moment my feet hit the sand, I dig my toes beneath the grains, enjoying the slight warmth they still hold from the sunny day.

Luna walks a few steps further, until her toes hit the wet sand and a small lull of water comes and curls around her toes.

"Why do I keep having this dream? It's like it's trying to tell me something," she says into the distance.

For the life of me I can't figure it out either. I'm not a mind reader and I don't know anything about the future, or premonitions, or anything like that.

"I don't know," I mumble honestly.

She whips around and stares at me, alarm and desperation in her eyes. "Will you take me there someday? To this cliff on the water?"

"I told you I would. We'll go to where the mountains meet the sea. And we'll stand there, and this nightmare can go to hell because sand isn't going to come and swipe you over the edge."

She shivers, a tremor racking her entire spine. "You don't know that."

"I do." I lift my feet from the sand and take a step toward her. "I wouldn't let you fly over the edge."

Her shoulders drop, and she finally nods. I walk up to her, the cold water crashing around my feet as well. We stand in silence and the only thing that can be heard is the sound of the water lapping at the shore.

"What did you say to Duncan today?" she asks out of nowhere.

I can't look at her. Shame and embarrassment hit me. But another part of me doesn't feel embarrassed or ashamed, because I don't want anyone else to like her. I don't want anyone else to even talk to her, to be honest.

"I told him that he can't like you."

I can feel her eyes sinking into mine, shock and a hint of anger in her gaze. I finally look at her. Her eyes are burning mine, enough so that I have to blink to rid the ache.

"Why?" Her voice echoes into the distance, bouncing off the sand, and water, and my heart.

"Because I don't want anyone to like you."

"I can't have friends?" Her voice raises.

I shake my head, too tired to get into it.

"He can't like you, Luna. You're *my* friend. I won't let him."

"What will you do? Beat him up? Give him a wedgie?"

"If I have to," I say seriously.

She laughs, her voice incredulous. Like I wouldn't actually beat someone up. For her, I would.

I'd do anything for her.

Just that thought makes goosebumps break along my arms.

"Sometimes I feel like I know you from somewhere," she says, stepping closer to me. Our arms are flush now, her cool skin aligned with mine.

I look at her. "That's not possible. I just met you."

She nods. "I know. But my mom calls me an old soul."

"What's an old soul?" My eyebrows furrow. That's a weird thing to call someone.

"Like, I should've been born before my time, or I lived a life before this one. Either way, it feels like I know you. Like, maybe we knew each other in a past life. Don't you think so?"

I think about her words. The craziness of us meeting and knowing each other in a past life. The possibility that our lives somehow connected in this small town in Wisconsin with a whole world surrounding us. That somehow, maybe we were meant to meet.

"My mom says that when you know your soulmate, you'll be able to feel it in your fingers and your toes. That your chest will feel like you can't get enough air and are getting too much air at the same time. That the world stops, the ripples in the waters settle, and everything else in the world ceases to exist." Her eyes are wide, like everything her mom told her, she feels. Down to her bones. "Don't you feel it?" she asks again.

I take a deep breath, letting my hesitation and worry and everything inside of me expel with the air from my lungs.

"I feel it."

CHAPTER FIVE

Luna

"Do you have everything you need?" Mom asks from the living room. She's crocheting a blanket and is on the last few rows. It's a colorful mismatched pattern of burnt oranges, browns, and creams.

"Yep!" I shake my paper bag full of candy.

"Okay, have fun!"

I burst out the door with my winter boots, and red coat zipped up to the neck. It's Valentine's Day tomorrow.

For school we get to make cool boxes so we can pass out Valentines to our other classmates. I'm making a special Valentine's Day card for Roman, even though he's a year older than me. I leap across the yard, making sure to step in the already made footprints in the snow. My boots crunch with each step, the snow packing down with each push of my weight.

The door opens before I even knock, Nora's bright smile and spindly curls bouncing with excitement. "My dad comes home today!"

My eyes widen. Wow. I kind of forgot Roman even had a dad. His mom does such a good job taking care of both Roman and Nora, it's hard to believe he's ever had a dad at all.

WHERE THE MOUNTAIN MEETS THE SEA

"Wow. Really?"

I step inside, the cold air making my legs chill.

"Yeah! We've told him all about you. You'll have to come to dinner tomorrow. I would say tonight but he's not going to be home until really late. My mom already said it would be okay if you had dinner with us. Do you want to?" Her words fly out of her in rapid succession. I can barely follow her, her excitement making her vibrate in front of me.

"Um, yeah, if my mom and dad are okay with it."

"Okay!" She starts walking through her house, her red shirt with a bright white heart in the center shining at me. It smells of banana bread and chocolate chip cookies, and as if on cue, my stomach rumbles.

Then he appears.

"I can hear your stomach growling from the other room." He lifts an eyebrow.

I set my bag full of candy and supplies down on the table, feeling a bit embarrassed.

Roman has become my very best friend. I mean, Nora is my best friend. But Roman, he's something on a completely different level.

It's like he's a part of me.

"Do you want a cookie? They're still warm." Nora picks one from the cooling rack and bounces it from hand to hand as she walks over to me. "Here."

I take it from her and take a bite, the cookie falling apart the moment it hits my tongue. The chocolate chips are still melty, and I can feel the sticky goo spread to my lips.

"You've got…" Roman lifts his hand, then drops it at his side when we hear his mom's footsteps. "You have chocolate on your lips."

"Great! You're here! Let's get started on those Valentine's boxes, shall we?"

We all sit around the kitchen table and munch on cookies and banana bread while Roman's mom helps us build our boxes. We get to pass out Valentine's cards to other kids in class and make a cool box however we want. Mine is full of pinks, reds, and whites with a glittery pink trim around it. Nora's looks similar to mine, except she adds purples and instead of a glittery pink she uses a glittery red.

Roman opted out of all the glitter and pinks. He chose reds and blues and put cardboard wheels on the sides of his to make a car out of it. The top is an open slot so people can put their Valentines straight into the car.

It takes us most of the afternoon to finish up our boxes and get our candy ready to pass out to our classmates. By the time we're finished, my hands are sticky with glue, the table is full of scraps of paper, glitter is all over the dark wood, and my teeth throb from all the sweets.

I glance outside, my eyes widening when I see complete darkness. "I better go home before my mom comes looking for me." That, and I want to finish up Roman's Valentine, and I can't do that with him right across from me at the table.

As if he knows I'm thinking about him, he looks up and locks eyes with mine.

"Can't you stay for dinner?" Nora asks. I feel bad for her. I love hanging out with her and I do all the time, but sometimes, I feel like my mind and body drift toward Roman.

Like, every time.

"Oh, not tonight, Nora. Daddy's coming home tonight." Her mom pushes a finger through one of Nora's curls, pulling it down and releasing it. I watch as it springs back up and bounces a few times.

"Okay," Nora grumbles.

Roman is still watching me, and I find that this is happening more often than not lately. We watch each other. Stare at each other.

The groaning noise from the legs of Nora's wooden chair being pushed against the floor snaps me out of my trance. I straighten my striped shirt and bell-bottom jeans as I stand up to gather my things. "Thanks for letting me come over, Mrs. Hall."

"What did I tell you, Luna, call me Goldie. Or Mom, for all I care."

I smile at her, loving that she has become like a second mom to me.

I slip my boots and coat back on, and with my bag in hand, I head home.

The next morning, I have my velvet red skirt with a white top on. For once, I'm the first one outside waiting for the other three to make their appearance for our walk to school. My backpack is tight on my shoulders with Roman's Valentine's card slipped into the front pocket. I'm holding my bag with my box and candy.

Soon, everyone else stumbles out, half asleep and bundled up in their winter gear. February is freezing in Wisconsin. I thought it was cold during the winter back in Illinois, but Wisconsin takes it to an entirely different level. It's been below freezing most days, making it impossible to spend any time outside. I can't wait for the summer again. I hope this summer I can spend it at the lake again with Roman. I hope we can do that every summer for the rest of our lives.

"Ready?" Harper asks. Since she's in middle school, she doesn't do anything for Valentine's Day. But she's still dressed in a red dress. I've got a heart shaped barrette holding the front of my hair back.

Roman's hair is unusually tamed today, and Nora has her curls pulled back in her own barrettes.

We walk silently, our feet trudging through the thick snow. My cheeks burn from the cold wind, and I tuck my face behind the front of my coat. Nerves start to take hold once school comes into view. I spent so much time on Roman's card, and I hope he likes it.

What if he doesn't?

What if he didn't get me one?

"I'll see you after school," Harper says, jogging across the street toward her own school. We all make our way inside, and Nora rushes off to her locker. Roman is about to make his way to his own locker in the second-grade pod when I wrap my freezing fingers around his coat-covered arm. "Wait."

"What is it?" His nose and cheeks are red from the cold, and his hair looks wet from the winter frost. I slip my backpack from my shoulder and pull out the card that's peeking out from the front pocket. The card itself is in the shape of a heart, with red and white tissue paper bunched up on the front. In a black magic marker, I wrote *Happy Valentine's Day* on the front.

I hand Roman the card with shaky fingers. He stares at it for a moment, his brown eyes darkening and brightening at the same time.

He takes the card, holding it with both hands as he tips it from one side to the next. He looks up at me, down at the card, and back up at me again. His finger clips underneath the fold, peeling the card back, and his eyes drop, falling to my girly and swirly scrawl.

Roses are red,

Violets are blue,

I may just be your friend,

But I like you.

Will you be my Valentine, Roman?

It's an admission of my feelings, and not very poetic, but I didn't want to go as deep as my heart was telling me to. I think if I told him how I really feel, he would run for the hills.

I wish he wouldn't stare at it for as long as he is. It seems like he isn't even blinking as his brown eyes spear the rough pink paper. Then he folds it up, a little rougher than necessary. He looks up at me, his eyes a little lost but also a little found. Like he wants to tell me something, but he doesn't know how. I want to ask him, and I'm about to as my mouth drops open and the question rolls across my tongue, when the bell rings.

"I've got to go," Roman says, hefting his backpack over his shoulder and walking toward his locker without another word, my card clutched in his left hand.

Tears fill my eyes as I stand there. I feel lost, confused. I don't know why his reaction was like that. So cold. Does he really not like me? He finds even being my Valentine for a stupid holiday so horrific that he can barely talk to me?

He didn't even get me a card.

A tear leaks from my eyes, tickling my cheek as it makes its way down to my lips. I bat it away, embarrassed to be the new girl crying in the hallway on Valentine's Day.

"You okay?" one of the office staff asks me as she checks the nearly empty hallway.

I nod, barely sparing her a glance as I make my way to my own locker. All I wanted to do was tell him how I really feel, but he finds me so unlikeable. Like I'm some freak. A monster.

Maybe he wasn't who I thought he was in the first place.

"Luna!" I can hear his voice call my name from down the road. I didn't wait for Harper, Roman, or Nora like I usually do. The moment we were released from class, I grabbed the rough strap of my backpack and hauled it out of the school. I didn't even put on my winter boots or zip up my coat. I just shoved everything on as quickly as possible and started racing home.

I've been in a horrible mood all day.

I don't want to talk to Roman. Or Harper. Or Nora. I want to go home and stay in my room all by myself for the rest of the day. Valentine's Day stinks. Love stinks. I hate all of it.

"Luna, wait!" I can hear Roman's heavy panting as he tries to catch up to me. "Please, Luna!" he groans when I don't stop.

I've been holding back tears all day, and I'm still trying to hold them back. They want to break from the surface and spill over the edge. The cold wind can't even dry my eyes until they're scratchy and burning from the cold. The sadness from earlier overpowers the cold and turns my body to fire.

"LUNAAAAAA!" Roman screams from the top of his lungs, sorrow and anger ripping from his throat like a never-healing wound.

I turn around, the second tear of the day making its appearance as it rolls down my cheek. "What do you want, Roman?"

His eyes widen for a split second when he sees my raw emotion. He recovers quickly, straightening his face and catching up to me in the next second. "Why are you crying?" He wipes my face, his somehow warm palm brushing my raw cheek. "Stop crying," he pleads.

"Why would you care?" I ask, shoving his hands away.

His eyebrows furrow, his face turning sharp as he scowls at me. "Why wouldn't I? You're one of my best friends."

I shrug, not wanting to get into it. Not wanting to embarrass myself any further than I already have.

I start turning around, wanting to get somewhere warm. My breath comes out as pants and I can see it puff in the air with every exhale.

He steps in front of me, blocking my exit. "What? What did I do wrong?"

Another tear falls, and he wipes it before it can hit the apple of my cheek.

"You don't like me," I whisper, the words passing through my foggy breath louder than they sound coming from my chest.

"What?" His eyes widen incredulously. "Yeah, I do."

"I gave you the card this morning and it's like you didn't even care. It's like you were mad about it."

He stares at me, his teeth going to his bottom lip and he starts chewing on it. *Bite, bite, bite.*

"See?" I step to the side, ready to get away from him. I knew he didn't like me. *I knew it.*

He steps in front of me again. "Wait."

72

I look up at him, my nose starting to drip from the cold. I bring the back of my hand up and swipe away the moisture.

He drops his backpack into the pile of snow, and it sinks in deep. Bending over, he unzips the main pocket and pulls out a blue piece of paper. Standing up, he hands it to me without looking me in the eyes, keeping them averted to his backpack. This time his hand is the one that's shaking.

I slide it from between his fingers, feeling the smooth paper. It's a large rectangle with the words *Happy Valentine's Day* on it. Reds and whites mix on the blue paper, but it's still perfect.

I take a deep breath as I open it, seeing his barely legible handwriting scratched in the middle.

Roses are red,
Violets are blue,
You're my best friend,
But I like you too.

A drop splatters on the letters, blurring them and making the ink run. I wipe my eye, realizing I'm crying again.

I look up at Roman, seeing him looking at me. A bit shyly, maybe. Unsure of himself.

"You like me?" I whisper.

He nods. "I've been working on it all week actually. I just haven't known what to write." He looks up at me. "You made it easy."

"But… but…" I'm at a loss for words, when he leans forward and presses his lips against my damp, cold cheek.

My heart stops.

My world stops. Everything stops as Roman's warm, soft lips press against my skin. He lingers for a moment, the air from his nose rushing against my cheek. My chest hiccups like a huge leap that I can barely contain from falling out of my chest.

Finally, he steps back, staring at me with an uncertainty but a need that I feel in my own blood.

"You mean it? You're not lying to me?" I ask, my entire body thrumming with excitement. Anticipation.

"I do. Now come on, let's go home and get warm." He wraps his hand around mine and pulls me home.

I'm no longer cold, though.

I'm so, so warm.

"Luna, you ready to go?" my mom shouts from down the hall.

"Coming!" I prop Roman's card up on my dresser after reading it for the millionth time. Since he dropped me off earlier, I haven't been able to stop reading it. Touching it. When the phone rang a short while after I got home, I ran to it in hopes that it was Roman wanting to play.

It was his mom.

I forgot that Roman's dad, Cypress, got home from tour yesterday. I was going to eat dinner with them, but Goldie actually wanted our entire family to go over so he could meet all of us. She told my mom we're basically family at this point.

I walk down the hallway and into the kitchen. It's smoky from their most recent joint that my dad is stubbing out into an ashtray. My dad is dressed in blue jeans and a button-up shirt. My mom is wearing one of her many dresses. She doesn't own much else besides her dresses that she makes herself. Harper sits in the kitchen, her hair in a tall ponytail and she's wearing jean bottoms and a matching jean top.

I'm wearing a dress as well, though mine brushes just below my knees and it's matched with a pair of long socks and Mary Janes. We all bundle up in our coats and make our way up the hill to Roman's house. Their outside porch light is on. My dad holds a bottle of wine while my mom knocks on the door. My parents aren't rock fans, they're more folk fans. But they're still meeting a celebrity of sorts, and they've been raving about it since Goldie's phone call.

Nora opens the door, a bright smile on her face while she takes us all in. She's in jeans and a dark gray sweater. "Luna!"

I wave at her, pushing through my parents to get in the house. "Hi." I look around for Roman, but he's nowhere to be found.

"Oh, hi, guys!" Goldie walks into the kitchen with an apron on. "Come on in." She gives my mom a hug and smiles at my dad. "You did not have to get anything! I told you that earlier."

"We just had this lying around." My mom waves her hand in the air to brush off her lie. Harper snorts, clearing her throat to cover it up. She actually made my dad rush out of the house to go buy one of the nicest bottles they had at the store. I think Goldie knows this, too, from the smirk on her face.

"It smells good in here. Can I help with anything?" Mom compliments as she follows Goldie into the kitchen.

"Oh, thank you. It's just a pot roast with some potatoes and carrots. If you want to slice the bread, that would be great."

My dad takes our coats to hang them up, and Harper walks to the living room with her cassette player and headphones. All she does is listen to music nowadays. She can't stop listening to The Ramones and Aerosmith.

I look around for Nora, but she's nowhere to be seen now.

And where's Roman? And Cypress?

I can feel a low hum on the bottom of my feet, like the floor is barely vibrating. Curiosity gets the best of me. I look over my shoulder, seeing my dad talking to Harper, and my mom and Goldie laughing and giggling in the kitchen. Turning around, I walk through the living room with their davenport, striped chair, and television. Opening the door to the basement, the sound of humming has turned into a low thrum of music—a guitar and what also sounds to be a voice singing.

As quietly as possible, I make my way down the stairs and walk toward the music studio. I've only been in here once, one of the first times I came in their house and Roman showed me around. He said this is where his dad records and practices with his band members. The door is shut, and I press my hand to the cold brass knob and as slowly as possible, turn it and pull it open.

My steps falter as I watch the sight in front of me.

Roman sits on a stool as he fumbles through the notes. He strums most of them perfectly, save for a few times when his finger squeaks down the guitar strings. His dad stands at his side, belting out the lyrics to *Highway to Hell* by AC/DC. He sounds just like the main singer, and Roman sounds like he could be the guitarist.

They are perfection.

Then Roman's lips open, and he follows along with his dad, his voice a bit raspy, even if it's still smaller than his dad's voice. The guttural passion in each word he sings sinks into my stomach and makes my chest twitch with emotion. I don't know whether to cry or laugh.

Roman is *everything*.

Nora notices me from the couch against the wall. It's covered by a crocheted blanket, something that my mom would make by hand. I walk over to Nora, the boys too into their music to notice me entering the room. It's warm in here, warmer than it is upstairs. A little stuffy, but the guys don't care.

Cypress is an older version of Roman. His hair is longer, dark like Roman's but with a slight wave. Like it tries to be curly like Nora's but can't quite get there. It brushes his shoulders and shifts back and forth as he bops his head to the song.

He's wearing a band shirt and a pair of jeans with his bare feet, his large toes wiggling as if he's playing the drums.

Nora rocks back and forth to the music, her curls bouncing, and complete euphoria written on her face.

Roman is good.

He's really, really good.

His eyes close a few times, his mouth splitting into a smile as he sings the lyrics of the song. He looks at ease next to his father. I always thought he was laid back, but now I realize there was something about him that's been missing since I met him, and that was his dad. Now that Cypress is back, Roman looks whole.

And sitting here watching him, I feel whole too.

My fingers pop through the holes in the crocheted blanket and I squeeze, pulling the fabric and stretching it as my crush hits me harder than it ever has.

I'm going to marry Roman one day.

CHAPTER SIX
Roman

1990

Isit on top of the monkey bars at the park, letting the sun beat down on me. The bars are hot beneath my palms and I grip the metal. The park has always been the go-to place around here, but it's always been a bitch when the sun is so hot it makes the metal burn you like a fried egg on a skillet.

This park has been a monument in my life. I've been coming here since I knew what a park was. In a few weeks I'm heading into high school. This park might not be what it once was, but I still like to come here from time to time. Me and my friends will still play basketball on the court if we need to take a break from playing music.

We started up a small band last year, just playing cover songs and fucking around in my basement. Until I realized my friends can really play, and they realized I can really sing. Together, we started making real music, scratching down terrible lyrics that will never make it an inch out of my basement, but still. It feels good to do this.

Not to mention, Luna has been even more dedicated to her ballet over the past few years, from going one night a week to multiple nights a week. With this summer being full of her ballet and my music, we haven't had a lot of time to spend with each other.

But that's why I'm here tonight, waiting at the park for her to get done with ballet. I wanted to hang out with her. Spend the last couple of weeks before school starts just doing what we do best: being around each other.

At this point in our lives, people just know that if there's one of us, there'll be both of us. We're best friends, but it's more than that. We are so much more than friends, even if we haven't ever done anything with each other. Sure, I kissed her on the cheek all those years ago, but that was the only time—the time we told each other we liked one another.

We've been tight-knit, her and I. Spending as much time with each other while also finding time to hang out with our own friends. She's best friends with Nora, and they hang out every minute she's not with me. And I hang out with the guys whenever I'm not with her.

But things are changing now. I'm going into high school, and she has one year left of middle school. We're both growing, and although I'm excited as hell to start high school, a huge part of me doesn't feel great about leaving Luna behind.

I don't think Luna is stoked about it either. She's been in a bit of a mood since summer hit. She tries hiding it from me, but I've known her for years. Her sadness hits me straight in the chest like it's my own pain.

I don't think it helps that Harper graduated high school this last year and moved to Iowa for college. She's living in a dorm, and according to Luna, she calls frequently, but I know she misses her sister.

I watch as small kids play on the swings below me. Their parents sit under nearby trees, stretched out on a handmade blanket as they watch their kids from a distance.

"Roman," a voice calls from below.

I brush my hair from my forehead as I look down, seeing Cindy from school. She's in my grade and has always been a bit of a flirt. A little too much, to be honest. She's pretty, but my eyes aren't for her. Whether or not she wants to believe it, I think my heart has been taken my entire life. It doesn't stop her from trying, even though I wish she would.

"Hey, Cindy." I hop down from the monkey bars, feeling a zing of pain shoot up my calves. She has on a pair of shorts and a tank top. I can see the straps of her bathing suit peeking from beneath her clothes. Her blonde hair sits in waves around her head, and her short bangs give a small shadow around her eyes.

"What were you doing up there?" she asks, adjusting the long strap of her purse over her shoulder.

"Waiting for Luna." Her eyes darken at this, clearly displeased with my answer. "What're you doing here?" I ask after a minute when her stare becomes too much.

She nods toward the beach. "I'm meeting Lori down at the beach. Do you want to come hang out with us? We're just going for a little while, then maybe go down to Mickey's Diner afterward."

Didn't I just tell her I'm waiting for Luna?

"Uh, I'm waiting for Luna." My tone comes out less friendly this time. My eyes narrow as I watch her.

She lets out an unsure smirk, pulling at the ends of her hair while she lets out a breathless giggle. "Yeah, but, she's not here right now, is she? Didn't you, like, grow up with the kid? Isn't she like a baby sister to you or something?"

I'm shaking my head before she can even finish her sentence. "I'll pass, and she's not a baby sister." Not in the slightest. Furthest thing from it, actually. I've been watching her straight, lanky body pop with small curves this last year. I've been watching her chest grow, to her embarrassment. Her mom and sister had to go with her to buy some training bras. I pretend that they don't exist, because if I do, I'm going to want to cross a boundary we've never even treaded on.

Trust me, I've wanted to cross that line since I hit seventh grade. When I knew what girls and boys really are. What my parents do when my dad isn't on tour. How babies are made. The thrumming between my legs turned torturous as Luna has gotten older. She's fucking beautiful. She always has been.

"Well…" she digs in her purse and pulls out a scrap of paper and a pencil. Scribbling on it, she sticks it in my palm. Her fingers are tiny and warm as they wrap around mine. She closes my hand, and the paper crumples in my fist. "Here's my number. Call me if you change your mind." She starts to walk away, then pauses, turning around to stare at me. "I don't want to be mean, but what do you see in her? She looks kind of weird, doesn't she? Her dark hair and her gray eyes. Some people think she's a witch."

Disgust and rage light in my chest as I turn away from her. I bet it's the girls that say that, since I've been threatening the guys ever since Duncan in second grade. They all think she's pretty, so I bet if someone has a problem with her, it's one of Cindy's immature friends.

A flash of color catches my eyes. I look up, seeing Luna walking this way. She's in a blue leotard with pink leggings underneath. Her hair that she's kept long, even after all these years, has been taken out of her tight bun. It falls down her shoulders in a messy heap, with the slightest wave on the top of her head where the ponytail made a kink.

And she's barefoot.

Since the moment she moved here, she prefers to be barefoot. I think at this point, her feet are stronger than mine. I remember back to when we just met, I was always barefoot, and she thought it was the oddest thing. She started copying me, and within a few days she had blisters and bruises and cuts and scrapes worse than mine have ever been, but she's never looked back.

She has her headphones on over her head and her cassette tape. Her head bobs back and forth and it's like she's floating, more than walking, down the sidewalk.

Hippy.

She's followed in her parents' footsteps in that regard. Where I'd rather listen to Black Sabbath and AC/DC, she'd rather be listening to John Lennon or The Beatles.

"She's everything," I mumble, barely paying any attention to Cindy as I walk away from her and toward Luna. It's like the sun directly shines on her. No matter where she is, no matter what kind of day it is, she has a brightness around her, making her black hair shine and her gray eyes glow. She's unlike anyone I've ever seen, ever met. She drew me in the first moment I met her, and I've never wanted to walk away. I don't think I'd ever be able to, if given the chance.

She notices me as I cross the street. Lowering her headphones, she asks, "Hey, what're you doing here?"

"I was going to see if you wanted to hang out?" I ask, suddenly unsure. *Why do I feel unsure?*

She looks at me a moment, then shrugs. "Sure, why not? What did you want to do?"

I shrug. I never got to that point in my plans. I just wanted to be around her. "Whatever."

She laughs, and we start walking home. I've thankfully sprouted in height over the last couple of years, and now I'm almost at six feet, finally towering over Luna. It took years, and she kept growing, but one morning I woke up and I was suddenly too long for my clothes.

Now instead of looking up at Luna, I get to look down at her.

"What's wrong?" I ask her once we make it to our street. Her ballet slippers dangle in her fingers, the ribbons wrapped around her wrists, so they don't drag on the ground.

"I don't want school to start." She pouts.

I don't want school to start either, because I don't want to go to school without her.

"Why? It'll be just another school year for you. For me it'll be totally different. I'll be the small fish in the big pond."

She scoffs. "You'll be fine. I'm the one that has to go through a whole year without you." Her voice rings with a sadness I didn't expect. We're in a different grade, so we never have any classes together anyway, and barely see each other unless it's in passing or at lunch. But I'm realizing her sadness runs deep.

She's sad.

I can feel that she's sad all the way to her bones.

I stop us in the middle of the street, the hot wind blowing at my back as I wrap my arms around her. Her arms fold in front of me, her slippers squishing against my chest and her face burrows deep into my neck. I can feel her inhale me, breathe me in. I do the same, burrowing my face in her hair, inhaling her floral scent. She smells like vanilla and flowers with a hint of marijuana that her parents are always smoking in their house.

She backs up, sliding her hands down my arms until she hits my palms. I don't realize I have the stupid note from Cindy still clutched in my palm until I hear the crinkling of paper as her fingers run over it.

"What's this?"

I squeeze the paper tight, but she still manages to pull the damn thing from my grasp.

"What is this?" she asks again. Straightening out the sheet, she reads the girly phone number, staring at it a moment too long. The only sound I can hear are the cicadas in the cornfield behind me, and her perfect scent is replaced by cow manure from the dairy farm down the road.

Her eyes roll up to mine, fury radiating from her form. "Who's is this?"

The words choke in my throat, and I feel like a fucking idiot for not throwing the damn note in Cindy's face like I wanted to in the first place.

"Cindy gave it to me." I sigh, tipping my head toward the clear sky and running a hand down my face. Fucking idiot.

"Cindy... Cindy Paulson?" She seethes. "Why the heck do you have Cindy Paulson's phone number in your hand?"

"She gave it to me..." I see the look on her face, and I put my hands up. "But it's not what you think. I was waiting for you when she came up to me and gave it to me. That's all it was."

Her hands fist at her sides, the crumpling paper losing its life between her fingers. She slaps her palm against my chest, mushing the paper into my shirt. Then she drops her palm to her side, leaving the paper against my chest. I don't grab it, though, and it falls to the ground between our feet.

"Call her," she says, the hurt in her voice palpable. Raw. She sounds utterly wrecked.

"I was never going to call her!" I shout, kicking at the stupid piece of paper on the ground. "I saw you and I forgot all about it."

She shakes her head, taking a step back from me. "It doesn't matter. I knew this would happen. You'll be in high school. I'm still in middle school."

"What the fuck does that mean?" I take a step toward her, and she takes another step back.

"It means that our lives were bound to go their separate ways eventually." Her voice is empty, withdrawn from the entire situation.

From me.

No, fuck that.

"No! Hell no, Luna." I snap my hands out and wrap them around her, pulling her against me. "Go our separate ways? We've done this before, when I went to middle school and you had one more year of elementary. How is this any different?"

"We were just children then."

"We're barely any older!" I shout in her face.

She shakes her head. "You don't get it."

"So, explain it to me!" My hands squeeze her bare arms, goosebumps raising on them even in the humid summer heat.

She squirms until she's out of my arms. Then she unwraps and rewraps her slippers around her arms.

"You don't understand. I've had to watch for years—*years*—as girls looked at you. Doesn't matter where we go. Doesn't matter who we're with. Guys want to be your friends. Girls want to be with you. I won't be there in high school, and you'll meet someone you want to be with. And what we have… what we've always had, will be over. I know it will." Her groaning words rip from her throat and bleed all over the ground in front of me.

"It's not going to change. We will never fucking change."

She shakes her head, a sad smile on her face. "You say that now." Turning around, she walks away, toward her house, leaving me in the street.

I don't follow her this time, too shocked and sad to fight with her on this.

She thinks what we have will change. She thinks I'm going to change.

Doesn't she know?

I've loved her my entire life.

"That was perfect," Flynn says from the drums. He twirls his sticks around in his hands.

"Ah, there's something missing. Let's go again," I say, wiping the sweat from my forehead.

I'm standing in the front of the room, my guitar slung over my shoulder and microphone on the stand in front of me. We're working on a combination of cover songs and making our own. Right now, we're trying to go through one of our own songs, but I'm not feeling it today.

I just can't get into it.

I haven't been able to sit still since Luna walked away from me yesterday. I tried going to her bedroom window last night, but she wouldn't open it for me. Now the guys have been here all day, and we're really behind on practicing. I'm trying to put it behind me for just a couple hours so I can focus on the shit I need to do, but I can't.

I can never put her behind me.

We roll through the song one more time.

By the time we're finished, I have sweat dripping down my temples, and I want to scream. My mind is too disorganized, I can't get shit straight. It's messing with my music.

"Perfect, Rome. Let's call it," Clyde says from the bass.

I shake my head, feeling like something's still missing. "No, not yet." My fingers run up and down the smooth guitar strings, wishing it would just play perfect for me so I could go see Luna.

"Dude," Lonnie says, "What's going on?"

I frown at him as I lift the guitar from over my shoulder and put it in its stand. "What? Nothing." I grab my glass of water and down it, letting an ice cube slip into my mouth. I crunch on it, feeling angry and embarrassed that they can even tell I'm torn up over something.

If they knew it was over Luna, they'd laugh at me until they were blue in the face. They love Luna, and they think of her as a little sister, but they have been making fun of our relationship since they met her.

"You love her."

"She has you whipped."

"You look like a fucking puppy dog."

Always. Always fucking harassing me about it. If they knew I was pouting over something so trivial, I think they would smash my guitar over my head.

"Kathleen and Leslie are going to the movies tonight and were wondering if we wanted to go," Flynn says, thumping the bass drum with his foot.

I sigh, not really interested. Although I can tell Clyde and Lonnie are by the way their ears perk up. "What movie?" Lonnie asks.

"The new Psycho is what Leslie said. Hey, Roman, Leslie said Cindy is supposed to be there tonight. Maybe if she gets scared enough, she'd jump on your lap." Flynn shrugs, like it isn't a big deal.

I hear a tinkering, and look over my shoulder, seeing Nora and Luna standing in the doorway. Nora is staring at Flynn; she's had a crush on him since I could remember. I would intervene on it, except my eyes are locked on Luna's and the devastated look on her face.

I take a step toward her, but she's already gone, only a wave of black hair flowing in the doorway before that disappears. Nora follows her a second later, after a fierce scowl in my direction.

I turn around, glaring at all three of my friends. "I *do not* fucking like Cindy. Why does everyone keep thinking that?"

"Dude, Leslie said she's going to try and pull big moves on you now that you're going to be in a different school than Luna."

I snort. "She can fucking try, but I'll shut her down every time."

Silence.

"Go get her, Rome. You always play like shit when you guys are fighting. It'd be a waste for us to sit here and pretend like the music will be good."

I nod, walking out and shutting the door behind me. They can either wait until I get back or leave whenever they want. I'm sure they'll end up going to the movies, and they know that I'm not going to be going with them. They've been around my house enough times to know their own way out of there.

I slip out the back door, walking in my shorts and t-shirt across my backyard and into Luna's. I walk to her window, tapping on it a few times.

No answer.

"I'm not leaving until you talk to me, Luna." Don't ask me how I know she's in there, I just do. I can sense her sadness radiating from the other side of the wall. I can smell the tears that are falling down her face right now. "Please, Luna. I'm not leaving."

Her curtain rips back, and there she stands. Her black hair sticks to her wet cheeks, and the small amount of mascara I wish she wouldn't wear runs down her face in dark rivers. "What do you want, Roman?" she asks, her voice clogged with tears.

"I don't like Cindy," I emphasize.

She rolls her eyes, the whites of them bloodshot and watery. "Quit lying to me."

"I'm not!" I shout, but her voice is muffled through the closed window. "Open your window so your mom or dad don't come see what's wrong."

She looks over her shoulder, gnawing on her lip a moment before turning back to me.

"Open your window, Luna. Right now."

She does as I ask, raising her window up only an inch. I push it up the rest of the way, bending down so I can slide inside. Her room smells salty, like it's full of her tears. "Stop crying," I groan, hating this feeling in my chest. Like it's shredding apart in a meat grinder. I can't take it anymore.

Her ballet slippers hang on her wall on a hook, and the rest of her walls are filled with pictures of me, Nora, and her family. Some ballet artwork also decorates her walls, but the focus is me and her.

It's *always* been me and her.

Without a second thought, I grab her arms and pull her to me. "I don't like her, and I never will like her. You don't have to worry about her. Not now. Not ever." I punch each word out with so much certainty her face freezes. She stares up at me, trying to decipher the realness of my words.

"I'm being honest with you. I promise."

Her face crumbles, lines forming in her eyes and forehead. Her body shudders as she takes a deep breath. She falls into me, her body sinking against mine. "I don't want to lose you," she whispers.

"You'll never lose me. Never," I mumble against her head.

Because I'll never let her go.

CHAPTER SEVEN

Luna

"Hey, Luna." I look up, seeing Travis staring at me from my table in the library. School started a few months ago, and as much as I hate being here without Roman, I just tell myself I have one more year to get through and then I'll be with him again.

Jealousy gnaws at my insides just thinking of him at the high school by himself. Imagining Cindy talking to him, flirting with him.

Ugh.

"Luna?" Travis asks again, adjusting the books in his arms. His letterman jacket is blue and yellow as it sits on his chest. Being on the football team, he's handsome and one of the guys in my grade that all the girls have a crush on.

Except me.

The library is quiet, and it smells like old books. The one place I like to be in school. My favorite place.

"I'm sorry, what?" I look up at him, setting my pencil down inside my notebook and closing it. It has a huge lump in it, the cover tilted halfway toward the ceiling.

I'm supposed to be studying for my upcoming math test, but I've been drowning in thoughts of Roman. I'm pathetic, but my life is consumed by him, and it has been since I was a child.

"I asked if you wanted to go to the winter carnival with me."

I blink at him, not sure where this is even coming from. I don't think I've ever really spoken with him before unless we were working together on a school project or something. He's never just searched me out for no reason, so I'm kind of wondering why he suddenly wants to take me to the school dance.

"Wait, what?" I let out a small chuckle. "Where is this coming from?"

The librarian gives me a harsh look, and Travis quickly slinks into the chair beside me, his knees knocking against mine. He leans forward, the smell of minty gum coming off his breath. He smiles with his perfectly straight teeth that had braces removed from them this last summer, and it's infectious with the dimple in his cheek. It has me instantly smiling back at him.

"It's not a new thing. I've always wanted to ask you out. I've just never had the chance," he says.

I frown at him. "Why not?"

He gives me a look like I'm stupid. Like whatever he knows is obvious.

"What are you not telling me?" My eyes narrow in suspicion. What the hell is going on?

His face drops a little, turning serious as he stares at me. "You really don't know?"

I shake my head slowly, feeling my stomach weigh down with lead. He leans closer, his knees pushing further into mine. I push my chair back a little, releasing the contact. I'm suddenly feeling cold inside.

"Roman wouldn't let any of us ask you to any dances. None of us could do anything, really. Now that he's not here, though, I figured now's my chance."

"Who is us?" I feel like my eyes are about to bug out of my head. "Chance for what?"

He scratches his jaw, looking like he's got all the secrets in the world stuffed in his pockets. "Everyone. All the guys in our grade. Some from even the grade above us. We've all wanted to ask you out multiple times, Luna. Some have even tried. Roman shut everything down before we could even ask." He taps his finger on the table, the *tap, tap, tap* loud and echoing in the quiet library. "He honestly never told you? You never knew?"

"How would I know?" I nearly shriek.

"*Shhhhhh!*" The librarian, with her glasses and colorful chain hooking from them behind the back of her head, looks at me like she wants to hit me with the newspaper. "Quiet down or else I'm going to have to ask you to leave."

I cringe and mouth an apology before looking back at Travis. "No, he never told me," I whisper.

The look he makes is a cross between the cat that ate the canary and the kid who stepped in his neighbor's dog poop. "Don't tell him I told you, okay?"

I glance up at the clock, seeing it's about ten minutes from the last bell of the day. Roman gets out earlier than I do, so he's probably already outside waiting for me.

I slam my book closed, the boom sounding like a gunshot. Shoving everything in my backpack, I don't even care that my pages are wrinkling, and my pencil pouch is opened, spilling everything to the bottom. I stand up too quickly, my chair making an ugly groaning noise even against the carpet. I wince, pushing it back in quietly.

I'm going to kill him.

I pause on my way out, turning around to a shocked Travis. "Oh, Travis?" He looks up at me, a little nervous from our conversation, I'm guessing. "Yes, I'll go to the dance with you."

His uneasiness drops, a genuine smile popping up in its place, and his dimples reappear. I feel like sticking my fingers into them.

A voice clears her throat behind me, and I look over my shoulder to the librarian standing directly behind me, pointing at the exit.

"I'm already leaving." I huff, walking out without another word.

The librarian will want me to go to the office to wait the last few minutes until the bell rings, but I'm not. I take a detour to my locker and grab the rest of my things. I pull my jacket off the hook and slam my locker closed so hard the door wiggles on the hinges. Slipping my arms into my purple sleeves, I stomp toward the exit with only one purpose in mind.

Roman.

Shoving the doors open, a blast of cold air immediately hits my face. This December is ridiculously cold, with our first snowfall being in October this year. As soon as that first flake melted on my skin, I knew it was going to be a hellish winter.

I let out an angry breath when I see him, sitting on top of the monkey bars as he usually does. Even in the winter, he finds his way to his park. That's what I like to call it. His park. It's been a part of him since I met him. I think if he could, he'd lift it up and put it in his backyard.

Roman blocked guys from seeking me out? Screw that.

The wave of breathy fog escapes my lips with a shuddering, angry breath. I can't believe that asshole.

I'm going to kill him.

I trudge through the freshly fallen snow. My feet go deep, snow instantly making its way into my shoes and socks. He notices me before I cross the street, and a worried look crosses his face. He slips down, landing effortlessly on his feet and brushing the snow from the back of his jeans as he walks up to me.

"What's wrong? The bell hasn't even rung yet. Are you okay?"

I press my cold fingers against his wool coat and give him a shove. "You jerk!"

He stumbles back, slipping on a small patch of ice, but rights himself before he falls to the ground. "What was that for?" he shouts at me.

"I think you'd like to know that I just got asked to the winter carnival."

His brows lower, and it's like a shadow takes over his face. "Who?" he growls, the fierceness in his tone not something I've ever heard from him before.

I go to shove him again, pure anger heating my cool skin. He wraps his hands around my wrists, his long and strong fingers warm even though he's been sitting out in the cold for at least ten minutes. "Who?" he questions.

The tone in his face automatically makes me answer him. "It was Travis."

His eyes widen, rage lighting his brown eyes to gold. "Travis Schwinn?" he roars.

"I told him yes!" I rip my wrists from his hold, shoving him away in the process. "You told him, and everyone else for that matter, that they couldn't ask me out. You have been making me feel like a leper for years, all for your own happiness? I thought I was some freak because no guys talked to me, no guys wanted to hang out with me. Now, I come to find out you've been pissing a circle around my leg?"

I kick snow toward him, and it puffs into dust instead of chucking at his legs like I'd hoped. "*I told him yes.*"

He laughs. "No."

"I'm going with him." I smile. "And I don't care if you like it or not." I take a step away from him, ready to rush home and get away from him before he lures me back.

He *always* lures me back.

His soft words and his calming, protective presence make me melt around him. I'm nothing but weak when it comes to Roman Hall. He has a power over me no one ever could. I'm a crumbling petal in his strong hand.

"You've never gone to a dance without me. We've always gone together. *Every. Single. Time.* Now you plan to take Travis *fucking* Schwinn? I don't think so, Luna. Over my dead fucking body."

I hear the bell ring across the street, and only a minute later are kids flooding out of the doors. I take a step away from him, hating that he's hurt me like this. That he's kept me from experiencing what every girl should experience. I would choose Roman every time, no question. But he never gave me the chance or trusted me enough to believe he'd always be my number one.

And that's what hurts the most.

"I don't think you really have a choice in that matter." I see Nora start to cross the street with a curious look on her face. I know she'll want to know what happened, she always is nosy when it comes to mine and Roman's relationship. She thinks we're going to get married someday, and I usually never deny her claims.

I've always wanted to marry Roman too.

But today, right now, that's the last thing I want to do.

I turn away from Roman and Nora, speed walking toward my house. I ignore both of them shouting my name. Telling me to wait. Nora asking me what's wrong. Nora screaming at Roman for being an asshole. I ignore them as I walk home. I don't answer the door later, or the window tap late at night. I tell my mom that I don't feel good. Because I don't. I feel terrible.

It feels like I'm falling apart, my body like the tied ribbon of my ballet slippers. One easy pull, and I'll collapse into a pile of nothing.

"You look so pretty, Luna," Nora says from beside me. We're standing in my bathroom, dolled up for the winter carnival.

"Ugh, I don't know." I look down at my dress. It's a faded pink, almost creamy in color. The satin fabric goes down to my ankles. The neckline is high, all the way to my collarbones. The sleeves are sheer, save for the two small scraps of satin strips separating the fabric. It's pretty, and my mom made it, so even if I didn't like it, I'd be forced to wear it.

Nora stands beside me in a satin red dress. A big thing that flares at the waist and has a large bow on her hip. Puffy sleeves cap her shoulders and look like oversized marshmallows.

"Are you sure you don't want to wait for him?" she asks, readjusting a curl from her up-do.

She's talking about Roman.

The first thing she told me when she walked in was that Roman was getting ready and planning to take me to the dance.

Hell no.

"I'm not waiting for him. I'm going to the dance with Travis." I run my hand down my dress, from my chest to the tops of my thighs. The dress is light and cool against my skin, the shiny fabric gentle as it kisses my body.

I watch as she frowns through the mirror. She doesn't like that we're fighting. She never likes us fighting.

"Knock, knock." My mom walks in with her Polaroid camera. She's been excited all day for the dance. Finishing last minute hemming on the bottom, helping me curl my hair into a subtle wave. I decided to leave it down, and it cascades down my back. "Wow, you guys look so pretty. Are you ready to go?"

"I'm ready." I take one last glance in the mirror and turn to my mom. "Ready to go?"

"I am." She turns toward the hallway. "Charlie! The girls are ready to go!" Both Nora and I grab our clutches and follow my mom into the living room.

"I want to take a couple pictures before we leave."

I sigh at this, hating the ridiculous picture taking.

"Well, don't you girls look lovely! You'll be the most beautiful girls at the dance!" My dad comes over and presses his lips gently on the crown of my head.

We take some pictures in the living room, since it's too cold outside to stand out there in our dresses. Once we have our coats on, we hop into the Oldsmobile and are off to school.

It's packed by the time we arrive. Cars parked along the curb, doors opening with colorful outfits spilling out. A rainbow of bodies filling up on the sidewalk.

A light snow is falling from the darkening sky, the evening sun setting early this time of year. The flakes are light and powdery, the kind that brush against your skin without actually seeping into you.

I see Travis standing in the hallway, his letterman jacket covering his suit coat. His black trousers fit his slim form nicely. A smile breaks out on his face when he sees me.

"You made it!" He wraps me into a hug when he sees me, and my eyes widen slightly.

Okay. I didn't realize we were on this friendly of terms.

Beside Travis stands George, Nora's date, another player on the football team. They've been casually flirting this year, although I know Nora's sights have always been on Flynn, Roman's best friend.

We head into the gym, where hundreds of white and blue balloons are hung from the rafters. Streamers dangle down, spinning from the constantly running vents along with shiny decorations. A disco ball hangs from the ceiling, creating glittery triangles to shine all throughout the room.

A boombox sits on a table in the corner of the room with *Piano Man* by Billy Joel screaming from the speakers. Next to the boombox is another table with a glass bowl filled with a red juice brimming to the top. There's also a platter of cookies and a bowl of chips.

Riveting.

We walk through pools of people; their different colored dresses and outfits making them a vibrant kaleidoscope of colors.

"Want some punch?" Travis shouts over the music.

I nod, clutching my purse with both hands, suddenly feeling a little uneasy.

I miss Roman.

I've only ever gone to dances or school events with him. I'm used to him standing beside me, and I'm so much more comfortable with him. Not that Travis is a bad guy, he just isn't the guy my heart beats inside my chest for.

Roman is.

But I'm so mad at him, and he shouldn't have kept guys from talking to me. Because now I have to spend my time with Travis instead of him, all because he wanted to be a possessive asshole who only thinks about himself.

Though, the thought of Roman seeing me have fun while he stands on the sidelines is a knife to the gut. Hurting Roman isn't something that interests me. Watching the blanket of sadness cover his face shreds my insides.

The gnawing in my abdomen grows, and I rub at my lower stomach, hating the ache that missing Roman does to me.

"Here you go." Travis and George come back with four cups of juice in Styrofoam cups. I take mine and watch as Nora takes hers. We stand on the sidelines, watching everyone dance and have a good time, while we stand there awkwardly.

"Want to dance?" Travis asks me once he's done with his juice.

I look down at my cup, seeing the mostly full cup with watered down punch. It tastes gross, and Travis has a little red mustache on his upper lip from his own drink.

"Sure." I swallow down the sigh that wants to break free and set my cup down on a nearby table. Glancing at Nora, I see her watching me with the same sadness. She wants what she can't have, too. Not only does she like Flynn, but Roman would never let her date him. And she thinks Flynn only looks at her like a sister, anyway.

"You okay?" Nora asks as I'm setting my cup down.

I nod. "You?"

George grabs onto her wrist and pulls her out into the dance floor before she has a chance to respond. We split off, Travis pulling me left and George pulling her right. People are spinning around, dancing with couples or with their friends. Smiles on faces and screams and laughs fill me from every which way.

I can't let tonight get to me.

I can't let my night be ruined by Roman.

So, I let loose. Even with the gnawing in my stomach and the ache in my heart, I dance with Travis.

Because that's what I'm meant to do.

I might be a ballerina at heart, but I can still twirl, jump, and dance like the rest of them. We dance until we're sweaty, hot messes. Until my waved hair is flattened into a sheet and strands of hair stick to my temples.

Travis's clammy palm wraps around my hands and he spins me around and around until I'm dizzy. I giggle, stopping in place until the world rights itself.

And my eyes connect with Roman's as he stands in the front doorway.

My heart lurches at the sight of him. Standing tall and too old to be in middle school. His suit presses nicely and curves around each muscle and bone in his body. He looks around the room, and I can tell from the look on his face that he's looking for me. He's scoping me out between each and every person, his eyes weaving like my mom crochets her blankets.

I duck a little behind Travis, pressing my hands to his chest. "I'm thirsty all of a sudden. I'm going to grab some punch."

"Oh. Let me. I could use some too. I'll bring some to our table."

I dodge Roman's eyes as I duck down and tiptoe around people. All the way to the table where Nora is already sitting down, looking bored out of her mind.

"How's it going?" I ask once I reach her.

"Wishing I was literally anywhere else in the world," she groans.

I sigh. "I know. I saw your brother."

Nora nods. "I know."

My eyes widen. "You saw him too?"

She shakes her head. "No, he's standing right behind you."

My jaw drops and I turn around, seeing him stand behind me. He looks so tall, so strong standing there in his suit. So much like an adult, and I suddenly feel like a small child who's about to get in trouble.

"I told you to wait for me," he mumbles.

"I told you I was going to the dance with Travis." At that very moment, Travis decides to make his appearance with a cup of punch in each hand. He blanches when he sees Roman, faltering in his step a moment before he continues his walk up to us.

"Roman. What're you doing here?"

Roman blinks in slow motion, like that's by far the stupidest question he's ever been asked. "I'm here for Luna."

"Uhh…" Travis looks between the both of us.

"Heard you were running your mouth, Schwinn." Roman says, taking a step toward Travis.

Oh, hell no.

"Roman, stop." I stand up at the same time as Nora does. She knows her brother, too. The tone is his voice makes the hair on my arms stand up. *Terrifying.*

"I didn't say anything, man. I swear."

Roman takes another step toward him, brushing by my side without a second thought. "I don't like people talking about me behind my back. Got something to say? Say it to my face." Roman slaps his chest, this being the very angriest I've ever seen him.

Roman doesn't get angry. Roman gets irritated, he gets annoyed, but Roman never, ever gets *angry*.

"Let's dance." I pull Roman away, because I'm scared more than anything he's going to punch Travis, and that will just get him into trouble.

I don't want that.

Travis looks forlorn as I walk away from him, and I wince and give him an apologetic look. He takes my seat, downing the contents of his Styrofoam cup.

Roman ends up being the one to pull me, yanking me until we're in the center of the gym. Directly underneath the disco ball we stand, listening to the last few notes of a song I'm unfamiliar with. It's upbeat, and Roman doesn't seem to be in an upbeat mood right now.

The first notes to REO Speedwagon's *I Can't Fight This Feeling Any Longer* comes on, and Roman snaps his arms out and wraps them around my waist, pulling me against his chest. My arms go around his neck automatically, my fingers lacing together at the base of his head. My fingers tickle against the messy hairs that have grown too long, threading through the soft strands. He bends down, crooning the notes in my ear, singing so softly, his voice so low and raspy, a tone that has recently turned deep, manly, and I melt. Every inch of me melts into his arms.

Our feet go from left to right, an easy two step that takes little effort or concentration. "Why do you have to fight this? Why would you go to a dance without me? With him?" he mumbles into my ear as he pulls me even closer.

My insides weep from his sad voice. I curl into him, wanting to hop inside his chest so I can hold him, cuddle him, make every inch of him better.

"You hurt me." I nuzzle against his chest.

"I didn't mean to." He pulls back, his hand going to my jaw as he tilts my head up. "I never meant to hurt you. I just couldn't handle it. I can't take it, Luna."

"Can't take what?"

"I can't watch you with someone else. All it takes is one guy, one moment, and maybe you'll realize they're the one."

I shake my head before his sentence is even finished. "It would never be like that."

He narrows his eyes. "How would you know? You met me, and you say it only took a second for you to realize I was going to be your best friend. You say you're an old soul, that maybe we were supposed to meet. But what if someone else is an old soul, too? What if Travis is an old soul, and he was the love of your life in a past life?"

I want laugh and snort and cry and scream at the same time.

"You know very little of me if you think that's how it'd ever be. You are my soulmate. Couldn't you tell from the moment I met you? All those years ago, you told me you could feel it. Don't you feel it, Roman?"

He takes a shaky breath, the hand on my jaw trailing to the back of my neck, his fingers gentle and tantalizing as they tickle from my neck and down my spine. "I feel it, Luna. I've always felt it." His hand moves down my back to my hips. His hand slips down over my hips, grazing my backside ever so gently.

His eyes widen, and his footsteps halt. He brings his hand up, and my eyes widen at the look on his face. I glance over, seeing a streak of red on his hand.

Oh, shit.

I start sweating, my body popping with goosebumps as a shiver racks my spine. My jaw becomes unhinged, and I swallow, mouth opened, as I realize what this means.

Roman snaps into action, spinning me around and pushing me through the crowd of people. We don't stop to tell anyone we're leaving. He just pushes me out of the gym and into the hallway. His fingers are strong against my arms, so tight and slightly shaky. I start sweating. I'm panicking, tremors making my teeth chatter as I come to terms with what's going on.

I got my period.

My mom kept saying it was taking a while. My sister got hers in the summer from sixth to seventh grade, and I'm in the middle of eighth grade and still haven't gotten it.

Well, I guess now I have.

It makes sense, though, why I've had the gnawing in my stomach all day.

Oh my God. I'm bleeding through my dress.

Did everyone see?

I look over my shoulder, seeing everyone dancing and talking and partying like they usually would. No one is staring. No one is pointing. It's just another dance for them. A teen dance with a ton of hormonal teenagers.

"Oh, no." I start to cry.

"Shhh." Roman rips his suit coat off his shoulders and wraps it around my waist. "You're fine." He's acting calmer than I am, even with his palm full of red.

Nora even got her period over the summer. Roman has been dealing with her PMS attitude one week a month for a while now, but it's still gross.

And *embarrassing.*

"Shit," I whine, wrapping his coat tightly around my waist. "This is so embarrassing."

"It's not embarrassing. You knew it was going to happen. Come on, let's just go home." He pushes me out the front door, keeping his arm on me as we walk home. I'm not in the right dress to walk in the snow, but it's only down the street, and it's supposed to be a while before my mom is supposed to pick me and Nora up.

The walk is quiet, the lightly falling snow heavier than it was earlier. It brushes over my toes and the sheer fabric on my arms does nothing to hide the cold. It's beautiful outside, and any other night I'd take a moment to enjoy the tree branches weighted down by the blankets of snow. To listen to the crunch of snow being compacted beneath my feet, or to smell the crisp freshness of the cool air.

Tonight, I can't do any of those things. Tonight, I'm distraught over bleeding through my dress and making a mess on Roman's hand.

Would Travis have done the same? No, I don't think he would have. I think he would have cringed, maybe gagged, and made up some excuse to spend the rest of the night away from me.

The nervous chattering of my teeth turns into a chatter from my freezing body. Soon, we're walking down Roman's driveway. I make a turn to head home when he shakes his head and pulls me into his house.

"Where are we going?" I sniffle. "I need go home."

He shakes his head again, pulling me into his house. I don't see his mom anywhere, but he pulls me straight through his house and into his bathroom. He crouches down, opening the cupboard underneath his sink and pulls out Nora's pack of feminine products.

He hands me a square package from the box, wrapped in yellow packaging. "Do you, uh… do you know what to do?"

My cheeks flame, embarrassment hitting me, and now I realize the gnawing is cramps, and they aren't getting any better as time goes on. Only worse. "I know what the heck to do," I snap, even though it's partly a lie. I think I know what to do, living with my sister and mom, and hanging out with Nora. I've just never done it by myself, so I really hope I don't mess something up.

"I'll go get you some clothes." He looks slightly embarrassed himself, and that only makes it worse.

"I should just go home," I whine when Roman starts to close the door.

He shakes his head. "Will you hang out? Just for a little bit? Let me take care of you." His eyes are pleading, his face screwed up in pain.

I stand there for a moment, and we're both staring at each other. "Fine. But my mom needs to know where I am. She'll freak out if she goes to pick us up and Nora is the only one there."

He nods his head and shuts the door. The moment I hear the click, I reach forward and press the small button to lock it. I loosen Roman's coat, letting it fall to the floor and turn around so my backside faces the mirror.

And I sob.

There's a big, circular splotch of red over my butt. A dark but bright red that is unmistakably blood. My sobs are silent but rack my chest and make my ribs hurt. My chest pounds as I grab the fabric around my sides and start inching it up. I continue pulling my dress up until it's around my waist, and my cream-colored panties are showing.

Hooking my thumbs into the waistband, I pull them down and cringe, my eyes watering as I see the stained red inside of them.

I go to the bathroom, wiping myself, hating the red smear that comes away on the toilet paper.

Knock, knock.

"I have some clothes here, and, um, a bag to put your… stuff in. I'll be in my room."

I don't say anything, my embarrassment making my face turn hot and the tears won't stop flowing.

Once I can hear the knowing creaks from the floorboards groaning from his weight as he walks back to his room, I get up, hobble to the door and as quietly as possible, I open the door and pull everything inside. A pair of Nora's underwear sits in between a pair of Roman's sweats and t-shirt. I wouldn't fit in Nora's clothes. I'm too tall and she is too short. Which is probably why he chose his own clothes for me to wear.

I slip everything on, opening the pad and putting the sticky side against my underwear. When I pull them up, I want to sob all over again.

It feels like I'm wearing a fucking diaper.

It feels gross and uncomfortable, but I don't see any other choice. With the small paper bag, I roll up my old underwear and dress, shoving them inside. I hope my mom can get the stain out of the dress. I really liked it.

I open up the bathroom door, and there stands Goldie. I'm sure my eyes are red-rimmed and puffy, but the sympathetic expression on her face makes me think she already knows what's going on.

"Oh, honey. I'm so sorry that had to happen tonight." She pulls me into her arms and squeezes me tight. "I'm going to pick up Nora, so your mom doesn't have to. Your mom did want you home in a couple hours, though, if you wanted to hang out here for a while longer." She has a knowing expression on her face, and all I can do is nod. Like she knows everything.

She knows us.

"Okay, you let me know if you need anything."

"Thank you." I sniffle, rubbing my eyes as I turn around and walk my bare feet across the tannish, yellowing carpet. Roman's bedroom door is opened, and he has his guitar in his lap as he sits on the side of the bed. On his nightstand sits a tall glass of clear liquid—I'm assuming water—and two little red pills.

He notices me when I step inside and props his guitar up against his bed as he stands up. "Are those clothes okay? I was going to get something of Nora's, but I'm guessing they would all be too small."

I nod. "These are fine." I glance at the table again, incredibly thirsty, since I was never able to drink that punch Travis was supposed to get for me earlier.

"Oh, here. Here's some water, and my mom said that Advil will help if you have a stomachache."

I nod my head, walking over to the table and swallowing down the pills with the water, gulping down large mouthfuls until the entire glass is empty. My stomach cramps, and I frown. "Maybe I should go home. I don't feel good."

"I can take you if you want. Or you can stay here, and I can play a little for you?"

I think about going home, and my mom's excitement over me getting my period. She'll hound me and ask me a bunch of questions, ask me how I'm feeling, and talk about womanhood. Or I can stay here with Roman until I'm forced to go home.

"I'll stay," I whisper.

He smiles, and I crawl under his blue comforter that smells like him. It's heavy and thick and I would sweat like crazy if I used this every night, but right now I'm freezing, like I have the chills. Probably from the blood loss, so I'm grateful to slip between the sheets that smell so much like Roman and burrow underneath its thickness.

I face away from him, keeping my back toward him as I curl up into a ball. My knees press against my chest and my toes brush against his cool sheets.

I can feel the other side of the mattress sink and can hear as he gets comfortable on his side of the bed. It's not a big bed, only a double size, but it's bigger than my twin-sized bed at home.

Roman starts plucking notes on his acoustic guitar, the one he rarely uses. He's a rock-and-roll guy like his father, but when he picks up his acoustic, I can't help but melt at the sounds. The soft tunes, the easy melodies. He plucks each note with ease.

"Roman?" I ask, my eyes closing as I imagine his fingers tugging on each string of his guitar, his fingers getting small red line indentations on the tips.

"Hmmm?" he responds, not stopping his random notes.

"Thank you for coming. Thank you for helping me."

He stops playing at this, a sharp, awkward note fading off into the distance and I imagine him pressing his palm against the strings.

"I wouldn't have had it any other way, Luna."

He starts up again, playing the notes until a tune starts, and then his voice starts crooning gently and quietly. Each note trails through the room until it reaches me. His voice swirls around my neck, my arms, my aching stomach, until they slip into my mouth and wrap directly around my heart.

I close my eyes and listen to the notes until they lull me to sleep.

CHAPTER EIGHT

Luna

My body bends as I spin in the air, my toes pointed, and my arms bowed above my head. I come down, landing on my toes and tiptoe across the stage. I can feel the pressure of my toes against the hard, wooden floor. I bend myself back, arching my spine and then I snap up, running forward and going into a split. I come down onto my toes, and then spin with my leg out, toes pointed. I end softly, going into a gentle bow.

The crowd goes wild and the curtains close, and every other dancer in The Nutcracker comes out. The curtain opens once more, and we all do a group bow as everyone stands and claps. Whistles and cheers are heard, and I think I even hear Roman in the crowd shouting my name.

The curtains close for a second time, and then it's chaos in the back. Everyone undresses into their regular clothes. Parents walk into the backstage area and greet their kids and give hugs. Soon my mom and dad are wrapping me in their arms, and my sister stands behind them. It's winter vacation, so Harper was able to come home for school break.

"You were wonderful, Luna!" My mom praises. I played Clara in The Nutcracker, a ballet that I have been practicing for since school started this year. I'm beat and tired, and I'm ready to go relax for Christmas in a couple days.

I say goodbye to my teacher and the other dancers, and then we walk off to the front, where Nora, Roman, and Goldie are all waiting for us.

"You did great, baby!" Goldie wraps me in a hug that I take willingly. I wrap my arms around her, loving the smell of Roman and their house that I've come to know as my second home.

"I so wish I could dance like that. How you can stand on your toes like that is beyond me." Nora scoffs and I laugh.

Roman stares at me, a proud and happy look on his face. Since the winter carnival when I got my first period, Roman and my relationship has been so much deeper than it's ever been before. We spend so much time together. We always have, but we're closer now. The simple touches, and the gentle glances— it's like my breath is stolen. He steals it easily, with only a glance, and I let him.

I let him swallow my breaths and my heart, and he takes them greedily.

He gives me his heart back.

It's thumping and wild, and a little erratic at times, but what we have together is undeniable, and I think we're both realizing we're tired of fighting the inevitable.

Not that we've made anything exclusive. Not that we've ever kissed. Our time together is something special in itself, even if I do look at him longingly every single night, waiting for the time when he finally presses his lips against mine.

"You owned that stage, Luna," Roman says as he walks up to me. I nuzzle against his chest as he hugs me, his warm, strong arms wrapping around my tired frame. My body is bruised and weary from practicing these last few months, and I'm glad to finally get a break.

"Thank you."

"Let's get going, or we'll be stuck in the parking lot forever with all these cars."

We walk out, and I see Travis talking to another classmate. He glances at me, his eyes barely passing over mine before he looks back at the girl. Our time was short-lived. Whatever we had lasted until the moment Roman walked into the winter carnival and stole me away. Travis never asked for an explanation. I don't think he even wanted one. Maybe he was glad to be rid of me.

That's okay, because being with Roman is the only place I want to be.

"Merry Christmas," my dad says when I walk into the living room a couple days later. It's Christmas morning, and as expected, there's a pile of presents under the tree. My parents never go easy on Christmas, even if they don't have a lot of extra money to spend. But whatever extra money they do have, they spend on us kids for Christmas and our birthdays.

"Merry Christmas." My mom stands over the stove, cooking French toast and sausages. Steam seeps off the skillet, the smell of cinnamon permeating the room. I walk up to her and give her a kiss on the cheek, then give my dad a hug. His morning beard scratches against my face and he smells like coffee. "Harper still sleeping?" I ask. I'm always impatient when it comes to opening gifts.

"She is sleeping. You'll have to wake her up if you want to open gifts now. College has her sleeping until the afternoon," my dad says as he grabs his cup, taking a sip. His newspaper is laying on his lap, with one leg crossed over the other.

I roll my eyes, knowing he's right. I walk back down the hall, passing my room on the way to Harper's. I stop, heading into my room. Getting down on my knees next to my bed, I reach under blindly, searching for the small package. My fingers grasp the tiny box, and I pull it out. It's only slightly bigger than a ring box, but I spent a lot of time and energy wanting to make this perfect.

My gift for Roman.

We've always gotten each other something for Christmas. Whether it be something silly like a handwritten card, or something from the candy store in town. But this year I saved up money I earned over the summer by babysitting some of the kids nearby, and I knew exactly what I wanted to get him.

I pull on the lid, and it makes a little squeaky noise as it props open. Embedded in a small pillow is a guitar pic. It's black marbled and engraved.

Soulmates.

R & L

It's not much, but I know how much playing the guitar means to him, and if he likes it, maybe he can use it forever. When he's famous, playing in front of thousands and thousands of people, maybe he'll remember the little girl from his old neighborhood. The little girl who he had a crush on and who had a crush on him.

I snap the box closed and tuck it back underneath my bed. Only a few more hours until I get it give it to him. My belly flutters with butterflies.

I hope he likes it.

A small tap on my windows makes me spring up in bed. I wipe my sweaty palms against my tight-covered legs and walk over to my window. I know who it is.

I always know who it is.

I slide my window open a crack, enough for Roman to get enough grip to raise it the rest of the way. He slides it open, the window squeaking on its hinges, and slips inside. His shoe slaps on my carpet, and a puff of snow explodes on the floor, instantly seeping into the carpet and disappearing.

"Sorry," he mumbles.

He looks handsome. He has a sweater on, and his hair is tamed a bit to the side today. He left to go to his grandmother's house, so I haven't been able to see him all day. I didn't have much to do.

After opening presents this morning, I spent the rest of the day watching Christmas movies with the family and hanging out in my room.

We don't have family nearby, and my parents didn't have the money to travel this year. So, we spent our day at home together. It wasn't as bad as I thought it'd be. I actually welcomed the peace and quiet. That, and I've been a ball of nerves all day. I've barely been able to touch my food, and I could barely focus on the words of our movies—my entire family laughing while I stared blankly at the screen.

I've just been so damn nervous.

About his gift, and about us. There's this… tension building. I don't know what it is, and I don't know how to tame it. Or whether it even wants to be tamed.

We're this low boiling chemistry that only needs one flick of a wick to burst into this incombustible heat.

Am I ready for the heat?

"What's the matter?" he asks. He has a small package is in his hand, wrapped in a green and red striped paper with a small bow on top. My heart rate speeds up, until I can feel the thumping in my ears and his voice sounds like it's coming from down a tube. "Luna." Roman gives me a small shake.

I shake my head clear of the fog. "Hmmm?" His fingers grip my bare biceps, his fingertips rough from playing his guitar as they press into my smooth skin.

"Are you all right?" His fingers give another squeeze of my arms.

"I'm fine. Are you?" I ask, sensing his own nervousness.

"I'm good." He releases me, stepping back and toeing off his boots. He shoves them with his black sock-covered foot up against the wall near my window. Walking over to my bed, he sits down on the edge. The springs creak and groan from his weight as he moves to take off his coat, tossing it on top of my pillow.

"Thanks." I chuckle.

He shrugs. "Do you want to open your present yet?"

"You should open yours first." I feel nervous again, large butterflies flapping against the cage of my belly, their wings tormenting me as they fly about. I walk to my nightstand and pick up his gift and extend my hand toward him. "Here."

"You should open yours first." He hands me my gift, and I shake my head.

"No, open yours first."

He grunts. "Always a pain in my ass." He takes the small box from my hand, his hand dwarfing the tiny box underneath his large fingers. He's grown so much over the years. He went from being my size, maybe a little smaller, to being one of the tallest guys in his grade. He is easily six feet tall, his chest trim but the muscles in his arms are strong. He looks more like a man than a boy, even with him only being in ninth grade.

He cracks the box open, displaying the pick I spent all day staring at. Hoping and praying and wishing that he'll love his gift as much as I do. He stares at the pick a minute, then pulls it out and drops the box. It tumbles, knocking against his knee before falling to the ground.

The pick sits pinched between his thumb and forefinger, the tips of his fingers turning white from the pressure in which he holds it. He flips it over, then flips it over again. When he looks up at me, his eyes are shining with such awe and adoration that I nearly crumble to my knees.

"This…" he snakes his free hand out, wrapping it around my waist and pulling me close. "I will play with this forever. Until the letters are faded, and the edges are worn, I'll use this. I'll keep playing with it even then and after. This is perfect. I love it. Thank you, Luna." He squeezes me tight, his arm slightly trembling from emotion.

"You'll use it when you're big and famous, and that way you can always remember the little neighbor girl from Wisconsin."

His eyebrows drop, nearly covering his eyes with a scowl. "Little? You'll be bigger and more famous than me as you reach for the stars and dance in the most famous ballets. I'll be singing shitty lyrics and playing cover music while you're dancing at Julliard Academy in New York with the best dancers in the world. You are so much more than just the little neighbor girl from Wisconsin." He palms his pick and hides it from sight while he grabs the little box from on top of my comforter and hands it to me. "Now open yours."

I take it with shaky hands, feeling the smooth surface beneath my palm. I feel for the little tape flap, bringing my finger beneath the crease and ripping it open with care. I grab the small box, very similar to my own present, and pull it out of the wrap.

"You didn't wrap this yourself, did you?" I ask. The wrapping job is too perfect, no way were his large hands able to manage this by himself.

He smiles sheepishly. "Just open the damn gift, Luna."

I do as I'm told. Opening the small box, my eyes instantly burn with unshed tears as I see what's hiding underneath the top.

"Wow," I whisper, my eyes filling with tears. I run my finger over the gold chain. It's dainty and small, feminine. The chain of the necklace is gold and lightweight as I pick it up. In the center is a tiny pair of ballet slippers. There is detail with the ribbons, fluttering to the point they look real even though they are also solid gold. The wrinkles carved into the tiny slippers are so beautiful, so realistic, a tear flows down my cheek slowly, the same speed my finger runs across the slippers. "This is… is it real?"

He rolls his eyes. "Of course, it is."

"It's too much." My voice comes out clogged, too full of emotion.

"No, it's not. Turn around, let me put it on you." He lifts the box from my hand, grabs my shoulder and spins me until my back is facing him. I can hear him as he takes the chain out of the box. Soon enough, his hand lifts my hair and brings it over my left shoulder. His hands come around me, the shiny gold chain glittering in my darkened room, the only light in this darkness. He clasps the chain, and the ballet slippers weigh heavy but light against my neck, right between my collarbones. I lift it up, feeling its texture and heaviness between my fingers before placing it back against my chest. His hand comes down, and he grabs it himself. He lifts it, inspects it, and drops it against my chest. His hand goes down, and he presses it against me, as if he wants it to mold against my skin.

Feeling my voice echo through my chest and against his hand, I whisper, "I'll wear this every time I dance. With every bruise and ache in my bones, I'll think of you. Every time I bow at the end of a show, I'll think of you. Every time I lace my slippers around my own feet, tying my bows with perfect precision, it'll be you I think about."

His hand leaves my chest, and I'm spun around again, this time facing him. We're close, closer than I've ever been to him. I can feel his breath against my face and breathe it in, loving the thought of taking something of his. Anything. I breathe in as he exhales, and I watch his own chest expand as I exhale. "I have one more gift. Well, more of a question, actually."

I look up at him, his eyes dark and swirling. My own eyes watery with emotion. "What is it?"

He takes a breath so large it grazes my face. The breath he puffs out blows the black hair from my cheeks, a blast of wind drying my eyes. "Will you be my girlfriend?"

Another wave of tears hits my eyes, and they're quick to spill, running down my face in quick motions that even I can't contain. He brings a hand up, brushing his palms against my cheeks as he tries to stop the flow. I can't stop, and his tenderness only makes me cry harder. A sob rips from my chest, and I'm not even sure where it comes from.

Relief, maybe.

Happiness.

Excitement.

I've wanted this boy since I was six years old, and here I am today. Finally going to be his girlfriend. Is this elation? This tugging in my chest? It almost feels like it's breaking, and I can't help but want to clutch my chest to stop the ache.

"Say something, would you?" He laughs.

I laugh too, the sound watery and garbled as tears clog my throat. "Yes. Yes, I will."

"Oh, thank fuck." His fingers thread through my hair, pulling me to him, as he finally, finally presses his lips against mine.

He kisses like he's practiced, even though I know he hasn't. I'm his first kiss, just as much as he is mine. He takes control, his lips swallowing my bottom lip, and then my top. Not too wet, not too dry. Perfect. I barely peek my tongue out, and he takes that as an invitation to slide his tongue against mine. I bring my hands up, clutching his shoulders.

I want him.

I want all of him.

This need swallows me, heating me up below the belly. A feeling I've never experienced before, but one I've heard of from girls at school. One kiss from Roman and I'm turning into a raging fire, one that can't be put out.

My hands move from his shoulders to the back of his hair, threading through the messy strands and pulling on them.

He grunts.

We kiss until my tongue hurts, my jaw hurts, and I can literally feel the dampness drenching my panties between my thighs.

Knock, knock, knock.

Roman rips himself off me, flinging himself back so he's lying on my bed. My eyes widen when I see the bulge between his pants. He notices my look too, and he cringes, sitting up and hunching over just as my door opens and my mom walks in.

"Oh! Roman! I didn't know you were here."

"He came through the window, Mom." I hope like hell she can't tell something just happened between us. My cheeks are surely flaming red.

Both Roman and my parents have known that we sneak through each other's windows since, well, forever. It didn't take them long to figure it out, and back then we were so little they knew nothing would come of it.

Now, though, I'm starting to wonder if my mom might say something about it. Or make some weird rules.

"Did you open your present?" My mom directs her question to Roman. His face softens from his shocked look and he opens his fist, revealing the small pick still sitting in the center of his palm. "What do you think?" she asks.

He swallows, and I watch as his Adam's apple bobs a few times. "Best gift I've ever gotten."

My mom's face softens to the point she looks like she's going to cry. I intervene before she does so. "Look what Roman got me." I walk up to her, lifting the pair of ballet slippers. She grabs it, laying it on her palm as she looks at it.

"Wow," she whispers. This time her eyes water, and she blinks them away before they can fall. Suddenly, she steps back and clears her throat. "Don't stay too late, Roman."

She smiles at us, giving me a *be smart* look.

Once she shuts the door, Roman looks over at me with a *holy shit* look on his face.

"That was close." I giggle, pressing my knee on the mattress. I'm seconds from hopping on top of him when he slides off the bed quickly, standing up on the opposite side of the bed and putting his hands in the air.

"No. That was *too* close." He takes a deep breath, running his hands through his hair. "I better go." I look down at his waist, seeing the bulge gone from his jeans.

An ache starts in my chest at the thought of him leaving already. "You're leaving? Already?"

He walks around the foot of the bed, stopping when the toes of his black socks touch my bare feet. "Only until tomorrow." He leans down, pressing his lips to mine again. "I just don't want to get caught." Another kiss. "Not today, at least." I smirk against his lips, and I feel his teeth. He's smirking, too.

After one more kiss, he grabs his coat and slips it on and goes to shove his feet into his boots. With one more smirk, he raises the pick to his lips and gives it a kiss and is out my window a second later.

I flop back onto my bed, a sigh leaving my chest with my arms extended at my sides. My pillows and comforter billow around me like cotton candy before settling against my body. They smell like him.

Roman Hall is my boyfriend.

I'm on the cliff.

It's particularly dark today. Raging storm clouds swirl up above, like a tornado getting ready to pick me up and swallow me whole. The soft sand swirls around my ankles like bracelets, tickling at my skin and making me want to reach down and scratch the itch away.

The sand starts to pull me, and I step backward, away from the edge. The water crashes angrily against the side of the cliff, the noise loud as if I were inches away from the waves. The wind picks up, and I fall to my butt, the jagged rock beneath me scraping the back of my thighs.

That's when I look down and realize I'm in my leotard. My ballet slippers still on my feet.

What? How?

I get back up, running away from the edge, when a huge gust of wind picks me up and blows me right over.

I shoot up in bed, sweat running down my temples in terror as my dream comes back to haunt me, once again.

I told my mom about it, this recurring dream, years ago. She brought me to a psychologist, but they thought nothing of it. Blamed it on the move. But that was years ago, and I haven't seen them since.

It has to mean something, though, right?

I breathe deeply, feeling a weight between my collarbones. I lift my hand to my necklace, clutching it in my palm as I lie back down. Snuggling beneath my comforter, I close my eyes as tears flood my pillow.

This nightmare has tormented me for years, and it feels like at this point, it will never go away.

Maybe someday, though, I hope. When Roman takes me to where the mountains meet the sea.

CHAPTER NINE

Roman

"Have fun tonight. Don't do anything stupid. No drinking. No sex." My dad says with his arm around my mom as they head out the door.

Tonight is New Year's Eve.

"We won't, Mr. Hall," Flynn says next to me, his hand coming up to slap my back. I shove his hand away, shaking my head in the same manner that my dad shakes his head at me before he shuts the door.

"You're an idiot." I shove him once my dad is gone. If they decided to stay here tonight, that would essentially ruin the damn night. It's just me and the guys tonight, and Nora invited Luna, even though everyone knows we're dating at this point. It only took a day.

One damn day.

From the looks on our faces when Luna's mom walked in, she instantly knew. She told my parents, who questioned me about it. Nora heard, and then blurted it to my friends.

Now everyone knows.

It doesn't matter. Not really, anyway.

Luna is my world. She's my entire life and signifying her as my girlfriend was inevitable. I need her in my life just as much as I need air. My heart doesn't beat for me. It beats for her. It beats with her. Nothing else matters.

And tonight, I finally get some alone time with her.

We're going to watch the ball drop. Nothing serious. Lonnie brought some beer, but I'm not letting Nora or Luna drink. Luna hates the smell of beer anyway, so I won't be drinking either.

When I hear giggling downstairs, I know Nora and Luna just arrived from Luna's house.

Flynn looks at me as he cracks open a beer. "Let's get this party started."

"Well, this sucks ass," Clyde says, adjusting the antenna on the top of my box TV.

"It's because it's snowing outside. We always have bad reception when it's snowing," Nora grumbles from the couch. Her arms folded across her chest as she pouts.

"I don't want to miss the ball drop." Luna walks up to the TV and takes over, fiddling with the antenna.

I walk over to the window, watching the snow fall lightly over the ice-covered lake. It's light and fluffy, but sometimes even the lightest snow will mess with the reception on our TV.

"You got it!" Clyde shouts, and soon I hear the crackling voices shouting over the TV.

I turn around and see the fuzzy screen making out the massive shiny ball in New York City. There isn't much time left. It has to be close to midnight.

I look at Luna, and she's watching the TV with a rosiness in her cheeks and a smile pulling her lips up. Her straight white teeth shine as she talks with Nora. Her dress is long, all the way to her ankles. I know underneath her dress she's wearing long wool socks that slide up her calves, and her worn brown boots that go up to her knees.

She's a lot like her mom in the way she dresses. Long flowing dresses, long flowing hair. Luna has the hippy blood in her, but it looks good on her.

I want to kiss her.

I want to kiss her when the clock strikes twelve. I want to kiss her minutes before and I want to kiss her for minutes after, but I don't know how to walk up to her and lay my lips on hers without making a fool of myself.

"I brought something," she says, bending over to reach into her purse. She pulls out a small white paper, and I realize what it is instantly.

"You brought a joint?" I laugh. She's never shown interest in smoking weed or drinking for that matter.

She shrugs. "It's New Year's Eve."

Like that's enough of an answer.

"Anyone have a light?" she asks, swinging the paper around. The guys look at her, enthralled by the joint. We've smoked once or twice, but not enough for me to want to buy some for myself.

My mom wouldn't be too happy either.

"We should go out on the deck," Nora suggests.

I point at her as I walk to the kitchen to grab a pack of matches. "You aren't smoking."

She plants her hands on her hips. "Uh, yeah I am."

I grunt my displeasure and go to our kitchen, opening the drawer and pulling out a spare pack of matches with an ace symbol on it. My parents always hoard packs of matches when they go to the casino for some reason. I couldn't explain why. They don't even smoke.

Everyone is huddled on the back deck when I get back to the living room. Luna holds the joint between her fingers, poised to her lips for me to light. I slide on my shoes and step outside. Walking up to her, I stare at her a moment. She stares back at me, her gray eyes in the nighttime sky nearly glowing, looking translucent, like a liquefied silver or mercury as she beams up at me.

I strike the match, lighting up her eyes and her pale face. Her eyes turn gold beside the yellow flame. I cup my hand around the joint and watch the tip grow a bright orange. She sucks on the joint, her eyes going wide before she pulls it out of her mouth and starts coughing. She coughs and coughs until there are tears streaming down her face, rivers of mascara trailing from her cheeks to her chin.

I take it from her, knowing from that one hit she's had enough. I take a hit and pass it around, skipping over my sister. She scowls at me fiercely, but all I do is give her a shrug.

She doesn't need this shit.

Luna wanders over to the edge of the deck, her back to us as she watches

121

the snow fall over the water. Snowflakes flitter into her dark hair. The blackness splotched with crystals of white snow.

She looks angelic.

When I hear the countdown from twenty start inside the house, my feet walk of their own accord. They wander over to Luna, my shoes crunching against the snow. I wrap my arm around her waist. She looks at me, her eyes glazed red and her smile loose. I can feel her counting down in her head, every second inching just a little bit closer to me.

Three.

Two.

One.

I press my lips to hers, and she exhales deeply. I breathe it in. I breathe her in, taking her lips and her body in mine as I wrap my arms around her. I can hear everyone go inside, their quiet footsteps on the deck as they give us space.

Her lips are warm and soft, even though the rest of her is cold. I kiss her until her body trembles, and I'm not sure if it's from the crisp air or her need. Her chilled hands go up to my shoulders, squeezing me tight.

"Let's go inside," I mumble against her lips, pulling back enough so I can see the look in her eyes. They're wide, wondrous, a little hesitant, and a whole lot turned on. "We don't have to do anything you don't want to."

"I want to." She grips the front of my shirt, pulling on me. As if she wants to touch every inch of me. Like she can't get enough.

I kiss her once more and pull her inside. No one is on the main level, and I'm assuming they all went downstairs to hang out. We should go down there with them. I trust my friends more than I trust my sister. I know she's had a crush on Flynn forever. I'll cut his nuts off if he ever does anything with her. I'd be pissed if she did anything with any of my friends for that matter. She's too good for them.

I pull Luna through the house and down the hallway, not even bothering to take off our shoes. The wet soles seep into the carpet, leaving dark footprints. We end up in my room, and I shut the door behind us. Suddenly it's quiet, so quiet the only thing I can hear is the heavy breathing of both Luna and me. I walk up to her, lifting the ballerina slippers from her neck, holding them between my fingers. I have yet to see her take this off. Every time I see her, she's wearing the necklace.

She brings her hands to the front of her coat, sliding it off her arms and drops it to pool at her feet. She grabs her dress around her waist, bunching it with her hands. She keeps bunching more and more of her dress, until the hem brushes the tops of her thighs. Her bare thighs are pale, and her brown boots click together as her knees tremble. She glances up at me through her long dark eyelashes as dark as her hair that brushes against her pale cheeks, tinged pink from the cold.

She's asking for permission.

I take a step toward her, slamming my mouth to hers and grab her dress between my fingers. I squeeze the soft fabric, bringing my hands around to the small of her back, pulling the dress with me so it stretches taut against her front. It raises a bit, showing off a sliver of her panties.

She lets out a sigh against my lips. "I want to touch you."

I swallow, not sure how far I should take this or how far she wants to go, but my strength is only so strong when it comes to her. I bring my hands underneath her thighs, lifting her into my arms and walk to my bed. Once my thighs are against my bed, I drop her, and she falls onto her back, her hair and dress splaying out around her.

I climb on top of her, pressing every inch of my body against hers. She grabs onto my hair, pulling me to her. I kiss her, licking against her lips and into her mouth. My hand drops to her shoulder, and I trail my fingers down her side. They dip and swell, her newfound curves giving her hips that she's never had before.

Once my hands brush her bare thigh, I move up, bringing her dress with my hand until it's bunched around her waist. She snakes her hands between us, grappling at the hem of my shirt and inching it toward my head. I push myself up, grabbing the fabric behind my head and pulling the shirt off in one yank.

Her hands plant on my chest. Gone are her cold fingers and now they are warm, burning as they press against my chest. She trails her fingers around, testing the boundaries and feeling me intimately for the first time. We've touched each other before, obviously, but never like this. It's like we wanted to search each other's hearts and souls to find the sole purpose for us being together first.

There has to be a reason, right?

There has to be a reason for us to have this infinite need to be in each other's presence. It's grown over time from playing with each other as children, doing simplistic things like playing in the water or riding our bikes to the park, to touching each other. To kissing each other. My rough fingers against her soft skin. Her bruised feet from ballet tangling with mine.

Her lips constantly pressing against mine.

We are an undeniable hunger that cannot be sated.

My fingers brush her panties, and I swipe against damp fabric. It's then I notice her scent in the air, swirling through my nose, and I grow impossibly hard, my erection painfully straining against the zipper of my jeans.

I grunt. No amount of jacking off would take away the swelling of my cock whenever I'm near Luna.

Luna's hands trail down my back, ending at my waist. Her fingers tentatively brush underneath the waistband of my underwear, her curious fingers scraping against the muscle where my ass meets my back.

Her fingers dance around my waist, moving to the front of my jeans. She plays with my button, flicking it a few times with her finger until I feel it loosen, and then the distinct sound of my zipper lowering.

"What're you…?" I move away from her lips, looking down at her in shock. She's not ready to have sex, whether or not she's high as a kite right now. I'm not taking her virginity with her best friend in the other room and my friends downstairs. When my parents could be home at any time.

"I just want to touch you," she moans, lifting her hips against my hand until my fingers swipe against wetness again. She tucks her hand beneath my boxers, and her fingers wrap around my erection, solid and hard as a rock.

Luna sucks in a breath. "It's… smooth, and… warm." Her fingers brush up and down the length, figuring out what feels good and what doesn't.

I bring a hand down, shoving my pants just below my ass, enough where my erection can spring free. It slaps against my stomach. Luna looks down, transfixed and in awe as she watches her hand move against the soft skin.

I have to hold my breath, so I don't ejaculate like a fucking child.

I snake my hand between her thighs, pressing against the wetness a little bolder this time, rubbing her over the panties. She likes this, I realize, as she gives my erection a tight squeeze. Her hands are shaky as I continue to rub her, and the wet spot on her panties grows larger, until most of the fabric is translucent. Her pale pink panties against the dampness become see-through, and I can see her naked slit through the fabric.

I bring my fingers up, curling them around the hem of her panties and pull them down over her thighs. They rock back and forth on her ankle, and she kicks her foot, flinging them to the floor.

Then her bottom half is on display, naked for me for the first time ever. I sit up, my erection sliding out of her hand as I try to get a better look.

"Can I?" I nudge at her knees, and her cheeks flame red, but she does as I ask, dropping her knees to the side to show me the slickness between her legs. Her juices spread to the insides of her thighs. I bend down, looking closer, inspecting every fold and crevice and perfection that is a part of her.

"Oh my God, what're you doing?" she shrieks, closing her thighs on each side of my head.

I push her legs apart. "Stop. You're... fucking hell." I let out a heavy breath and watch as her folds tense and quiver.

Fucking. Shit.

I can't *not.*

My tongue peeks out, and I swipe between her folds. My eyes roll in the back of my head at the flavor, the sweetness as it touches my tongue. A slight tanginess that lingers in my mouth. I can't help but go back for more, licking up her wetness.

Her hips jackknife off the bed, and I bring my hand to her stomach, pushing against the softness of her belly until her butt hits my sheets once again.

I continue licking her, continue ravaging her, swallowing every drop of juice I possibly can, until her pants turn into moans, and I bring my hand to her mouth so everyone in the house doesn't know what we're doing in here.

Her body starts trembling, and I know she's orgasming. I suck on the bud at the top of her folds, flicking my tongue against it until her trembling stops, and she sinks into the mattress like a wilted flower.

I lean back on my knees, my erection straining and nearly purple, and wipe my mouth with the back of my hand.

"I've never..." she pants.

My eyes widen. "That was your first time?"

She nods, rolling over and glancing down at my erection. "My turn?"

She crawls toward me, grabbing it in her hand. She grips it tightly, moving her hand awkwardly up and down. I place my hand over hers. "Like this." I show her how I like it, and when I release my hand, she does exactly as I showed.

My eyes roll in the back of my head.

It doesn't take long. Her tiny, firm fingers wrapping around my erection make it painfully hard. Soon enough, I grunt, "Going to come." That doesn't stop her, and she keeps pumping, until I'm spilling all over my stomach and all over her hand.

Perfect.

She brings a finger up to her mouth, dipping it between her wet lips and places the pad on her tongue, tasting me.

"Mmmm. Tastes good."

Fucking shit.

CHAPTER TEN

Luna

1994

"Ugh, isn't he hot?" Nora says from beside me.

I stare at Roman, singing his heart out as his fingers fly over the strings of his guitar. He owns the stage; he owns the guitar. He owns everything that he walks on. There's just something about him that's so... *possessive*. He's an enigma, and I guess I've known it since we were little, but as he gets older it only gets more real.

But now... now he's in his last year in high school, and the little boy that I used to know is now a man. His long, dark hair is damp at the ends from sweat as he shakes it to the beat of his music. I watch as droplets of sweat fly into the air. He doesn't look anywhere besides his guitar, otherwise his eyes are closed. He doesn't play for the crowd. He plays because he was born to do it.

"Can you stop watching my brother like that?" I look over at Nora and see her face scrunched up in distaste.

"Shut up." I flick my bunched-up straw wrapper at her.

"I can't believe this year is almost over. Next year we're going to be seniors."

"I know." I frown. It's been good to be back in school with Roman, mostly now that we're dating. It feels natural. Never once have things been awkward or feel uncomfortable. Every little bit of our relationship has been flawless, seamless. We easily melded from best friends to boyfriend and girlfriend.

But I guess things are effortless when you're soulmates.

"Have you figured out what school you're planning to go to yet? You can still come with me to Madison."

I shake my head. "I'm still hoping for Julliard. You know that's my goal."

She frowns. "New York, though? That's halfway across the country. What am I going to do without you?"

I smile. "I'll come home. My parents won't let me stay away for long. And you can always come out to visit." I shake my head. "You don't have to even worry about that. We still have senior year before anything is set in stone."

"What do you think Roman's going to do?"

Those words make my stomach flop. It's been a taboo question that I haven't wanted to think about. One both Roman and I haven't brought up at all. I really hope it's because he plans to stick around until I'm done with school, and not because he has some plan I don't know about churning in the background.

But he wouldn't do that to me, right?

I couldn't imagine he would. The thought of being without him fractures my heart to no end. Being with him is like breathing, being without him would steal my breath and heart. Living would be impossible.

Everyone starts cheering in the little coffee shop turned concert. They have Thursday and Saturday night bands play, and since our town is so small, Roman's is usually the only band that performs.

Doesn't bother anyone much. They're so good at this point they could be famous. People from different towns come to see Roman and his band play.

Cataclysm.

Roman's band's name.

Everyone stands up, cheering and whistling. For the first time since his song started, Roman looks directly out at my usual table, locking eyes with mine. He smiles, and I smile back. He sets his guitar in his stand and gives his friends a nod before bending down, pressing his hands against the stage as he hops off, walking over to me.

Planting a wet kiss on me, he smiles. "What'd you think?"

"As always, perfection." I smile against his mouth, tasting the saltiness of his sweat as I lick my lips.

"Ready to go?" His fingers go to the ballet slippers around my neck. Ever since we started dating, Roman has been bringing me to ballet. He stays if he can, watching me dance and practice until my toes are bloody and bruised, and then he brings me home, lying with me and my tired body until I'm asleep.

"Ready." I grab my bag with my leotard and slippers. Sliding my fingers through Roman's, we walk out the door together and down the street toward the dance studio. The evening is quiet, only a few locals walking in and out of the shops. I can see the sun setting over by the park, the red sun lighting up the metal swing set. Inhaling deeply, I smell the familiar cornfield and beachy lake only blocks away.

"You can just drop me off if you need to go back there and grab your things."

He shakes his head. "We can stop there afterward. The guys will pack everything up so all I'll need to do is grab everything."

I nod, and we walk quietly through the evening spring air. Soon we're there, and I use the key from my purse to unlock the door.

My teacher, Leona Ivanov, used to be a famous ballet teacher in New York at Julliard. But her sick mother eventually led her to moving out here, and she's been my teacher ever since. I was little when I met her, only a short while after I moved here. She's always been the teacher that has me practice rigorously. She even prefers I go when no one else is there to stay focused and get my work in. I think she's even more determined than I am that I need to get into Julliard.

Roman turns on the lights and goes to sit in his usual booth that's built onto the wall. I go into the back, getting dressed quickly. I put my hair into a knot on the top of my head, and walk out barefoot, the ribbons of my ballet slippers wrapped around my fingers.

My feet slapping again the wooden floor make Roman glance up. He smiles when he sees me, patting the spot next to him when he sees my bare feet.

I hand him a slipper when I get to him, propping my foot up on his lap. He slides the slipper on, having watched me since I was a child, he knows exactly what to do. He replicates my movements that I'm doing with the opposite foot, crisscrossing the ribbons over my foot until it's at the back of my calf, and then he ties a perfect bow.

I smile at him when its finished, knowing its perfect, maybe even more perfect than the one I did, only because he did it himself.

"What're we listening to today?" he asks, the CD player next to him with a stack of CDs on the floor.

"Mmmm. You choose today."

I've practiced with every type of music. From rock that Roman listens to, to folk that my parents listen to, to classical that I've grown up on while dancing to ballet. I can dance to anything and everything.

But classical is always my favorite.

He pops open the top of the CD player, putting a disk in the middle and clicking the top down. Switching the player to turn it on, he clicks Play, and *Canon in D* starts by Johann Pachelbel. I smile at him knowing this is one of my favorites.

I stretch a little bit as I walk around, feeling my limbs and muscles flex and bend. I go up on my toes, and back on my feet. I spin around, doing a plié and going back down again. I twirl, bending and moving to the music as gracefully as the melody tells me to. It speaks to me, it always has. No words are needed with this type of music, it bleeds into my skin and I move however it wishes me to.

I spin and spin, floating through the air from one side of the studio to the next. I don't even pay attention to Roman, although I know he's paying attention to every move and step I take. He knows my dances well enough to know what needs to be improved on. He's listened to my teacher ream me out about the silliest, smallest things. But they aren't small to her, and if I want to get into Julliard, I need to be as focused as she tells me to be.

The crescendo of the song builds, and I can feel my heart expand with emotion. My eyes well as I dance, feeling the emotion rip through me as I give it my all. Suddenly, I spin around, and there is Roman. He stands on the other side of the studio in the middle of the wooden floor, arms at his sides.

He waits.

I run to him, as fast as I can, and when I'm within reach, he lifts me at my waist and extends me in the air. His arms don't shake. His body is certain, still, strong. Perfect as he keeps me in the air and suspends me above him. I point my toes as he spins me around, and then he slowly brings me back down his body. I wrap my legs and arms around him as I hold him tight, laying my lips on his.

I love him so much.

"You dance beautifully. Every single step you take has the most breathtaking emotion in it. It's almost heartbreaking to watch you."

My eyes start to water again, and I nod. Because I know how he feels.

Sometimes it's sad when I dance. A sadness buried deep within me comes out, and it's a darkness I only show when I dance. I'm not a sad person, and there's nothing depressing about me, but sometimes, when I dance, this uncontrollable grief hits me in the center of my chest.

I dance until the heaviness goes away. Dancing always makes me feel better. Every. Single. Time.

He sets me down. "Keep going. I want to watch more."

I do.

I dance and continue dancing, pressing all my weight in my toes until I can feel them start to crack and bleed. I float myself in the air until I feel like I'm going to touch the clouds, and I extend my arms as if I can wrap myself around Roman from across the room.

Wandering over to the bar, I stretch into a split, curling and stretching my back to rid the ache. Only soon enough I can hear Roman's footsteps behind me, and then his hands are there on my waist, lifting me off the ground as he spins me around. He sets me on the bar, and I wobble a bit.

"This won't hold me." I worry, trying to grab onto his shoulders for support.

His eyebrows lift. "You weigh five pounds. It'll hold you just fine."

He walks between my legs, keeping his hands planted on my waist. I roll my spine, bending down until my lips press against his. He kisses me deeply, plunging his tongue into my mouth. His kiss is heated, turned on. He swallows my moan, his fingers going between my leotard and pressing against my sex, which is already damp.

"Stop, we can't do this here." I look to the left, where the windows are. They're big and wide, no curtains to shield us from pedestrians. Anyone could see us. This town is small enough where everyone knows everyone. One look in here and our parents would know we were fooling around.

Not like they don't already know.

But there's one thing—we haven't had sex. Not yet, anyway. Not that I haven't tried. Roman puts it off, telling me I'm not ready.

That doesn't mean we haven't done everything else.

Why he won't go that extra step is beyond me. I've practically begged at this point, but all he tells me is that it should be special. *He* wants it to be special.

And that is exactly why I'm in love with him.

"I know we can't. I just can't help it when you dance like that. You're so

133

fucking breathtaking." He lifts me off the bar, sliding me down his body. I reach up on my tiptoes, giving him another kiss. I push him across the studio, back through the back room where I change for the evening.

I press him against the wall, raising my leg so it's over his waist. "I want you," I moan. "I want you now."

He groans. "Not here. Not now."

"When?" I whine.

"When it will be special." He presses his fingers between my thighs, rubbing the ache that grows whenever I'm around him. "I can make you feel better now, though." He slides his fingers beneath my leotard, finding my naked folds wet and ready.

I'm ready. I've *been* ready.

He sticks a finger in, and I grunt around the pressure as he starts fingering me. I reach down to his erection and squeeze, knowing he's just as pent up with tension as I am. I drop to my knees, grappling at his button until his pants are loose and I'm shimmying them down his waist.

"N-not here, he stammers, although I know he won't turn me away.

I shake my head. "Please. Let me." I pull his erection out, seeing him rock-hard and red with need. I lick the tip, tasting the dollop of precum there. Placing my lips around the head, I suck until I get as far to the base as I can.

Roman's head tilts back to the wall, the back of his head knocking against it as he lets out a tortured groan. "Shiiiiiit."

I lick him faster, hollowing out my cheeks and sucking him hard. My hand goes down to the base, cupping his balls and giving them a small tug. He grunts, his hips jacking forward slightly. It makes me gag, and I let him slide out of my mouth a bit while I struggle to swallow.

His hand goes to my bun, and I go back down, my other hand going to the base of his cock and pumping him a few times while I get him as wet as I can with my tongue, my head going back and forth until I can feel him harden even further in my mouth.

"I'm going to come," he grunts, and that makes me pump him faster with my hand, my other hand pulling on his balls as I flatten my tongue on the underside of him and suck until he starts throbbing. He comes, the salty warm cum filling my mouth. I swallow, but there's so much it leaks from the corner of my lips.

He pulls me up roughly once he can breathe again, his hands going under my armpits as he yanks me up like a child. His fingers pull my leotard to the side, diving between my drenched folds as he sticks two fingers inside of me. There's a pinch of pain, but he uses his thumb to rub my clit until I'm grinding against the heel of his hand.

He fucks me hard, and I grip the back of his neck and pull his lips to mine, groaning into his mouth as I hump his hand. I want to fuck him—not his hand, but this will do.

For now.

He rubs my clit harder while he fingers me, and soon I feel the low burning in the pit of my belly. It starts slow, tingling from my stomach and spreading to my toes.

"Oh, fuck," I moan against his lips. I lose my standing, and Roman sweeps and arm around my waist and holds me up against his body while my orgasm takes hold. He holds me until I come down, and he holds me long after, too.

"I love you, Roman." I've said the words a million times, but I've never said it like this.

He leans back, looking at me with a soft expression. A smirk lifts his mouth, his pouty lips quirking up on the sides. "I love you, too, Luna. Now and always."

"Now and always."

CHAPTER ELEVEN
Roman
1990

This is it.

Tonight is the night.

I'm bringing Luna down to a secluded spot by the beach, and I'm going to sleep with her. She's been wanting it, and I've wanted it to be special. How can I make it special, though? What can I do that would possibly be enough and special enough for *her*?

I've wanted to fly her to a different country, but even that doesn't seem like it would be special enough.

Nothing would ever be perfect when it comes to her, but I realize she doesn't want perfect. She just wants me, and I just want her. Together we are as perfect as we'll ever be.

I found a small secret area of the beach, a place where we've been only a few times while exploring around the lake. A place that's hidden from people and sights of everyone. The only things that I've ever known to explore this area is wildlife.

But today it's quiet. Not a sound, not an animal.

The sun sets over the lake, creating a glistening appearance on the water. A few boats are out, but we're hidden by trees and brush. The sun is tinged red as it sets, the clouds a burnt orange as they shine back at me.

I have my guitar here, a blanket, and a small basket I found in my kitchen. I packed a few things, even though I don't think Luna will want to eat anything when she knows what my plans are. She's eager, a nymph. It only makes me want her more.

I left her at ballet this evening and told her I had to meet the guys for something. She didn't bat an eye. I left as quickly as I could, packed everything up and brought it to this secret spot. I'm hoping she likes it.

With one last glance at the area I put together, I grab my car keys and head to my car. It's an old thing, a Ford Escort, not something I ever actually drive in unless I'm going out of town for a show or something.

I drive to the studio, where I see Luna dancing and stretching her body like a bow as her body flips and turns and twirls to the music I can't hear. I watch her for a few minutes, as other people walk by the outside window and stop to stare at her too.

She's something different. Not anything anyone has ever seen before. She's beautiful, and unique. Her long black hair is tied in a small bun on top of her head. Her long body, longer than most girls her age, is thin but strong. Her toes are always pointed, whether she's at home or in ballet. It's like her feet were made for the slippers she always wears.

I turn my car off, hop out, stepping onto the curb and opening the front door. Classical music plays through the stereo, and Luna's spine snaps straight when she hears the small bell above the door ring. A smile breaks out on her face when she sees me, love and adoration filling her features.

"You're here early," she says, her forehead damp from exertion.

"I have something to show you. Are you ready?"

Curiosity lines her face, her gray eyes sparkling in anticipation. "A surprise?" She smiles. "Let me grab my things."

She runs to the back, her toes holding most of her weight while she floats to grab her bag. I walk over to the stereo and turn it off, then flip off the lights and pick up the CDs while I wait for her. It doesn't take long, and soon she's back, her bare feet slapping across the floor with her slippers slung over her shoulders.

"Ready?" she asks, a smile on her rosy face.

I nod and lace my fingers through hers as we walk back out to my car.

"You're driving today?"

I nod, pushing her into the car without another word. I don't want to spoil anything.

I hop in, and she instantly fiddles with the radio while I turn on the car and pull onto the street. I take a right, and it doesn't take long for her to notice we aren't driving home.

"Where are we going?"

"You'll see." I smile, bringing my hand over to her thigh and giving her a squeeze. Her skin is hot against my palm, smooth and creamy white.

I drive to the other side of the lake and pull off the road when I get to our spot.

Her eyes light up when she notices where we are. "We're at our secret spot?"

I nod, getting out of the car and walking over to her door. "You can leave your things here."

She does as she's told, leaving her slippers and bag at the foot of her seat.

I grab her hand, pulling her from the car and through the brush. She slaps at her bare legs when the weeds brush against her skin. I know it feels like spiders and other bugs as it tickles her legs. I pull a tree branch back for her, and she ducks beneath it as she steps onto the sand. "Oh my God," she whispers, looking back at me with wide eyes.

I smile at her, not sure what to say.

"What is all this?" She waves her hand around, seeing the plaid blanket spread out on the sand and the small basket sitting in the corner. She looks at my guitar, propped up against a tree. "What is all this?" she repeats.

"I told you I wanted it to be special. Do you like it?"

She looks at me, her face draining of color and filling at the same time. "You mean… really?" Her hand separates from mine, and a brightness fills her features as she walks over to the blanket. She sits in the middle, her toes staying in the sand as she buries them beneath the grains. "This is perfect. Absolutely perfect." She lies back, her eyes going up to the evening sky.

Out here in Shallow Lake, Wisconsin, the night sky is always filled with stars. So many stars, you never realized there were that many hanging in the sky. The stars that are far, close, small, and large all shine at you, making its own light as it shines on you at night. Her eyes flit over the different sparkles in the sky, and I know she's naming them off in her head. We've spent enough of our childhood studying them and memorizing the names of the different constellations.

She sits up as I walk over to her. Toeing off my sandals, I sit next to her on the blanket and wrap my arm around her waist, pulling her against my side. "I love you, Luna. More than all the stars in the sky."

She looks over at me, her face soft and nervous. "I love you, too, Roman."

My free hand goes to her jaw, and I cup her slim face, bringing her mouth to mine and pressing my lips to hers. She gasps, as always, and I breathe her in. I lick along the seam of her lips until she opens, sliding her tongue against mine. I swallow her, my greed and need taking hold, and I finally let it. I gently push her back, until her back once again presses against the blanket. I mold my front to hers, pressing into her body and settling between her thighs. "This should be perfect, and I can't take you to the moon, so I hope this is good enough for you."

She runs her fingers through my locks, slightly tugging on the ends. "This is perfect. *Anywhere* with you would be perfect. It doesn't matter where it is. I don't care if the sun is up, or the moon is shining. I don't care if there are stars in the sky or the rain is falling. I don't need your guitar, and I don't need a blanket. All I need is you next to me, and I know it'll be perfect."

I press into her further, grinding my growing erection in the crux of her thighs. I nip at her plump bottom lip, licking away the ache and going back to nip at it again. Her fingers go to my cheeks, and she scratches along my jaw as her hips rise to meet my grinding. She wants the friction, and this time, I'm not going to stop her.

Her hands drop to my shirt, and she tugs on it. I reach behind my head, grabbing the collar and pull it over my head. Her palms plant on my chest, and she brings her nails down, lightly scratching my tan skin. I grab at the strap around her shoulder, the light pink leotard that she never changed out of. I snap it against her skin, and smirk at her when she raises an eyebrow. I lower it, letting it loosen around her bicep, allowing me a glance at her naked shoulder.

I bring my lips down, planting them gently against her collarbone, kissing my way up her neck and back up to her lips. She lets out a quiet sigh, tilting her head to the side and giving me better access to her neck. I loosen her other strap, letting it fall so her leotard sits just above her breasts. Her chest heaves, and my hand goes up to palm her breast, giving it a squeeze while I kiss along her cleavage. My finger goes beneath the fabric, pulling down until her nipples appear. They are peaked, hardened by the cool night air and my teasing. My finger brushes against its bumpy but smooth texture, and I give it a tug.

She moans, her chest arching into my hand. "Yessss."

I give her other nipple a tug, bringing my tongue down and swiping against the tender peak. I bring it into my mouth, sucking and running my tongue along the pink skin. My hand goes to her leotard, and I keep pulling until it's bunched against her belly. Her stomach quivers, and I press my palm against her to calm her nerves, settling her skin.

Her arms go around my back, and she holds on as she brings her lips to my shoulder, kissing along my skin while I continue teasing her breasts.

She arches into me, alternating between raising her chest and her hips to grind against my jeans.

Needy.

I release her, grabbing her leotard and pull it off the rest of the way. The fabric glides against her hips, and I pull her underwear along with it. It slides down her smooth, pale thighs, down to her ankles. I toss her leotard into the sand, covering her naked body with my own. Her skin is warm against mine, and I press my naked chest to hers.

"Take your pants off," she whispers. "I want you."

Her needy voice springs me into action, and I grab a square package from my pocket before I unbutton my jeans and shimmy out of them, wiggling them down my legs and kicking them into the distance.

She stares at the square package, a little hesitation filling her features.

"Are you sure?" I ask suddenly. "We don't have to if you don't want to." Fuck, I hope she doesn't back out now. I think I'd have to jack off for a week straight if she turned me down.

She shakes her head. "I want to." She grabs the package from my hand, ripping it open with her teeth. She takes out the slimy condom, cringing at the stickiness of the rubber.

"How do I...? She looks up at me, confusion in her features at the weird circle.

I take it from her, knowing I've spent enough time in my room practicing on myself to do it with no issues. I'll show her another time.

I push up, pinching the tip as I roll the condom down my length. She watches, enthralled, until it's secured at my base. I look back at her, and hesitation lines her features once again.

"I'm not hesitating. I know you're about to ask again," she says, wrapping her hands around my back and pulling me against her. "I'm scared, but I'm not going to back out."

"It's going to hurt. It's going to hurt you, not me. Do you understand that?"

She nods. "I don't care. I want it to hurt. And I want you to be the one to make it hurt."

"I don't want to hurt you."

"You'll help the pain go away, too. Don't you know? You always make me feel better in the end."

I nod, breathing through my nose as I stare down at her. "I love you."

"Now and always," she murmurs.

I grab my length, positioning it between her legs and push my hips forward. My tip enters before it meets a barrier, and I watch as Luna starts wincing, pain lining her face and filling her gray eyes. I bring my hand up, wiping her dark hair from her forehead that's fallen from her bun.

"Tell me to stop," I whisper.

"Keep going." She leans up, pressing her lips to mine. "Don't stop," she mumbles against my lips, her voice choked, pained.

I press forward again, feeling like I'm stuck at a wall that I can't get through. I push harder, giving one small shove and break through the barrier, sinking in deep. Luna lets out a cry, tears flooding her eyes and flowing down her temples.

I bring a hand up, wiping the wetness away from her cheeks as I keep still.

"Move. Please move."

"I don't want to hurt you," I groan. Her warmth and tight walls envelop me completely. I could come just from sitting in her like this. It's been a long time. Eighteen long years of me not having sex, and at this point, just looking at Luna could make me fire off like a fucking rocket.

I do as she asks, though, pulling out until only my tip is inside of her. I see my cock painted red from her cherry. A part of me loves it, that I've taken a part of her no one else has. That she's given herself to me, and only me. It will always only be me. Us. Another part of me hates that I've given her this pain, that I'm making her bleed. I bury that part of me deep, not wanting my worries to taint this moment.

I plunge back in slowly. The friction makes me grit my teeth, the sensations too much. I want to stop and pound into her like a fucking animal. I want to ravage every single inch of her.

Her whimpers eventually turn into soft moans, and her nails scoring my back soften, the tips of her fingers pressing me closer until not an inch of air separates us.

"Feels good," she moans, searching for my lips. I press mine against hers, speeding up. My toes dig into the sand, gaining momentum and quickening my pace until I'm pounding into her, sand flying around us while we make love in our secret area.

"I think I'm... I think I'm going to—*ohhhhh*."

Her walls tense around me, and I grind my jaw until my teeth turn to dust, my thrusts becoming erratic and uncoordinated while she flutters around me. I empty myself into the condom, throbbing against her walls while my own orgasm takes hold.

"Fucking shiiiiittttt."

I bury my face into her neck, kissing and nipping at her while she claws at me to get closer and tries pushing me away at the same time.

I can feel her heartbeat against my chest, beating in the same rhythm my own heart pounds. I flatten against her body, burying her into the sand between my body and the earth.

Her breathing settles, and my sweat cools as I pull out. I peel the condom off, noticing the red streaking the rubber as I toss it in the sand.

I lift her into my arms, my legs shaky and her body limp as I wrap her around me. I walk into the water. It's cool against my skin as it laps against my ankles. Luna tenses once it hits her, and I only hold her tighter. She wraps her legs around my waist, cinching herself to me. I wade in until we're waist deep. The water slides between our skin, our stomachs growing wet as small waves roll between us. My toes dig into the grainy rocks on the ground. Burying my fingers into her loosened bun, I bring her lips to mine, breathing her in as I give her a kiss.

I breathe with her.

I breathe for her.

Everything she does is what's made me who I am. She is a part of me. Wholeheartedly. We're one. There is no her without me. There is no me without her. Nothing could tear us apart. Nothing could fracture our love.

She drags her tongue against my own, and I grow hard between her thighs, even though I know she'll be in too much pain to go again. My hand goes to her ass, and I squeeze the soft skin there, loving the way she squirms in my arms. Loving the way she attempts to get as close to me as she could ever be. Like she wants to bury herself inside of me. Like she wants to be in me.

We stay in the water; kissing, touching, feeling, loving, until our skin is pruney and prickled with goosebumps. I walk out, and Luna's limbs are lazy in my arms, her exhaustion hitting her deeply. I walk to the blanket and lay her down, my feet coated with sand from being damp. Lying next to her, I roll onto my side, bringing her with me so I'm spooning her. Her cool body meets my cool body, and I wrap my arm around her, nudging her so she's flush up against me. Together, we warm up, our heat and love making it bearable in the open night sky.

I give a kiss to her naked shoulder blade. The sun has officially set now, the sunset long gone and the stars out in full force. The moon sits high in the sky as our only source of light on the lake. My eyes shift to the water, and it's crystal clear, a mirror image of the moon reflecting on the surface, bobbing and dancing with the light lapping of the water.

I nudge my head back down, curling half on the blanket and half on the sand, closing my eyes.

"I love you, Roman," she murmurs, her voice already hazy, half asleep and drunk on sex.

"I love you, too, Luna." I bring my hand up to the stray pieces of hair that've fallen from her bun and are damp from the water, brushing them over her shoulder. I give her one more kiss on the back of her neck, curling back down and shutting my eyes.

I love her. I love every inch about her.

I just hope after the news I give her tomorrow morning, she still loves me too.

The sun rises, and my eyes crack open. I'm cold, but I'm warm with Luna's limbs tangled in mine. At some point during the night, she must have flipped and twisted her body to curl against me.

I slide out from her arms, walking over to my guitar and pick it up. Brushing the sand from the bottom's smooth surface, I walk back over and sit beside her, lifting her head so she can prop it on my lap.

She's always slept like the dead.

I play a soft tune, nothing in particular. Just soft notes that spin together into a song I'm not even trying to create. I hum along, thinking of songs I could make or new tunes I can piece together to build. There's a sadness in my notes, and the sadness is because I want to be with Luna, with every piece of her, every day.

But with growing comes opportunities, and unfortunately, I've taken an opportunity I couldn't deny. My bandmates wouldn't let me not take it.

I know Luna, and I know making a big decision like this without having talked with her about it first is going to rip her apart. She's going to be heartbroken, because I know she feels the same about me as I do about her.

And the thought of being apart from her for any length of time causes a sharp pain in my heart. I just hope she understands that this isn't forever. It'll be a blip in time, and then we can be together again.

But we don't have to be apart. Not really. She can still be mine, and I can still be hers.

There are phone calls, and letters, and even holidays when we can see each other. And it'll only be for a little while.

It doesn't take long for Luna to stir, and when she does, she rolls onto her back, looking up at me with her big gray eyes that drive me straight to her soul— to her heart that looks so full of love for me.

I second-guess bringing up my bad news, but I can't wait, because I've already put it off long enough, and my time has run out. I have to tell her now.

There's no other choice.

"Good morning, baby," I mumble, continuing on with my tune. I bend down, my humming lips pressing against her plump ones.

"Morning." She stretches, her naked body pale and beautiful in the morning light. Her long limbs are thin and glowing against the yellow-gray sand with a milkiness that's always been a part of her body—exquisite. Her bruised toes are full of the rough grains, and she wiggles them. I watch as the grains fall back to the earth. Her nipples are peaked as they point toward the sky.

"Hey, what's wrong?" she asks, her hand reaching up to brush some hair from my face. I smile at her, setting my guitar aside and picking her up so her back presses against my chest.

"I have to talk to you about something." I trail my fingers along her shoulder and down her collarbone, to the ballet slipper necklace. It's a permanent fixture on her body. Like another arm or leg. It's a part of her.

It's a part of me.

"Uh-oh. That doesn't sound good at all." She tilts her head up, her hair bunching on my neck as she frowns at me. I tweak her cheek and press my thumb against the soft skin between her eyebrows to smooth out the crease.

"It's nothing too bad." I think about what to say. I think of how to say it. I don't know how to break the news, even though I've known myself for weeks. I've practiced a million times in my head, alone in my room. But when the time comes, I'm speechless, and no words will form on my tongue.

"Spit it out, Roman." She sits up, pulling the blanket over her lap while she frowns at me. The sand flies from the blanket, flinging onto my legs and face and arms.

But I'm rarely quiet, rarely have any bad news or anything negative to say, so I know Luna can tell something is up from my tone alone.

"Modern Records offered us a label."

Her eyes go wide, her jaw going slack before a wide smile breaks out on her face. Her gray eyes glowing with elation. She drops her blanket, rolling around so she can hug me. Her arms go around my shoulders, and she squeezes tight. "That's good fucking news, Roman!"

I don't say anything, emotion building in my chest to the point that I can barely breathe. She notices my silence, her arms going slack around me as she leans back, looking me in the eyes. "What's wrong? Isn't that good news?" She shakes me a bit, and I stare at her. My eyes want to water, and I blink them back.

"They want us to start a tour. I leave in two weeks."

Her entire body freezes as she blinks at me, her own eyes filling with tears. She moves back a bit, her hands fisting piles of sand. Clenching and unclenching. I watch as the sand seeps from between her fingers. Her eyes furrow, like she's confused at my statement. The impossibility of it.

"We have to go out to California. I got a small apartment there with the guys. It's the beginning for us, Luna. It's what we've always wanted. And you know, in a year, when you're done with school, you can come with me! We can tour together, and you can be on the road with me."

She chucks a handful of sand in my face.

"I don't want to go on tour, Roman! You know that! I want to go to Julliard in New York! You've always known this!" She starts breathing heavily, a panic building in her chest. I move toward her, but all she does is chuck another handful of sand at me.

"No! Don't come any closer." Tears fall down her cheeks now, sand mixed in, and she looks a wreck.

A beautiful, broken wreck.

"Why did it take you this long to tell me? How long have you known?" She stands up, grabbing her leotard. She slips it on, the straps snapping against her shoulders. The straps are rolled over multiple times, and I know she hates that. I want to straighten them for her, but I don't think she'd let me right now.

She looks at me. "Huh? How long?"

"One month."

Her eyes widen to the point that they're about to roll out of their sockets. They darken, the gray turning a murky brown that I've never seen in her before. *One month?* she screeches. A flock of birds leave the trees around us, flapping away and moving across the lake. "One fucking month, Roman? And I'm just finding out about this now? That you're leaving in two weeks? Right after we…" She shakes her head, tears streaming down her face as she stomps up to me. She shoves me, slapping at my chest and clawing at my skin. I let her, keeping my hands at my sides as my heart breaks for the girl in front of me.

The love of my life.

"I'm sorry." This time when my eyes fill with tears, I don't bother to wipe them away. My cheeks dampen as I stare at her. Her usual straight spine curled over in pain.

"Sorry isn't good enough. How could you…" She inhales a shaky breath. "How could you do this to me?" The last of her words come out in a whisper. A fractured whisper that can't be repaired.

I open my mouth, but once again nothing comes out. A silent breath of empty apologies and even emptier promises.

I failed.

She shakes her head, defeat in her features as she walks away.

"Wait. Where are you going?" I ask her, reaching for her arm. She yanks out of my hold, angry tears streaming down her face.

"Leave me alone, Roman. I'm going home."

"Let me drive you at least," I plead.

She shakes her head. "I want to be alone."

When she walks away from me this time, I let her. Her body curled over in sadness. She doesn't push the weeds or the branches out of the way. I watch as they scrape her legs, leaving red lines on her skin. She just moves straight past them. A complete zombie as she goes through the motions of getting away from me.

Her quiet cries shred me in two.

My chest quakes, breaking straight down the middle until I'm in two pieces.

Broken. Utterly broken.

CHAPTER TWELVE

Luna

Tears flow down my face as my toes scream in protest. I fall flat on my feet again, groaning at myself in pity.

"Fuck," I cry.

I've been useless all day. All week, to be honest. I'm sore between the legs and I'm sore in my chest. I feel lost. Confused. I haven't spoken to Roman in days. It's the most we've gone without speaking to one another since I moved here, and I feel completely broken. A shattered glass, broken and forgotten. No one to pick up the pieces of my shattered heart.

Roman has tried to talk to me, but I've feigned sickness to my mom. She knows better, looking at me with pity and a nod of her head. I'm sure she's talked to Goldie at some point, so she probably knows what's going on.

It doesn't matter. None of it matters at this point.

Roman is leaving.

Every day that I don't talk to him is another day that I'm losing being with him. Every day is a day closer to him leaving me. But I can't for the life of me go and talk to him.

I'm too broken, too stubborn.

I don't want him to leave.

I walk over to the bar and grip the wood with my hand, bending down in a plié. It feels forced—off. I know if my teacher were here right now, she'd whip me with a ruler for faking my moves. I'm so much better than this. But if I were honest, it all feels useless if Roman isn't here.

I feel like a fraud.

I slide down to the floor, my back scraping against the wall as quiet sobs rack my chest. I pull on the bows on the back of my calves and the ribbons release, floating to the ground in a quiet drop. I peel my shoes off my aching feet, slapping them against the ground in frustration.

I've avoided Roman everywhere. At home, in school. I'm surprised he hasn't shown up at the studio. But another part of me is hurt that he didn't.

Did he give up on me?

That thought alone makes another sob rip through my chest, and I feel like my heart can barely take the crying anymore. My chest feels bruised. My ribs feel broken. I've cried so much. Too much.

I wipe my face with the back of my hand and stand up. Grabbing my slippers, I go to the back and grab my things, turn off the radio and the lights, and lock up. Turning around, I come face to face with Bryce, one of the guys from school.

"Um, hi?"

"Oh, hey. What's up?" he asks, shoving his hands in the pockets of his jeans.

I toss my thumb over my shoulder, trying to act nonchalant even though I'm sure my face is a wreck, all blotchy, red and swollen. "I was just practicing."

He bobs his head. "I was walking by and saw you. You're really good."

I cringe. "Wasn't my best today." That means he saw me cry, and that makes me cringe even more.

"You okay?" His eyes rove over my face, checking each dip and curve.

"I'm fine." I smile, even though it feels forced.

"People have been talking in school, you know? That you and Roman haven't been talking at all this week. Are you guys okay?" Roman and I are the married couple in school. People barely pass us a glance when we're together, but I guess there are still eyes on us.

I shrug. "I don't really know." Tears try to make their way to my eyes again, and I blink them away.

"Well, whatever he did, he's an idiot. You're a catch, Luna."

"Thanks." It doesn't feel that way right now. Otherwise, why would he be leaving me?

Because at the end of the day, if he's moving to California, that'll be his home. In one year, my plan is to move to New York. I always thought our plans would align, but it couldn't have been further from the truth. We'll be in separate parts of the country in one year. The furthest we could possibly be away from each other, we will be.

Has it always been this way? Have our destinies always meant to be separate? Maybe we were never meant to be, and that makes me the saddest of all. I always thought we were soulmates. That's been our thing, him and I. How could that be true, though? If we're about to be apart, for who knows how long? Possibly forever?

A swallow down a sob and look at Bryce. He's staring at me with a sympathetic look on his face while mine turns red, my eyes water, and I hold back a gut-wrenching cry.

"He's an idiot," he says. "I'm guessing you aren't going to prom then?"

I frown. I've forgotten all about it. I got my dress, and Roman got a matching tux. That must be out of the cards now. "Probably not."

"Well, if you do, maybe you could save me a dance?"

"I'll do that." I won't. Without Roman, I won't be going at all.

I don't say that, though, because even though the thought of dancing in the arms of another man is nearly crippling, maybe this is how it's meant to be.

Us apart.

CHAPTER THIRTEEN
Roman

I sit on my bed, my foot bobbing with an empty bag in front of me. So much to do in the next week and a half, yet I can't find it in me to pack, or do any of the necessary things I'm supposed to do before I move across the country.

The only thing on my mind is her.

She's been avoiding me.

I don't know what to do, and it's killing me inside. My parents know this, her parents know this, my friends know this.

I don't want to leave her. My insides feel like they're tearing in two at the thought of being in a different state than her. But I have no other choice.

Everyone tells me to take the chance. That if it's meant to be, it's meant to be.

But how can something be right when it feels so damn wrong?

How am I supposed to leave when every bone in my body is aching to stay?

I let her be the first day, knowing that she might need a little bit of space. The second day I searched her out, and her mom said she wasn't feeling well. The pity on her face when she told me made it clear that we all realized she was lying.

I tried talking to her in school yesterday, but she fled my presence every chance I got. I could have held her down, shouted at her to listen to me. Forced her to understand. But that's not her, and that's not us.

We aren't angry with each other. We're seamless. And now things are messy, and it feels so fucking wrong.

Staring at my empty bag and guitar case sitting on the floor, I shake my head in disgust. If I know one thing, it's that I can't leave with us like this. I have to make it right, otherwise I refuse to go. Everyone will have to get over it.

I grab my keys from my nightstand, knowing exactly where she's at right now.

She's dancing.

I ignore my mom and dad in the kitchen and head outside. The sound of the birds and frogs oddly loud this time of day. They're usually their loudest in the early morning hours, or late at night when the sun goes down. Them being loud right now makes me think they're yelling at me. Telling me I'm a stupid fucking idiot who doesn't know what he's doing.

They would be right.

I hop into my car and back out of the driveway. Luna's mom is on her knees in front of her garden pulling weeds. She looks up when she hears my car, wiping her forehead with the back of her glove. It makes a brown streak of dirt mark her forehead, but it's the look on her face that catches my attention.

She's sad.

She gives me an understanding look, like she knows exactly where I'm going. Turning back to her plants, I take that as approval to make this right.

Our two families have combined into one. If something is wrong with one of us, our entire group is in dysfunction.

I need to make this right.

I fly down the road, my windows down as my brown hair blows in the wind. My arm hangs out the window, feeling the hot breeze slap against my skin.

The sun is setting, which means Luna will be done dancing any time.

But, what if she's not there?

That makes me speed up a bit, and my wheels screech on the road as I break to turn right toward town. I see Luna instantly, standing outside the studio with her ballet slippers clutched in her palm. She's talking to someone, and I abruptly turn into the first parking spot I see and hop out of the vehicle.

It's a guy.

I notice it's one of the fuckers from school, Bryce. He and every other guy in school has had a thing for Luna for as long as I can remember. She doesn't notice these things, too focused on her friends and me and dance. But I notice. I see how their eyes stray toward her as she walks past. I see how their eyes linger too long, and how they're all always willing to help her at the drop of a hat. It doesn't matter what it is; they all want to befriend her. Boys and girls alike.

I slam my door shut roughly, the entire car shaking from the force. It snaps Luna and Bryce from their conversation. Luna's eyes widen in surprise, then lower in sadness. It makes me falter in my step, and I want to fall to my knees right there and beg her to forgive me.

Bryce looks uneasy, and I'm sure it's because my face is screwed up in anger at his presence. He shouldn't be there. What is he doing there? Is he watching her? Stalking her?

My thoughts take a dark turn, and I suddenly don't know if I can leave her alone at all.

"Luna," I say, staring at her and trying to convey my thoughts once I reach her. She can't catch my eyes, her own averted as she looks down at her bare feet.

"Roman." Her voice is broken as she speaks to me, and I want to stick my hand in her chest and rub her heart well again.

I can't see her face well, but from what I can see of her, I notice her cheeks are red, the skin underneath her eyes a little swollen. Like she's been crying.

I scowl, looking up at Bryce. "What did you do to her?" I step up to him, towering over him like I do everyone in school.

"Nothing." He looks at me in irritation, like I'm ruining their moment.
Fuck off.

I point at Luna. "Then why the fuck is she crying? What the hell did you do to her, huh?" My hands land on his chest, and I push him. Because I'm pissed. At him and myself. But mostly because I just want him to step the fuck away from her.

"Roman!" Luna shouts at me. She grabs my arm, her nails digging into my skin as she pulls me away, scratching me in the process.

"Stay away from her," I growl at him, standing down because I'd rather have Luna's hands on me more than anything right now. Luna doesn't like violence. She grew up with hippy parents and is half hippy herself. Violence is the last thing she ever wants, and I know I'd just disappoint her more if I did what I wanted to do, like punch a dent right into his ugly face.

Bryce shakes his head at me, like he's embarrassed and angry at my actions. His eyes glide to Luna. I follow his eyes, stepping right in his line of sight so he can't see her. "I'll see you, Luna. Maybe at prom?"

I laugh, a bitter bark ripping from my throat at the words. "No, you fucking won't."

Luna's fingernails dig into my skin, breaking the first layers as her rage takes hold.

"Roman, you're a fucking asshole." Her head tilts over my shoulder, "Maybe you will, Bryce. Talk to you later."

I can feel my face heat, my cheeks warming as fury boils through my entire body. "Maybe? Maybe? Are you fucking kidding me, Luna? Maybe you'll see him at prom?" I rip my arm from her hold, seeing little moon crescents from her nails, blood dolloping on a few of them. "Who are you right now?"

She scowls at me, pure anger in her gray eyes. "Who am I? Who are you, Roman Hall? How could you make such a life-changing decision without talking with me about it first? Do you know what that's done to me? Do you know how I've been feeling these past couple of days?" Tears flood her eyes again, streaming down her cheeks.

My hand raises, ready to wipe the wetness, but she shakes her head, stepping back and out of my reach. "No. You don't get that right. Not now."

"Luna, I made a mistake. I'll stay. I won't go. Please, I just can't have you mad at me."

"No!" She swipes her hand through the air. "I don't want you to stay. This is your dream, Roman. You'd never forgive me. I'd never forgive myself. I just wanted you to talk to me. I just… *what about us?*" Her voice drops, sadness dripping from each letter like rainwater dropping from a petal. Slow. Tortured.

She's broken.

I step up to her, and this time she lets me. I grab her shaky hands, trembling with the same fear as I have. Of us losing each other. Forever.

I can't let that happen.

"Do you want me to stay?" I ask her honestly. Because I would. At the end of the day, she is the most important person in my life. If she wants me to stay here, I would in a heartbeat. Fuck the record and fuck my friends.

Her body loses its tension. "No. I want you to go. This is what you were meant to do."

"Come with me," I plead. "Please. Just come with me. That way we can still be together."

Her eyebrows furrow, her toes curling against the cement as surprise rocks her body. "What? How?"

"Just do it. Come with me. You can finish school later. Or not finish at all. Or, hell, have your mom homeschool you, for all I care. It doesn't matter to me. As long as you're with me, right? Now and always?"

"Now and always…" She bites her lip, the skin around her teeth turning white from force. Her eyes water again, and this time I reach my hand out, landing it against her cheek to catch the tear before it can fall. "I can't," she says on a shaky breath.

"Why not?" Panic seizes me, and I grab her hands again and press my fingers into her nails, turning the light pink of her fingers a ghostly white.

"Because your dream is music. My dream is dance. I can't give that up. I have practice. I have my family. I have Julliard, Roman. You are meant to play songs for the world. I'm meant to dance for the world. Maybe our dreams lead us on different paths, after all."

I pull her close, until her leotard-covered chest brushes against my shirt. She smells of sweat. She smells of sadness. So, so much sadness. "No. One year, Luna. In one year, I'll move to New York with you. We'll get a place, and you can go to Julliard. I might have to tour, but I'll be home with you as much as I can. We'll be together. In one year, Luna. Don't give up on me."

She cries, her chest shaking against mine, vibrating down to my veins. My blood stops pumping as I stare at her. As I watch her translucent tears float down her cheeks. They hit her lips, and she licks them away. "One year, Roman. One painful year. But you have to promise you'll write to me and call me at least once a week."

I squeeze her to me. "I promise, baby. I'll promise you anything."

"One year," she murmurs against my lips.

"One year," I echo, sealing her lips to mine.

CHAPTER FOURTEEN

Luna

My bed feels soft beneath my hands as I run my fingers over the quilt. My mom made it for me last year, the different patches made from soft squared patterns. It's *so* my mom, and my mood right now makes me want to curl over and burrow my face in the fabric, letting its softness dry my tears.

My baby pink dress floats around me like a princess gown. It reminds me of my leotard, the color such a soft and feminine pink. The bottom half of my dress is a tulle, making me feel like a princess with the many layers. It poufs around my waist, and I press down on it, only for the fabric to fluff back up.

The top half of my dress is a soft pink satin that hugs my curves with its small trim. It's strapless, silky smooth and bunched on the side.

I look beautiful, even though I feel anything but. My heart is breaking. I can feel the small crack starting at the top, slowly shredding down the rest of my heart. It hurts to breathe. It hurts to be awake. It hurts to talk. Everything aches, a sharp pain that burrows deeply within my soul. I don't want tonight to happen, because that means this will be it. It'll be over.

Tonight, is the last night I'll spend with Roman for an entire year. Yeah, I might have a holiday here and there where he'll be in town, but overall, tonight is the last time until he'll be mine, only mine, for an entire year. Being away for him for an extended time is something I don't even know how to handle. I haven't been away from him for more than a day, maybe two, since I met him. The thought of not seeing his face, touching his skin, hurts. It hurts so fucking bad.

This last week has been filled with him getting ready for his tour. What I thought would be days of us talking and touching and spending every moment together that we possibly could has turned into a week of him making phone calls, packing, coordinating with his band, and being overall—*busy*.

I'm feeling alone.

Tonight is prom, and he really wanted things to be special. He rented a room at a hotel just a few towns from Shallow Lake so we could be alone. I should be excited to have this alone time with him. To be intimate with him again. But I feel like a knot that's fallen loose over time, and I only have one more tug before I fall apart.

"Knock, knock." My door opens, my mom peeking around with a soft smile on her face. "Oh, Luna, you look lovely. Look at how beautiful that dress is." Her eyes start to water, and my eyes drop back to the quilt, not able to take any sort of emotion from anyone else. I'll fall apart. Completely.

I only have enough strength to deal with myself. And even with me, I'm barely hanging on.

"What's the matter, Luna?" She walks up to me, sitting next to me on the edge of my bed and tucking my curly hair behind my ear. Her fingers are warm as they graze my temple. She smells so warm, so comforting. Like the garden outside and a hint of a joint. I want to curl into her, burrow underneath her skin and beg for her to take the pain away.

I shrug, my throat growing tight with emotion. I don't want to cry, because I just spent the last hour perfecting my makeup. I made sure all my cries were out beforehand, but ever since I did the last swipe of mascara, my sadness has hit tenfold.

"Tell me," she urges, her fingers dropping to my bicep and giving me a small squeeze.

"I just don't want him to go," I choke out, tipping my head toward the ceiling and blinking rapidly. "I don't know how to do this without him."

She lets out a breath, a heavy sigh that I feel deep in my bones. I'm dead tired with exhaustion. It's like Roman was the piece that put me together. He made me motivated. He made me feel alive. Now that he's leaving, he's taking my life with him. I don't want to dance. I don't want to eat. I barely want to function. All I want to do is sleep and cry.

How will I survive this way for an entire year?

"He's not gone forever, Luna. It'll be a year and then you guys will figure it out. You should focus on what's important. What's right in front of you. You haven't worked this hard in ballet for nothing. You should put all this sadness into dance. Work it out with your moves. You're getting into Julliard one way or another, but take this time to really focus on your own dreams. Doing what you love."

Do I really love it, though?

It feels like Roman is my muse. Because I suddenly don't know if dance is what really tics in the center of my heart. Without him, my drive and motivation are just… depleted.

"It's just hard." I pull at the tulle of my gown, feeling silly crying like a baby in a princess dress.

"I know it is, baby. But time will fly, and then you'll look back and wonder why you were so sad in the first place. But right now isn't the time for this. Nora and Roman and some strange guy are outside waiting for you." She squeezes me into a hug, bringing her mouth to my ear and whispering, "Roman got a limo."

My eyes widen as I turn to look at her. "Are you serious?"

"Serious as your dad in the morning without his coffee. Let's go outside and take some pictures so you guys can go have fun tonight. Enough with the sad talk. We'll worry about that tomorrow once he's gone."

I nod, and my mom stands up, pulling me with her. She grips my fingers, pressing on my knuckles in reassurance. I feel like I'm in a fairy tale as the dress poufs around me, my white heels the final touch.

I walk out of my room, my heels clacking on the floor as I make my way out of the house. Nora and her date, Corman, are nowhere in sight. The only one I see is Roman as he stands up against the passenger-side door, his arms folded across his chest as he looks at the ground.

His look is exactly how I feel.

So incredibly lost.

I press on the small handle of my door, opening it and stepping outside.

Roman hears the squeaky hinge as the door opens, snapping his head up to look at me. His jaw goes slack, and he straightens up from the limo, adjusting his suit coat as he walks up to me. He looks over my shoulder, and I can sense my mom and dad waiting. Probably with huge smiles on their faces with a camera in hand. I don't look at them, though, only keeping my focus on Roman as he steps up to me.

"Wow," he says, rubbing his jaw with his palm, "I really don't know what to say." He grabs my hand, lifting it over his head as he twirls me around. The tulle of my dress raises in the wind, floating around me before settling once I'm facing him again. "You are *so* damn beautiful, Luna." His voice is hoarse with his words.

I smile, my cheeks hurting from the unused muscle. "You don't look so bad yourself." And he doesn't. His hair is a little messy, his brown waves unruly, like he's run his hand through it one too many times. His black tux fits him perfectly, from the trim shoulders down to his narrowed waist. He tops it off with a pair of black shoes. Shiny and glistening against the black pavement.

"Here you go." My mom comes up behind me, giving me the baby pink corsage we picked up earlier today.

I take it from her, smiling gratefully as I loosen the pin. Roman steps up to me, getting right in my space. I can feel his breath on my face as I pin the flower to his coat, barely able to look him in the eye. I can feel him looking at me, his eyes on the crown of my head. He wants me to look at him. I'm afraid with one look, I'll collapse.

Once I'm finished, I don't step back. I stand there, inhaling his lightly scented cologne, the manly scent combined with his usual outdoorsy smell.

He smells like Roman.

My knees grow weak once I realize I won't be able to smell it for an entire year. Roman notices this, wrapping his hands around my arms to steady me. "Hey, look at me."

My eyes raise, my mascara-covered eyelashes growing wet from tears. I can feel the thickness of my wet lashes brushing my cheeks with each blink.

"We're going to get through tonight, and we're going to have a smile on our faces while we do it. Tomorrow we can be sad, but I'm not going to let you be sad during prom, okay? Not tonight."

"But—"

"No buts. Okay, Luna?"

I nod.

"Good, now…" He steps away from me, turning around and bending down to get a small box off the ground. I see a small flower inside, realizing it's my corsage. A beautiful bunch of pale petals, elegant and perfect. Not too big, nor too small. I hold out my wrist, and he slides it on gently. He holds my wrist afterward, trailing his fingers along my palm. My breath stops, the pads of his fingers gentle and firm at the same time. Then he lets go of my hand, and it falls to my side.

"Ready?"

No, I'm not ready. Not at all.

"Ready."

The dance is torturous. Long and chaotic. People with smiling faces, slightly red-rimmed eyes from the secret alcohol they've snuck in, skin glistening from the stuffy auditorium. Everything is perfect… for them.

Roman and I haven't done anything besides dance. No refreshments, no visiting with our classmates. Straight out of the limo, he brought me to the middle of the dance floor. Wrapping his arms around me tightly, his palms feeling every curve of my sides and waist, pulling me until not an inch of air separated us. This is how we've been, where we've been, for hours now.

Roman's arms wrap around me, holding me close to his body as *Time After Time* by Cyndi Lauper plays through the speakers. My cheek rests against Roman's chest, and his hands rub against my naked shoulders. His skin grazes mine gently, a caress full of love that only Roman provides. "I love you, Luna."

I don't say anything, nuzzling closer to him. I just want to stay like this forever. Stay wrapped in his arms and never leave. *But I have to.*

I never want this night to end.

"Are you ready to go to the hotel?" he asks, not stopping his dancing. "We should go," he adds after I don't answer him.

I nod my head against his chest, knowing that once we leave here, I'll be one step closer to Roman leaving me. I take a large, shaky breath and separate from him. "Okay."

He pulls back, his fingers wrapped around my arms as he gives me a sad smile. With a breath that's just as unsure as I'm feeling, he pulls me along while he says goodbye to everyone important. He tells his friends to meet tomorrow morning at his house so they can load up their new van to take off.

Nora sees me and walks up to me, a sympathetic look on her face. She knows me. She knows how every step has been difficult, nearly impossible with the amount of pain I'm feeling. My heart is leaving me, and she can see it in my gray eyes. Wrapping her small arms around me, she whispers, "It'll be okay. I'll sit with you in your room and cry all day tomorrow if you want, okay? Just have a good night tonight."

I nod, giving her a squeeze before releasing her and walking back up to Roman. He waits for me by the entrance, outstretching his hand to lace his fingers through mine. He pulls me along, and we hop into the limo, driving silently the twenty minutes it takes to get to the hotel outside of town.

It smells like leather in here, the limo so large, easily fitting twelve people, possibly more. There are lights throughout, like we should be throwing a party. Instead, we're quiet, not saying a word as Roman's side leans up against mine, his arm tossed over my shoulder while he holds me tightly. We look out opposite windows, not sure what to say, not wanting another minute to pass, wishing we could freeze time.

Once the limo pulls up to the front door, Roman passes the driver a few dollars and hops out, grabbing the small bags he must have shoved in there earlier. I don't remember packing a bag. I wonder if my mom or Nora packed it for me.

But who knows, I could have packed it myself. I've been so out of it lately, it's not totally out of the question.

I stand silently beside Roman as he checks in, grabbing two keys from the front desk before bringing me to the elevator. The hotel is nice, soft muted tones and a cream-colored carpet. It smells like cleaner in here, and I realize this is one of the nicer hotels Roman must have gotten for us. Soft music plays from the ceiling as we wander through the lobby, our feet silent as we walk. A grand piano sits in the corner of the room, and I imagine Roman playing it, a soft tune breaking across the room with me sitting on top of the shiny wood, my legs crossed over one another as tears leak down my cheeks.

We hop inside the elevator and Roman stands behind me, snaking a hand around my waist as he presses a kiss to my naked shoulder. "You doing okay?"

I nod, faking a smile for him. "I'm okay."

"No, you're not." He knows me too well. "But it's okay. I'm not okay either."

The music is louder in the elevator, drowning out my lonesome thoughts. I tap my toes to the upbeat music until the elevator dings, snapping me out of my trance. As the doors roll open, Roman grabs my hand, pulling me along the patterned yellow and red carpeted hallway until he finds our room.

He slides the key card in the door, and when it clicks, the red dot turning to green, he presses down on the handle to open it. I walk in ahead of him, glancing around the nicely-sized room. The bathroom is directly to the left, and what looks to be a coat closet on the right. The same patterned carpet extends into our small suite. There's only a double bed which sits in the middle of the room, with a grayish poufy-looking comforter and two white pillows at the head of the bed. Two small nightstands sit on each side with lamps on them. In front of the bed is a small table with a Bible in the center. There's also a TV stand with a small boxy TV sitting on top.

It smells like clean linens and air freshener in here.

"This is it." Roman sets our bags at the foot of the bed, loosening his tie and taking his coat off before he tosses it onto the foot of the bed. He looks up at me as he untucks his crisp white shirt and lifts his hand to his wrist, unbuttoning the sleeves. "What do you want to do? Want to watch TV? You tired? Hungry?"

I fold my arms across my chest. "I could kind of use a bath. Or a shower. I'm kind of cold and want to wash the school off me."

He chuckles at that, nodding his head. It was stuffy in there, crammed with a bunch of sweaty teenagers. "Want to take a bath? I can see if there's bubbles or something."

I nod, but he's already halfway to the bathroom. I listen as he tears open the shower curtain, and it squeaks against the bronzed metal pole. "Found some!" He shouts from the other room.

I toe off my heels and pad toward the bathroom. My feet ache, and glancing down, I see red marks where the tops of my heels pressed into my skin.

As I walk into the white bathroom, the white tiles on the floor are cool against the soles of my feet. It's simple, with a white porcelain tub and sink. The lights are warm, turning the color of the room a light yellow. Tiny soaps and toothpastes sit next to the sink, with folded up towels shaped into triangles on top of the toilet. Roman is bent over on his knees, his fingers underneath the spout as hot water pours into the tub. He grabs the miniature white bottle, tipping it over and pouring in half the container. I want to open my mouth to tell him that's too much, but I can't muster up the energy to tell him so.

He tests the water once more, knowing I like it slightly hotter than boiling. "I think it's good. Want to test it?"

I shake my head. "You know how I like it."

He stands up straight, wiping his hands on his slacks as he walks up to me. "I do know how you like it." He wraps his arms around me, pulling me into a hug. "I love you, Luna. Everything will be okay."

I nod, turning around to give him my back. "Can you help me out of this?"

His fingers trail along the edge of my dress, tickling my skin as he grazes along my shoulder blades. He stops at the zipper, and I can hear the metal clink. He gives a tug until my dress loosens, and pulls slowly, releasing inch by inch of my skin until he reaches my waist.

And lets go.

My dress pools around me, and I step out of the pink fabric flooded at my feet.

I'm braless, which is typical for me. I don't wear one with my leotard, so it didn't bother me to not wear one tonight. I have on a pair of black panties, a little sexy, but nothing overboard.

Roman likes it, though.

"Jesus," he groans from behind me. His hands go to my waist, circling around before going back to my backside. His hands squeeze, rubbing against my ass before hooking his fingers underneath the waistband of my panties, pulling them until they slide down my thighs. He leans in close, and I can feel his warm breath against my skin. I shudder, my skin prickling with goosebumps.

His fingers hook around my ankles, giving them a squeeze before his hands trail up the outside of my legs, moving up my thighs. He goes around my waist, up my sides and to my breasts until he reaches my neck. He tilts my head back, and I give him a soft kiss, closing my eyes as emotion catches in my chest. "Will you come in with me?" I whisper against his lips.

He separates from me, his eyebrows lifted as he looks down at me. "You want me to come in with you?" He gives a quick peek at the tub before glancing into my eyes. "It looks a little small."

I shrug. "I don't care. Please?"

He takes his clothes off without another word and steps into the tub. His form is lean, strong, tanned. Perfect. His muscles flex and bend with his movements.

He outstretches his hand, and I place my small one in his large one. His fingers curl around mine as he helps me in, the water perfect, the bubbles about to boil over the side. He settles down, helping me in so I'm sitting against him with my back against his front.

He gets some bubbles in his hand, spreading them across my arms, up my shoulders and neck, and down to my fingers. He pays attention to each one, spreading bubbles between my fingers, to my palm, to my fingernails.

"Tell me about your plans," I whisper.

He sighs, my body floating up and down against his heavy breath. "I don't really want to talk about it right now, Luna."

I turn my head toward his, the back of my hair getting wet against his chest. His eyes are sad, a small frown playing at his lips.

"I want to know what your plan is. Please," I beg.

He sighs again, bringing some water up to my hair, washing the loose curls from my head. His fingers are gentle as they comb through the strands from root to end. "We got a place in Los Angeles, close to the record label. We'll be going there a lot at first to record, practice and shit."

"What about your tour? Where are you going?"

He pops open a bottle of shampoo, squirting some in his palm before massaging it into my scalp. My head tilts back, my eyes closing as the scent of lavender fills the room. "We'll start in California, then head to Los Angeles, San Diego, Sacramento, San Francisco. Eventually, we'll head up to Seattle, then over to Las Vegas, Miami, Atlanta, Chicago, New York. Our manager says he wants us to eventually go abroad, but first we need to get through the US tour."

"Wow. You'll travel the whole country then." A part of me is jealous that he's going to experience this without me. Something I've always wanted him to do, but with me standing by his side. The fact that he'll be hopping state to state when I'll still be stuck in high school leaves a bitter taste in my mouth.

"And between tours, when I can, I plan to come to Shallow Lake, Wisconsin, so I can visit my beautiful girlfriend."

I shake my head, not sure of the words that are about to come out of my mouth. They just do, spilling across the bubbles and throughout this small bathroom. "Are you sure you want to even date me still? Will we even be together? What if you meet some girl on the road or something? You'll be this big rock star. You aren't going to want to be tied down to some little kid who's still in high school."

He's silent for a moment, his hands still in my hair. He doesn't say a word. Then his hands drop into the water, a light splash heard as he grabs my waist, turning me around so I'm facing him. My legs wrap around his waist as he holds onto mine. A fierce scowl sits on his lips, condensation dampening his face as he looks at me with anger. The tips of his hair are damp, brushing against his forehead. "Why would you say that, Luna? You know how I feel. It's you and me. Forever. My heart beats because you are alive. That's all. I don't care about anything, anyone else in the entire world. Now and always, remember?"

"I remember," I whisper, my voice echoing throughout the room.

"This right here," he presses his hand to my naked breast, right over my heart, "your heart beats for me. The love I feel for you runs through my veins. I know you feel the same. I see the flutter of your heart in your neck and know that the reason your heart beats is for me. We're one in the same, Luna. One doesn't exist without the other. I'll seize to even be alive in a world without you in it. Why would you think I'd want to experience someone, anyone else in this world? You'll be far away, but you're engraved in my heart. I don't care about miles, Luna, not when you've already imprinted on my entire being."

I lean forward, slamming my lips around his. I listen as the water splashes between us, flooding over the side of the tub and slapping onto the floor. Roman grabs me around the waist, pulling me closer until I'm straddling him, his hard-on directly under my butt. I grind against him, the water splashing against us with our movements.

My moans echo through the bathroom, banging against the walls and floating through the air.

"I love you," I moan.

"I love you, too." He brings his hand up to my sudsy breast, smearing the bubbles around and giving my nipple a tug. I groan, arching my chest into his hand.

I need more. So much more.

I move my hips against him, feeling him harden into a rock beneath me. My fingers go beneath the water, my nails scraping against his abs that are flexing with coiled tension. The room grows steamy, cloudy with the hot water and our heavy pants.

I grab his cock beneath the water and line him up when he stops me. "Wait. I need a condom." I slide off his waist as he leans over the tub, water splashing and dripping all over the cream rug. He grabs his pants, digging into his pocket to pull out his wallet. He flops it opens, pulling a condom from the inside pocket.

With quick movements, he dips his hand beneath the water to slide the condom on, then gives me a heated look, pulling me back on top of him.

I line him up, giving his base a squeeze before sinking down on top of him. There's a pinch of pain, but it's less so than last time. There's a lick of pleasure in there too, and it makes a shiver break out along my spine.

I wrap my arms around him as I lift up, sinking back down slowly. I try to make a rhythm, each motion making water splash over the side of the tub. It's difficult, though, because the combination of pleasure and pain makes my legs so shaky it's hard to move.

Roman pushes on my chest and I lean back, my body floating on top of the water while we're still connected at the waist. My hair floats around me in a black sheet, my breasts glistening with soap and water between my breasts. Roman grabs onto my hips, holding me tightly while he thrusts into me from below. I bring my hands up over my head, pressing them against the end of the tub so I don't knock my head against it. He rocks us, slowly but forcefully. Each motion climbing me higher. A slow burn starts in the pit of my belly, a tingling sensation that I'm becoming familiar with when I'm with Roman. I want to squeeze my thighs closed from the sensation, but our position makes that impossible.

I can feel Roman hardening further inside of me, his cock rock solid as he slides against my tight walls. I tense, and he lets out a grunt as he starts to speed up. It doesn't take long, our rocking becoming manic, our moans simultaneous as we chase our release.

We come together.

Our moans shake the walls, and I'm sure our neighbors can hear us as I scream Roman's name. My walls flutter against him, and I can feel as he twitches and tenses, the hardness of his cock pulsing against me.

He lets go of my hips, and I continue to float, staring at the ceiling as my body begins to cool. It's hot in here, foggy, and I have a thin sheen of sweat covering my skin. My mind became as cloudy as the room, our heat and love dulling my brain. But moments pass and clarity comes, and my bones start to chill, just like my heart.

I close my eyes, listening to our breaths settle and our heartbeats slow. My ears are under the water, and I listen as Roman pulls the plug on the drain. The pipes groan as they swallow the water. Soon, Roman's arms are around me. He lifts me from the tub, and I open my eyes, watching his wet hair drip onto my chest as he carries me out of the bathroom.

He brings me into the bedroom, pulling back the comforter and sliding my wet body between the sheets. He follows me under, covering my body with his hot one and brushing my wet hair from my face. It hits the pillow in a quiet slap. "You're so beautiful," he whispers.

His other hand has a condom in it, and I'm surprised he wants to go again so soon, but I don't complain. He tears open the condom and slides it on, and this time when he enters me, he stares right into my eyes. He moves slow, keeping only inches away from me as he rocks against me. My legs go up, wrapping around his waist as I curl my arms around his stomach. My fingers trail along his skin as he moves against me, our wet bodies warming beneath the sheets.

His eyes, not once, leave mine.

How can I last a year without this man? *The love of my life.*

My throat starts to close, and I can barely tamper down the sob that wants to escape. Tears fill in my eyes, trailing down my temples and into my wet hair. Roman doesn't wipe them away, keeping his fingers threaded in my messy strands as he continues to slide into me.

We're silent this time, our soft breaths the only sounds filling the room.

I don't want him to leave me.

My tears don't stop, and they make his face blurry. I open my mouth, taking a shaky breath as the loss of him begins to consume me.

When he comes this time, he stares me right in the eyes. I stare at him too, a soft cry floating from my lips as my own orgasm burns through me. He leans down, kissing my tears away, wetting his lips. He licks them, tasting the saltiness before he brings his mouth down to mine.

Gripping the condom, he slides out of me and tosses it over the side of the bed. His arms go around me, pulling me close so that he can spoon me. I bring his arm beneath my cheek, and I know he can feel my tears tickle his skin as they continue to river down my face, but he doesn't say anything. He just lets me cry in his arms on our last night together.

I fall asleep like that, with his wet arms, filled with tears, clutching me while I fall apart.

I'm on a mountain.

I'm on the mountain.

The wind blows around me, a swirling tornado. It's dark this time. Like I'm on top of the mountain at night. Looking up, the sky looks identical to the night sky at the beach with Roman and I. Completely identical. But when I look down, I'm not at the beach.

I'm on the mountain. The cliff.

The sand blows as always, making my eyes burn and my skin ache. I instantly start crying, because I don't want to be on the mountain tonight. I never want to be on the mountain, but tonight especially.

I want to go back to the bed with Roman, where he can keep me safe and protect me. I want to cry in his arms and never leave. I want to beg him to stay and not leave tomorrow, but I know I have to.

So right now, I don't want to be on the mountain. I just want to be in the hotel with Roman.

I look behind me, down the trail. A place I've never been or had the opportunity to explore. I'm always on the edge of the cliff, watching the waters churn below. Angry. They're always angry.

I walk away from the edge of the cliff, but the sand doesn't let me, pulling me back, a huge gust of wind knocking me toward the tip of the sharp rock.

I fight against the tornado-like winds, attempting to push through it. To escape. Now more than ever, I just want to escape this nightmare.

But the winds won't let me.

I try to sprint, doing my best to break free, but it's as if the wind and the sand have hands, turning me around and plunging me over the edge.

I shoot up in bed, a sob breaking from my chest as my nightmare comes back to haunt me.

Again.

Roman sits up a moment later, his hand going to my back. "The mountain?"

I cry, "And the sea. Again. The cliff." I can't make out my words coherently, but Roman gives my shoulder a squeeze, knowing exactly what I'm talking about. He pulls me down, bringing the blanket to our chins and snuggling us back in tight.

"You're not on the cliff. You're here. With me. I'll always keep you safe." He presses a kiss to the back of my neck. "Try and get some sleep."

My chest shakes with fear. With terror of my nightmare. In fear of Roman leaving. I cry silent tears as Roman falls back asleep. It takes me a while, but I finally succumb to a dreamless sleep. My eyes flutter closed, and I slip into nothingness.

My eyes crack open, burning and feeling swollen. My nose is plugged, but I know it's because I fell asleep a wreck last night. I grab a tissue from the box on the side of the bed, blowing my nose and wiping my eyes before I turn around.

Roman sits with a pair of jeans and nothing else on. Sitting on the edge of the bed, he stares out the window. He doesn't move, or flinch, or say anything. Even knowing I'm awake, he does nothing besides stare out the window.

I slide out of the covers, crawling across the bed to him. I wrap my arms around his neck, settling my chin on his naked shoulder. "Good morning." I press a kiss to his cheek.

He doesn't turn toward me.

"I don't know if I can do this. I don't know if I can leave you," he murmurs.

My heart shatters. I know it's today. I knew before I even woke up that today is the day. I would do anything to go back to yesterday. But I know I don't have that power.

But I can't let him make a mistake.

"You can't stay. You know you can't."

He turns to me, finally looking me in the eyes. His face is stricken, his skin pale and white. He looks ill as he stares at me, with big bags beneath his eyes and his hair a mess, as if he's spent all morning with his hands in his hair.

"I can't leave you, Luna. I never knew why I thought I could do it. Because I can't."

"Yes, you can." I crawl around him until I'm sitting on his lap. I wrap my arms around his neck, burrowing my head beneath his chin. I can hear his heavy, broken heart without even pressing an ear against his chest. "This is your dream, Roman. I'll wait for you. On our small lake in the middle of Wisconsin, I'll be waiting for you. I'll dance every day and think of you. I'll look out on the crystal lake every morning and think of you. There's nothing that I won't do for the next three hundred and sixty-five days that isn't going to involve you being on my mind. You will be. In my heart. In my soul. Every second. Every moment. Every minute. Every day. You, and only you."

His face breaks, pure torment filling his eyes and screwing up his mouth in pain. "Fuck, I love you so much, Luna." He crushes his mouth against mine and I kiss him back with vigor, plastering myself against his body and getting as close to him as I possibly can.

I have only hours.

Hours.

We kiss and hold each other for a long time, staying silent. No words are spoken as we just enjoy the time together. But too soon, the time comes when the front desk calls to say our limo is out front.

I dress in a pair of pajamas, draping my princess dress over my arms and slipping into a pair of sandals. I look like a disaster, but I don't care. I hold Roman's hand as we leave the hotel, with tears streaming down my cheeks and torment written across my face.

We sit in the back of the limo on our way home, keeping each other as close as possible. Our arms are entwined, and our hands are linked.

The only thing I can hear is a clock ticking down in my mind.

The hourglass with only a few grains left.

Their tour van is already out front, ready for them to leave. The guys will be driving all the way to California. He squeezes my hand as we pull up, and I let a quiet sigh leave my body.

I can't let him know how tortured I am feeling.

How shattered my insides are.

"I'm going to go inside for a bit. Want to come inside with me? We aren't supposed to leave for a little while yet. I'm sure my parents want to smother me before I go."

"Isn't your dad going on tour soon too?"

He frowns. "Yeah, he's doing a small one, but I'm still worried about my mom. I'm glad Nora is here with her. I really don't know if I could leave otherwise."

My chest feels bubbly. Like a cry will burst out of me at any moment. "We'll take care of her. And my mom will visit with her all the time."

He smiles, but we're both forcing it at this point.

"I don't want to leave you. I really wish you'd come inside with me." He squeezes my hand.

I shake my head. "Go spend some time with your parents. I'll be over in a bit."

We slide out of the car, and he leans down to kiss me. "Don't take too long. I love you."

"I love you." I clutch my dress in my fingers, strangling the fabric as I walk my bare feet across the yard and toward my house.

My mom opens the door before I even make it there with her long dress flowing in the morning breeze. She gives me a sympathetic look, and I break down instantly, dropping my dress and bag into the grass as I run into her arms.

I watch as the guys pull up outside Roman's house, their parents getting out of the car and crying while they say their goodbyes. I wait until the parents leave, feeling too much like of an emotional wreck to deal with their pitiful stares.

My mom hasn't left my side for the last hour, being a mother hen and asking if I want food, a drink, a shower, anything and everything, she has asked.

I just need Roman.

She held me while I cried, and then I took a shower and freshened up. Now I'm in a summer dress, staring out my front window as I try to find the strength to go say goodbye to my soulmate. The love of my life.

"He'll be over here soon himself if you don't make your way over there." My dad says from the kitchen table. He's got his morning coffee and paper in hand. His favorite place to be. That way he can watch my mom as she works on the garden and see a sliver of the lake too. He's happiest in his spot.

"I know," I mutter.

"Come on, Luna. Let's go." My mom grabs my hand, and I inhale a shaky breath as I follow her outside. She lets go of me, and I cross my arms across my chest as I make my way to Roman's yard. Lonnie, Clyde, and Flynn are already outside. Nora and Cypress are outside too. No Goldie.

No Roman.

I bypass everyone, my mom turning the opposite way as she walks over to talk to them.

I go to the front door and stare through the screen, seeing Goldie hugging Roman. Her shoulders shake as she sobs in his arms, and he looks just as distraught.

As if he can sense me, he looks up, and Goldie separates from him, wiping her eyes as she gives me a smile. "Oh, honey, come on in."

"I'm okay, if you guys want a minute."

"Oh, no. Roman couldn't take any more of my crying. I'm just going to miss my baby boy is all."

Roman smiles sadly.

"I'm sure he's going to miss you too," I say, my voice cracking.

Roman opens the screen door and steps outside. He instantly wraps me in his arms. I go willingly, wrapping my arms around his back and holding him tight.

"I guess it's time," he says.

"I guess so," I whisper.

The guys have already loaded up their things, and I watch as Cypress and Goldie grab Roman's bags and guitar, loading them up in the van.

I guess it's only Roman now.

He goes around, giving his mom and dad one more hug. Then he goes up to his sister, whispering something in her ear, and I watch as she nods and cries on his shoulder. He gives my mom a hug next, and my mom is the one who whispers in his ear this time. He nods his head, looking so sure and certain with whatever she's telling him.

Then he turns toward me.

The guys get in the van, and my mom and Roman's parents walk off toward Roman's deck.

Roman walks up to me, wrapping me in his arms once again.

"Tell me to stay," he tells me.

"You need to go." Even though everything in my heart is telling me to beg him to stay, I know that would be wrong of me.

"Come with me then," he pleads.

I shake my head against him, knowing that I want to, more than anything, but that I can't. I have my own dreams. And he would never take me away from them. Not really.

"I can't. You know I can't," I sigh.

"I know, this just sucks." He slides his fingers under my chin, tilting my face up until I'm looking him in the eyes.

"Now and always," he tells me.

"Now and always," I echo.

"I'll call you once I get to Los Angeles. Whenever you miss me, look out at our lake. Dance to a song. Know that I'm standing next to you. Maybe not here, but in here." His finger grazes below my collarbone, right next to my necklace.

"Please be my soulmate in one year," I beg, tears flowing down my cheeks.

"I was your soulmate when we were seven and six. I am your soulmate today, just as I was yesterday. I'll be your soulmate next year, and fifty years from now. Now and always."

"Now and always," I sob quietly.

He wraps me in his arms once more, and I clutch him to me, feeling like I'm breaking straight down the middle. My fingers grip his back, holding him as closely as I can to me. If I had a stethoscope, I swear I could put it against my heart and feel it shattering into a million pieces. I feel so broken, so unrepairable, and he hasn't even left yet.

I hear him sniffle, and feel a drop touch my forehead. Looking up at him, I see tears of his own flowing down his face.

I bring my hand up, brushing his face dry with my fingers. "Now and always," I repeat.

I grab his cheeks, bringing his face down and give him a kiss. He kisses me back and doesn't stop until I'm breathless and my knees are weak.

Then he stops.

I squeeze my hands around his arms, clutching him tightly as he pulls away from me.

"I don't want you to go," I say suddenly.

He grabs onto my hands, releasing them from his arms. He brings them to his lips, giving them a kiss before dropping them at my sides. "I'll call you when I arrive, Luna. I'm always here with you. Always."

"Now and always," I cry.

He steps back, and his parents walk up to him, wrapping him in another hug as they walk him to the car. My knees feel weak again, and this time they do collapse. I fall to the ground, and my mom is there suddenly, wrapping her arms around me as Roman gets in the car.

He gives me a sad look, so tortured. Like he wants to come help me, but he knows.

The moment he comes back to me, he'll be here to stay.

The van turns on, and I cry, gripping the grass beneath my fingers and pulling with all my might. The roots rip out, blades of grass and dirt littering my fingers and embedding beneath my nails.

He pulls out of his driveway, giving me a small wave and a broken-hearted look. Then he goes blurry, as the tears flood my eyes again and he disappears down the road. My sobs turn into screams as he leaves. Roman's parents, Nora, and my mom and dad help me up, bringing me to my room and tucking me in bed.

I cry for hours.

I cry for days.

He's gone.

PART *Two*

CHAPTER FIFTEEN

Luna

1995

Red hats float in the air above me, suspended for seconds while cheering and clapping ensues around me. I stare up at the ceiling, watching my square hat fly back down to me. It's a wave of red gowns, a sea of blood in the claustrophobic gym.

This is it.

Graduation day.

I catch my cap from the air, picking up the soft tassel and setting it on the opposite side. Everyone starts to vacate their folding chairs, the feet creaking and groaning, banging loudly against the next one as everyone moves too fast, too eager. Their gowns float around them as they walk toward their friends and family.

"Congratulations, Class of 1995!" The principal says from the podium. Everyone is already off, though, and I watch my classmates around me with their bright smiles and tears in their eyes as they're finally finished with one of the biggest milestones of their lives.

Nora runs up to me, her arms extended so she looks like a red bat as she wraps me in a hug, squeezing me tight. "We did it! We did it!" she screeches. A wave of her fruity perfume slaps me in the face. I hug her back, laughing and smiling, even though a part of me feels empty, lacking.

Half of me, actually.

I look up at our families, seeing Nora's parents sitting next to mine. Harper and her boyfriend sit beside my mom. She waves at me, and I wave back, my eyes jumping to the empty seat next to Cypress.

The spot where Roman was supposed to be.

Only he's not.

I promised myself I wouldn't cry today, and I'm trying too hard to keep that promise. Even though beneath my gown feels broken, like any misstep and I may shatter into a thousand pieces.

I bite my lip as Nora pulls me along. Our families get up from their seats, walking down the metal steps to meet us on the gym floor. The entire auditorium echoes, the voices bouncing off the walls and the clacking of heels so noisy it feels like I'm in a tunnel.

My dad has me wrapped in a hug the next moment, lifting me off my heels and spinning me around. "I can't believe my baby girl is all grown up." His voice is clogged with emotion.

A tear springs to my eyes, and I wipe it away once he puts me down, smiling up at him. I can't think of any words to say, my entire mind is scrambled and a little fractured.

"What's the matter, baby?" my mom asks, brushing her fingers through my straight hair.

I feel my chest shaking, and I press my palm against my satin gown, directly over my chest, hoping to calm the quaking. "I just wanted him to be here," I whisper.

She gives me a sad smile, the same smile that I've been seeing over the past year. Ever since the day he left, it's been pitiful, sad looks given to me in every direction.

"Why don't we head home, huh? I can grill for us down by the lake. It's a beautiful evening," Cypress says from behind me, wrapping me in a hug of his own.

I inhale a shaky breath, giving him a smile and a nod. We all head out, going in our separate cars back to our houses.

A year ago, after Roman left, he called that same day. He found a payphone on the road, using the spare change in his pocket to give me a call. He didn't call his parents; his friends didn't call their parents. He only called me. It left me with an inkling of hope that everything would be okay. That our time together could be filled with phone calls and letters. If I closed my eyes, it was like he was almost there, lying next to me on my bed. That's how soft his voice was. It was low, echoing in my chest and making me feel like if I reached out, my fingers would thread through the thick strands of his hair. I could pretend he was with me every time he called, and the next time I'd open my eyes, it'd be a year from now, and Roman would be in front of me.

I'd get letters. The beginning weeks and even the first couple of months consisted of my mailbox being stuffed with letters upon letters from Roman. Love letters, really. Small trinkets that he'd find and mail to me. Things he knew I'd love to see. Promises of places that we'd travel to when I would go on the road with him someday. Stories he'd tell, people he'd meet. The letters were filled with each moment of his life. He wanted to share those moments with me, and I swallowed every word, every curl of every letter. Every dot and period, every crease in the paper. I'd smell the letters, hoping for a small scent of him. A remembrance, something normal that I could hold on to. I'd feel the texture of the smooth paper, running my finger across the bumpy seal where I know he'd licked. I begged and pleaded for time to fly by.

Unfortunately, time seemed to slow.

Roman never made it home for Christmas. They were too busy in the recording studio to make the trip, their manager too strict and kind of a hard ass, Roman would say.

Then New Year's came, and I waited by my phone, curling the cord around my finger until my blood ran cold. Once the clock struck midnight, and the new year was here, I still hadn't received a call. I clutched my phone in my arms all night, waiting for the obnoxious ring and Roman's timbre voice to relax my frayed nerves.

It never came.

He called days later, telling me how chaotic things had been in California. Now they were getting ready to head out for another tour.

I cried. I cried so hard through the phone he had to have felt the tears. He pled with me to stay strong, that nothing has changed between us. That before I knew it, we'd be together again.

But now, here I am.

I'm alone. I haven't heard from Roman in weeks. I know he's okay, because the local paper always loves talking about the local boy turned rock star. He's on tour, traveling and making friends and being famous.

No phone calls. No more letters. Our connection has gone silent, just as my heart has. It no longer beats. My blood no longer pumps. I'm a walking zombie as I float through the days. Senior year in high school was supposed to be filled with happiness and good memories, but I barely remember a day of it.

I'm so lost, I don't even know what tomorrow brings.

I stretch my unused feet in front of me, feeling useless and sad. My body isn't as flexible as it once was. Just a few months without dance has turned my body into something it's never been before.

The moment Roman left, my love for dance dwindled. Don't get me wrong, it's always been a part of me, and it always will be. I went to the studio for a long time after he left, trying with everything in me to get that strength, that power, that drive back that I've had in me for thirteen years. But the moment Roman left, it's like he took my ability to dance with him.

I can dance just as good as I always have, but my heart isn't in it. My mind isn't in it. And ballet isn't a sport that you do half-assed. Do it with everything in you or don't do it at all. Ballet doesn't deserve me when I'm like this. My slippers don't deserve my blood and my leotard doesn't deserve my sweat. Not if my heart isn't in it.

My heart isn't in it.

It just makes me wonder, how Roman can be such a big impact on my life, but I'm such a little impact on his? If he can continue to sing and make music, but I can't even find it in me to tie my slippers around my ankles, were we ever soulmates at all?

Is it possible that he's my soulmate, but I'm not his?

The thought pulls me into a dark, dark pool of dread and tragedy, dark as my black hair. It curls around me like a cold blanket, and I chill.

All the way to my soul.

My toes curl in the cool lake, and I watch the minnows swim around them. They float up to my toes, getting a sense of what the unusual thing is floating in their home. I move my foot and they flitter away in the blink of an eye.

The edges of my dress are damp, floating on the surface of the water as I kick my legs. My butt is planted on the end of Roman's dock, and I watch the sunset over the horizon. A few fishermen still linger about, creating small waves as they drive by. Mr. Sorenson from across the lake comes by in his pontoon, his grandkids sitting on the edge, half of their bodies suspended in air as they look at the water. Their bright orange life jackets choking them to death.

My eyes flit back down to my toes.

None of it matters anymore. It's all meaningless.

It's been two weeks since graduation, and I still haven't heard from Roman. I sent him a letter with the date and time of the ceremony, and I figured he'd be there. I'd hoped, but now that weeks have passed, the hope is long gone that I mean anything to him at all.

He's forgotten about me.

My spine curls over, and I pull my legs from the water, curling my knees up to my chest and wrapping my arms around my shins. My head goes between my thighs, and I let out a silent cry, the never-ending flood of tears seeming to be turned on even though I so desperately want them to turn off.

My fist clenches, the letter I wrote to him on graduation morning clutched in my fingers. I was going to give it to him the night that he got home. The letter that speaks about my undying love, and how I'll give up dance to go on the road with him.

It's all meaningless now.

I cross my legs over one another, wiping my eyes with my free hand as I straighten out the letter, staring at my dainty scrawl in front of me.

Roman,

I'm writing you this letter with shaky fingers. In only a few hours, I'll be able to hold you in my arms again. I'll be able to kiss you and see your face. It feels like it's been forever. It has been forever. I've been waiting a full year, and I know with my heart and soul that a piece of me left with you that morning after prom.

I don't want you to give it back to me.

I just want you by me, and I know everything will be right again. I have some news that I've been waiting to tell you, but I can't hold it in anymore.

I'm going on tour with you.

I already have my bag packed, sitting at my feet as we speak. I don't want to dance anymore, not when it means being away from you. I want to tour with you, watch you sing, watch the arms of thousands of fans shake into the sky at your beautiful words.

I want to listen to your voice blare through the microphone and float into the ears of hundreds, thousands, millions of people.

I don't care where we go. Let's go everywhere. Across the country and across the world. It'll be worth it as long as I'm with you. I want to travel the universe and experience this journey with you.

I'm ready, and I don't want to wait another second.

I can't wait to give you this letter tonight.

I can't wait to spend the rest of my life with you.

I love you, Roman.

Now and always,

Your Luna.

A tear drops onto the middle of the heart right next to my name, blurring the ink and breaking it into two pieces. It's fitting, really, and it's exactly how I'm feeling right now.

I bend down, placing the letter in the lake. The water swallows it up quickly, wetting the center of the paper before it seeps onto the edges. Half of it falls underwater, bobbing up and down as it turns translucent. And then it floats away, taking the rest of me with it.

I'm a shell of the person I used to be. It feels like I was never a person at all. Not really, anyway. Like I was an addition to Roman, and now that he's gone, I'm a box without the contents. I'm a shell of a human.

The dock rocks, footsteps vibrating all the way to me from up on land. I turn around, seeing Nora walking up to me. She has that sad look on her face. The same face I've been looking at for the past year.

"Hey, what's up?" she asks, coming to sit next to me. She grabs her sandals with her hands, placing them on the dock beside me and dipping her own toes in the water.

I wipe my face, tucking my hair behind my ears as I look at her. "Just enjoying the sunset." I clear my throat, hating how full of tears it sounds.

"You don't have to pretend you weren't crying, Luna. It's all you've been doing for a year. Everyone knows."

I tip my head toward the cloudless sky, blinking away the tears that instantly spring to my eyes. I let out a groan. "I'm so tired of crying. I feel so weak."

"You aren't weak. You're just in love," she says softly, rubbing her hand down my arm.

"Have you heard from him?" I ask, bringing my head back down and looking into the distance. A bald eagle flies over the trees, and I wish I was as effortless as him. I wish we could fly through the trees together. Maybe I'd just fly away. Never come back.

"No. None of us have," she sighs. "I'm sure we'll hear from him soon, though. There has to be a reason he hasn't reached out."

I shrug. "Doesn't matter too much anymore."

"What do you mean?" I look at her, seeing her heavy frown directed my way.

I bend down, dipping my fingers in the water. Creating a ripple, I make a constant figure eight. Over and over again, I watch, entranced as the water tornados around my fingers.

"Luna?"

I sit up, looking over at her. "I'm done crying about him, Nora. I can't keep doing this."

She nods. "I know." Leaning over on one butt cheek, she brings her hand to the back pocket of her shorts and pulls out a white squared paper. My heart drops, thinking it may be a letter from Roman. "I was just down at Coffee Joe's and saw this flyer. I thought of you instantly."

I take it from her, keeping it folded up. "What is it?"

She nods her head toward it. "Take a look."

I wipe my wet fingers on my dress and unfold the paper, seeing blue skies and oceans and palm trees.

"What is it? A vacation? I don't even have a job. I certainly can't go on vacation. I don't have the money."

She rips the paper from my hands. "Well, you'll never know what it is if you never read the fricken words. It's a once in a lifetime opportunity. This company in Hawaii is offering young people to come live on their farm for free. You work on their farm and get paid a little, but otherwise you get free housing, and *hello*, it's Hawaii. I'd take it myself if I wasn't leaving for Madison in a month."

I take it from her, finally reading the words. She's right. It's a once in a lifetime opportunity. Doing manual labor on a farm, but in exchange, I get to live in Hawaii for free. I even make a little extra money from it. All I need is a plane ticket to get out there, but this past year I've saved enough from dog walking and babysitting. I'm sure I can find a way to get a one-way ticket out there.

"I think I'm going to take it," I breathe, finally feeling like I have something to look forward to. "This actually sounds like a really good idea."

Her eyes go wide. "Oh my God, really?" She stands up with me, "Please don't tell my parents or yours that I'm the one that gave you this idea. I think they'd all bury me at the bottom of the lake."

They probably would. At least try.

"I won't. I promise." I grab her for a hug, wrapping her in the first true hug I've given anyone since Roman left. Over a year ago at this point.

It's almost like he never existed at all.

"Oh my God. I'm actually really excited for this." I squeeze the paper in my fingers, such a different reaction to when I was squeezing a different paper in my hands only minutes before Nora showed up. "I'm going to go talk to my parents."

She cringes. "They're going to be so mad."

I shake my head. "You know what? Maybe not. I've been so sad for the last year, maybe they'll be happy that I'm finally excited over something."

She smiles at that, her face brightening against the setting sun. "Yeah, you're right. That makes me happy, too." She wraps me in another hug before stepping back to head down the dock. The wood is warm beneath my feet from the afternoon sun as I make way toward the sand. The water slaps against the bottom of the dock as it rocks from our movements. "I'll let you know how it goes."

"Should I come rescue you if I hear screaming?"

I roll my eyes, "I'll talk to you tomorrow!"

I run to my house, the bottom of my wet dress slapping against my ankles as I run into the front door. I let the screen door slap against the frame, and it startles my mom and dad from their spot on the couch. "Hey, honey, what's wrong?"

I walk up to them, sitting on the coffee table between them and handing them the piece of paper.

My mom grabs it, not looking down at it as she stares at my face.

The excitement.

"What's going on?"

"Read it."

They bend down, reading the words. Heads bent together. Eyes roaming in the same rotation. I watch their eyes read it. Once. Twice. Three times before they look back up to me.

"What are you trying to say?" my dad asks, taking his glasses off and setting them next to me on the table.

"I want to do this." I tap the top of the page with my fingers. "I want to go to Hawaii."

"But…" my mom starts.

"How will you get there?" my dad asks, "You know we don't have that kind of money to get you a plane ticket to Hawaii."

I shake my head. "I have some money saved."

"You do know you have to fly to California and then to Hawaii, right? There are no direct flights from Wisconsin to Hawaii. It's going to be an expensive ticket."

My fingers fall from the paper into my lap. I didn't think about this. But I'm determined, and for the first time in a year, I'm actually looking forward to something. I want to hang onto the last shred of humanity I have left in me. This beating heart in my chest feels alive, like it's awakening after a long sleep. The creakiness in my body after being stiff for so long. I feel new, alive.

I have to do this.

"I want to do this. Please, guys." I put my hands in the prayer pose.

My dad sits against the back of the couch, folding his arms across his chest, and glances at my mom.

She has tears in her eyes. "Is this about Roman? Because—"

I whip my head from side to side. "No. For once in my life, this is about *me*."

"But what about dance?" She dabs her wet eyes with the back of her hand. "Ballet has been such a huge part in your life. You just want to throw that away?"

"I think dance is a part of my past." My own throat starts to close up, and I clear my throat to rid the emotion. "I'm ready for a fresh start."

She blows out a shaky breath between her teeth, handing me back the piece of paper. "When would you leave?"

"Right away. Next week, probably." Obviously, I need to figure out the finer details, but getting away from here is what would be best for me and my health. Sitting here and moping over a guy isn't doing me any favors. I need to start over. It's time I find myself.

She nods her head, turning toward my dad. "What do you think, Charlie?"

He wraps his arm around her, pulling her against him. He knows she's having a hard time with this, and so do I. "I'm okay with it if you are. She's an adult now. I think if she wants to go and experience life, we can't stop her."

My mom looks back at me. "You'll talk to me all the time? Send me emails and call?"

Tears spring to my eyes, the reality of what I'm choosing smacking me in the face. "Of course." I lean over, wrapping my arms around the both of them. "All the time."

"Then, okay. We're okay with it," Mom says.

I fold the paper up and stand up from the table. "Thank you. Thank you! I'm going to go look some stuff up on the computer." I head to Harper's room, which has been converted into a guest room slash computer room. It takes a while to log on, since our dial-up internet is so terrible out here, but I find a Greyhound that leaves here in a week, heading to California. From there, I can take a flight out to Maui. It's the cheapest route and would save me a little money along the way.

By the time I shut down the computer, my body is humming with excitement. The hair on my arms stick straight up on my entire body, actually.

One week.

One week, and my life begins again.

CHAPTER SIXTEEN
Roman

The yellow taxi hops off the highway, and I'm instantly hit with nostalgia. It's been a long time since I've been in my hometown. A long time coming.

I was hoping to get home a while ago, but tour stop after tour stop, and things couldn't be avoided. That, and our van broke down in Iowa. The guys are there, but I couldn't wait anymore. I had to get home. I have to talk to my family, and I have to see Luna. It's been too long. Every time I'm about to pick up the phone and call her or get a piece of paper out to write her a letter, I get pulled in a different direction.

I know I'm in the wrong. I made a promise that I kind of fell off on, but once she hears how busy I've been, how popular we're becoming, and how busy things are going to be in the upcoming months, I know she'll be happy for me. She'll be proud that I've finally made it.

I'm hoping she is ready to move out to New York with me. I'm planning to let the guys take over the rent fully in our little apartment in Los Angeles, and me and Luna can go live in New York. I'll come stay with the guys whenever I need to be in town, but I always want to come back to Luna. That's the plan, at least.

I just want to be with her agai

This last year has been crazy. ...wn over our band. The number of topless and naked women I've seen begging for a piece of us, a piece of me…

I shake my head.

The guys love it. It makes me wonder if this is the type of stuff my dad deals with when he's on tour. Naked women throwing themselves at him.

Not only women, but the drugs. They're hardcore.

In Wisconsin, we deal with weed, we deal with alcohol, but hard drugs are hard to come by in our sleepy town. We don't have much crime. It's safe here. So, when I see lines of white powder left and right, or pink, yellow, and white pills, or needles filled with a brownish liquid, I barely know what to do with myself.

I've dabbled, yes, but it's not really my thing. The guys are more into the women, and they like to do cocaine, but otherwise, we stay out of it. For the most part, at least.

We drive down Main Street, and I see the studio where I've spent so much time watching Luna. I hope she's still dancing. I hope her body is ready because what I've heard of Julliard is that it's rough. It's not pretty, but once you get in, it's totally worth it. I know it's what Luna has been meant to do; she always has. Her body was made for it.

The way her toes are always pointed, the way her body is made. Her spine is always straight. She's a ballerina at heart.

I crack my window down, smelling the lake, the slight smell of fish from the bait shop, the cow manure. I take a deep inhale, closing my eyes as all my memories come back to me.

Home.

We pass the school, then old Tip Town park, and I watch little kids play on the playground. It's a new era here. My generation is gone, and in its place is an entirely new group of families, kids, and friends who get to explore the land of Shallow Lake, Wisconsin.

It's funny. Shallow Lake actually isn't shallow at all. It's a pretty deep lake, really. Not sure where the name came from, but it stuck somehow.

We turn on our long road, and I see the cornfields that I've lived across the street from for my entire life. I see a hint of the lake in between the houses. I only got a glimpse, but I can't wait to swim in the water again.

I may only be here for a couple days, but I plan to take advantage of every second.

First things first, though. I need to see my girl.

"Right here, on the right."

I point to our houses, which look exactly the same. They seem a little smaller than they used to, whether it be because I've grown or maybe it's because of all the grand places I've experienced over the last year.

The brakes squeak as the taxi parks, and I go in my wallet and hand him some cash. "Thanks for the ride." I was able to Greyhound up from Iowa but decided on a taxi home instead of calling Luna or my parents.

I wanted to surprise them.

I walk around to the back of the car as the trunk pops. I grab my black duffle, wrapping my fingers around the worn straps and shutting the trunk with a slam.

The sun is setting. The orange glow over the dark blue waters is something I'll never get sick of. This place is not something even a bone in my body could ever get sick of.

Someday, I'd like to move back here. Takeover my parents' house if I could. Maybe buy my own house on the lake. Start a family with Luna and raise our kids in this small town. That's my goal. Way down the road. Not something I've ever spoken with Luna about, but I know she feels the same.

The taxi driver pulls out of the driveway, reversing and heading back the way he came. I shield my hand over my eyes as the sun glares at me, and walk toward Luna's house. Just as I'm walking up to her door, it opens, and there stands Jane.

"Hey, Jane." I wrap her in a hug, not thinking anything besides hugging my second mom.

She's stiff for a second, shock covering her face before she melts and gives me a hug back.

"Roman, I didn't know you were coming home."

"Yeah, it was kind of a surprise. Is Luna here?"

Her eyes blink a few times at me, shock in her gaze again. It makes me raise my guard a bit. She's not acting cold toward me, but something is definitely wrong. I'm not sure what it is, but it makes my stomach turn sour.

"Um, yeah. She's in her room." She opens the door, and I walk in after giving her a smile. I could ask her what that look is about, but the only thing on my mind is seeing Luna.

The house smells of the same marijuana and herbs that I've smelled my entire life. I inhale the familiar scent as I walk through the home, knowing each creak and groan on the floorboards. With my bag in hand, I walk to Luna's room. Her door is cracked open, and when I see her, my entire body freezes.

God, she's beautiful.

She sits with her back to me, looking out the window at the lake. A bag sits on the ground at her feet, and a smile breaks out on my face.

It's like she knew I was coming, and she's ready for anything.

She's wearing one of her dresses, the creamy fabric full of a thick lace that is so hippy, so her. Her dark hair sits in a mess as it tumbles down her shoulders, falling to the small of her waist.

My beautiful Luna. So much the same.

"Luna," I say.

Her body freezes, and it takes her a moment. Like she thinks my voice was in her head. Like she's not sure if it was real or not. But then she turns, so slowly, like she's moving in slow motion as her body rotates and she ends up staring at me directly in the eyes.

They're wide, wonder and shock filling her features.

"Roman?" She stands up, walking around her bed and stopping in front of me. Her hand raises, touching my bare arm. Like I'm a vision, a dream.

"I'm here," I whisper.

"Roman." Her voice is sad, so depleted and so happy at the same time.

I don't waste another second, grabbing her around the waist and pulling her against me. She smells the same as I bury my face in her hair. It's soft, the scents of the lake and the sand and the sun hitting my nose. "Holy shit, I've missed you." My voice is raspy.

I can feel her body shake against me, tears and surprise racking her body in silent sobs. "Shhhh, I'm here, Luna. I'm right here."

She looks up, tears streaming down her face as she looks at me in wonder. "I can't believe you're here. How... how are you here?"

"Our van broke down in Iowa. We were stuck for a few days, so I decided while they stayed there, I'd come home to see you. I've missed you. Fuck, I've missed you so much." I wrap her in my arms again, giving her another squeeze.

"It's been too long." She smells so familiar. She feels so familiar.

She doesn't say anything, holding me so tightly against her, her shaky arms and her trembling body feeling so small against mine.

"Let's sit down. Tell me everything. How are you?" I drag her to the bed, sitting down in the middle of it, shoes and all. I pull her on top of me, and she lays curled up in a ball on my lap. Her hand goes up to my hair, feeling the long strands that I've let grow even longer since I've been gone.

She shakes her head. "I want to hear about you."

I let out a breath, feeling so at home here. With her. It doesn't matter that we've been apart for an entire year, that our contact has been lessened. One moment with her and I'm back right where I started. This is why I've gone a year without bringing a girl in my bed. It wasn't even a contest, no question at all whether I should stick to my word and stay faithful to Luna. It wasn't hard, not in the slightest. Luna is it for me, and she always has been.

One moment with Luna and everything is exactly how it should be.

"It's been crazy, Luna. I can't even begin to explain it to you. It's been city after city. Concert after concert. People come to the shows! We have sold out venues. It's like nothing I ever expected when I started this."

"I've heard your songs on the radio," she whispers against my chest.

"I know. I can't believe we have an actual hit. I grew up with my dad having hits all the time, I just never expected that I would actually have a song on the radio of my own. It's just crazy. Our manager is a hard ass, but I've told you that."

She nods.

"I know I missed your graduation, and I'm sorry. I had the dates mixed up, and when I realized it, my manager wouldn't let us bail since we were about to have a huge show in Chicago. So, I was going to come afterward, and we ended up having car issues. Shit, it's been a hell of a last couple weeks. I'm just glad I'm in a home, on an actual bed. You don't realize how good you have it until you're cramped on a bus with a ton of dudes. Shit sucks."

She giggles, even though it sounds sad.

"We have a couple more stops after this, and then we're heading back to LA. I was thinking about packing up my things and heading out to New York. Like we planned. How does that sound?"

She stiffens against my body, her limp form turning still as a statue.

"Luna, what's wrong?" I ask, tilting her face up to mine.

She nudges her head out of my hand, rolling off the bed. She stands, keeping her back toward me.

An instant chill breaks out over my body, and dread seeps into my vision, darkening everything around me. I nearly black out in fear. Fear of something being wrong. Fear of her no longer loving me. Fear over her having found someone else.

That one brings a bit of rage as well.

I grab onto her shoulders, turning her around so she's facing me. "Tell me. Whatever it is, just tell me. We'll figure it out."

Her eyes water, turning glassy just inches away from mine. A tear spills, and I'm too frozen, too panicked to wipe it away this time.

"What is it, Luna?" My voice is sharper this time, and I can't do anything besides grip her shoulders. I loosen them a bit when she winces, but I can't let go of her.

Doesn't she know? I will never let her go.

"You're too late, Roman." Her eyes avert to the ground, and tears fall on top of her bare toes. I can barely find the reflex to swallow as I take in her words.

My hand goes to my hair, running my fingers through the rough strands before bringing them down to my cheeks, scratching at the stubble there. "What do you mean, I'm too late?"

She looks up at me, her eyes bloodshot with regret. "I mean you're too late. I waited for you. I waited an entire year. And then longer. I *mean*, Roman, that you. Are. Too. Late."

I glance down at her bag on the floor, bulging at the seam and ready to go.

"So, what's your plan? Go to New York without me? I saw the bag, and I don't know, had this hope that you were planning to come on tour with me. Maybe you had a sense I was on my way." She says nothing. "That's not it? Then what could it be? You meet someone else?" She still says nothing. I give her a little shake, and she wobbles around like a bobble head. "Tell me, Luna!" My voice raises, rage and fear clutching my throat like a snake is wrapped around it, slowly suctioning every last bit of air, of life, from my lungs.

"I'm leaving."

"To where?" I grit through my teeth.

"I'm moving to Hawaii."

My eyes nearly bug out of my head. "Hawaii? What the fuck is in Hawaii? What about New York? Julliard? What about your ballet, Luna? I can tell you right now that there isn't some good fucking ballet school in Hawaii."

The next words that come out of her mouth rip my soul straight from my ribcage.

"I don't dance anymore."

My hands drop from her shoulders, and I take a step back. It feels like someone reached their bare hand into my chest and took my heart out with their sharp, five-inch nails, scraping along my walls and inflicting wounds every inch of the way. "W-what?"

I blink at her, and she says nothing as she continues to silently cry, her slim shoulders bobbing up and down from her sadness.

"What do you mean, you don't dance? That's your entire life!"

She whips her gaze up to mine, torture and tragedy in her gray eyes. They are empty, the life she grew up with zapped clean, drained, completely wiped dry of the girl she used to be. She might as well have blue eyes; she looks so different to me.

"*You* were my life! You left me, Roman. I wanted you to leave, to take a chance at your dream, but the moment you left, a part of me died. I haven't been able to dance, not in months. I don't even *want* to dance anymore. All I do is cry, and cry, and cry some fucking more. I begged and pleaded for you to come home on graduation night. When you didn't, I lost hope. Days, and days, and more days passed without you coming home, and eventually, *I gave up*."

I open my mouth, but nothing comes out besides a painful breath.

She doesn't dance anymore.

"I gave up, Roman. I gave up on you coming home. I gave up on us."

"Luna, I told you—"

She holds a hand up, stopping my reply with a slice through the air. "I waited for you, Roman. For months! No calls, no letters, nothing!" She takes a deep breath, lowering her voice, "When an opportunity came up, I felt life fill me for the first time since you left, and I realized I can't keep doing this. I'm done waiting, and I'm done allowing myself to bleed dry. I'm going to go live, for once. For me, and me alone."

"Luna." I step toward her, grabbing her in my arms and making her look me in the eyes. My thumbs press against her cheeks, keeping her gaze pinned to mine. I spear her gray eyes, begging for this to be a joke, a fucking dream. Begging for her to relieve me of the pain I'm currently feeling. "I'm sorry. I'm so sorry that I made you wait. That's my fault, and I take total responsibility. But are you telling me you're going to give up everything that we have, our entire existence, because of this? So you can, what, flee to Hawaii?"

She scowls at me. "I'm not fleeing." She rips her arms from my hold and steps back. "It's time I learn how to be my own person, Roman."

"So what does this mean? For me? For us?"

When she looks at me this time, her eyes are completely void of all emotion.

"No, don't you fucking say it, Luna." I point my finger in her face, shaking, fucking trembling in terror. "Don't say it to me, or I swear to fucking God."

"I think we're over, Roman."

Tears spring to my own eyes, and I go to grab her, but she freezes up, sidestepping my grab. "Please, Roman. I think you should go."

"I'm not leaving like this," I grit through my teeth. "I'm not leaving us. I'm not giving up on us. *Are you?*"

Her eyes fill with tears again, and I watch as one falls down her cheek. It bobs on her wobbly chin before falling. I reach my hand out, palm up, and catch her tear in my hand. I close my palm, keeping her tear, because it looks like she's going to keep my heart.

"I don't want to give up on us, Roman. But my life has been *nothing* this past year. I need to go do this. I need to go figure out who I am. Without dance. Without… you. I need to find me."

I step back, feeling a coldness in my body I've never felt before. The summer heat should be sticking to my skin, the heavy humidity creating a glaze of moisture on my face and arms and neck. But instead, I feel like I stepped into a walk-in freezer, locked myself inside, with no way out. I feel like my entire body is dropping degrees by the second.

I feel dead.

"So, this is it then? This is it for us?"

"This is it," she says, her voice void of emotion. I drained that from her. I bled her dry. She has nothing left to give, and it's all my fault.

I run my hand down my face, so much shock rocking through my chest. This is not how I imagined this reunion going. Quite the opposite, actually. I don't know how to take it. I barely know how to breathe at this point. It feels like I have a knife sticking from my heart, but when I look down, it's just my plain black shirt, lifting and dropping with my heavy breaths.

"I guess this is goodbye, then," I say, bending down to pick up my duffle.

I turn around, seeing sadness bleed from every pore on her body. "Can I… can I give you a hug at least? One before you go?"

She opens her arms without another word, and I drop my duffle, stomping over to her and lifting her in my arms. I don't think twice, my hand going to the back of her head and bringing her lips to mine. If this is the last time that we kiss, I'm going to make it worth it.

I inhale every last bit of her, my greedy lips taking and taking and taking until I can't take anymore. I kiss her until she separates, gasping for air. I settle her down on her feet, tucking her hair behind her ear. "I will be here. I will always be waiting. One week. One month. One year. Maybe never. But I will be waiting for you. We're soulmates, and that doesn't just go away. I love you so much, Luna. Now and always."

"Now and always," she whispers, the words barely leaving her mouth.

I brush my thumb over her lips one last time, staring into her gray eyes. I'll never meet another Luna. Never again. She is it for me.

I just hope that when this all ends, I'm it for her.

I turn around, because I won't be able to take it if I'm in this room another second. Bending down, I lift the straps of my bag once more, walking out of her room without another look.

I only take a few steps down the hall when I hear her sob and a small crash, like she fell to the floor. I stop in my steps, wanting so badly to turn around, but knowing if I do, I'll never let her go.

Instead, I squeeze the straps on my bag, imaging I'm squeezing the life from them. I continue walking, heading toward the kitchen, and stop again when I see Luna's parents. Jane stands in the kitchen, her shoulder propped against the wall. She holds a Kleenex in her hand, pressed to her face as she silently cries. Charlie stands behind her, his hand on her shoulder and a sad look on his face. He looks at me unhappily, like he feels bad for this entire situation.

No one seems mad at me.

Everyone seems lost.

I don't say anything as I walk out, the door slapping behind me.

I walk across our yards, feeling so lost and confused. Almost like I'm drunk or on drugs. I don't know which way to walk, or how to form words on my tongue. Mosquitos are out, and I don't even swat them away as I walk aimlessly, the incessant bugs buzzing around my face. When I get close to my yard, my outside light turns on. The door opens, and my mom stands there, her own face wet with tears as she holds her arms open for me.

I drop my duffle, my eyes flooding with tears as a gut-wrenching groan rips through my chest. I'm not a man that cries, but for some reason, when it comes to Luna, my emotions are heightened.

I walk straight into my mom's arms, my cries heavy and deep, my pain aching down to my bones. My heart broken.

I lost her.

I lost her.

I lost her.

CHAPTER SEVENTEEN

Luna
1997

The sound of water trickling between rocks trails into my ears as the soft tunes of *The Sound of Silence* by Simon and Garfunkel play in the background. My toes dip into the cool water, the sun hot on my exposed back as my fingers wrap a piece of chrysocolla between twine, perfecting another one of my dream catchers.

I press my hand to my eyebrows, seeing the sun hot, round, and bright as it sits high in the sky. The jagged red mountains of the Apache Trail don't make it any less hot here in the desert. It's like the sun heats the sand, the sand heats the air, and the air makes it so dry and stifling, it's hard to breathe. Luckily, we've got a nice spot along the river.

It's nothing like Wisconsin, where the air was a bit humid, smelling like a mix of cow manure, fresh air, and lake water. The thought makes my feet stop tapping to the beat of the music.

I miss my parents. I wonder how they're doing. Is my mom still gardening outside? Is my dad's favorite spot still at the kitchen table, where he can get a clear view of the lake and my mom outside at the same time? Does he still like his coffee scorching hot and black?

I shake my head.

He'll always like his coffee black and boiling.

After they dropped me at the Greyhound station, I hopped on the bus heading to San Diego, where I'd then catch a flight to Maui.

Sitting on the bus that smelled like dirty socks and sweat, my tearful face pressed against the window, half wanting to jump out and run home, hoping that Roman was still there so I could beg him to take me back. Beg for his forgiveness.

The other part of me wanted the bus to move faster, to flee as far away from my past and create a new future as quickly as I could.

Then I met Willie, Neil, Shauna, and Trish. All of us headed to different locations. A little lost, not really sure what we're looking for. Just something new, something fresh to dip our toes into with hope we come out the other end okay.

I showed them the flier, passed each of them the wrinkled, folded-too-many-times piece of white paper with my destination on it. I watched as four sets of eyes lit up, each of them thinking it was a great idea. They wanted to take this journey with me, hoping they could find what they were looking for on the beaches of Hawaii.

But first, they wanted to make a pit stop in Arizona. The pit stop ended up being our home. My dream is still to make it to Hawaii, but right now, I'm enjoying the red desert of Arizona. The red mountains, the cool rivers, the ranches, and the cowboys.

At times I get to see wild horses, their hair blowing in the wind as the ground shakes beneath their feet, their hooves pounding the sand as they run from place to place.

Wild.

Free.

Nothing gives me greater happiness than watching them roam the world. That's what I want. To be free, without heartbreak, without obligations or people assuming what I need. I've dealt with that. I've lived a life with pitiful eyes watching me, assuming what was best for me. I don't want that life.

I want to make my own path, build my own life.

We hopped off the bus in Phoenix, not really a destination in mind. It was Neil's destination, and he wanted to at least check it out before we continued on our journey. We all walked off the bus, our legs stiff and our backs sore. We were all in desperate need of a shower, maybe a bed too.

But none of us had much money, so we wandered, hiked, found small jobs here and there. I'd find small stones on the ground, and with the days long and the nights even longer, I'd twine things together, until one day I made a dreamcatcher. Then I made two, three, until I had an entire stack of them.

We'd head down to town, and the locals and tourists loved them, their hands anxiously going to their pockets to pull out any spare change they had. I took it greedily, in need of food and water. Anything, really.

Neil and Willie found a small job with a rancher, cleaning up his fields and tending to his animals. In exchange, the old man gave us a half broken down Winnebago. We brought it to our spot by the river, making a small little home here.

Most of them sleep in the van.

I prefer the stars.

I always have.

It reminds me of lying on the sandy beach and watching the glistening stars both near and far. I feel like if I reach up, I'll be able to pluck one from the sky and put it in the satchel with my dreamcatchers. I'd keep the star, though. I'd hold onto it forever.

Though, there's something about the sky here. It's different. The constellations are still there, in the same distinct pattern I've studied since I was a child, but a part of me feels like it's not the same.

It's like I'm looking at a different sky. It makes me feel like a different person entirely, like who I was is not who I am now.

The guys constructed me a makeshift bed outside, made of sticks and stones. I sleep out here most nights, unless the air gets too cool. But I like it out here, the night is silent with the occasional coyote howling in the distance, or the sounds of horse hooves pounding against the earth.

But no traffic. No pollution. No people.

Just us.

Sometimes Willie sleeps outside with me.

Willie.

What is Willie? I don't know. A boyfriend? Absolutely not. A friend? Something in between? Probably.

He makes my heart hurt a little less and hurt a little more at the same time.

He'll never be *him*, and I knew that the moment I met Willie. But his long blond hair and cheeky smile make him so boyish, no girl would be blind to his charms.

My fingers subconsciously go to my necklace, the chain hot in the sun. I want to take it off, once and for all, but I know even telling myself that is a lie, because it's just as much a part of me as the rest of my body is. I can't separate from my soul, as much as I beg myself to at night underneath the stars, crying into the night because all I want is to be free of him. Be free of this love and pain that I feel day and night. But that freedom never comes. My love is too strong, too sure.

The pain and love mingle together and run through my blood, hot as fire. Nothing will stop it.

Nothing.

I shake my head, clearing these thoughts as I finish the dreamcatcher.

Pressing my toes against a slippery rock in the creek, I push myself back until I'm flat on my back.

"What do you think?" I ask, showing the dreamcatcher to Neil and Willie behind me.

Willie checks out my stomach, his eyes grazing from my rib cage all the way to the waistline of my skirt. My nipples protrude, poking through my white shirt that I've shredded to crop right below my breasts. Out here in the desert, less clothes are better. He settles his guitar on the ground, crawling over to me in his shorts, no shirt. His blond hair fans around his face as an evil smile crosses his face.

He bends over, kissing me upside down. His hand slips beneath the collar of my shirt, tweaking my peaked nipple in his fingers. I roll away from him, a sharp bush poking me in my naked side. "Ouch."

"You shouldn't have rolled away from me, then," he chuckles.

I roll my eyes, sitting up and sliding the dreamcatcher into my satchel with the pile of other ones I have. We'll probably drive down to Globe tomorrow, the Wild West town with the mines and all the cowboys. It's a smallish town, reminds me of home a bit. The locals and tourists love my dreamcatchers.

I need to sell them because we're running low on our canned foods. We cook outside, around our makeshift firepit in front of the Winnebago.

My skin still can't tan, not even in the hot sun of Arizona. I turn red with a burn that hurts for days, even the slightest touch causes pain, then once the burn

210

subsides, I'm back to my palish hue—the milky-white skin of someone who doesn't ever see the light of day.

We sleep by the stream, because most of the other canals in the area are dried up, only filling after a heavy rain. We have to boil the water, cleaning out any contaminants, but it's better than packing our things up and driving into the closest town for water.

We live off the land.

A part of me loves it, this feeling of living completely different from everyone else. Being able to sleep, eat, and bathe in the wild. We live in a place that isn't full of pollutants, chemicals, metals, and everything else wrong with the world. I've learned a lot about the good and bad of the world on my travels. We've been to Flagstaff, Phoenix, Globe, and my favorite, the Apache Trail. It's all so much different, but one thing remains the same.

Every place I go, the moment I leave, I still feel a little lost. That part of me that I search for remains missing. That piece that I desperately search for between the dried bushes and on top of the red mountains, it's not there. Whatever I'm looking for, it just isn't here.

I'm worried that in the bottom of my heart, I know what it is I'm looking for. Or rather, *who* I'm looking for. I don't want to be tied to him; I don't want to need him as much as my soul aches for him.

I don't *want* to want him, even if I know he's the only one I need.

Crossing the border, I only felt a loneliness that dragged my heart across the state lines, leaving fractured pieces along the way. I can't lie about that, and my friends all know I left something behind that was soul-crushing, so hard that I've never been able to speak about it.

Unfortunately for me, I've come to realize that what I had with Roman was love, and I don't think I'll ever experience it with anyone else. Not with anyone else.

I don't know where Roman is. I don't know if he's still singing. I stay away from the newspapers and televisions and radios whenever they're around. I'd prefer not to speak of it. And the rare times I'm able to call my parents to check up on them, they know not to bring him up.

What we had was cataclysmic, and we destructed.

While we've been traveling across Arizona, this is by far our favorite place to be. We've been talking about heading to California soon, though. We still have talks of heading out toward Hawaii, and I think I'll make it there eventually. But I like not having a plan, no schedule, nothing to tell me what to do or when to do it. I live for me, and me alone.

Shauna and Trish walk up the stream, their shirts clutched in their hands and their naked breasts on display in the bright sun. It's extra hot today, the red mountains and dry air always making breathing a little heavy. Nothing like the sticky, wet humidity in Wisconsin. The air is dry here, making my skin chip and crack more than it ever has before.

Shauna stumbles on a rock, nearly going down into the water. Trish grabs her around the arm, helping her back up.

"What the hell are you guys doing?" Neil laughs.

"It's hot today. I wish we could go swimming somewhere," Trish whines.

"Sun will be goin' down soon. Best stick near camp for the rest of the night. Coyotes will be comin' out," Willie says, walking over to the Winnebago and grabbing two cans from our stash.

We're five people, none of us knowing the next person, who met under unusual circumstances and found a bond.

I don't know where any of us will end up, but I do know that somehow, my life will never be the same after this journey.

I'm on the cliff. A cliff I can almost count as home with the number of times I've been here. It's sunny out, the first cloudless and clear day I've seen in a while. I look into the distance, seeing nothing but endless blue waters as calm as the night. Not a ripple in the water, not a wave cresting against the shore. It's almost eerie. I don't hear a sound. It's like I've lost my sense of hearing, except when I take a step forward, I can hear the rocks roll underneath my bare feet.

I stand on the edge, my toes curling around its sharpness. A gust of wind comes, no sand this time. Only a clear breeze that blows my long hair from the back of my neck, waving into the wind.

I inhale, tasting the saltiness of the sea on my tongue.

Bang, bang.

The sound comes out of nowhere, snapping my body into shock. I curl over, my body wiggling forward. My arms windmill around me, trying to keep my balance on the cliff, but it's no use. I tumble over the edge, a silent scream

making it to the back of my throat.
And I fall.

I shoot up on my wooden bed, the night sky still and silent.

"What's the matter?" Willie asks, his arm curling around my naked waist. I look up at the stars, feeling the need to tell him, tell anyone about the dream that has plagued me for years. Roman and my parents are the only ones that know about it. I feel a little lost, a little alone at the moment.

Bang, bang.

Willie shoots up, snapping his body out of the bed in a flash.

"Gunshots!" he whisper-shouts.

My heart rate runs a mile a minute. For once, it wasn't a dream. The bang I heard wasn't fake, it was real.

Bang, bang, bang, bang, bang.

Continuous shots fire off in the distance, and what sounds like a scream.

Not a coyote scream, but a human scream.

"Did someone just get shot?" I cry out.

Trish, Neil, and Shauna all clamber out of the Winnebago.

The gunshots cease, but the echo still lingers in the air. I can smell the gunfire, the powder making my nose wrinkle. They were too close. So close I don't hear any animals around. No coyotes in the distance, no snakes hissing in the night. The usual wildlife is the loudest in the dark, always lurking, looking for food or anything to stay alive.

"I want to leave," I whisper, tears flowing down my face. "Please, let's go."

"Everyone, into the van," Neil orders. We all scramble inside, and Neil shuts the door, locking it behind us. "We'll be safe in here."

"Are you sure about that?" Shauna asks, her voice shaky. *Worried.*

I walk around Trish, grabbing a large shirt that's sitting on the fold-up table and slide it on. I'm unsure of whose it is, but I'm suddenly freezing, my naked body trembling. Due to fear or the desert night chill, I'm not sure.

"Let's just get over on the bed. Be quiet, don't make a noise," Neil orders.

We do as he asks, huddling on the small, full bed. None of us will be able to sleep tonight, that's for sure. Our skin touches, our arms clinging to each other as we listen for a noise, a cracking branch, a footstep, a gunshot, anything.

We hear nothing. *Nothing.* Sleep doesn't hit any of us, and we sit and stare at each other, holding our terrified breaths in the depths of our chests, remaining in complete silence until morning.

CHAPTER EIGHTEEN
Roman

Dark hair flashes in front of my face, and my gaze shoots up. Seeing one of the VIP members with long, dark hair, so familiar that I want to wrap my hands in it and see if it feels the same as hers does. I want to turn her around and see if her eyes are as gray as I wish they were.

They aren't.

I know they won't be.

They'll be a dull brown that looks like melted chocolate poured straight into the pits of her eye sockets. She's a beautiful girl, maybe a little loose, but she keeps my bed warm when I need her to.

I lean down, slicing the blade down between the piles of coke in front of me, cutting out a thick line. My foot bobs against the footrest—erratic, hectic, chaotic.

I need a bump.

"Brandy, come over here." I open up my arm toward her. She turns around, her muddy brown eyes locking with mine as she tosses her hand on her waist. She walks over, strutting her hips heavily and sliding into my lap with ease. I wrap my hand around her waist, sliding my fingers over her jean skirt and squeezing the side of her ass. Bending down, I place my thumb over my nostril, inhaling the thick powder with the other. It burns, sending a shock through my brain that has me tilting my head back and closing my eyes.

Brandy is there in the next moment, dipping her tongue into my mouth as if she can taste the cocaine on my tongue.

Once the head rush clears, Brandy separates, bending over to cut out her own line. She takes it with ease, her hair creating a sheet around her face as she leans down. She wipes the residue from below her nose with her pointer finger and sucks the dust off with her tongue. Her eyes grow wild, the fire burning through her veins as the hit flows through her.

"Rome, on in five!" one of the set stage crew says before walking back out.

"Want to have a quickie before you go on stage?" she asks, whipping her dark hair over her shoulder. She turns around, straddling me in my chair. Her skirt inches up, and I can see the tiny pair of panties between her thighs.

I sigh, her persistence and eagerness a turn-off more than anything else. She brings her hand up, ready to dig her long nails into my hair. I tilt away from her. My stage look has already been perfected—my face is powdered, and I'm in blue jeans and an AC/DC shirt, with my leather jacket covering it. I don't want to fuck around with her when I'm about to go on stage, and she knows that.

Lonnie, Clyde, and Flynn are probably somewhere around here. I glance up, looking over at the couches and chairs in our back VIP section, seeing them empty. We're so used to shows nowadays that we just do what we want until we need to go on.

We've been doing this for three years now. Our fame has only grown. So substantially, our shows are almost always sold out. We even went on a short tour with my dad last year, but he's getting older now, and tours aren't really in the cards for him anymore.

He stays home with my mom, since my sister doesn't live there anymore. She's living in Milwaukee in a small apartment of her own, almost finished with getting her bachelor's degree in some art shit. She tries to go home a lot, visiting with our parents, but she says it's not the same.

She tells me there's something about our town. The air is different. It doesn't feel good like it used to, she says.

Nothing is the same anymore.

I try not to go back there, although I do it for my mom. It's painful to be in

Shallow Lake. The waves don't crash against the shore in the same way. The sun isn't as bright as it used to be as it sets over the trees. The air doesn't feel as good when it brushes my skin.

I can't even look at her house, haven't spoken to any of her family since the day I walked out of there. My parents still keep in touch with them, as far as I know they're still best friends. Their faces still visit me in my dreams. It's scarred me, to be honest. Their crying eyes as they stared at me with such a heavy sadness. The day my heart was literally torn from my chest.

I don't know where she is.

My sister doesn't talk about her. At first, I pried, asked for every little detail about Luna's life. Where she was, who she was with, what she's been doing. When I found out she went to Arizona with a group of people she'd never met, I knew.

I've lost her. *For good.*

I don't know who she is anymore, and it's a pain that sits so heavy in my chest that it feels like I'm bleeding directly onto my shoes. Every minute of my life.

I try my best to move on. I do everything I can to get her out of my thoughts, and out of my mind.

The only thing that helps is music. Music and drugs.

Cocaine is a high that I wasn't looking for. Something I barely dabbled in back in the beginning days of my tours. Not something I even needed, because I knew Luna wouldn't be happy about it. So, I usually steered clear.

But now that Luna's gone, there's nothing else in my life that I'm looking forward to more than smashing my face into a pile of white powder. I want to ingest every last grain, until my brain is so far gone, I'll never think of her and her gray eyes again.

It's never that easy.

Her face, her body, every single thing about her bleeds out on the pages as I write lyrics. My songs are songs about love lost, soulmates broken, and hate, so much fucking hate for a world that doesn't give me what I want.

The upside is, is that the music is fucking good.

Apparently, broken hearts lead to good music.

We create number one hit after number one hit, surpassing even the major record labels and the most powerful voices, shoving them out of the top seats with just a simple fucking vocal.

"Where'd you go, just now?" Brandy says, scratching her nails down the back of my neck.

I look over at her, hating her muddy eyes and her hair that is two shades too light. Her body isn't right, either, but that doesn't stop me from wrapping my fingers around her thick thighs as I plow into her from behind. Anything to dull the pain, even though it doesn't dull it.

Not even an inch.

"Nowhere, I'll see you after the show." I push her off me, grabbing my aviators and slipping them on my face. Nothing is worse than being high as fuck and having the heavy, bright lights blast me in the face. It's painful. The glasses help.

Standing up, I press on Brandy's shoulders, slipping past her just as Lonnie walks in. His eyes are bloodshot, and I know he just had his own bump of coke.

The guys were the ones that got me into it, being way more willing to try out the different drugs the rock-and-roll life had to offer. They had their eyes open, and their arms splayed wide for any girl and any drug to fall into their laps.

After Luna left me, I took the reins.

They don't partake like I do. I dip, and I dip heavy. I fuck, and I fuck hard. I don't want the easy life, not anymore. I want the gritty, raw, edgy part of being on the road all year. I don't want to live on the surface, I want to bury myself in the wrongdoings of the world.

Being on tour with my dad, he learned quickly what kind of life I was living. He understood, since being a star, drugs and whores come with it. A package deal of sorts. But he didn't want me to lose myself in the process. He asked me to slow down.

Doesn't he know? I lost myself that day back in Shallow Lake.

I fucking died that day, and no one seems to realize that.

"Ready?" Lonnie asks, adjusting his jean vest over his naked shoulders. Tattoos line his arms all the way down to his wrists. I slap him on the back as I walk past him.

"Let's do this shit."

The moment I walk through the door, the screaming crowd blasts me in the face. I walk down the hall, the voices shouting *Cataclysm, Cataclysm*, their voices vibrating through the ground. I can feel their shouting hit me directly in my chest, making my heart race as I head for yet another show.

It's the only place I can go and show how I'm really feeling. The place I can openly reveal that I've been dying a slow death. Show them the blood that's been dripping from me since that day in her room. The pain I feel every single day, I scream it with my words. I howl out the pain that rips from my chest. I can't take the pain. It builds and builds, and with each show, I can expel it from my lungs. It's the only place I really feel at home anymore.

We get to the back of the stage, where Clyde and Flynn are already waiting for us. I give them a nod, unable to say any words to them with the crowd shouting so loudly.

In the next second, we're walking through the back of the stage. The crowd goes wild when they see us. Flynn walks to the drums, while I walk to the center of the stage and grab my guitar from the stand. Clyde walks to my left, grabbing his bass, and Lonnie walks to my other side, grabbing his guitar.

The four of us are Cataclysm, and we rock shit like no other.

The lights are dim, and the crowd is a sea of heads. Black leather and blue jeans fill the entire floor. Women stand in the front, and I watch as one with a crop top lifts her shirt, showing off her large breasts. They jiggle with her jumps, her friend going wild and screaming when she notices what she's doing.

I shake my head. *People are fucking wild.*

I slide my guitar strap over my shoulder, testing a string and stopping it quickly. I walk up to the microphone, smiling at the crowd as I mumble, "How're y'all doing tonight?"

They go wild, screaming so loud it makes my ears pop. The room is hot, the bodies creating heat and making a thin sweat break out on the back of my neck.

"Let's have a little fun tonight, huh?" I smirk at them, my white teeth shining in the bright light.

My hand slips into the pocket of my jeans, my fingers curling around the small piece of plastic that is my *everything*. I pull it out, barely glancing at it as my fingers slide over the *R & L*. My eyes close and I take a shuddering breath, wishing so badly that life was different, wanting to say *fuck you* to fate for screwing me over.

Begging for my ballerina to come back to me.

Please come back to me, Luna.

Opening my eyes, I start one of the fan favorites, a dark song I created last

221

year that the guys ate up like candy. The words flew out of me, flying onto the page from my broken pen as I scribbled on the thin lined paper.

I stop on a slow note, and the crowd goes absolutely wild, screaming and jumping. My head spins from the coke, and I feel jittery. A fucking mess. I want another bump, and I want Brandy. But she's not what I really want. She's just the closest thing. It makes me hate myself, to be honest. Pretending. Acting like Brandy is the one I want, even though that's furthest from the truth.

But I settle.

I'll settle for the rest of my life, because the woman I love broke my heart and tore it to shreds. She lifted it from my chest and threw it into the lake. It sank to the bottom, lifeless. Bloody.

So fucking ruined.

Because, what else am I supposed to do? My broken soul doesn't even want to find second best. I don't want anything that isn't her, but my empty heart needs to be filled, so I fill it.

I fill it with mindless drugs and mindless women, until I can't think, and I can't see. My life darkens until I black out, and I start again the next day.

We play a few more sets, until sweat drips from my face and down my arms to my wrists. I grab a cup of water nearby, downing half of it and tossing the rest into the crowd. They go wild, their arms flailing in the air as they try to catch every last drop. The cup bounces from their fingers, each hand trying to catch something that I've touched.

It's weird. That I'm wanted like this. I like to pretend it isn't real.

Sometimes, I like to pretend none of it is real. I mentally go back in time to the lake. To the night on the beach when I laid with Luna, our feet digging into the sand, my hands gripping the grains as they rushed through my fingers. The sound of the water crashing against the sand. The sight of the stars, hanging so low I felt like I could have reached up and grabbed them out of the sky. I wish, and I pretend.

Because the alternative is coming to terms with my reality.

And that's just not something I can do.

Ever.

After the show, the stage crew loads up our things and packs them up, getting ready for our next stop.

I find Brandy instantly, and she's already ready and waiting for me. In a pair of black shorts and a slinky tank, her dark hair tossed over her shoulder in messy waves. She lines her eyes too dark, the thickness making her look messy, too much of a road whore. She should treat herself better. Too bad I don't care. Not about her, or about our relationship, or whatever the fuck it is.

"You played fucking great, Roman," she says as I walk up to her.

I say nothing, wrapping my arm around her waist and pulling her out the back. No one is here, we have enough security now that we can come and go without being flocked by groupies.

We walk through the night, straight to our RV. The sounds of the crowd in the distance, but the back gated off to where the only sounds I can hear are my heavy boots and her heels clacking against the ground.

The guys are off somewhere, probably finding their own groupie to fuck. Brandy sticks with me. She travels with the stage crew. Her dad grew up on the road, traveling her from place to place, working with larger bands as their stage crew. It's all she knows, and she's good at it.

I pop open the door, and Brandy rushes in, instantly pulling out a small white baggie from her bra. "I thought you'd need a pick-me-up."

I take it from her hands, pulling off the rubber band and walking to the small dining table. I slide my wallet from my back pocket, grabbing a credit card from one of the slots. Pouring some coke on the table, I slice up two lines. Bending down, I take them both, snorting the grainy, rough powder through my sinuses. My fingers go up, squeezing my nostrils as the burn hits my head. My eyes automatically shut as my entire body flushes hot.

I can hear Brandy beside me, lining up her own line of cocaine. I listen as she snorts it, and then her front presses against my back, her breast pressing into my shoulder blades.

I spin around, grabbing her around the waist and setting her on the table. She grabs the button on her shorts, popping it through the hole and shimmying them down her thighs. The table is wobbly beneath her, the smooth, lightly colored wood only held by two small hinges.

I don't care. I pop my own button, taking out my cock and grabbing a condom from my wallet before sliding my jeans down my legs. I rip the foil package open with my teeth, sliding the condom on with quick motions. Brandy is already ready, her legs spread as she touches herself between her thighs. Her wetness dampens the table, making a small wet spot form on the light wood.

I slide her forward, her ass easily sliding through the wetness beneath her. I plunge into her, grabbing onto her thick ass, my fingers digging into the meat of her backside as I thrust into her. She moans, her head tossing back and her dark hair brushing along my fingertips.

I flick her hair to the side, not able to deal with the feeling of the dark strands. Not wanting to associate her with my black-haired, gray-eyed Luna. *I can't.* Not tonight.

I'm feeling extra empty tonight.

"Give me another bump," I slur, continuing my aggressive thrusts. The table squeaks and groans with each pump.

The lights are off, the entire RV blanketed in darkness besides the lights from the nearby building, illuminating a small glow through the windows.

Her head leans up, her eyes glazed and red as she stares at me. Her hand lifts from the table, her fingernail filled with coke. She brings it up to my nose, and I inhale, breathing as deeply as I can. The burn hits me deeply, going all the way to my chest. She pulls her finger away, but I snap my hand out, bringing it to my mouth. I wrap my tongue around her fingertip, sucking the sweetness from her nail. I run her fingertip beneath my upper lip, along my gums.

My eyes close. The flavor. The hit. It turns me on more than the girl in front of me does.

I fuck her until I can't see. Until my blood runs hot and a heavy load of cum empties inside the condom.

It's Luna that I imagine coming inside of. It's her body I imagine wrapped around me. And when I pull out of her, tossing my condom into the trash bin, I imagine it's her melodic voice I hear, not the raspy one coming out of Brandy as I tuck myself back into my jeans.

I watch her through hazy eyes as she leans down, taking another bump. "I have to fucking crash. You coming to bed?"

I shake my head, feeling the world spin with me. It doesn't stop when my head does, continuing on in a tilt-a-whirl that feels like it'll never stop.

"Okay." She stumbles off the table, ripping off her shirt and tossing it on the floor on the way to my room. She's naked by the time she walks through the door, climbing on the bed and falling straight on her stomach, face in my dark pillow.

She's out within seconds.

I stumble down the hallway, picking up her clothes and tossing them on top of her. I close the door, giving her some fucking decency because the moment the guys walk through the door, they'll be able to see her naked ass.

Not like she would really care. She really is a fucking road whore sometimes.

I shake my head in disgust, running my fingers through the sweaty strands of my hair before grabbing the heavy laptop from beside the sink. I walk over to the table, sitting down in the red and blue fabric booth. It squeaks and puffs, the air releasing from the cushion as my weight presses on it.

Cracking the laptop open, I run my hand across the smooth black screen. The screen lights up when I press on the small red circle, and my heart starts racing, wondering if today is the day.

I rarely find time to go on my laptop, this clunky thing that has shitty internet and barely works. But I bought one the other year, tired of finding time to get access to a desktop computer when we're always on the road. So, I splurged on one, and the first thing my dumbass did?

I emailed her.

Which is stupid, since I have no idea if she even looks at her emails. It's something we made back in high school, something that neither of us ever actually used.

But now, it's the only shred of communication I have left. The only possibility I have when it comes to connecting with her. Without it, I don't know how we'd ever speak again.

Will she ever go back to Wisconsin?

It's been over two years, and she hasn't gone home. I don't know what she's doing. I don't even know if she's alive, honestly.

That thought alone makes me want to scream until my throat bleeds.

Starting up the internet, my fingers tap on the edge of the black keyboard while I wait for this slow fucking computer to work. The dial tone is obnoxious, making my ears screech and my head throb. My foot taps on the floor, so loud and so heavy that the entire RV feels like it's shaking.

I can barely see straight, and the only way I know the internet is working is from the loud computer voice telling me I've got mail.

My heart thumps, stops a beat, and starts pumping again.

I click on my inbox, hoping to see an email from the *loolooluna* email.

Once my inbox loads, my heart drops, all the way to the linoleum floor beneath me. It splats and smashes, and I even punch my boot to the floor a couple times, making the floor shake in frustration.

I have an email, but it's not from Luna.

Just another one from my mom.

She tells me she misses me and hopes I'm planning to stop home for Easter. She tells me my sister is well, and the heavy winter led to a high rise in the lake this spring. They had to put sandbags by the house, because the water rose so much, they were worried it would leak into the basement. She tells me she misses me, and that she watches the news and reads the paper for updates.

She tells me she loves me.

She doesn't say a word about Luna. I re-read the email, checking twice to make sure I didn't miss it, even though I know if I saw her four-letter name, my eyes would have gravitated toward it before any others.

She doesn't speak about her, though, or Luna's parents.

I click out of her email, knowing if I responded now, it wouldn't make much sense. I'm too high, and me typing on a keyboard wouldn't create any coherent words or sentences.

I go to my sent mailbox, needing to double-check that my emails have even been delivered. Sometimes the internet is so bad that I think my emails have gone through, only to check back later to see I have received an error message.

But when I scroll down, and I continue scrolling, all I see are message after message of sent emails. Me to Luna, me to Luna, over and over again.

None responded to.

I don't even know if they've been read.

I shouldn't be so stupid, but when I click on the little envelope to compose a new email, all I can do is type in *loolooluna* in the *To* section.

Luna,
Do you miss me?
Are you still mine?
Do you still feel it, Luna?
I still feel it.
I'll always feel it.

226

Still feel it, Luna.
Fucking. Feel. It.

I can barely see straight, but I think my words were at least understandable. I slam my computer shut, cringing, hoping I didn't break it. I slide it to the other side of the table, knowing my destructive behavior will easily go south from here.

Why?

Why can't she just fucking respond to an email? I want her back so badly; I can feel my soul in pieces inside my chest. It's like a piggy bank, every step making a small rattle. That's my fucking chest, with my soul and my heart racketing around my rib cage, broken and fucking fractured.

Standing up, I stumble into the table. I glance at my bedroom door, where I know Brandy will be sleeping naked. Probably ready to wake up in the morning and go for round two.

She isn't *her.*

She'll never be her. I know she'd like to be. She'd accept a proposal if I had one for her. But I don't, and I never will. I should probably shut it down now, but I'm a fucking bastard. I'm not the nice guy I used to be. My life isn't what it used to be.

She isn't her.

With that thought, I turn around, heading toward the two-cushioned sofa. It's uncomfortable, too short and too thin. The fabric too rough against my back. I'll wake up with a sore neck and an aching back, but it's better than pretending to be something I'm not.

I flop down, my eyes rolling to the back of my head as the high hits me. This is the worst part. My mind is exhausted, it always is. But the coke gets my body going, and I could thrum and fucking rock out all night.

Tonight, I don't have it in me.

My body twitches and shakes, my fingers trembling so badly I have to smoosh them beneath my legs. With my eyes closed, I wait for sleep to take me.

It doesn't, not until morning. And the only thing in my dreams is a gray-eyed Luna.

CHAPTER NINETEEN

Luna

My eyes are heavy, and my body is tense, from the night before. We're all a little skittish, leery of staying here. None of us are comfortable anymore. Our easy spot has turned into… *what, a murder scene?*

"What do you think happened?" I ask, squeezing the water from my hair. I took a quick bath in the creek, feeling gross and sweaty from nerves and a night of restless sleep.

"Do you think someone got shot?" Trish asks.

"Maybe it was just a hunter or something? Maybe they were shooting an animal," Shauna suggests.

Neil shakes his head. "Didn't you hear how many shots there were?"

"Or that fucking scream?" Willie chimes in, a shiver taking over his tanned, naked back. "I'm pretty sure it was a murder."

I stand up, wrapping the worn towel around my body. "I need to get out of here. Does anyone else need to get out of here?" It's like there are eyes on me, or one million spiders crawling over every inch of my body.

I've seen some creepy critters out here. Scorpions, snakes, huge-looking spiders that would make me run across state lines if they were on me.

But nothing, *not one thing*, has scared me as much as hearing those gunshots and that scream. *Nothing.*

"That's a good idea, babe," Willie says, and my stomach hollows out from the nickname. "Where should we go?"

"Dude." Neil stands up from his spot by the fire. "Hold on." He hops over the flat rock he was sitting on, running barefoot inside the Winnebago. The small home rocks as he jumps up the front steps. Coming back out, he has a map that's been folded one too many times. The middle crease is ripped, and some of the locations are so worn you can barely see the names on them.

"I've been wanting to go to Superstition Mountain." He points at a spot on the map not far from where we are. "We can hike there today, get away from here for a bit. Clear our heads."

We all look at each other with excitement and relief that we get to get out of here for the day.

"Yes! Let's do it!" Trish stands up, Shauna right behind her.

"Ugh, thank God." I grab my things, packing up the little belongings I have and put them in the Winnebago. I don't trust any of my stuff out here now. I just feel like this entire place is unsafe.

"Are we going to walk there or drive?" Willie asks. He grabs a bucket, walking to the river to fill it up. Carrying it to the fire, he pours it over the flames. It sizzles and steams, the logs smoking once the flames burn out.

"We'll walk. It shouldn't be that far." Neil looks at the map again, using his knuckle to check the miles. He looks up at the sky, checking the sun. "We'll just make sure we bring enough water for the day."

We all nod, not really caring what we do or how long it takes. We just want to get out of here.

"Shit, it's hot," I gasp, grabbing the canteen from Trish's hip. The strap snaps around her hip, yanking her toward me. I don't care. I'm so thirsty. I take a small sip, knowing we're only a short way up the mountain. We've got a long way to go and make it back to camp before we'll be able to get more water.

"What's the story of Superstition Mountain, anyway?" Shauna asks, looking at the rock walls and jagged peaks. The canyons are beautiful, but it's very dry out here, and the higher we climb, the drier it becomes—the closer we get to the sun.

It's bright, and I don't have sunglasses. My eyelids ache, each blink dry and heavy.

"From what I've been told, there's a gold mine here somewhere that was hidden by the Lost Dutchman."

"So, you're saying we might come across a fucking mine of gold?" Willie asks, his own glasses going to the top of his sweaty head as he looks around.

I roll my eyes, panting, "Don't even try. You'll never find it. I'm sure people come here all the time scoping it out. It's probably not even real."

He lifts an eyebrow at me. "I wouldn't count it out until I've scoured every inch of this mountain." He continues looking around, and I let him, too hot, too tired to argue.

"It is really fucking hot today." I look up at the sun. Today, there isn't a cloud in the sky. The sun burns bright. I want to sit down, but everything is sharp in the desert. Beautiful, but one wrong move and you get stabbed with cacti or a bush or bitten by some kind of fucking animal.

"It really is hot," Shauna whines, "maybe we should head back early."

Yes. Please yes.

Neil laughs. "We can't head back yet. We've barely started. And honestly, would you rather go back to that place already? Or would you rather stay out here, far away from those gunshots?"

We all nod, knowing even if we're hot and uncomfortable, we'd rather be here than back at camp.

We walk through the red-colored mountains, the smooth rocks looking hot and almost shiny from the sun. Unlike anything I've ever seen. The bushes are a light yellow, all types of greenery dried of any water source. The canyons and dips in the earth where there should be small pools are all dried up, the ground cracked and dehydrated. Nearly as dehydrated as I'm feeling.

It takes a while, and the further we get away from our camp, the hotter it gets. The sun beats down, my skin past the point of sweating, instead keeping each drop of fluid I have stored in my body.

"Can I have some more water?" I plead, holding my hand out. I don't care who hands it to me, I'm getting so thirsty I'm starting to feel sick. Nausea builds in my stomach, and my head is starting to throb.

"I'm out," Neil says.

I whimper, still holding my hand out.

"Oh, well, that's not good. Looks like I'm out, too," Willie grumbles.

I turn my head toward him. We have three large canteens, and we drink it all before we even get to the top of the mountain?

"Uh-oh," Trish whines. "Me too."

"Are you serious?" I whip my head around toward them, feeling my heart speed up. "Are you telling me we're out of water?" I gasp. They're joking, right? They have to be fucking joking.

"We should turn back." I stop, my knees screaming in protest. My entire body feels like it's locking up. I've never been this thirsty in my entire life. "I don't feel good. Something is wrong."

Willie walks up to me, taking his shirt off. "You're getting too much sun. Do you need to sit down?" He wraps his shirt around my head, but it feels too heavy, just another added layer on my body. I whip it off, throwing it on the sandy ground. A plume of dust floats up, coating his white shirt in orange.

Every move is starting to become excruciating.

Shauna stops, her face filling with fear. Her skin pale, and her hair sticking to her forehead and cheeks. Her top is rolled up beneath her breasts, her stomach bright red, burning from the sun. It doesn't matter how much time we've spent in the sun; the Arizona heat burns your skin no matter how tan you are. "We need to turn around."

Neil spins around, walking backward up the hill. His face is sweaty, his own shirt wrapped around his head. "Come on. We're almost to the top!" He points up the hill. He's right, we're so close. We'd be stupid to turn around now without walking to the peak.

But the sun is setting, and at this rate, we're going to be walking back in the dark. That's stupid, with mountain lions and coyotes. You never know what you're going to run into in the dark.

"We're out of water, Neil. We have the entire walk back. Do you know how long it's going to take us? We've been walking all day." Shauna's face is beet red, but her lips are pale. We're all getting dehydrated.

Everyone's outer edges of their figures are turning fuzzy. A little blurry. My eyes are burning, every blink a struggle. It feels like there's sand beneath my lids, the scratchiness making my eyes feel raw.

The world turns on its axis, and I stumble, falling to my knees. My knees knock against rocks, and instant rock burn hits my skin. My hands plant onto the ground, the hot gravel burning my palms.

"Whoa, you okay?" Willie comes up to me, his hot hand wrapping around my bicep as he hauls me up.

"I don't feel good." My body is starting to get cold, which doesn't make any sense since the inside of my body is burning up. I shiver, feeling feverish. "I think I'm getting sick."

"Probably a little heat exhaustion. Do you want to sit down? Hey, guys! Let's sit down for a second!" he shouts to our group.

I wave his hand away, stepping out of his hold. His hand is only making me hotter, and it feels disgusting to be touched by anyone right now. "No. No, I don't want to sit down. I won't be able to get back up, and there's no way I'm going to sleep some place that's called Superstition Mountain."

His hand comes to my back, rubbing against my tank top. The fabric rubbing up and down feels like scrapes along my already irritated skin. "Stop. Fucking stop, Willie."

He puts his hands up, stepping back. "Just trying to help."

"Well, all you're doing is hurting me," I whisper to myself, although from his silence, I know that he heard me.

We walk in silence, and all I can think about is home. How I could dip my toes in the cool water of the lake, floating on my back with my hair drifting around me. Or how I could go to Roman's house in the middle of the night, and the grass would be cool, maybe even a little damp and dewy on my feet. Everything cool, everything refreshing. I wish it were on me.

I wouldn't mind a torrential downpour right now, making mudslides left and right. Any kind of coolness or water would alleviate the immense amount of pain I'm in right now.

We reach the top a short while later, and my knees give out again. Everyone falls to the ground, but I collapse. My eyesight goes in and out, and I know this is the worst I've ever been, illness-wise.

Shauna groans from the ground, not looking much better than me. She blinks, but it doesn't look like she sees anything. Her gasps are pained, her limbs looking tense against the ground.

It feels like we're going to die.

And the scary part is, I think it's a real possibility at this point. The desert in Arizona is dangerous, but the desert in Arizona at night is almost forbidden.

People die all the time in the desert. We came across a dead body when we first arrived. Half turned to bones in the sun, leaning against a side of a mountain. Lost, or maybe found. I don't know, but it was sad to see, the decrepit skeleton rotting away in the sun.

We've heard the horror stories of people walking into the desert and never coming out. People get lost, people get sick, people get attacked. It's the fucking wilderness, and unfortunately, we we're stupid enough to follow their lead, heading straight into the desert without enough water.

"I want to head back. It's getting dark out," Trish's voice is shaky, her eyes wide as she continues looking over her shoulder. Like she's moments away from being eaten.

I try to move, but my muscles have started cramping. My calves hurt, a horrible charley horse making my entire leg lock up. "Shit," I cry, my hands going down to the cramp. I can't clench my fingers around my calf, though; my fingers are completely unusable, locked up and in pain.

"You okay?" Shauna rolls over, sounding just as bad as she looks. I can't imagine what I look like, but it has to be just as bad. Probably worse.

The rocks and bushes dig into my back, scraping my skin to shreds, but I can't find it in me to even move.

"I don't think so," I gasp.

"Come on, let's get back. You look really bad." She bends over, helping me to my feet. It's nearly dark now, the path in front of us meshing in with the rest of the mountain. Or maybe my vision is going dark. Either way, I can barely see. Shauna nudges me toward the path, and the five of us start making our way down the mountain.

It doesn't take long for me to start hallucinating.

Half of the mountain starts turning into a cartoon, and I close my eyes, rubbing my sockets with the heels of my palms. It hurts, my entire body screaming in agony. When I open my eyes, everything is back to normal. We keep shuffling forward, and after a few steps, the world starts turning into a cartoon again.

I bend over, dry heaving. I feel like my spine is about to split in half when my back folds over, my muscles screaming at me in horror. The ground moves, like it's turning into water below me. I dry heave again, the mixture between cartoon and real life churning my stomach like and angry tornado.

234

"What's wrong?" Willie walks up to me, not touching me this time, but still getting close enough that I can feel his hot breath on my shoulder. Nothing is coming from my stomach; my dehydration having sucked up everything in my body. But it doesn't stop the gags from rolling through my throat.

"Hallucinating." I breathe when a gag passes. I reach my hand out, placing it in his outstretched hand. When I stand upright, my eyes widen.

Right off the path is a wild horse. A giant, white stallion. Its tail swishes back and forth, the thick, coarse, white hair blowing in the wind. It looks like mine, except mine is a midnight black, where the pony's is a stark white. I stumble off, not scared of this hallucination.

The hallucinations terrified me before, made me feel sick.

This hallucination... it centers me. There's something about it. It's not looking at us, but it has to sense us, right? Five loud, stomping, dehydrated kids walking down a mountain at night? Our feet shuffle across the desert ground, our pants echoing throughout the open air. The horse has to know that we're here.

But why isn't she scared?

I nearly fall over a bush, but right myself as I get close. It's looking down at the ground, looking for some type of food or something. Maybe it's hallucinating from the hot too, and wants this day to end.

But as I get closer, she looks up, looking straight at me.

This *has to* be a hallucination, right?

I feel like it's a sign. And it makes me feel sick, makes me want to cripple over in agony, but I look at this white horse and I only think of one thing.

I think of Roman.

Why? Why is he always in the back of my mind? When you cut ties with your soulmate, shouldn't they leave your heart? Shouldn't their soul separate from yours? Why would my soul still be tied with his? Why would my heart still ache? Why would my mind and body still weep for him? For his closeness, for any ounce of Roman that I could get, I would swallow it just as greedily as I would swallow a glass of water right now.

I want to go home.

I want to go back to him.

The horse looks at me, her black eyes blinking slowly. Her tail swishing heavier now, to a beat almost. It swishes back and forth every time my heart beats. Like we're in sync, connected in some way.

My hand reaches up, wanting to touch her. Wanting to feel her and wondering if it would feel like going home.

What is she trying to tell me?

The moment my hand is about to graze her coarse hair, her body twitches, and she runs off into the distance, her feet galloping heavily, pounding against the ground. Her white hair blows in the red sunset, and a tear leaks from my eye.

My chin quivers.

Come back. Please come back.

"Did you guys see that, too? Or am I hallucinating?" Neil utters.

My head whips around, my eyes wide in shock as I stare at them. They're all looking at me with wide eyes, their jaws slack as they stare into the distance.

I turn around, looking where my hallucination just was and only see the dust settling to the ground, the pale-yellow sand tinged red from the setting sun.

"You saw her?" I cry.

I thought it was in my mind. But it wasn't. She was real. She was real, and I don't know what it means, but the fact that my heart beats heavier, my body shot with adrenaline, makes me know what it means.

It was him. It was my soulmate.

It was Roman.

Don't give up.

If he were to tell me anything right now, it would be to not give up.

"Guys?" comes a wobbly voice.

I turn around, seeing Trish staring at Shauna. I glance at her, seeing her eyes barely open, her knees shaking for only moments before she collapses to the ground. Her lids open wide, rolling in the back of her head, showing off the whites of her eyes. Her jaw tenses, the entire muscle along her face and neck going taught.

Then she starts shaking. Trembling heavily as her spine arches. Her entire body tense, her arms twitching against her sides as her body rocks against the ground.

"What's wrong with her?" Trish screams.

"She's having a seizure!" Neil shouts, running up to her. He pushes her on her side, his body pinning her against the earth. He brings his fingers to her cheek, tilting her face to the ground.

"What are you doing?" I scream, my fingers going to my hair. I pull on the ends, feeling helpless, feeling sick, feeling out of fucking control.

"I'm trying to help her!" he shouts.

Trish cries, "It looks like you're hurting her."

He scowls at her, keeping her pinned to the ground. Shauna continues to thrash beneath him. What feels like hours, even though I know it's only been minutes, goes on with all of us staring at Neil trying to control Shauna so she doesn't hurt herself.

"Shauna!" I cry, wanting this to be over. Wanting it all to end.

Finally, it does.

Shauna's body goes limp beneath Neil. He rolls off her instantly, his knees in the sand as he lays her on her back.

She's motionless.

Her eyes open wide.

"What's wrong with her?" I whisper, my jaw slack.

"Shauna!" Trish screams, falling to the ground. Trish shakes her shoulders, her fingers burying into her skin as she attempts to wake her. "Wake up, Shauna! Wake the fuck up!"

"Shit," Neil mumbles from beside me.

I look at him with a frown, taking a step away from him and toward Shauna. I squat down, my knees creaking and aching as I grab her hand. My fingers trail along the warm skin of her palm, sliding up until I hit her wrist. I press my fingers against the tendons, holding tight and closing my eyes.

Please.

Trish cries beside me, but I keep my focus. Hoping for something. Anything.

Please.

Nothing.

My eyes pop open, and I look over at Neil. "She's gone."

His jaw clenches and he looks away from her, off into the distance. "We better get back to camp."

Trish shuffles around, the rocks noisy beneath her. "I'm not leaving her here!" Her voice echoes into the distance.

He looks down, not passing Shauna a glance as he stares at Trish. "Who's going to carry her, huh? We're all fucking dehydrated. Unless you want one of us to have a heat stroke and a seizure, too? Huh?" His arms go wide, splaying out at his sides.

We all stare at him, the sun barely illuminating his outline. We're all shrouded in the dark at this point, all visibility on this mountain gone.

I look down at Shauna, tucking her brown hair behind her ear. Trish brings her hands up, placing her palms over her eyes and closing them. I sniffle, feeling like tears need to release myself, but I'm all dried up.

"Can we move her, at least?" I whisper, staring down at Shauna's peaceful face. I didn't know her, not really. I don't know much about her parents, or her life. I just know she's from somewhere in Virginia. She was a free spirit. A really cool chick. We got along well.

I hear footsteps around me, and Willie and Neil come up, Willie grabbing her feet and Neil grabbing her arms. They lift her, her body in the shape of a U as they bring her up against the mountain. They prop her up, settling her behind some brush.

"I feel like we need to bury her or something," Trish cries.

Willie shakes his head. "We don't have the energy. We need to get back before another one of us goes down."

We all stare at Shauna, knowing that he's right, but wishing it weren't true. We're too tired, too dehydrated to do anything else. We need to get back to camp, and we need to get back now.

With one last glance at Shauna, we turn around, continuing on our hike, each of us dehydrated, but the sun lowering and the moon raising gives us a much-needed cool blast of air.

My body aches, my mind weeps. But I keep going.

For him.

CHAPTER TWENTY
Roman

My knee shakes, the white notebook on my lap sliding off the side. My hand snaps out and catches it, only for me to set it back on my lap, and the process starts all over again.

I'm fucking edgy.

My words won't come today. I feel lost and confused.

Last night I had the weirdest dream.

I dreamt of Luna. She was sad. She was so sad and fucking broken, and she was just staring at me. Staring at me like she desperately needed help. The pleading in her eyes was gut-wrenching. She needed saving, wherever she was, whatever she was doing, she needed me.

I know that in the pit of my soul.

I look into the night, the California sky absent of any and all stars. The city is loud, polluted, always busy. I fucking hate it, if I were to be honest. I hate the noise, and I hate the people.

This is getting old.

I don't know what I want anymore. But that's a lie, because I do know what I want.

I want her.

I look up at the sky, my neck aching as I stare into the darkness.

She's somewhere out there, and she needs fucking help.

The moment I was about to reach her, touch her, open my mouth and speak to her, I woke up, and I haven't been able to go back to sleep. So out here I sit on our condo deck, watching the nightlife that never tires. Wishing my brain would turn off but knowing it never will.

I came out here to get some writing done, but a bump of coke later and I can barely see straight. My anxiety is at an all-time high. Thoughts of Luna are swirling in my mind and making even sitting here fucking painful.

I fucking love her. After all these years, I love her so damn much and I can't do a thing about it. Now after this dream, I'm thinking the worst. I want to go back to sleep and start where I left off. Stay in my dream forever if I have to. I'll do anything I can to talk to her, just make sure she's okay.

But I don't have that ability, and because of that, I'm fucking wrecked.

Torn into shreds, inside and out.

My bare torso burns even when I feel like ice is in my heart. The muscles twitch and roll with each movement of my body. I push my finger into the tip of my pen, wanting it to penetrate my skin, just for the fact that it'll distract me from the feeling I feel so deeply inside of me.

The smooth pen glides across my finger. The lined paper in front of me is filled with nothing but scribbles about hate and heartbreak. It's all fake, though. It's a fucking rouse.

I want to hate Luna for what she's done to me, but if anything, I love her more. I can't hate someone who wants to better themselves. Mostly her, I could never hate her. But if she wants to go and do what she thinks is right, what am I going to do, hold her back? That'll only have her resent me in the end. I had to let her go, even if it meant leaving me alone and empty.

I'll stay alone for the rest of my life, waiting for her.

I glance over my shoulder and straight into my bedroom, seeing Brandy's form underneath my sheets.

She follows me, and it's just about time to cut her off. I can't deal with her anymore. She's falling for me. I can see it in her eyes, and I'm not even in the same dimension of being able to give her something back. I couldn't even give her a mindless relationship, even though she'd already probably say we're dating.

We're not. We're really fucking not. I let her suck my dick because she gives me a bag of coke every day.

"Baby, what're you doing out here?" The raspy voice of Brandy rings into the night. I don't turn around, don't give her my grimacing face.

"No. Not right now," I grumble, half to myself and half to Brandy.

The door slides open, the screen rolling and making the floor beneath my feet vibrate. I close my eyes, knowing she's going to touch me when it's the last thing I want right now.

Within a second, her long, thin fingers wrap around my shoulder, giving me a gentle squeeze around my collarbone. "Trying to write some music?"

I lean forward, sliding out of her hold. I put my elbows on my knees, pressing my face into my palms and gripping the front of my hair. I pull, wanting to pull until I rip out every last strand.

I just want to be alone.

But that's a lie, too.

I don't want to be alone. I only want her.

"*Trying.* I just want to be alone right now." I haven't looked at her yet. Not once. I can feel her eyes boring into the back of my head. She wants me to look at her. She wants the affection I'm not able to give her.

"Are you sure? Maybe I can help?" Her finger threads into the back of my hair, and I turn around, my head whipping toward hers.

"Brandy, I want to be alone right now. Go back to bed." Her face falls, her eyes wanting so badly to fill with tears, but she's tougher than that. She grew up around men. She can hold her own.

She's nothing like Luna. Luna would have broken down already, fallen to her knees with emotion. She's always been emotional, wearing her heart on her sleeve.

They're black and white. Night and day.

Maybe that's why I've perused her, if you could call it that. She came on to me, and my shattered soul didn't know anything but to let her do whatever it is she wanted.

I've been a zombie, a shell of a human throughout our entire relationship, and if this is what she likes, well, then I kind of feel bad for the girl.

"Sorry, I didn't mean to snap. I'm just not in the mood." I'm not a total fucking asshole, but I wish she would take the fucking hint.

With a nod, she slinks back inside, shutting the door behind her. I drop my notebook and pen to the ground, listening as the pen rolls and falls off the edge of the patio.

Fucking hell, that was a good pen.

I put my feet up on the railing for a second, wondering if I should just jump over the damn thing. End it once and for all. Be done putting myself through the pain I feel every single day.

Is this how it'll be for the rest of my life?

I don't doubt it, honestly. But maybe this is how it's supposed to be. Maybe I am an old soul, like Luna told me a long time ago. Maybe I was a bad person, and this is my penance for the sins I've committed. In this life and the last.

It doesn't matter, anyway.

Luna is my heart and soul. If she's out there somewhere, then I'll be here. My heart will be wide open, bleeding at my feet. My body will ache, my mind won't be right, but if she's out there, then I'll be here.

I'll fucking wait. And if I'm waiting forever, well, at least I tried.

"Dude, you okay?" Lonnie side-eyes me backstage.

I haven't been able to sleep. Not since that dream. I've tried, trust me, I've tried, but I just can't. It might have something to do with the lines of coke I've done. My body feels electrocuted, and everything around me is shaking, or maybe it's just me.

Yeah, I'm fucking shaking.

"I'm good."

"Dude, you don't look good. You look like you're seizing." He's about to reach out and touch me, but I step away from him.

"Don't touch me right now, Lon. I'm not in the fucking mood."

"He's never in the mood. Rome is a shit lately." Clyde walks in, a beer in his hands. When he notices me, he stops, his eyes going wide. "What's wrong with you?"

"I'm fucking fine!" I roar.

He points his beer at me. "You aren't fine. And you have coke on the tip of your nose." His eyebrow lifts.

I narrow my eyes, my fingers lifting to my nose, and he's right, the side of my pointer comes away with white grains streaked across the skin. "Fuck off."

I push off the wall, walking toward my chair, but the world is moving in slow motion, and I'm walking too fast.

I run straight into something, and looking down, I see it's my guitar case laying on the ground.

"Dude! Watch what you're doing!" Lonnie shouts at me.

I flip him off, walking around my guitar case and falling into my chair. The world spins, and I turn the chair so I'm facing the mirror. My eyes are red, my hair is sticking up in all directions, even though it was just done by hair and makeup.

I see a baggie of coke on the table, a line already missing. I pour out another, slicing up a thick line. We're due to be on in ten, and I don't usually take this much before a show.

But after my dream last night, fuck it. *Fuck it so hard.*

"Dude, you've had enough," Clyde says, walking up to me.

I ignore him, cutting my line into perfection. The white powder is like snow, making everything painful in my life go away. Not fully, not even for a long time, but it dulls the ache, and fuck, if it even dulls the slightest bit, I'll take it.

"Dude." Clyde walks up to me, pulling my chair back. I jump out of my seat, pushing my chair toward him. It groans against the floor. He stumbles, nearly falling to the ground. He rights himself at the last second, glaring at me, his dark eyes alit with fury.

"Fuck. Off," I growl. Bending down, I take my last line, plugging my nose as the burn hits and the head rush flushes through my head, spreading down my body.

I twitch. Twitch again.

Fuck. Yes.

"Let's go," I say once I open my eyes.

They're staring at me, hesitation and worry in their gazes.

I point at them just as Flynn walks in the room. "Look at me like that again and I'll lay you on your asses."

I walk past them, opening the door so roughly it slams against the wall. Brandy is on the other side with a headset on, and she jumps about a foot in the air from the noise. She sees me, her face softening. She's about to take a step toward me, and I stop in place.

She frowns. Stops. Then starts walking again. "You okay? You don't look good."

"You're fired."

Her eyes widen, shock slackening her jaw. "W-what?"

"I want you off the set, Brandy. Go find someone that wants you."

"Are you… are you breaking up with me?" She places her hand on her chest, her cleavage heaving with emotion.

I smile, sickness filling me, cooling my bones. Cooling my heart.

I feel dead inside.

"We were never together, Brandy. You were just a pussy to slide into. I don't love you. I've never loved you."

For the first time since I met her, years ago, tears spring to her eyes. They tumble down her cheeks, and I watch as she holds herself back from reaching out to me. She wants to beg; she wants to plead. I watch her patience thin.

It's so fucking thin.

"I don't love you, Brandy. I've only loved one girl in my entire life, and you aren't her. You could never be her." With that, I walk away from her crumbling form, not even waiting for my bandmates before I walk onto the stage.

The crowd goes wild. I don't give them my usual smile, my usual playful demeanor. I grab my guitar, making sure it's tuned, keeping my face on the smooth, black wood.

I pull out my pick, flicking it against my fingers. Wanting to throw it, wanting to burn it. Wanting to fucking cry on it.

I can hear the guys walk out behind me. I can feel their heavy, solemn footsteps. The crowd even quiets down, still cheering, but not nearly as excited as they were when I walked on the stage. Bringing my hand up, I run my fingers through my hair.

I feel fucking wild right now.

My blood pumps extra hard. I feel crazy. Like everything in me is colliding at once. Like whatever has been laying low, is rising from the ashes, ready to break free.

My heart and soul have fucking had enough.

Flynn starts the drums, and my fingers poise to start the notes. I know exactly what song he's starting with.

The tips of my fingers are shaky, my body running hot.

It all feels fucking wrong.

Why am I doing this? Why am I here when my heart isn't? Why am I doing something I no longer love? Music is a part of me, it's always been a fucking part of me. But if my soul is lost, am I really even here?

What's the meaning of it all, at the end of the day? Is there even a point of living if you're missing half of yourself?

My breathing picks up, and the moment comes when I'm supposed to start strumming my first note.

I don't play.

I stand there, and I can feel the guys around me grow irritated, worried. Waiting for me. Lonnie starts his notes, trying to fill in for me, and then Clyde starts his.

Waiting for me.

Fuck this shit.

I grab the head of the guitar, swinging it over my shoulder. Gasps ring out, collectively, as if everyone breathes in at the same moment. The air gets sucked from the room as I swing the guitar over my head.

Crash.

It slams to the ground, my favorite guitar, the most expensive wood I've ever had, collides to the ground in a loud—*so fucking loud*—crash.

Everyone stops.

The crowd goes silent. You can't even hear them breathe. I don't look at the guys behind me, but I can tell they're shocked, fucking furious at me.

They know.

It's over.

Hands grab my arms, fingers digging into my muscles as I'm shoved off stage. I can hear three sets of footsteps behind me, heavy and angry, shoving me. Pushing my back.

Everyone is going crazy backstage. The stage crew have their headsets on, all shouting over one another.

I don't see Brandy anywhere.

I'm shoved into a closet, where all four of us cram inside.

Lonnie slaps the light, switching it on. We're shoved beside stage equipment, some random fucking signs, and a box of toilet paper.

Flynn's fist snaps out, hitting me straight in the nose. My head flies back, my hand going up to my nose. The back of my head slaps against the wall. "Fucking hell!" I roar.

I can feel the blood flowing before it pours out of my nose. I pinch my nostrils, but the blood still leaks through, seeping down my fingers and onto the floor. I can taste the blood in the back of my throat, and I lean forward, letting the thick red drip from my mouth.

Clyde bends down, grabbing a roll of toilet paper and tossing it at me.

"That's it, huh? That's how you wanted to go out?" He stares at me, his jaw clenching as his furious eyes bore into mine.

"It's not right. Not without her."

Silence.

Lonnie closes his eyes, tipping his head toward the ceiling.

"It's always been about her, huh?"

"You know it has." I narrow my eyes at him.

"You don't even know where she is. What is your plan, to fucking search the entire country until you find her?" Lonnie barks at me.

I shake my head, grabbing a handful of toilet paper and plugging my nose with it. "I don't know."

"You're fucked up, dude. You fucking threw the entire show because of your damn broken heart! You couldn't wait until after the show to fuck shit up?" Flynn barks at me.

I say nothing.

"You need help." He frowns in my direction.

"I'm fine." My voice is nasally, congested. The toilet paper gets soaked instantly. I pull it out, and I can feel the blood seep into the back of my throat. I bend down, spitting a pile of blood onto the ground.

"Are you really done? This is it?" Clyde asks. We all stand there, staring at one another. We've been doing this since we were kids. Since we knew how to create music, we've been doing it. It's all we know, really.

Music is in our blood. Being on the road, it's in our fucking veins.

But I also know that I love her. And at the end of the day, she's all that fucking matters.

"I can't… I don't think I can do it anymore," I say truthfully.

They all nod, knowing it's true before I even say the words.

My body is jittery, even if a part of me feels relief. I've been feeling this for a long time, and I didn't realize it. Not until I crashed my guitar on the stage.

"Go get some fucking help, dude." Lonnie slaps me on the shoulder.

I scowl at him. "Why am I the one that needs help? You guys all fucking snort blow, too. But I'm the only one that is an addict? We're all in the same fucking spot."

"Trust me, I'm definitely going to need a fucking therapist after this shit." Clyde runs his hands through his hair.

"Because, Rome, you deal with shit differently. We haven't been what you've been through. Whatever it is that you and Luna have, it's fucked you up. You've got a drug problem, but more than that, you're fucking broken, dude. You've been broken since we left Shallow Lake at eighteen years old."

I bite my lip, hating their accusing looks, but knowing they're right. They know me more than anyone. They're the ones who've been around me the past three years. Hell, they've been around me since I was young. They know me.

But more than anything, they know Luna and me. They know how we are. What she means to me. What being without her has done to me.

They know how broken I am.

I nod, and they collectively sigh in relief.

"Well, it was a good run, boys," Lonnie says, looking at us sadly.

This is it. This is really it.

"Thanks, guys. For everything." I blink, suddenly overcome with emotion.

Life is funny. It changes in just a blink of an eye. I could have not crashed my guitar on the ground, and we would still be out there playing. But one second, just one moment, and everything changed.

My entire life changed.

Everything changed.

CHAPTER TWENTY-ONE

Luna
1998

I walk along the beach, the sand so much different from home. My skirt blows in the ocean breeze, my bikini top full of sand. I look into the distance, seeing wave upon wave. Nothing but blue into the distance.

Nothing but time.

I hear my name and turn around, seeing my friends wave to me from our picnic bench.

San Diego.

It's where we've been for a year now.

Leaving Arizona was inevitable, mostly after that fateful night. It was traumatizing on all of us, mostly after walking back to the Winnebago with one less person. It was hard when we finally made it back, drinking water and watching our color return, knowing we left someone, empty, broken, dead, way up in the mountains.

My eyes water, and I wipe the tear from my lashes, flicking it off onto the sand.

It didn't take long for us to leave; a few days of mourning and we couldn't stand to be there another second. Between Shauna's death and the shooting the night before, we were all itching for something new.

Our goal was to finally go to Maui, but once we landed in San Diego, this place just… stuck. There are so many people here. It's not like Arizona, where you can go days without seeing someone. The beaches of San Diego are packed, people who are just like us. We sleep on the beach, we sleep under the stars, we sleep wherever we're meant to.

And no one cares. Everyone is happy here.

Neil loves it. He was in a dark bubble when we left, we all were. But Neil had this guiltiness in his eyes, a darkness I didn't want to inspect. Once we got here, and we met all the people on the beaches, the darkness left his eyes, and he's been the usual, free-spirited guy he was when I met him.

San Diego is different than Arizona in many ways. I'm grateful for it, actually. The air isn't as hot and dry, stifling with every breath you take. The ocean breeze cools your skin, even on the hottest of days. I watch the water, feeling a closeness to it. The water, it reminds me of my dreams.

But it also reminds me of home.

It reminds me of the lake, the smell of the water, the feel of the sand. It makes me feel like I'm home, even if that couldn't be further from the truth.

I called my parents when I got out here. They were glad to hear from me, maybe a little sad. It's been years since I've seen them, but I still can't find it in me to go home. What would I be going home to? What awaits me at the end of the road? I feel like by walking back there, I'd be going right back to senior year. Right back to a broken heart and a half missing soul.

I still miss Roman. I still love him.

I wonder if I'll ever stop loving him, or if there will always be a part of me that is broken, dead, and cold on the inside.

It's a chill that never subsides.

Life is different. Every place I've traveled to has been completely unique from the next. Arizona is dry, red, hot, dehydrated.

California is green, a combination of pollution and salt lingering in the air. There's always noise. Always traffic, people, waves. I could sit in silence for hours in Arizona, me and my thoughts drowning in memories of my past.

Now I don't have a moment to sit and think. Not during the day, at least. My thoughts are tucked away until nighttime, when they scream loudly, crashing with the waves as the tide rises. The water fills the beach just the same as thoughts of Roman flood my mind at night.

I haven't seen him in over three years.

It feels like a lifetime since I've touched him. Since I've felt his smooth, tanned skin. Since I've seen his brown eyes that match his brown hair. Sometimes my heart skips, small fragments of him fading. Did he have a freckle there? Were his eyes a light, or a dark brown? Time and memories fade, swirling out with the waves of the ocean. I want to grasp them, cling to them. Hold on to them for the rest of my life.

What does he smell like? Is his scent still like the beach? A little woodsy? Has his boyish scent turned into a manly scent? Does he have stubble covering his smooth face?

My mind goes to everything I'm missing, every moment that I've lost. So many minutes that I can't get back with my family, with Roman. What does Shallow Lake look like? Is the water still as blue as the sky? Is the grass still green, or has it dried and turned yellow? Is the beach still as big as it once was, or has the water risen and washed it away?

I shake my head, maybe I'll never know. Maybe I'll get lost into the world, fading away just like my memories.

I don't want to go home and hear that Roman met someone. Even just going back there, where he's touched every surface, walked on every part of that small town, eaten at every single diner. I can't go back there and stare at our memories in the face. I can't do it.

My heart won't survive.

So, I stay here, where nothing matters. Where my heart neither weeps nor rejoices. Where my soul isn't awake nor asleep. I just am. I float by.

I realized after some time, that maybe I'll never really find myself.

Though, maybe I'm not lost, but I know I'm not found either.

I'm stuck in this odd in-between, and I'm hoping someday I'll find it. Whatever it is I'm looking for. When I do, I'll go home. But until then, I'll stay here with my small crew, enjoying life, enjoying the sun, enjoying the warmth.

I breathe deeply through my nose to stop the tears as I walk to the bench where everyone is waiting for me. I find myself wandering along the shore a lot, looking for small shells that I can use to make my dreamcatchers. Selling them is just as popular, if not more, in California. People buy them, young and old, girl or boy.

"Luna!" Willie calls my name, waving me over. He has a brightness in his gaze, a familiarity in his smile. He likes me, a lot more than I like him. He wants what I can't give him. I wish I could, any girl would like to. He's handsome. His long blond hair brushes his shoulders, always a little sandy. Over the years, they've turned into dreadlocks, and in his spare time I always watch as he twists them. Over and over again.

Twist, twist, twist.

Willie shakes out his head as he walks up to me, tossing his arm over my shoulder and planting a kiss on my cheek. His lips are dry and warm as they press against my skin.

I've been wandering around most of the afternoon, enjoying watching the various tourists explore the beachy pacific. You can always tell the repeat visitors versus the newcomers. The people who have come here before barely spare the ocean a glance, but those who have never been here? Those people look at the ocean with wide eyes, an awe in their gaze that doesn't suppress after minutes, after-hours. They could stare out into the horizon for hours without blinking.

I don't blame them.

I curl my toes in the sand, the warmth should be scorching against my toes. After a lifetime of walking barefoot, my feet don't feel much of anything. The bruises, the cuts and scrapes, the broken toenails, they aren't affected by the ground anymore. It doesn't matter if it's soft or hard, cold or hot, my toes curl around the earth like they're meant to be there.

"I was enjoying the nice day." I look up, seeing the blue sky. It's a cloudless day, not even one in the sky. With a light breeze, the palm trees sway up near the beachside homes.

"Was starting to get worried about you." He pinches my side, and I wiggle out of his hold. Trish and Neil are talking to a guy I haven't seen before. He isn't part of our normal crew. His long dark hair is pulled into a bun, and he's shirtless, his jean shorts cut off mid-thigh. Frayed and worn. A woman stands next to him, her clothes threadbare, the colorful fabric faded over time to an almost pastel tone.

"That's Crow and Danae. They're Deadheads."

My eyes go wide, never having heard that term before. "Deadheads?"

He lifts an eyebrow. "You don't know about them?"

I shake my head.

"Hippies. Like, not the fake shit. The real, real hippies. The free people."

I look around, seeing everyone who we've been around for months. We're all hippies, in a way. Free people. We don't follow the rules like the people who have regular day jobs. We follow our own rules, and if someone doesn't like it, well, we usually just continue what we're doing.

"Aren't we all hippies?" I ask, my face scrunching up in confusion.

He laughs, "Not even close," he leans down, pressing his lips against my neck. I step out of his hold, feeling like every day he's getting clingier and clingier. Sometimes my body crawls when he touches me. My skin twitches when his fingers hover. I find myself more and more wanting to step out of his hold instead of into it. I need more breaths of fresh away, away from people, more alone time.

I've never felt an inkling of what I did when I was with Roman. After being with someone for so long, my feelings should be growing fonder instead of less. But I feel myself separating, my body disconnecting from it all.

I know that my feelings should've developed into something deeper, but there's an invisible wall around my heart. Only one person has ever been able to slither past that barrier. Knock it down until it's a rubble of dust at my feet.

That same person built that wall back up and solidified the bricks with the firmest cement. I don't think anyone will be able to get past that wall again.

Most of all, Willie.

What we have is so miniscule compared to what I had with Roman. Our love was unstoppable, but it was also tragic. Tragedy was our downfall in the end.

"What's the matter?" Willie asks, his tanned face lowering in concern. "You've been distant lately. Did I do something wrong?"

I shake my head, feeling like I've been keeping him on a string when there wasn't even a string to be kept on. I never should've let it get this far, yet here I am, wanting comfort and love all the while knowing he could never be the one to give it to me.

"It's nothing." I look at Crow and Danae, wondering why Neil and Trish look so excited. "What's going on over there?"

He looks over his shoulder, a crease between his eyes. "They're talking about going up to Santa Cruz." His eyes come back to mine, heavy, lost, a little angry. "Don't change the subject. Something's different with you. Something's wrong. What is it?"

My nostrils flare as my eyes connect with his. There's a volatility in his gaze that puts me off. None of us have ever even gotten angry with each other. Maybe a slight disagreement, but we aren't people to fight. We don't like conflict. I never have. The brashness in his tone makes me uncomfortable. "Why are you acting like this?" I take a step back from him, and that only makes his eyes darken further. His hand reaches out, his long fingers gripping my wrist tightly. Firmly.

"I'm just wondering what it is I've done to make you turn frosty. You've never been a particularly warm person, Luna, but it's like you can't even stand to be by me anymore."

I hold the breath in my lungs, my chest expanding and the walls screaming for relief. I know I need to tell him the truth—that I could never love him. That whatever we have is going nowhere. That our intimacy is meaningless to me because every moment with him is a moment that I wish I was with someone else.

"Willie, I think we need to cool off. Just remain friends for a bit. I... I've been hurt in the past, you know?"

He shakes his head, this being the angriest I've ever seen him. "No. I don't know, because you don't tell us anything! You don't tell *me* anything. The most I know about you is that you grew up in Wisconsin and wake up most nights drenched in sweat. Why? What is it that you dream about every night? What happened to you, Luna, and why won't you let me in?"

My body quakes, an unbearable scream barreling in the pit of my chest. It rages, banging against each rib and causing me immense pain.

"Because I will never love you," I say honestly, brokenly. Maybe I would give him my heart if that was a possibility. But maybe I wouldn't. He was a filler. Nothing more. Nothing less.

Anger flashes in his eyes, a wave of rage more turbulent than the ocean behind me. "And why not? Am I not good enough for you?" he asks, taking a step toward me. I step back out of instinct, the alarm bells ringing in my head.

I shake my head. "I can't love you because my heart belongs to someone else. Not a surface love, but an all-consuming love that changes a person inside and out. I found my soulmate, and I have to stop pretending with myself that what I can give you is anything like I gave him, because it's a lie. I'll never be able to give you my love, because it's not mine to give any longer."

His jaw clenches, the sun reflecting off his tense bone crushing against bone.

He's handsome, but my heart doesn't even leap for him.

"If you found yourself in this *all-consuming* love, then where is he? It's been me you've been sleeping with for three years, not him. Where is he then, huh? I don't see him anywhere." He extends his arms, kicking the sand as he spins in a circle.

"We broke up," I whisper on a broken breath. The words even slipping against my tongue are painful. Saying them aloud is gut-wrenching.

"You broke up," he huffs. "You're in love with a man you aren't even with and haven't seen in years." He shakes his head, anger and pity in his eyes. "I'm heading to Santa Cruz with them. Come with or don't, I don't even fucking care anymore." He stomps over, sand kicking over my feet in the process.

I watch everyone, feeling like this is a turning point in my life. I'm at a crossroads, and I can either leave this group I've been with for three years, or I can turn around and go back to the life I left behind. Who knows what is waiting for me, what I might walk into. That thought alone makes me pause, fear clutching my throat in a strong grip.

"Luna, come on! We're leaving!" Trish waves me over, a bright smile on her face. She's excited to move on, our time here coming to an end. Maybe that's what took me so long today. I knew I'd be leaving here soon, and I needed one last glance at the beach, at the water in southern California.

I don't know why, but for some reason, this feels like the last time I'll ever be here.

"You coming?" she asks again.

I bite my lips, my heart racing. I don't have enough time to think of what I want to do. I want to sit down, weigh the pros and cons, but I don't have the time.

It's now or never.

"Coming," I say, mostly to myself. I lift my skirt, the edges damp from the water, and walk off to my friends and the Deadheads. With every step I take, I question whether I'm making the right decision or not.

Only time will tell.

CHAPTER TWENTY-TWO

Luna

The ride to Santa Cruz is long and cramped. Hours upon hours of watching the coast fly by as we head north. Marijuana fills the car, and it reminds me of home so much that I close my eyes, leaning my head against the cracked fabric seat that smells like smoke, and listening as they play The Grateful Dead on repeat.

Crow and Danae are married and are somewhere in their mid-thirties. They've been traveling the coast for ten years, and before that bounced around from state to state, always ending back in California. They attend a lot of festivals and rainbow gatherings. I wasn't sure what that was, but I'm glad it was Trish who asked.

"What's a rainbow gathering?" she asks, her face screwed up in confusion.

Danae turns around, laughter in her dark eyes. Both Danae and Crow have dreadlocks, although I think they are more from lack of a comb or brush than anything else. Danae has her messy brown hair in a bun at the back of her head, a scrap of fabric holding it up.

"A rainbow gathering is like a peace circle. A lot of people come from all over the country to celebrate with us."

"Celebrate what?" I ask.

"Life," she shrugs, like it's the simplest answer in the world. "We pray for peace in the world."

"Just a ton of people that are looking for the same things in life," Crow mumbles.

"It kind of sounds like a cult. Is it a cult?" Neil asks, and silence in the car ensues.

"We aren't a cult." Is all Danae responds with.

The rest of the drive is silent besides the music. We drive up the coast, and I watch the landscape turn from flat to mountainous. It's beautiful, and I stick my face against the window like a child.

We eventually turn off the highway, heading toward the trees and into the mountains. The road turns bumpy, and Crow's van knocks from side to side with every rock and hole in the earth. I bump shoulders with Willie, who hasn't spoken with me since the beach. He's spoken with everyone else, laughing and joking. The minute I interject something into the conversation, his face drops, and he acts like I don't even exist.

We come to a point on the road where cars are lined up on the side. The ground dips off the side of the dirt road, and the way the cars are parked make it look like they're tipped sideways. Crow continues driving past them, past car after car after car. He drives to the front, parking near a clearing. My eyes widen at the sight in front of me.

Hundreds, and I mean hundreds of people sit in a large clearing. Small groups of people, people sitting alone, and huge groups of people make up the entire circle. The entire clearing. People with colorful clothing, topless women, and people of all ages fill the crowd. Smoke streams into the air, and taking a whiff, I feel comfort when I realize it smells like home.

More Marijuana.

"Here's home," Crow says, turning the ignition off on the car.

I look at my friends, although only Neil and Trish look back at me.

"You live here?" Neil asks.

Crow nods as he opens the door. "A lot of us do. Some travel and come back. A lot of people stay short-term, long-term, doesn't matter. This is home."

The sun is setting, and the trees are turning black in the shadows. Most people are barefoot as they walk around, and what looks to be a wild party is going on, or maybe it's only just the beginning of one.

We all step out of the car, and music plays off into the distance. The same type of music that played in the car on the way up here, and I'm beginning to think it's part of their circle—Rainbow Circle—whatever, type thing.

We follow Crow and Danae into the clearing, my toes pressing into the dried grass. It crunches beneath my feet. There's a chill in the air higher up in the mountains. I wish I had more than just this scrap of fabric over my breasts and this threadbare skirt, but I don't. Most of what I had was left in the Winnebago.

Only a short while after we came to California, our Winnebago went missing. Neil was parking it on the side of the road, out of sight from the beach, just over on the other side with the houses and shops. It took maybe about a week. We weren't sure where it went, and we had no way to look for it. Once it went missing, so did most of my clothes, and my rocks from Arizona.

My fingers go up, wrapping around my ballet slippers necklace. I'm glad I kept this on me. I've taken it off once or twice, only because I didn't want to lose it in the ocean if the clasp broke or something. But I kept it on the day our van went missing, and I'm so grateful I did.

The gold has faded from the sun and the salt over the years. I find myself clutching it at night, warming the slippers with my palm. I wonder why I don't just take it off, throw it in the woods, leave it in the desert, let it sink to the bottom of the ocean. But even taking it off is painful, and the thought of parting with it settles a panic in the pit of my stomach.

I shake my head, clearing my thoughts as I watch everyone talk to Crow, shaking his hand and shouting out a hello as he passes. It's like he's the top dog here or something. People worship him.

I walk past people who look like they're on another planet. They watch the trees, dazed out in their own world. My eyes widen as I pass a person fully naked, staring into nothing.

There's a blanket littered with items at one end of the circle. The music is louder here. Someone has a guitar, which is hard to look at. Music in general is painful.

It all reminds me of Roman.

Danae grabs a dropper and passes it to Crow. "Here you go, babe."

He takes it, tipping his head back and putting two drops on his tongue. He passes it to Neil.

"What is it?" he asks, tipping the small dropper and watching the clear liquid swirl around in the small tube.

"Acid." Crow's voice is lighter and heavier at the same time. He smiles at us, a loose grin on his face.

I look around, seeing everyone looking like they're in a completely different dimension.

Is everyone on acid?

"How much do I take? Two drops? The entire thing?"

Danae puts up a finger. "Only one."

Neil shrugs, tipping his head back and squeezing his eyes shut. I watch his fingers push on the rubber top, my throat dropping into my chest as I watch the liquid dribble out, and one drop slip from the seal and onto his curled tongue. He holds the dropper out, and Willie grabs it, repeating Neil's actions. No hesitation, no worries. His scrunched face relaxes the moment the liquid hits his tongue.

I try to swallow, but the lump in my throat makes it difficult. Trish looks as hesitant as I do as she grabs the dropper from Neil. Her fingers are shaky as she clutches it in her grip. She looks at me, fear in her eyes. "What do you think?" she whispers.

I shake my head. I haven't taken drugs. Not since that night all those years ago on Roman's deck on New Year's Eve. Not a hit, not a drop, nothing. None of us really have, mostly just keeping to ourselves most of the time while we traveled.

But now we've ended up in the Rainbow Circle, with drugs and Deadheads surrounding us.

I knew that feeling in the pit of my stomach before we headed here, that hesitation and worry. That time is now. It's here. *It's this.*

Without another thought, Trish tips her head back, dripping a small drop onto her tongue. She rolls it into her mouth. Her arm snaps out, the dropper ending in front of my chest. I take it, clutching the slippers around my neck with my other hand.

Where is Roman right now? What is he doing?

He wouldn't want me to do this.

But thoughts of Roman always lead me down a dark path, and today I don't want to end on my dark path. I close my eyes, tip my head back and squeeze the dropper, letting one drop settle on my tongue.

It tastes like nothing, and rolling it around in my mouth, it's light, slightly oily as the substance covers my tongue. Nothing happens, though, and I anticipated flying to a different galaxy immediately. I've heard stories of acid over the years, how dangerous it could be if not taken correctly. How wild the high is. Worry lingers in the back of my mind. *Uncertainty.*

We all sit down in the grass, and I pass the dropper off to Danae. She takes two drops and settles it back with her things. Crow sits beside her, curling his arm around her waist as they sway to the music.

"When does it hit?" Neil asks.

"You'll come up soon. Just let it ride," Crow rumbles. He pulls out a joint, sparking it up and passing it around. Everyone takes it, smoking the joint down until it's a tiny roach pinched between my fingers.

I suck in, a cough hitting me before the smoke even fills my lungs. My finger burns as the cherry brushes my skin, and I wince as I pass it on, my eyes watering as a flush takes over my body.

And then I feel *everything.*

It feels like my body is morphing into something else. An animal, a plant, the entire earth. My hand raises and I settle down onto the grass, letting the long green blades brush against my legs and ankles, tickling my feet. They feel soft, soft like butter, cotton, air, as my fingers wrap around them. My palm swallows them, and it feels like my body ingests them.

Whoa.

I roll onto my back, looking up at the sky. Night has come, pushing the sunlight to the other end of the earth. The air is cool, brushing against my bare neck all the way to my feet. It feels like every breath I take lifts me off the ground. I feel suspended in the air, levitating above the earth as the world expands around me.

I close my eyes, seeing the galaxy reflected behind my lids. Every time I open my eyes, the sky lights up, the tips of the trees swaying in the mountain air. Then I close my eyes again, seeing each star I've memorized since I was a little girl.

I name them off, just as I always have.

Ursa Minor, Ursa Major, Cygnus, Cassiopeia, Draco.

The list goes on, and on, and on. I feel like I name off constellations for a century, each one morphing into something else. It's like the stars come to life, moving and creating a movie in the sky.

I watch.

I feel the grass crunch beneath me, sounding like it's coming through loudspeakers. I look over, seeing Willie walk up to me.

"Feel it?"

I blink at him, not sure how to use my tongue. Not sure how to use my body at all.

It hit me at once.

He lies next to me, his body one hundred degrees as he sits flush against me. It feels too hot, like there are flames coming off his body. I look over at him, literally seeing flames curling around his clothes. He doesn't flinch, like it's not even there. But it looks like it is, so it must be me.

I shuffle away from him, only an inch. I can tell he doesn't like this. His arm slings around my stomach, pulling me flush against him. His arm feels like a weight, like it's a million pounds of fire as it wraps around my naked stomach. I breathe, not sure how to use words right now. Not sure how to tell him that I don't want this.

Instead, I close my eyes, riding the wave.

And let the world consume me completely.

I wake up the next morning, feeling out of sorts. My body feels overused, like I ran a marathon overnight. I sit up, looking around the open field. Most people are still sleeping, either on blankets or on the grass. There are some tents, but most people are sleeping underneath the open sky.

Willie lies next to me, his arm wrapped around my side.

What happened last night?

My skirt is bunched up to my thighs, and I frown, pulling it back down to my ankles. I slide out of his hold, rolling over and getting up.

I need to go pee.

I see Trish and Neil sleeping next to Crow and Danae. Danae is sleeping directly on top of Crow. Crow's arms are splayed out onto the blanket, and for some reason he reminds me of Jesus on the cross.

The grass is damp this morning, and my toes get wet with dew as I walk across the field and into the trees. There are a few people sleeping against the stumps, and I walk past them, tiptoeing across sticks and logs, hoping I don't wake anyone up.

I find a private spot and pull my skirt up, squatting down to the ground to relieve myself. When I'm finished, I get up, wandering back the way I came.

Willie is still asleep, but Neil and Trish are sitting up. They both look out of it, completely disoriented. Just as I feel.

"Hey," I whisper as I walk up to them.

"Dude, what happened last night?" Neil runs his hands over his face. "I feel like I got hit by a truck."

"You look like you got hit by a truck." Trish grimaces.

"We really took acid, huh?" He looks at us with wide eyes.

We both nod.

"What's the plan?" I ask, sitting down beside them. My legs cross beneath my skirt, and I run my hands down the length of it, attempting to get the wrinkles out.

"No plan." Neil shrugs.

I frown.

That's the thing. I really don't want to stay here. These people seem nice, but this isn't something I want to do long-term. I don't want to trip on acid for the rest of my life.

I didn't come all this way to lose myself.

"I want to leave," I whisper.

Trish looks at me, the same look on her face.

Neil frowns, confusion lining his face. "What's wrong? Did something happen?"

I shake my head, not really sure. It just doesn't feel right to be here. It doesn't feel like it did in Arizona or in San Diego. This doesn't feel like home. This feels like a stop.

And I'm ready to go.

"Little birdie looks ready to fly away." Comes from behind Neil. I look over his shoulder, seeing Crow staring at us.

"What was that?" I ask, confused.

"You. You look like you want to leave. Didn't you have a good run last night?"

I bite my lip. He doesn't seem angry, more so just curious. But there's something in his tone that puts me off. It worries me.

"It's just not really my thing." I cringe.

He shakes his head, pressing his hand into the ground so he can sit up. He goes into his bag, grabs his little dropper from last night. Sticking his tongue out, he lands two drops onto his tongue. He closes his eyes like it tastes like candy, even though I remember from last night that it was flavorless.

He gets up, walking over to me with his dropper in hand. He stands right in front of me, looming over me like a mountain. I stand up, and Neil and Trish do the same. We're all a little leery now, a little hesitant.

I look down as Crow opens his hand, leaking the rest of the dropper into his palm. Bringing his hand up to his mouth, he mumbles at me, "Fly away, little birdie."

Neil shoves me out of the way, just as Crow inhales deeply, blowing the entire palmful of acid in Neil's face. He coughs, stumbling, falling to the ground, wiping the oily liquid from his face.

"What the hell?!" Trish shouts, kneeling in front of Neil. He looks disoriented, a little confused.

I stand there, shell-shocked at the scene in front of me. *What just happened?*

"Bummer. It was meant for little birdie." He shakes his head, turning around and settling back down next to Danae, who hasn't even stirred.

Come to think of it, Willie is still passed out as well.

I look over to Neil, who hasn't said a word. He's barely blinked, actually. He's just staring, looking confused. Lost.

I walk up to him. "Neil, are you all right?"

He looks up at me, wonder in his face. His eyes travel around my head, down my body and back up again. He doesn't say a word.

"We need to get him out of here. Before they do something else," Trish says, a tremor of fear in her voice. "Help me get him up, would you?"

I go to the opposite side of Neil, lifting his arm around my shoulder and pulling him to stand.

Glancing over at Willie, I whisper, "Willie." He doesn't move, not doing anything besides lying in the grass, his mouth hanging open as he dreams his dreamless sleep. "Willie." I kick him, and this gets him moving. He snorts, wiping his mouth as he blinks away his sleep.

"What? What's going on?"

I nod my head toward the way we came, and he must notice the tension in the air, because he stumbles to his feet, looking disoriented as we walk away from Crow and Danae. People are starting to wake up, sitting up in the grass and staring at us in shock as we walk by.

We make it to the cars, walking down the gravel road and toward civilization.

I watch as a man lights up a cigarette near his car, staring at us as we walk past.

"What's wrong with him?" Willie asks, finally getting his bearings.

Tears form in my eyes. Whatever happened to him, was meant to happen to me.

"I don't know, but we need to get him to the hospital." My voice shakes with my words.

"Hospital ain't going to help him." Comes the voice from behind me.

We all pause, Neil stumbling but following our lead. He stands there, staring straight ahead. Like he's tripping hardcore.

He must have overdosed.

"What do you mean? Do you know what happened to him?" Trish asks.

The man nods, taking a large drag from his cigarette. The smoke trails through his nostrils as he walks around us and stares at Neil. He shakes his head, pity and regret in his gaze. "He ain't coming back."

"What do you mean?" Willie frowns. "He's just tripping, right? It might just take longer for him to come down?"

The man shakes his head. "He was puddled."

We all frown simultaneously.

"What's puddled?" I ask, looking over at Neil. He stands there, his head tilted to the sky as he watches the trees.

"Someone blew acid in his face, right?" The man asks.

Trish nods.

He shakes his head, taking another drag of his cigarette. "How much?"

Trish shrugs, panic in her eyes. "Like, the whole dropper."

The man winces. "Puddling is what happened to your guy here. Most likely, he'll be in his trip forever. If he comes down, and they rarely do, he'll never be the same. This guy is gone." He shrugs. "Sorry. These people aren't bad people at all. We just live life a little differently."

Tears fall down my cheeks, shock and terror that this could've been me.

I could've been gone, in just the blink of an eye.

Would anyone have ever known? How would anyone even find me? My parents don't even know where I am.

Would Roman ever know?

I swallow down a panic attack and look at Trish. "We need to take him to the hospital. Maybe they can do something."

The man shakes his head. "You're wasting your time."

Willie looks at the man, urgency in his gaze. "Can you take us to the closest hospital?"

The man takes a step back, his hands raised in the air, cigarette poised between his fingers. "Hey, man. I'm not getting into this. If he got puddled, he must have done something."

"It was supposed to be me," I cry.

Trish cries too, pleading, "Please, just take us to the hospital. We have no idea where we are."

The man grimaces. "I'll take you to the closest town, but I ain't taking you to a hospital. You'll be on your own from there."

We all nod, grateful for any kind of help.

The man nods toward his van, and we all shuffle in, shoving Neil into the middle. Willie sits in the front, his hands gripping his headrest as he turns around, staring at Neil. He tries to talk to him, asking him questions and shaking his knee.

Nothing happens.

I cry the entire time down the mountain and into town. The man doesn't say anything, doesn't ask us any questions. He just drives us directly into the closest town, parking on the corner of an empty street. There are shops nearby, but none even look open yet for the day.

"Thank you, man," Willie says, giving him a smile.

"Where's the closest hospital?" I ask through my tears, unable to stop the terror of this morning. I could be dead right now, or mentally, anyway. Who knows what kind of trip Neil is going through in his mind right now.

The thought of that terrifies me.

The man points out the passenger window. "Three blocks that way you'll find the emergency room."

We all nod, thanking him again before shuffling Neil down the road. He can walk himself, but his feet are wobbly, and we want to get him there as soon as possible.

My eyes glance at a sign that shows a nearby airport, and my heart lurches in my chest. This is the first time the thought of going home has hit me so hard. This is the first time I've felt as lost, as homesick as I do in this moment.

I don't want to be here anymore.

We walk into the emergency room, and the scent of disinfectant slaps me in the face. The doctors give us disappointed looks when we tell them what's going on. They put Neil in a wheelchair, the wheels slightly squeaky, and bring him to the back, telling us to stay in the waiting room and they'll update us when they can.

The moment Neil pushes through the pale white doors, I break down and cry, bending at the waist and burying my face in my skirt.

I can hear Trish crying beside me, and then Willie's hand pushes me off to the side, shoving the both of us into the waiting room chairs. The plastic bangs against my spine, and it only makes me cry harder. "It's not going to do us any good to sit here and cry. Let's just wait and hope for the best," Willie says.

"I want to go home," I cry, wiping the tears from my face. "I feel so lost. That could be me right now. But Neil saved me. He pushed me out of Crow's way. That could be me, and my family would never know!" A sob rips from my chest, and I feel so incredibly desperate. "I just want to go home."

"Let's just sit here and wait. We can talk about it when we get some news from Neil, okay?" Willie says, his voice a little uncertain, a little possessive. It makes me feel uneasy, and I grind my teeth together with unease.

"Luna, will you go to the bathroom with me?" Trish asks, standing up from her chair. She wipes her red face, her skin discolored and blotchy from tears.

I nod, standing up and wiping my own face. We look for the sign and find it right away, holding each other's hands as we walk into the bathroom. Pushing open the heavy door, I walk straight toward a pale blue stall when Trish's fingers wrap around my arm. Her hand is shaky, tremors so heavy that my arm twitches. "Luna."

I look at her, confusion in my eyes, "What? What is it?"

She looks around for a few seconds, like someone, maybe Willie, will walk in here any moment. She sticks her finger into her bra, pulling out a wad of cash. She looks uncertain, but so damn sure of herself as she stares me in the eyes. "Take this. I saw you eyeing the airport. This is your time. Willie will never let you leave. Did you see the look in his eyes? He'll *never* let you go."

I feel her words in the depths of my heart. I know he won't. There's been a look in his eyes since San Diego, a possessiveness that has no right to be there. Our relationship was never that serious, yet the look in his eyes is one that says he'll never let me leave him.

Never.

"But... where'd you get this?" I stare down at the money, eyes wide.

She winces, looking a little sheepish, "I left home with it. It's always on me." She rolls the money out, some of it faded, crumpled from being wet. "It's not in the best shape, and it's not much, but it should get you home. You want to go home, right?"

I nod, tears springing to my eyes. I don't know what waits for me, but I know I want to leave California. This place, it doesn't feel right.

But neither does taking Trish's money.

"I can't take your money." I push the money toward her chest, and she pushes right back.

"Yes, you can, and you will." She grabs my hand, forcing my fingers around the crunchy bills. "I'm going to take care of Neil, and then I'm going home. I can call my parents and they can send me some money to get me home." She takes a deep breath, her eyes filling with tears. "I know your family isn't as wealthy. So, please, go home, and don't come back."

My fingers squeeze, clutching the bills. I shove the money into my bra, my cheeks damp with tears and my fingers shaky. I look at her, the words forming around my tongue, yet I'm unable to say them. I'll be forever grateful to her, and for some reason, I don't think I'll ever see her again.

"Thank you," I whisper.

She smiles, tears springing to her eyes. "It was fun, wasn't it? We had fun?"

"We had so much fun." I wrap her in my arms, pulling her against me. She comes willingly, her arms cinching around my ribs and squeezing tight.

"I wish Shauna would've made it home," she cries.

I step back and wipe my face, feeling my heart in my throat. Shauna was a good girl. She didn't deserve what happened to her.

"Me too."

"Well, I guess this is it." She turns around, pressing her hands against the sink. She looks at her reflection in the mirror, at our skin that feels permanently peppered with flakes of sand. Both of our hair is braided down our backs, since there isn't much else to do. Our clothes are faded and threadbare from the sun, and our eyes look like they've lived one million lives.

I have lived one million lives.

"This is it." I clench my hands at my sides, feeling like there's so much to say, but not sure how to say it. I don't know how to tell her how much her friendship has meant to me during some of my darkest days, how much I'm going to miss her. Saying what's written in my heart feels like an injustice in the emergency room bathroom, so I decide to say nothing at all.

"Goodbye, Luna." Her eyes lift to my face, watery as she glances at me.

"Goodbye." I turn on my feet, leaving her in the bathroom and walking back through the door. I stop, peaking around the corner, glancing out at the waiting room. I see the Willie's back turned, his blond hair dirty and messy as it falls along the back of his chair. His head is tilted toward the nurse's station, as if he is sitting on the edge of his seat, waiting for any type of news.

I take this as my cue, rushing in the opposite direction toward the doors. They automatically slide open as I walk up to them, and I run out, across the grass and away from the hospital. I end up back where the sign was and stop on the corner, bending down with my hands on my knees as I take in gasping breaths.

This is it. I'm going home.

I start running again, the soles of my bare feet slapping across the hot pavement as I make my way to the airport. People stop and stare at me, wondering why a girl is running barefoot through the city. I pay them no attention, excitement coursing through my veins at the thought of finally going home.

A part of me is glad I started this journey, but another part of me wishes I never would've left in the first place.

I get to the airport, cars and taxis and so many people walking about. Suitcases roll on the ground, and tears spring to my eyes as reality hits me.

There's no turning back now.

I walk into the airport, my skirt whooshing between my legs. The air conditioner blasts through the vents, and goosebumps break out along my arms. I rub my hands up and down my biceps, warming my skin as I get in line.

Slipping the money from my bra, I flatten it all out the best I can, just as the person in front of me walks away with a ticket.

"Next," the lady behind the desk says, barely looking up from her computer.

I take a step forward, placing my money on the counter and sliding it toward her. "I'd like a ticket home."

She looks up, staring at me.

Oh, right. "To Wisconsin. I'd like to buy a ticket to Wisconsin."

She blinks at me. "Which airport, ma'am? There are multiple airports in Wisconsin."

"Anyone. The soonest one you have available." I push the money toward her further, and she looks up at me this time, taking me in.

Her eyes travel from my dark, messy hair, all the way down to my bare stomach. It's like she can read my story in my appearance, and her face softens. "Let me see what I can do."

She clicks on her keyboard, her fingernails making the keys clack extra loudly. It feels like it takes her forever, her alternating between clicking with her mouse and clicking with her keyboard.

"Ah, here we go. There's a plane taking off to central Wisconsin in about four hours. Does that work?"

I nod my head, a smile breaking out on my face so wide my cheeks hurt. "That's perfect."

She takes my money, counting out what she needs and handing me back a much smaller stack. The small printer below her starts whirring to life, and a small ticket pops out. The lady tears it off and holds it out to me. "Do you have any bags you need to check?"

I shake my head. "No, nothing."

Her face frowns in confusion, but she nods. "Have a safe flight."

I take the ticket, sliding it from between her fingers and looking down at it. "Thank you." All I can read is the word Wisconsin.

I walk off, heading through the airport and looking for my concourse. There are small shops, restaurants, and gift stores. I curve left toward a small convenience shop, realizing I haven't drank anything in I don't know how long.

I grab a water, and a small bag of peanuts, slipping a twenty-dollar bill from the stack and setting my things on the counter. A younger guy behind the cash register gives me a smile, staring a little too long at my stomach. I wrap my arms around my midsection, drifting my eyes away from his and toward the magazine stand.

And everything stops.

Everything.

My hand reaches out automatically, almost in slow motion as I grab the magazine closest to me. Pulling it free, I bring it to my face and read the headline.

ROMAN HALL FROM CATACLYSM HAS MELTDOWN ON STAGE. TREATMENT? GIRLFRIEND TELLS ALL.

Girlfriend?

Roman has a girlfriend?

It shows a picture of him, looking so different, yet so much the same. He looks older, but I suppose he would after not seeing him in years. He has a pair of sunglasses on his face as he sings. It looks like this picture was taken during a concert. I don't need to look into his eyes, I already know what I'll see.

He's changed. Just as I've changed.

I drag my finger over the curve of his face, over the sharp edges that have formed over the years. Over his tan skin, and his dark brown hair. It's like I can really touch him as my finger glides over this piece of smooth paper.

Except I'm not, and I can't.

There's a heaviness in him that I can feel through the pages. A sadness and an anger that bleeds in the way he holds himself.

The pages crumple in my fingers as I pull it to my chest, lowering my head and letting out a quiet sob.

He met someone.

He's moved on.

"Miss, are you okay?"

I don't pay attention to him, taking this moment to grieve the loss that I know is gone forever. I thought we were soulmates. In the back of my heart, I always hoped one day we'd end up together again. I didn't even give it a second thought, just assuming that our hearts were one. I didn't anticipate him meeting someone else. Finding someone to give his heart to.

Maybe I shouldn't read too much into it, but if the media knows, it must be serious, right?

Another sob racks my spine, and I want to fall to my knees and wail. I don't do that, though. I just sniffle into the magazine and wish for the pages to swallow me whole.

"Um, do you need me to get someone?" the man behind the counter asks.

I shake my head, pulling my face out of the pages. I straighten it the best I can, sliding it back onto the rack. It's crumpled and wet, but I don't want it. I turn around, keeping my back to the counter as I walk out.

I know what I have to do.

"Wait, do you want your things?"

I don't pay attention to him, continuing my walk back toward the front desk. My eyes water, tears leaking down my cheeks. Someone comes up and asks if I'm okay, and I ignore them. My mind feels blank, zombie-like. I don't feel the cool air anymore. I don't feel the cold tiles against my bare feet.

I feel nothing.

I wait back in line, the tears seeming endless as they leak from my eyes. I don't wipe them away, feeling like they deserve their justice. They deserve to grieve, too. This will be the last time I cry over Roman Hall. I'm going to take this time.

The lady behind the front desk cocks her head to the side when she sees me again. Her eyes widen when she sees my tearstained face. "Are you okay?" She stands from her seat, leaning over the desk as if she can help me.

No one can help me.

I slide my ticket back across the desk, pushing it toward her. "I'd like to exchange my ticket."

She frowns. "Where would you like to go?"

"Hawaii."

She stares at me a moment, then sits back down, starting her clicking and clacking all over again.

"I have a flight that leaves for Maui in one hour."

"I'll take it." I feel dead inside as the words leave my mouth. It's not even something I'm sure I want to do anymore, but I do know one thing.

Home used to be wherever Roman was.

Now that he gave his love, his heart, his soul to someone else, I don't have a home anymore.

And I feel more lost than I ever have in my entire life.

CHAPTER TWENTY-THREE

Roman

1999

"We'll miss you, Roman. Don't be a stranger," my therapist, Mr. Hyde, says to me as he grabs my hand. His shake is firm, while his other hand goes up to my arm, giving my bicep a firm squeeze. His blond hair looks yellow in the Florida sun, swept and combed so perfectly to the side, not a hair out of place. He's a perfectionist, probably needs his own therapy, honestly. But him getting me to where I am now, I can't complain.

The last six months spent in treatment was the best thing I've ever done. Not something that I wanted to do in the slightest. But I came here with a chip on my shoulder and a hole in my heart. Treatment was something that was coordinated between my manager, my parents, and my boys. They thought I needed it, even if I denied I had a problem at every turn. But walking out of here, I have to say it's probably the best thing I've ever done for myself.

Six months ago, I was at the darkest point in my life. The only sustenance I had was drugs and sex. The high life of rock and roll and being famous gave me the fuel to keep going. But I realize that wasn't healthy, because I was sick on the inside.

"I won't," I say, sliding inside the taxi.

He taps on the roof of the cab, and I'm off.

Next stop? *New York.*

The taxi drives through the city, nothing but blue skies, palm trees, and green grass in every direction I look. I crack the window, and humidity and salty air slap me in the face. Florida is awesome, but this isn't my home.

My parents ask why I don't just come home to Wisconsin. Why I decide to continue being away from family, friends, and everything that I know and love. They're worried that moving out to somewhere I don't know anyone or anything is going to lead me down the same path I've been on the past four years.

They don't understand that I'm not just moving *anywhere.* I'm moving to where I was always meant to go. I'm going to the place where I was supposed to build my life with Luna. We were supposed to grow there, chase our dreams. She wanted it so bad.

I'm doing it.

For her. For us.

She might not be here with me now. I might not know where she is, or what she's doing, but she'll come back. Because she's mine. She always has been. She'll be mine before she'll ever be anyone else's.

I'll be ready, and I'll be waiting.

It hasn't been an easy road to get here, but here I fucking am. First, I had to come down from the drugs. That was terrible. Living off coke for years, you don't really realize how bad your addiction is. It takes a toll on you mentally and physically. I took it like coffee, because it kept me going when my life was always on the move. When I was broken and empty inside. Everyone on the road did it, and no one seemed like they were fucked up. We all seemed normal, just hopped up.

But coming down, I realized just how deep my addiction ran. I lost weight; I lost my color. My eyes lost their life. Coming back from that was hard, and treatment was something that I wanted to give up on multiple times. Say fuck it and walk out. But they wouldn't let me. Not the therapists, not my parents, not my friends.

They say this place is voluntary, but it wasn't. At least for me.

By far the hardest part was after I came down from the drugs. That's when I met my therapist, Mr. Hyde. He wanted to dive right into me. But not just into my thoughts, he wanted to delve deep into my soul. He wanted to figure out what made me tick. He wanted to know about each and every detail of my life.

My life isn't my life without Luna. I just didn't want to talk about *her*.

At that point, I hated Luna more than I hated myself. I was so angry at her for tearing apart the best part of me, of herself, of us. She threw us away without a second thought, and that made me so damn angry.

I didn't want to talk about her, I didn't even want to think about her. I was sober for the first time in years and my mind ran a thousand miles a minute. My soul hurt for the first time in I don't know how long, the ache so deep I felt it in my toes. I've been numb, and now I could feel every inch of pain I've been in, and my fucking God that shit hurt like a bitch.

But Mr. Hyde got it out of me, and it hurt worse than chopping my body into pieces. Figuratively, he made me bleed all over his ugly sofa. He learned about Luna, so much so that he grew fond of her. Of her ability to dance, of her love for me.

He ended up loving Luna nearly as much as I do. He told me he wants to meet her someday. I don't know how that would ever happen, and I even told him that. All he did was look at me and say, "I know true love when I see it. You'll meet again someday."

I fucking hope so, but every day that goes by is another day I don't get to be with her. It's another day wasted away. I think about her, it's something I can't stop doing no matter how hard I try. She's engrained in me, a part of me. There's no denying that. I don't even *want* to change it.

Mr. Hyde just wanted to find a way for me to learn how to live separately from her.

Isn't that what I've been doing for over four years now?

Living without her. Living my own life and letting her live hers.

He tells me no; I've done the exact opposite. Every song, every lyric, every fucking second of my life was spent drowning in her. I needed to learn how to live in the good, not in the bad.

He told me if I never learned how to be whole without her, I'd never be able to be whole *with* her.

I've been living in pieces for a *long time*.

Maybe longer than I know. All I've ever known was living on the road. Contact being fleeting. It's how I grew up with my dad being on tour most of the time. Luna was my rock when everything else was uncertain. She grounded me, she stuck by me, she loved every fucking piece of me. And I left her the first chance I got.

Mr. Hyde made me realize that what I did to Luna probably affected her more than I thought. Not that I shouldn't have went on tour, I just handled it shitty. I wish I could go back. I wish I could take it all back. Maybe we'd still be together now if I would've done things differently. I'll never know.

All I do know, is that I'm hoping one day our lives will realign again. I'm hoping that what we used to have is lying dormant somewhere, and our flame will be reignited one day.

Toward the end of my stay at the treatment center, Mr. Hyde asked me the biggest question.

What now?

It played on in my mind for weeks. I could've tried to salvage our band, but after six months of treatment, the guys decided it was just best to retire our name. With that out of the picture, I didn't really have anything else to do in life.

What could I do?

I have no college degree, no desire to attend a university, live in a dorm, or try a damn community college by any means.

I could find a job, work in a low-paying business that will bleed me dry.

But I had no desire for any of that. I didn't want to go into something that could possibly sink me back into the black hole I've been living in.

The day when Mr. Hyde came in with a stack of pamphlets and informational packets was a turning point for me. I was about to be released, and the fear of taking any steps backward was terrifying. The thought of living a normal life was terrifying.

The thought of living a life without Luna has been terrifying. Every day. For who knows how long.

I want her back, but if fate is as true as I think it is, we will be together again.

I spent hours, days, going through those pamphlets. My mind landed on one. It was something I've never thought about before, but it's something where I could make a difference in life. Something that would keep me busy and out of trouble.

Something that I could do that would help people.

It was a small black and yellow pamphlet that spoke about a program with the FDNY, New York City Fire Department. Everything I needed to do could be done online. I could finish treatment and go through the courses at the same time. New York was where I wanted to end up, anyway, so I felt like it was just another piece of fate.

Part of my destiny.

I showed Mr. Hyde the packet the next day, and he helped me set up the courses I needed to take. It didn't take long, and by the time I was awarded my firefighter certificate, I only had weeks left in treatment, and Mr. Hyde was able to land me a job at the FDNY.

I start next week. I'm fucking nervous. I've never had an actual job. Going from high school to being a rock star, I know nothing in between.

But I have to live my life. I have to be the best man I can be because the day when Luna comes back to me, I need to be ready.

Not *if* she comes back to me. *When*. Because I know she will. I'll be ready. I'll be waiting.

I can't fucking wait.

The taxi pulls up to the airport, and I take my small bag and throw the driver some cash. Looking at the busy, chaotic Tampa airport in front of me, I take a breath, releasing all the stresses and the worry I've been hanging on to.

I'm going to keep living the life Luna wanted us to have. I can feel her soul out there, out in the world. Missing mine. I know she aches as badly as I do. We've always been connected, maybe even before we met.

There's no doubt in my mind we'll meet again. I'll be able to look into her gray eyes and touch her black, silky hair.

And when that time comes, I'm never letting her go again.

It's four hours later when the second taxi drops me off outside my new apartment. New to me, I suppose. This thing is old, built out of stones with so much historic architecture curving the tops and sides of the bricks.

New York is… New York.

Loud. Chaotic. So many different smells. So much traffic.

My blood burns through my veins to think of Luna walking these streets, her ballet slippers slung over her shoulder. She'd walk down the sidewalk, people bumping into her left and right, cussing her out for being in their way.

She wouldn't even spare them a glance. She's always in her own world. A dance playing in her head. Some note or tune vibrating from her lips as she hums along to the soundless song.

Come home to me, Luna.

I unzip the side pocket of my bag, pulling out my new key. The condo unit comes newly furnished, something my parents and Mr. Hyde coordinated for me. I head inside the high-rise unit, and people are bustling in and out, not sparing a glance at the next person as they bark into their cell phones.

I walk through the entryway, my shoes clapping against the tiled floor as I walk to the elevator. It's about twenty floors high, each unit having their own balcony. I press the circular button with the up arrow, watching as it glows yellow. The elevator starts humming, and I look around as it descends to the main floor.

Tiny little gray slotted mailboxes line an entire wall. The ceilings are tall, old. It smells a little like mildew in here, but not terribly so. Old building smell, I suppose. Everything is expensive in New York, mostly since this building is in the heart of the city.

This place doesn't seem unkempt, just old.

The elevator dings, and the door rolls open. I step inside, and press floor eleven, watching as the doors glide shut behind me.

Taking a deep breath, I feel as the elevator lurches, bringing me to my new home.

I chose a one-bedroom unit, something small. I don't need anything huge, or luxurious. I just need some place that has a bed and a kitchen.

The guys all ended up in different locations after we split. Lonnie stayed in California. He took over our apartment and started working at the record label. He loves it there. Flynn and Clyde went home to Wisconsin. I spoke to Flynn not too long ago, and things are going good back home. He says it looks just as we left it all those years ago. Flynn is working with his dad right now, trying to figure out what he wants to do next.

Clyde, on the other hand, did start some classes at a community college. I hope it works out for him.

The elevator dings again, and when the doors slide open, I step out onto the dark carpet, looking in both directions to see where I'm supposed to go. I decide to head left, watching as the units go up. Once I get to unit 124, I stop.

This is it.

Sticking my key in the lock, I turn it, listening as it clicks. Turning the knob, I open the door, walking into a brightly lit condo. Neutral tones and a balcony that looks out onto the entire city. Skyscraper after skyscraper line my window. The glass is floor to ceiling, bringing in sunlight and brightening the entire apartment. The ceilings are tall in the apartment, too. Crown moldings of a dark wood line the ceiling, and the dark wooden floors are worn but sturdy. A few scratches here and there, but still glossy and shiny.

I bring my bag to the living room, walking over to the gray couch and settle in.

There's no TV. Going to have to fix that.

Unzipping my bag, I pull out my laptop, setting it on the glass coffee table in front of me. I told Mr. Hyde that I wouldn't obsess, that I wouldn't worry or head back down my dark path.

But I *have* to check.

I push the top of my laptop open, pressing the small button to turn it on.

The screen lights up and I log in, heading straight toward my email. I use a neighbor's internet that doesn't have a password, knowing I'm going to have to get my own soon if I want something reliable.

Heading straight to my email, I log on and click the inbox button. My email loads, hundreds of emails popping up. All unread. I've stayed away from the media and the press, knowing they're fucking vultures that will do anything to get a story out of you.

I know what Brandy did. Lonnie told me how she sold out the entire story of my breakdown to the media, painting me in a bad light and making me look like a fucking douchebag drug addict. My manager says I should sue her for breaching her contract and the fucking non-disclosure that's put in place for every worker to keep our lives discreet, but I didn't want the hassle. If she wants to be a bitch, then she can be a bitch. I'm done with her.

I scroll down, looking only for one name. I scroll through all six months' worth of emails, and go even a little longer, my heart sinking the further I go.

Nothing.

After all this time, she still hasn't reached out to me. It's been four years, and I haven't heard a peep from her. You'd think she would've reached out to at least say hello.

Does she know that I've been in treatment for half of a year? *Is she even okay?*

The thoughts and worry make sweat dot along my neck. I wipe it away, considering reaching out to her parents to see if they've heard from her.

I don't do that, though, because I made a promise to Mr. Hyde. I need to give her space. I need to give her time. If our destinies are as aligned as I believe they are, she'll come back to me.

She has to.

CHAPTER TWENTY-FOUR

Luna
2000

I sit in the forest, taking a break from my work and eating a fresh avocado. These things here are delicious, growing to be the size of my head. No one understands how good actual fresh fruits are. Go to Hawaii, you can have anything you want. Double the size. Double the flavor.

Juice dribbles down my lips, and I wipe it away with the back of my hand. *I made it to Hawaii.*

I live in a small hut, almost like a cabin, with a ton of other people that are here for the same purpose. To live in paradise and not have to worry about the stresses around us.

I get to live near the ocean, I get to live near the forest, I get to live near the mountains. I can choose to do anything that I want on any given day, and all it takes is a small trip and I can do what I want.

I've made a few friends out here, but after what happened in Santa Cruz, I've mostly just kept to myself.

The owners of the ranch are an older couple, Hawaiians that don't care too much for small talk. Most of the locals are the same here. They don't really care for tourists. They keep to their side of the island, and the tourists keep on the other side. The locals call it *the other side of the world.* I've traveled there once or twice, more out of curiosity than anything else.

It's beautiful there. It's beautiful everywhere, actually. Chickens roam free throughout the land. I wake up in the mornings to them talking to each other, their clucking loud and off tune. It makes me smile, and I love waking up in the mornings to watch them roam around the island.

I've only gotten in touch with my parents once since I got here. After I got off the plane, I walked here, worried that the job opportunity wouldn't even still be available. Luckily for me, they've been doing this for years, needing all the help they can get in the fields, in the gardens; anywhere they need help, we're put to work. Most of it is outside, full of manual labor that makes my body ache in places it's never ached before.

But living here has rejuvenated me, and I finally feel a little bit alive again. Not fully, and a part of me doesn't know if I'll ever be whole again. But that's okay, because I'm learning to live again. Learning to be me. How can someone be unhappy while living for free in Hawaii? It's impossible.

I think about Neil and Trish a lot. I'm not sure where they ended up, or what happened to Neil at the hospital. I also wonder what happened to Willie, as fleeting as my thoughts are, I hope he's okay, wherever he is.

I drop the shell of the avocado, wiping my sticky hands on my legs. Standing up, I walk through the dense, green trees and back out into the field. I've been growing a lot of kale, cherry tomatoes, and papaya lately. But my absolute favorite place to be is in the flower garden. There's a peace in watching a flower bloom from absolutely nothing into something so pure and spectacular. Nurturing it from a seed, taking care of it over time, watching it blossom under the bright sun.

There's absolutely nothing like it.

It's almost the end of the day, and tomorrow there's a big festival at the other end of the world. The owners of the farm invited us, and since we're never actually invited to any local events, we jumped on it instantly.

I wave to some of the other workers, kneeling down next to the vegetable garden. My knees turn brown in the dirt, and I slide on my gloves, going back to work.

My eyes open to the sounds of clucking outside. My legs slide across my white sheets, and I plant my feet on the cool wooden floor, stretching my arms over my head. The owners expect us to be up with the sun. So of course, on a weekend, my body just automatically wants to get up when the first chicken of the day starts clucking.

I slide on some shorts over my underwear and step outside, shielding my hand over my eyes as I watch the sun start to rise across the ocean. I head toward the beach, the sand cool against my feet after sitting under the dark sky all night. The tide has just lowered, so most of the sand is wet. Each footstep creates a footprint against the sand. I walk until the water covers my ankles, the cold waves crashing against my skin.

It's beautiful here.

How someone can feel so lost and so found is beyond me. This isn't home. It never has been, and unfortunately, it never will be. I know this, and I knew it the moment I stepped off the plane.

The long plane ride from California to here was torturous. My mind couldn't get off the fact that Roman has a girlfriend. For all I know, they could be engaged by now. She could be pregnant.

Just that thought alone makes my chest heave. My spine curls over in pain, my foot stepping forward on a particularly sharp rock as I catch myself from planting straight into the ocean.

Everyone watched me on that plane. No matter how hard I tried to hide my face against the window or bury my head in my hands as I tried to quell my tears, they wouldn't stop. The agony in my chest was excruciating, and if I were to be honest, that pain hasn't really lessened over time.

I've just grown numb.

I know at some point I'll go home. This is just another pit stop in my life. Another place I'm trying to find myself. The thing is, I know there's nothing to be found. Since the day I left, I knew who I was, it's just taken a while for me to figure it out.

I figure my time here must be coming close to the end. It's hard to leave a place this beautiful, though. Serene. Complete paradise. I've been living in my head for months, not having anyone to talk about things with.

I've spoken with Nora once. My mom passed her email along to me, so I was able to make one and reached out to her. It was brief, and I know she wanted to know more, but to tell her about my journey over email didn't seem right.

The water is cold this morning as it crashes against my ankles. The palm trees blow against the wind, my long hair flowing against my back and hitting my waist. I've barely cut it over the years, only trimming it when the ends grow frayed. I try to tell myself I don't keep it long because of him, but I know that's a lie.

I do everything because of him. I breathe air into my lungs because of him. It doesn't matter if he's across the world or if he has a ring on someone else's finger. He might not be mine, but I'll always be his. We may not be together ever again. Maybe I'll end up alone for the rest of my life, but Roman Hall has a part of my soul, and I don't ever believe he'll give it back to me.

I stay in the water until my feet are numb from the cold, then walk out, the sand sticking to the soles as I walk across the beach. I head back to my cabin, grabbing an avocado from a large basket sitting in front of the main house. This little area that I live and work in is smack-dab in the middle between where the tourists and the locals live. I call it the edge of the world, since I live neither on one side nor the other. There is a larger house, which is where the owners of the farm live, and they have small cabins and huts surrounding the main house, which are where all the workers sleep. Some end up bunking together, but I was lucky enough to end up in a one-bedroom cabin. The main house is almost hotel-like, with a kitchen and living area. Like a bed and breakfast of sorts.

Behind the main house and all the cabins, is the field where we work. None of us have to travel far, only feet from our house and we can begin our day.

Since today is the weekend, I have the entire day to pass until the party over on the local's side tonight.

With my oversized avocado in hand, I walk through the field, making sure to not step on any fruits or vegetables that I'm working so hard to grow, and into the forest. I find my spot near the oversized tree, with a trunk so large it's as wide as four trees at home. The tree has changed over time, and now the bottom slopes toward the ground. As the earth settled and the roots shifted, it created a curved chair, perfect for me. I've found this is my favorite spot, shaded from the sun, still close enough that I can hear the waves of the ocean if I listen closely. It's a spot I've spent most of my free time. Thinking, talking, listening to the earth around me. It's *my* place.

I settle in, slouching down and closing my eyes. The sides of the tree curl around me, and I burrow in, letting sleep take me once again.

I wake up to the feeling of a tickle on my leg. I twitch, the avocado falling from my palm and rolling onto the ground with a *thump*. I sit up, looking down and see a huge centipede the size of my palm crawling around my ankle. It's thin, but the legs are long, each one slapping against my skin as it walks up my leg. It's dark brown with orangish legs, and as my eyes widen, I swear I see it look directly at me.

Oh, shit.

I scream, shaking my foot and getting up, running as quickly as I can out of the forest, completely forgetting about my avocado. I've seen them before, but I've never had one *on me* before. I've never touched one, and I've never fucking wanted to, either.

I shiver the entire way out of the forest, slapping at my skin as a constant tickly feeling racks my spine.

Fuck, fuck, fuck. No, just no.

Once I'm out of the forest, my body calms, although I still scratch and slap at my legs as I walk back through the field. Looking up at the sky, I see the sun tilting toward the west. *Shit, I must have slept the entire morning away.*

The party will be starting soon.

I head back to the house and see the other workers loading into the back of a truck. They wave to me, and I put up a finger, telling them to give me a minute. I rush into my room, changing out of my shorts and shirt for a creamy dress. I run a brush through my hair, the humidity today making it a little wavier than it usually is.

I walk into the bathroom, looking at my pink-tinged cheeks. After all these years in the sun, my skin still hasn't turned as bronzed as everyone else's. I still have my palish hue. Although, it now looks like I have a permanent tint of blush on my cheeks and nose. A dusting of freckles has also popped up along my skin, dotting along my nose and the apples of my cheeks like tiny sprinkles.

I brush my hands over my face, running my fingers through my hair before heading out. These people don't wait around for long. If I take much longer, I'll be walking to the other side of the island.

When I step outside, they turn on the truck, and one of the older gentlemen holds his hand out. I grab it, his palms rough from work. He helps me onto the bed of the truck. There is sand, grass, and seed all along the floor. The grainy seeds stick to the bottom of my bare feet, and I run my palm along the bottoms, brushing them off.

The ride is bumpy, and some of the long-timers chat with each other on the ride over. I don't, because shouting across the blowing wind doesn't sound appealing. Instead, I watch the landscape, the hills, the mountains, the forest. I watch all of it. The ocean expands forever, somehow much bluer than the California waters. Where those waters were a dark blue, almost black in some places in California, the water in Hawaii is a bright blue, almost green. Like the rare, teal gemstones that I would find in Arizona.

I pull my hair over my shoulder as the wind whips my dark strands around my head. I grab a handful, securing it against my neck as we drive, and soon enough, we're pulling off the highway.

People with leis walk around. Groups with drums and other instruments, men and women dancing in the streets; it's a festival for as far as I can see. There are booths set up with games and food and little things to buy, and as the truck rolls down the street and swerves around this person and the next, the scents of authentic island foods swirl through the air and into my nose. The most colorful outfits are on display; men, women, children, everyone is out to enjoy the celebration.

The truck parks, and we all hop off the bed. Some of them stick together as they go to explore, while others head off in their own directions. I wander around, going by myself and checking out each booth.

I spend hours wandering around aimlessly. I take my time at the booths, picking up the different dishes that are homemade and deliciously hot. By the time the sun has set, lanterns are set on the streets and people are dancing as others walk around and play the drums. I'm incredibly full and all I can do is sit down next to a colorful building and watch the locals have the time of their lives.

This. This is bliss.

A smile breaks out on my face when I see a young girl and boy dance in the middle of the street, their swimsuits on as they run around and chase each other. It reminds me of Roman and I when we were little. Chasing each other. Soulmates before we knew what soulmates were. Best friends. I loved him then, even when I didn't want to. When I thought boys were gross and didn't want anything to do with them, Roman was always there. We both knew we were meant to be.

We were.

Are we still?

Life is cruel, and as I watch these kids, with a brightness lit in their eyes as they stare at each other, I just hope they don't end up with the same fate Roman and I went through.

"Luna?"

The voice shocks me out of my thoughts, and I turn around, coming face to face with the last person I wanted, or expected, to see.

There stands Willie, with his bag slung over his shoulder. He looks like he just stepped off the plane and walked straight to this party.

I stand up, straightening the skirt of my dress. I'm glad it drapes all the way to my toes, so he won't be able to see how badly my legs are trembling.

"Willie? What are you doing here?"

He shakes his head, his blond locks full dreads now. His eyes are a little lazy, a little unfocused, even as they burn down on mine. "I should be asking you the same thing. I thought you went home."

I bite my lip, hearing the accusation in his tone. He wanted me. He didn't want me to leave, and I left anyway. "I was going to, but plans changed."

He eyes narrow slightly, like he doesn't believe me.

"What about you?" I ask after a beat of awkward silence. "I have to say, it's kind of a coincidence," I laugh, nervousness filling my stomach.

He shrugs. "Doing what we've always talked about. Coming to Hawaii." He takes a step toward me. "Why did you leave me like that in the hospital? Why didn't you wait for me?"

I take a step back, the heel of my foot hitting a small crate. I look down, pushing it out of my way as I shuffle back. "I was going home. After everything that happened, I wanted to go home. I… I wasn't in a good spot. After what was happening to Neil—wait, what ever happened to Neil?"

His eyes darken, nearly turning black as he stares at me. "Neil is dead."

My eyes widen, my stomach dropping to my feet and my body breaking out in a chill. "What? How?"

"He killed himself in the hospital. He couldn't come out of his trip."

I shake my head, so fucking broken that another one of our friends is dead. "What about Trish?"

He shrugs. "She went home right after that. Didn't want to stick around."

"What about you? Where did you go?"

"I decided to stick around in Santa Cruz for a while."

My eyes narrow, already knowing where this is going. My blood cools, and I feel a betrayal at his decisions. How could he do that to Neil? "You went back to Crow?"

He nods, his face blank of all emotions.

"You went back to him? After what he did to your friend? What he meant to do to me?" My voice is raised, drawing the attention of some of the locals. I turn my back to them, lowering my voice to a quiet whisper, "How could you do that to Neil?"

He leans forward, his face only inches away from mine. His breath floats into my face, smelling of smoke and a grossness that makes me want to gag. "Because everyone left me, and I had no one to turn to. My girl left me, and my best friend died. What else could I have done? I had no one, I had nothing. I was eight hours away from San Diego. There was nothing for me to do!"

I take a step back, afraid of the heat, the anger that's boiling beneath his surface.

"So, how'd you get here?" I ask after a beat.

"I earned some money over the last year." He reaches into his pocket, grabbing the small dark dropper that's part of my worst dreams. Tilting his head back in the middle of the street, he drops two liquid drops on his tongue. Tilting his head up, he smiles at me. "Want some?"

I blink at him, shocked at his audacity. Horrified that he'd do that after his greatest friend committed suicide for being on the same drug. "You have no shame, do you?" A gust of wind hits, causing my hair to blow in front of my eyes. We stare at each other, and it takes me a minute before I can catch my bearings. My hand reaches forward, pulling the hair from my face and I turn around, ready to walk away from him for good.

That snaps him into action.

He grabs onto my bicep, pulling me back around. "Where are you going?"

"I'm heading back to my house. Not really in the mood to party anymore." I attempt to pull out of his hold, but that only makes his grip tighter. "Let go of me."

"Wait. Stop. What did I do? What's wrong?" A mixture of sadness and anger hits his eyes.

I shake my head. "It's nothing. I just want to be alone." I pull my arm back, but his hand comes with it.

"Where did I go wrong? Where did we go wrong? Didn't you have good times with me?"

I smile. It's sad, a little broken. "We had good times, Willie. But that's all it was. It was fun while it lasted."

"Why can't we try again? I can do better. I can be better for you now. We're finally at our destination. Where we always meant to land."

I shake my head, not sure when his mind got so skewed and why he thinks there is a *we* in this equation at all. "Willie." I pull my hand out, firmer this time. And this time he lets me. "I told you back in California why we won't work. I mean that. Every word I said, it was the truth. You *don't* want me. I'll never be able to love *you*." I look around, smiling at the happiness and peace surrounding me. "But there are some awesome people here, and I'm sure you'll find some beautiful women to spend your time with." Willie is attractive. Like, top-of-the-line hot. He has all the dips and muscles that a man should have. It's unfortunate that my heart has been given to someone else. But that's how my soul works. I only see one man. It was useless to pretend otherwise.

He takes a step back, another flash of that darkness slipping into his eyes. "Whatever you say, Luna." He walks off, not sparing me another glance.

A chill breaks off on my spine, and I walk the other way, checking over my shoulder constantly to make sure he's not following me.

It felt like he was a completely different person. He's not the man I first met. While being on the road changes people, it seems that it changed Willie for the worse. He used to be an easygoing guy, somewhat like Roman in that regard. I think that's what pulled me toward him, his happiness. His outgoing nature that everyone gravitated to.

Now I feel like there's a darkness around him. A darkness that I want nothing to do with. We have been through a lot, and he sunk deep into the evil. He's not a good man. Not anymore.

I don't see him the rest of the night, and I eventually catch up with the rest of the workers, hopping in the back of the truck. I let out a sigh of relief once the truck starts moving, and I watch the lights of the party fade off into the distance. I hope this is the last time that I see him, but a part of me knows it won't be. Maui isn't huge, and he isn't a local, which means we'll probably end up crossing paths again.

It takes a while for us to get back, and I lean against the side of the truck, the salty air and the rocking making me tired. My eyes grow droopy, and I do my best to stay awake.

I'm grateful when we arrive home, and I'm the first one off, waving to everyone as I head into my house. I slip inside, climbing straight into bed with my clothes still on. I pull the sheets up to my neck, burrowing my head into the pillow. Sleep comes quickly, and I'm pulled down into my dreams.

I hear the waves before I see them. I'd know the sound anywhere. It's not the gentle lapping like in California, and it's not the loud crashing like in Hawaii. The waves that I hear are angry, aggressive as they pound against the side of the cliff. My eyes slide open, and here I am.

It's been a while.

It's been since California, I realize. I haven't dreamed about my cliff in over a year, and for an odd moment, I feel at home. This place where I've spent much of my nights through my childhood to adulthood. It's dark out now, and I don't think I've ever been here at night. I can't even see the water, only darkness as I look over the edge. I can hear them below, and can imagine them now, sliding up the edge of the rock, each wave competing to reach higher than the next. The waves turning white from their aggressive force.

I can barely see anything because it's so dark, but looking up, I see the stars. So many of them reflecting down on me, giving me the only light I'll get. That and the moon, which is only a small crescent tonight, a sliver in the sky, placed delicately between the stars.

I take a step toward the edge of the cliff. Only a small one, but I can feel the soft sand beneath my feet. The soft sand that isn't sand at all. I've walked barefoot for years, and I know what sand from each part of the earth feels like. This isn't it. It's softer, almost powder-like as it disintegrates beneath my feet. I stop as the wind picks up, howling in the distance. It sounds like a whistle, and I take a step backward, feeling the sand pick up and swirl around my feet. It lifts higher, reaching my ankles, my waist, traveling across the skin on my arms and around my neck.

I feel like I could lean back into the air and the sand would lift me off the ground. I feel like it would carry me away from here, anywhere, if I really wanted. A gust of wind pulls me forward, and I don't fight it. I'm not sure why, maybe because I know this is all a dream. I've been through this before. I've danced to this tune. I know that no matter what I do, I'll always end up going over the cliff.

The wind pulls me toward the edge, with each inch the air turning colder and colder. It's freezing by the time my toes curl around the edge. My heart races. The hair on the back of my neck stands on end. I don't fight it. I let the sand wrap around me, creating a thin coating across my skin. It pulls me, bowing my body. My toes press into the rocks, just as I had years ago in ballet. My spine arches, my form bent so perfectly, but it's not enough.

All it takes is one small gust, and it happens. I fall over the edge. I keep my toes pointed, and my eyes closed. And I let the world swallow me whole.

I wake up, sweat dripping down my temples as a shiver racks my body. It feels so real. Every single time, it feels like I'm there. I can still feel the sand against my feet. I can still feel the chill of the air against my skin. Why didn't I try to get away this time? Why did I let the wind take me? It's almost like I wanted it to.

Not only that, but this time I was still in my dream when I fell. Usually, the moment I fall over the cliff, I wake up. Not this time. I could feel the wind blast my face as I descended toward the ocean below me.

Tap, tap, tap.

The tapping on my door makes me freeze in place. My breathing stops, and I can barely blink as I listen.

What was that?

"Luna? You in there?" Dread pools into my stomach at the sound of Willie's voice. I hold my breath, hoping he thinks he has the wrong place and walks away. But I can feel him out there, his intoxicated heavy breaths. The sand underneath his shoes crunching and swishing along the ground outside as he steps from foot to foot.

I get out of bed, tiptoeing to where the small bathroom is. If I can get out of here without him noticing me, I can run to the owner's house and let them know he's been following me. They don't like crime and they don't appreciate shit

297

happening on their island. He'll be on the next plane out.

That's if I get out of here first.

The wood creaks beneath my feet, and I wince, pulling my mouth into an O as I let out little bits of air. After a second, I move, rushing off to the bathroom. I slide open the window, the wood creaking against its hinge as it's pushed up. The front door opens just as the window fully opens. I can hear him in the front of my cabin, his shoes creaking on the wood. A gust of wind slaps me in the face, and I take in a shaky breath, fear pounding in my ears.

"Luna, what're you doing?" Willie's voice is slurred, hurried.

I jump through the window, literally diving through headfirst. The edge of the window scrapes my hip, and I whimper when I feel it cut through my skin.

"Come here!" I glance up, seeing Willie sticking his hand out the window to grab me. It waves back and forth, looking for a connection to my skin. When he can't reach me, his arm slinks back inside, and I can hear his feet as they pound across my house. That gets me moving. I put my hands on the grass, pushing myself up to run. I move as fast as I can, my bare feet pumping against the cold grass. I hear my door slam open, the knob knocking against a wall. As I look over my shoulder, I see Willie sprinting toward me.

He's bigger. Faster. Stronger. A whimper leaves my throat as I run as fast as I possibly can toward the house.

Willie cuts me off.

My feet cut left, toward the beach. He's stunted by my change, my quickness. He follows me, though, right on my heels. My feet punch the sand, instantly slowing me down with the density. I kick sand behind me, trying to get as much distance as I can. But it's useless.

He's here.

I feel my dress being pulled back, tight around my stomach. Then I'm halted, and I trip, falling against the ground. Sand shoots in the air, slapping against my skin and into my face. Willie falls on top of me, pinning my hands above my head.

"Why are you doing this?" I cry, my tears mixing in with the sand. The tide is higher, so close to my hands at this point. If I reached out another few inches, I'd touch the wet, cold sand.

"Why do you have to run? Why are you always running from me, Luna, huh? What did I ever do to you? Why can't you just be with me?"

"Please. *Please.*" I try to get up, but it's useless. My face falls to the sand, the grains hitting my lips. I bite down, the crunchiness of the sand getting between my teeth. "Please let me go. Please, Willie, I beg you," I sob, feeling useless. *Helpless.*

"How can I let you go, Luna? *I love you,*" he croons against me, his body lowering over mine. The weight of his body pinning me against the ground makes it hard to breathe. I gasp in air, wishing someone would see me. Wishing someone could help me.

"Please, Willie," I cry, "Please, oh my God. Help me. Someone, help me." My cries are whispers, my voice choked from his weight. His breath is heavy against the back of my neck, blowing my hair into the sand, across my face. It only makes it harder to breathe.

"Why can't you love me? I just want you to love me. Don't you think it's fate? Me coming here and the first thing I see is you? There has to be a reason for it." His hand yanks on my dress, pulling it up around my calves. His hand falls to my skin, the heat of him making nausea build in my stomach. He trails his hand up, sliding it on the inside of my thigh. Between my legs.

"I'm sorry. Please don't. *Please, please, please*, Willie. I won't tell anyone. Just let me go. Please. *I don't want this.*"

His fingers press against my heat, grasping my panty-covered sex, squeezing tight. "You don't want this? After all our years together? What was I? Just someone to pass the time? This has been mine for years." He squeezes again, and I swallow down a gag.

No, it hasn't. It's never been yours. It will never *be yours.*

He starts pulling on my panties, yanking them down my thighs. I pin my legs together, but it's no use. He's much bigger than me, much stronger. I can feel the cool air between my legs, my dress bunched around my waist.

In the middle of the night. In the middle of the dark. In paradise. And he will take me. Even if I don't want it.

I wish for peace. I wish for the waves to roll over me and carry me out to the sea. I'd rather drown than have this.

I'd rather have *anything* than have this.

I can hear rustling on top of me, and then he's there. Pressing against me. Pushing between my legs. My hands reach forward, clutching the sand, squeezing it between my fingers. The sand packs beneath my fingernails until I feel pressure. It hurts. It hurts between my legs. My chest hurts. My entire body hurts.

My heart hurts.

Whatever was left of my already fractured soul shatters, floating into the ocean, far, far away from me.

I feel empty. I feel numb.

It burns as he sinks in, grunting above me. His breath is hot against the back of my neck. It feels like the centipede, slithering across my skin. I squeeze my eyes shut, hating the feeling of him inside of me. *I don't want this.* Yet he doesn't care.

"Doesn't this feel good?" he grunts behind me. "It almost feels like it did in Santa Cruz, huh? Underneath the stars. High on acid?"

My body tenses.

It tenses so stiffly that he pauses on top of me, but only for a second. Then he settles back in, continuing his slow pumping. "Oh, yeah. That's right. You were passed out last time. Sleeping on the forest grass while I fucked you. People watched, too. They enjoyed it. Seeing you. Your beauty. You're so *fucking beautiful*, Luna."

I bite my lip until blood leaks between my teeth, dripping into the sand.

He defiled me. Like a fucking animal.

He raped me then.

He's raping me now.

He keeps pumping, unaware of my boiling body beneath him. He thinks I've submitted to him. He thinks I've given up.

My hand swings back, my knuckles hitting him directly in the nose. He flings back, letting out a shout. But that's all I need.

I shove to my knees, flying to my feet. And I'm off. Sprinting into the water. No destination in mind. I just need to get away. Get as far away from him as I possibly can.

I dive into the waves, my dress pooling around me in the cold, as I slice through the black water.

Sounds are muted.

Smells are muted.

The world is muted beneath the water. I open my mouth.

And I scream.

Bubbles float up from my mouth as I sink to the ground, pure horror filling every inch of me. I only have a moment, though, because in the next, my hair is pulled, and I'm yanked to the surface.

"Bitch," he gasps, his wet face dripping with water. "Why the fuck did you do that for?" Blood mixes with water as it dribbles down his face, spilling out of his nose in a constant flow.

I put my feet against his stomach, pushing off from him. His hand is tangled in my hair, and the threads break from my scalp. I let out a scream, falling back under the water.

Then he does it.

His hand goes to my neck, grasping the chain that is as much a part of me as my heart is, and *he pulls.*

I feel the clasp release on the back of my neck, and my eyes shoot open under the water. I can barely see Willie, the dark night and the dark waters making him only an outline, but I can see my gold chain as it floats in the water in his grip. I rush toward it, my tears mixing with the salty water as I swim after him.

No. No, please, no.

His arm reaches out, grappling for my waist. I reach for the ends of my necklace, and my fingers wrap around the gold that shines in the dark. I clasp the slippery pieces, and I pull. *Hard.*

It yanks around Willie's neck, right below his chin, and his hand releases from my waist, searching for relief. He tries to pull the chain away from his neck, his fingers attempting to wrap around the necklace. I have it so tight, though, that his fingers can't slide beneath the gold.

My feet go up his back, and I pull with all my might.

I'm losing air. Barely able to hold on. But I do, pulling as hard as I can, worried about the chain snapping from the force, feeling him struggle beneath me, still attempting to pull the necklace away from his neck. He tries, but he can't get a grip.

I hold on.

A sob rips from my chest, my ribs heaving as he loses his strength. I can feel the life leaving his body, and I keep holding on.

Then he grows heavy. The struggle stops. He starts dropping to the floor of the ocean. I pull on the chain, releasing his body as I swim to the surface, and stop as I'm yanked back.

What?

I pull on the chain again, but it's stuck on something. I yank as hard as I can, but it's impossible.

Again, my arms pull back as I try to release the chain from whatever it's stuck on. No air is left in my lungs. I can feel them contracting, screaming for air. My face must be a dark, deep purple. The pressure is building, and the tears won't stop flowing from my burning eyes. I pull once more, but it's no use. I look to the surface, and with a gut-wrenching sob, my fingers loosen around the ends of the necklace. I release my chain, swimming to the surface.

As soon as I breach the top of the water, a guttural scream leaves me.

"*Noooooooooooooo!*" I sob, kicking my feet to keep me in place. My body is freezing, the night water cold and vicious around me.

I can barely see the sand of the beach in front of me, and I know I should swim to land. I'm tired. Depleted of everything.

But I can't leave my necklace. I look below me and see nothing but water. So much water. It's black. Black as the night.

With a huge breath, I dive back under, my hands pushed out in front of me. Feeling for gold. Feeling for a body. Anything. I swim to the bottom, my fingers brushing the sand. I feel around, but I'm exhausted, and there's nothing. There's no one. Nothing besides rocks and shells. And sand. So much sand.

With a cry, I put my feet on the ground, pushing off and swimming for the surface. Another sob leaves me when I break through the water, my body feeling ripped in half.

I can't leave without it.

I take another deep breath, diving under again. Suddenly, I'm pulled to the side, a vicious rip current swallowing me and pulling in different directions. I kick as hard as I can, attempting to pull myself out of it, but I have no energy left to fight. The water is too strong. The force of the ocean is too aggressive as it whiplashes me from one direction to the next. But I don't stop, kicking, my arms waving with all my might, my exhausted limbs screaming in pain.

The waves keep swirling. My legs give out, finally having enough, and I swirl around, almost like a tornado, pushed to the bottom of the ocean. I can't fight it, it's too much. It's too strong.

My body bows, my feet pointed, and I float to the bottom, out of my fight.

Out of my energy. Darkness pulls me down, and I feel like I'm losing life. I can feel it draining out of me with every second that passes.

Is this it? Is this the end?

I don't want this to be the end. I don't want to die.

Roman, please don't let me die. This isn't the end. It can't be.

My butt hits the sand, and I'm pushed from side to side as the rip current keeps fighting against me. My eyes start to close, my lungs pummeling against my chest, begging for air. I'm about to open my mouth, gasp in water, when the wave pushes against me, shoving me off the ground and up toward the surface.

My arms windmill, my legs automatically kicking. My eyes open, and I look around me, expecting hands. Expecting anything, really, but there's no one. Nothing. Just darkness and water. Pushing me toward the surface.

I break through the water, gasping in mouthfuls of air. I cough, wiping my eyes with my fingers as my legs kick to keep me afloat.

"Hey! Hey, are you okay? Help is coming!" A man shouts from the shore.

I wave at him, wanting to ask him for help, but not having the energy. My hands cup the water in front of me, and I float on my side, hoping the riptide doesn't come back and sweep me out into the ocean. I'm able to make it close enough that the guy and one other person rush into the water, grabbing me around the biceps and pulling me to shore.

"What are you doing out there? Do you have a death wish? You're lucky you're alive!" The older man shouts.

The moment my feet hit the ground, I collapse, my knees and palms slamming against the sand. I curl my fingers beneath it, clutching it to me.

It was Roman. He helped me.

I know without a doubt, somehow, it was him.

"I want to go home," I sob. "I just want to go home."

"Okay, okay." The men help me up just as more people rush out with a blanket and flashlights. I hear an ambulance in the distance, but I don't want any of that.

I just want to go home.

My hand goes up to my bare neck, bare for the first time since I was a child. I look over my shoulder just as a blanket is draped over me. "My necklace is out there," I mumble. To them. To no one. I don't know. I just want it back.

"Well, it's probably swept way out to sea by now, sweetheart. Sorry to tell you, but you probably aren't going to see it again."

My head dips, and another cry breaks from my chest. My hands drop from my neck and go to the front of the blanket, holding it tightly against my chest. The ambulance arrives, and I'm ushered into the back of the truck. Lights flash in my eyes, and I'm hooked up to I don't know how many different things as they check to make sure I'm okay.

They ask me a million questions, but I don't remember any of them.

"I just want to go home," is all I could say on repeat.

"I think she's in shock," one of the men says.

"Miss, would you like to go to the hospital?" the paramedic asks, flashing a light in both my eyes.

I shake my head. "I just want to go home." I can't stop my eyes from glancing to the water, wishing I would see my necklace float on top of the waves. But it never does. It's gone.

Forever.

After another handful of questions, I'm cleared to not need a hospital visit. They drive off, and the men surround me, looking at me curiously.

"What were you doing out there, anyway?" The man cocks his head to the side, half looking at me like I'm crazy, half curious.

I open my mouth, about to tell him I was attacked, but the words won't come. I hope Willie stays out there, gets buried in the sand and swallowed by the waves. I hope he stays out there forever, drowning in the darkness.

I shake my head, "Nothing. I was just taking a swim."

They all shake their heads at me, and I know how stupid that is. That's the number one rule—to not go swimming in the ocean like that. Never alone. Never at night.

"Do you need anything?" One of them asks me.

"I'd actually like to use the computer quickly. To schedule a flight home."

They nod, letting me in the main building. It's not usually allowed after-hours, since the owners sleep upstairs and don't like the disturbance. But under these circumstances, they must think it's okay.

I head to the main living area, wrapping the scratchy blanket around me as I sit in the chair. It takes a few minutes to power on the computer, my eyes zoning out as I wait. My fingers float to my neck, feeling the nakedness of my skin. Feeling somewhat empty. So much alone.

Lost.

The screen lights up, and I squint against the bright light. My eyes pound against my skull. My fingers go to the keyboard as I log onto my email. They're tired, weak. It takes extra force, extra muscles to press down each square, plastic key. Once my email is loaded, I search through my inbox, finding the one phone number I'm looking for.

Lifting up the phone next to the computer, I press in the numbers, biting my lip when the phone starts ringing. Nerves fill my stomach, and my hand that's holding the phone starts shaking.

"Hello?" comes a sleepy voice. My heart drops into my stomach from the familiar voice. I want to press rewind and play it on repeat, but I can't.

"Nora?" My voice cracks, and I swallow down my sad sigh. *What am I doing here? Why did I ever leave?*

"L-Luna?" Sounding much more awake this time, and instantly emotional. "Oh my God. What's wrong? Is everything okay?"

I shake my head even though she can't see it. I have to bite my lip to stop the sob that wants to break free. It tickles my chest, my entire body jerking from keeping my cries silent. "Do you have your brother's phone number?"

She's quiet for a second before she lets out a sob on the other end of the phone, and it instantly makes me start crying. My cry breaks from my chest, my chin dipping down, tears rolling down my cheeks as emotion overtakes me. My chest aches, and I bring my free hand to rub the pain away.

I don't know if Roman is still dating that girl. I don't know if they're married, or have kids, or if he's in the middle of a tour. All I know is that he saved me in that ocean whether he knows it or not, and he's the one I want to see right now.

Once Nora calms down enough to speak, she tells me to hold on. I nod, wiping my face while I listen to her sniffle on the other end of the line.

"Ready?" she asks, her voice clogged with tears.

I nod my head, grabbing a pen from the desk and a little yellow sticky note. "Ready," I whisper. I've never felt more ready in my entire life.

She gives me his number, each number building a weight in my heart, and asks, "Does this mean you're coming home?"

"I'm coming home." My voice breaks off at the end as I start crying again, and so does she. It's painful as the tears flow from my eyes, my chest aching with each breath I take.

"I'm never going to be able to fall back asleep now," she laughs, still in the midst of crying.

"I'll talk to you soon, okay? I really want to get out of here."

She pauses at this. "Is everything okay? Seriously?"

I bite my lip. "It will be."

"I love you," she says on a whisper.

"I love you, too."

We hang up, and I place the phone back in its holder, staring down at the phone number I scribbled, my handwriting shaky and barely legible. My fingers run over the pen marks, smudging the ink.

My heart races and slows down, like it knows something life-changing is about to happen. It's been so many years since I've talked to Roman. So many years since I've heard his voice. Has he thought about me? Does he miss me?

With a deep, shaky breath, I pick up the phone, pressing the buttons extra slow. My fingers tremble, and tears fill my eyes. I'm so excited, nervous, worried, hopeful, regretful. So many emotions fill my stomach, and I can't do anything besides breathe deeply.

And hope that he answers.

It rings. And rings. And continues to ring. I'm almost worried it's going to hit voicemail, that maybe I won't be able to reach him, after all.

Then the phone clicks.

"Hello?"

My mouth opens, a gasp coming out. It's *him.*

He sounds so much the same, but so different.

The letters of his name curl around my tongue, but nothing leaves my mouth. Nothing besides breath. Nothing besides love.

He doesn't say anything on the other line, listening to my heavy breaths as they come through the phone. Then I hear his sharp intake of breath, and I know.

He knows.

"Luna?" His voice comes out quiet, hushed.

I nod, still no words coming out of my mouth. My throat squeaks a little, and I can hear his heavy breath on the other line. Tears rush from my eyes, my cheeks drenched as his voice awakens a part of my soul that has been sleeping since he walked out of my room all those years ago.

"Luna, is that you?" he asks again, his voice rushed this time.

"It's me," I whisper.

He says nothing, his breathing labored. I imagine him sitting there, his eyes pinched closed. His fingers running through his hair as shock covers his face.

"Are you okay? Where are you?"

My mouth opens, and all that comes out is a cry.

I hear him groan on the other end of the line, pure agony ripping from his chest. "Please… *please*, Luna, don't cry. Please don't fucking cry." His voice is pained, ripping from his throat.

"I want to come home," I cry, not able to answer any of his questions. Because I'm not okay, not in the slightest. So much has happened. So fucking much in my life has changed.

"Home?"

"Yes. Please. I just want to come home." This time it's a sob that rips through my throat, and I can literally feel his pain coming through the phone. He hates my pain, just as much as I hate his.

We're connected. We always have been.

"I'm in New York," he says.

I blink, shocked. I guess I didn't even think of where he might be living again, and then suddenly, thoughts of his girlfriend come back to my mind. Of him possibly sliding a ring on another girl's finger. His voice rushes out, "I can get you a ticket home, to Wisconsin, if you want. Or I can get you a ticket to me. Whatever you want. I'll do it."

"You. I want you," is all I can say. I don't think about the girlfriend, or the fact that I might be walking into him with a baby on his hip. I need to see him, more than I need air. I need him more than anything else in this world.

I hear him move around. "Stay on the phone. I'll get you a ticket right now." I listen as his fingers fly across a keyboard, his mouse clicking. We don't speak, and I don't need to. My heart settles in my chest, maybe for the first time since I last saw him. It's like it knows everything will be okay. That this, now, is right.

"Where are you?" he asks.

My mouth opens, pain seeping from my lips with my words. "I'm in Hawaii. Maui." He says nothing and I know he can hear the agony in my words. He doesn't know what has happened to me, and he doesn't need to know the story to know I've been through hell.

"Okay. Can you get to the airport now? I can get you a plane out at about five a.m. there." I check the clock on the computer, seeing it's only two a.m.

"Yeah, I think so."

"Okay." More clicking, and then he lets out a deep breath. "Okay, you're good to go. I'll meet you at the airport."

My heart races at that, and I press my palm to my chest. "Okay," I whisper.

We say nothing, breathing through the phone.

So much to say.

So, so much to say to each other.

"I'll see you soon," is all he says instead.

"I'll see you soon." I'm about to hang up the phone when I hear him call out my name.

"Luna?"

"Yeah?" I clutch the phone to my hand, nerves, excitement, worry, everything swirling in my stomach at once. A riptide in the pit of my belly.

"I missed you," he says softly.

My face scrunches up, tears flooding my eyes instantly. They fall down my cheeks, dripping onto the blanket around me. "I missed you, too." I choke out.

I hang up, grabbing the Post-it Note and standing up, leaving the blanket on the chair. After shutting down the computer, I head to my cabin, ready to pack up and get out of there.

It's time to go home.

PART
Three

CHAPTER TWENTY-FIVE

Roman

People rush by me, the world spinning. Scents and sounds and colors fly by, but it's all a blur. It feels like I'm underwater or wearing headphones. The only thing I can focus on is my heaving breaths. I can feel my heart pounding against my chest, my black shirt twitching with each beat.

I look at every single person that walks by, their blurring figures only a blip in my sight. My eyes can't connect with one person. One glance, and I know it's not her. Then my eyes move on to the next person, and the next person.

I feel my shirt sticking to my back, my nervous sweat making me feel damp, my blood boiling beneath my skin.

I was getting ready for work, just out of the shower and getting dressed, when the phone rang. It could have been anyone. The station, my family, my asshole friends.

The very last person on the list I thought would be calling me is Luna.

Luna.

It's been so long. Years since I've heard her voice. Just my uttering her name made her break down. I couldn't take it. I couldn't take her sadness, the agony ripping through the phone. I wish I could have reached through and taken it from her. Lifted the sadness from her soul and pulled it through the phone. She sounded exactly the same. Her soft lilt, feminine and so melodic that I nearly fell to my knees.

Nothing could have prepared me for her call. I have no idea what she's been through. I don't know where she's been, or who she's been with. I don't know anything about her, honestly. But at the end of the day, I do. I know every single inch of her. I know her depth, what makes her tick. I know her inside and out.

I swallow down my groan as I look around, worry hitting me at the idea of her never making it on the plane. Fear that she changed her mind. I'll stand in this airport all day if I have to, waiting for that moment where I get to see her again.

I glance out the floor-to-ceiling windows, seeing the Delta plane descending from the west. I know, without a doubt, that's her plane. I can feel her getting closer. My heart starts to calm, like it's finally able to rest after all these years. My hearing clears, and the voices grow louder around me.

It's been a year since I got out of treatment. One year since I started working as a firefighter. Living in New York has been different. Not bad, but it's been missing one thing.

Luna.

This was our dream. Our dream to move to New York together. It's felt wrong being here without her.

A part of me is worried that this is only temporary for her. That she'll come, say hello, and leave again. But the other part of me knows that won't happen. That the moment she steps into my arms, I'll never let her go. Never again. It was foolish of me to walk away in the first place. To experience life without her is the same as not existing. I need her to live. She is my sustenance, the bits and pieces that make me, me. If it weren't for her, who would I be?

It took her whispers of saying she wanted to come home for everything to change. Just her pleading made me drop everything. I called my boss at work and told him I had a family emergency. He's easygoing, so he didn't mind me needing the time off.

I don't anticipate me being there tomorrow, either. I didn't tell him that, but once I get Luna back, I don't think I'll be able to be away from her. There's so much to talk about. So much to catch up on. I need her near me, as near to me as she can possibly be. I'll never get enough of her, and being away from her for so long, I don't anticipate that need being satiated any time soon.

Another flood of people start walking this way. I take a deep breath, blowing it out between my lips as I wait.

She's coming.

My skin starts to hum, and I know she's getting closer. It feels like electricity, like our souls are reconnecting. My insides pull, and I want to walk forward, but I keep my feet planted where they are. Just waiting. Everyone walks around me, the flood of people splitting on either side of me as they pass by. My fingers go up to my hair and pull, feeling uneasy. On edge, like I'm fraying. I can barely think. Can barely stand still.

Each step she takes toward me, my body starts to hum louder, until I can barely take another breath.

Then she appears.

I can see her gray eyes shining from across the room as she looks around, a plain pair of shorts tight around her thighs, making her legs look a mile long. A small backpack sits on her back, her fingers playing with the straps as she looks from left to right.

Her hair, just as long as it's always been, is draped in long, dark waves down her back.

She looks the same, but there's a weight of sorrow surrounding her, a sadness that I can feel from here. It tears my insides apart, watching the sadness drip from her. Luna isn't a sad girl; she never has been.

So, what happened to her?

I take a step forward, just as her eyes lock with mine. They widen, and she stops in her step. Her plain sandals slapping against her feet pause, her toes pressing into the ground just like the ballerina she's always been.

Her face crumples as she looks me over, pure sadness covering her features and darkening her eyes. I take another step, and that gets her moving. She walks toward me, slowly and carefully. I walk too, and we end up in the middle of the room, only steps from each other. Tears stream down her face, and my own eyes burn with emotion.

"Roman," she whispers. But even with all the noises around me, her voice rings straight into my soul. It ricochets around the cage of my chest, burning straight into my heart.

"Luna."

She drops her bag onto the ground, running the last few steps. My arms swing out, catching her around the waist and pulling her toward me.

Her body molds to mine, each curve of her sinking into every inch of me. She smells like the ocean, salty with a hint of Luna. I'll never forget how she smells. Girly, like she spends her days in the sand, outside, with the wind blowing in her hair. My hand goes up to the base of her skull, pressing her against my shoulder, her body trembling against mine.

I bury my face in her hair, inhaling in every inch of her. My fingers clench, her hair bunching between my fingertips. My throat feels like it's closing, and my sinuses burn. I wipe my face in her hair, feeling like it's too much. Our connection is too much. But I can't get enough of it.

"Roman," she cries against my shoulder.

I let out a shaky breath, not sure how to speak the words I'm feeling right now. Not sure how to articulate the emotions that are roaring through my body.

"I missed you," she cries, her tears wetting my neck. I grip her neck, pulling her back so I can see her face. Her cheeks are damp, reddened. Her gray eyes are bloodshot, and her bottom lip trembles, puckered out like she can't control her emotions.

My palms go to her cheeks, wiping her wet face. "You have no idea how much I missed you."

She wiggles, and I set her on the ground. She bends down to grab her bag, suddenly seeming shy.

I hold my hand out to her, not ready to let her go just yet. "Are you ready?"

She looks down at my palm, my large fingers waiting for her small ones. She reaches out, her skin is still so pale, even though the tip of her nose is red, like she's spent a lot of time in the sun. There are bags beneath her eyes, giving away the fact that she hasn't slept in a while.

Like maybe she hasn't slept since the last time she saw me.

That's how it's been for me, at least.

I grab the strap of her bag from her fingers, taking it from her hands. She smiles up at me, and I turn, pulling her through the crowds of people coming and going. I hold her tightly, and I can feel her fingers flexing against mine, as if she doesn't want to let me go either.

Once we're outside, I pull her toward my Jeep. I open the back door, tossing her bag into the back, and slam it shut. She stands with her hands at her sides as she looks at me. I walk up to her, pulling open the passenger-side door. She walks past me, her body brushing against mine. My hand wraps around her waist, and I lean in, needing to touch her again. Needing to smell her. It doesn't feel real. But if this is a dream, fuck, I never want to wake up.

"I can't believe you're here," I breathe in her hair, whispering in her ear. "This doesn't feel real."

Her hand reaches up, running along my jaw. Testing my stubble against her fingers. I haven't shaved in a few days, and it's new to her. She hasn't seen me since I was a teenager. "I'm here, Roman. I'm finally here." Dropping her hand, she slinks into her seat. I shut the door behind her, taking a moment to breathe in the New York air.

This is it. We're finally here. Together.

The drive home is silent. Not much is said. Luna spends her time looking out the window, at the place she's always dreamt of living. She watches all the taxis, the people, the noise, the tall buildings. Everything crammed into a small city.

I do nothing besides reach my hand out, grabbing her fingers that are draped over her lap, lacing my fingers through hers. Her skin is smooth and hot, as if the sun seeped into her body.

She glances over at me, her face a mixture of sadness and relief.

I'm here, I tell her by squeezing her hands. I don't say the words. I don't need to.

Her fingers squeeze back, ever so slightly. *I'm here, too*, she says.

Her eyes go back out the window, and I finish driving us the rest of the way back to my apartment. I park in the underground parking garage, grabbing her things and opening her door. "Ready?" I ask, holding her door open.

Her face twists, worry and indecision in her gray eyes. "Before we go up, I have to know, are you seeing anyone?"

I frown. *What the fuck?*

"No." I shake my head, disgusted by her question.

"Do you have any children?" Her voice squeaks out.

A snarl takes over my face, and I take a breath, so I don't snap on her. "Are you kidding me, Luna?"

317

She frowns. "It's a valid question."

"It's a fucking stupid question, is what it is." I reach in the car, pulling her out. She rocks on her feet, and I steady her, stepping into her bubble. Her hair is dried, a little messy. I push it off her shoulders, revealing her slim neck. "If you needed to ask, then you can ask. But you should know me enough, Luna. I've been waiting for you."

Her body relaxes, the tenseness draining, spilling onto the cement ground. It's dark down here in the parking garage, and every noise and step echoes. "You were that worried? I ask her, her body melded against mine.

She nods against my chest.

"I'm yours, Luna. My mind, my heart, my fucking soul. Every inch. Every breath. It's yours. Yesterday. Now. Tomorrow. Don't ever forget it." My shirt grows wet, and I know she's started crying again. "Come on, let me show you upstairs."

She nods, stepping out of my hold and wiping her face. We walk silently up to my room, using the elevator and walking down the hall. She stands behind me as I unlock the door, and I can feel her nerves heating my back.

She's nervous.

Why the hell is she nervous?

The door opens, and I cringe at the mess. In a hurry to get to the airport, I didn't have time to clean up. It's not like anyone comes over here, anyway. If the guys from the station have something going on, we usually go to one of their houses. Most of them are married, anyway, or are dating someone.

The few of the guys who aren't with anyone spend their weekends at bars. That shit isn't me anymore. That was me about four years ago. Not anymore. Work has been my life this last year. I've been biding my time. Waiting. Hoping. Dreaming.

And here she is.

"I'm sorry it's not much," I say, dropping her bag by the door and walking to the kitchen, grabbing trash from the counters and shoving it into the trash bin.

She stands by the door, her sandals next to her. She looks around, taking it all in, her gray eyes flitting from one piece of furniture to the next. She looks out the window, looking at the tall skyscrapers around her.

"Do you need anything right now? Are you hungry? Thirsty?" I look in my fridge, cringing when all I see is an old pizza box and a case of beer. I close the fridge, pulling out a stack of takeout menus. "I'll have to run to the store to get some food, but I can grab us some takeout if you're hungry?" I look over, my eyes widening when I see an empty space. Her bag and shoes are still there, but Luna isn't.

I step out into the front room, looking into the living room. "Luna?"

The menus drop to the floor, scattering all around me as I rush to the bathroom, hoping she's in there.

She's not.

The bathroom light is turned off, the door opened. Just how I left it.

"Luna?" My voice rises, hysteria making it crack. I burst into my room, stopping in the doorway. My hands clutch the wooden frame, feeling my heart stop.

She's wrapped in my blankets, her face buried in my pillow. Her black hair splays over the pillowcase, nearly falling over the side of the bed with how long it is. Her eyes are closed, like she's already asleep. But the crease between her eyes is present, creating a frown on her pale face.

I step into the room, wanting to confront her, wake her up and ask if she's okay. Demand answers from her. But I stop, not knowing what she's been through. Not knowing what made her contact me in the first place.

What happened to you, Luna?

I want to wrap her in my arms, feel her body mold against mine. Feel her heartbeat against my chest, see if our beats are still synchronized. I want her. I just want all of her. Every bit.

But I don't do those things. I walk over to my windows, shutting my blinds to darken my room. I walk out quietly, leaving the door opened.

I don't know what to do when I get to the living room. I think about heading to the grocery store, but I don't want her to wake up while I'm not here. I could order food, but I don't want to get something if she's not going to like it.

I walk to my couch, sitting down and grabbing the remote from the coffee table, switching on the TV.

And I wait.

CHAPTER TWENTY-SIX

Luna

I smell Roman.

All I smell is Roman.

I burrow deeper into the marshmallow pillows, never wanting to wake up. I'm so comfortable, so peaceful. I haven't felt this rested in so long.

Roman.

My eyes fly open, and I whip up in bed. Looking around, all I can see is his darkened room. Dark cherrywood furniture, very minimal. Not at all Roman. When we were children, the walls of his room were filled with posters of musicians and albums. There wasn't an inch of his wall showing. There isn't a picture, or a poster, or anything. Except…

I fold the sheets back, crawling on my hands and knees toward the edge of the bed. A lone picture frame sits on his dresser, propped right in the middle in front of his mirror. My hand reaches out, and I grab the black frame, pulling it toward me.

My fingers trace the young faces, my smiling one as I look at Roman. His arm is tossed over my shoulder, and I'm smushed up against his side. He's smiling at the camera, a genuinely happy smile covering his face. Pure happiness is seen on both of our faces.

Where did we go wrong? What happened to us?

Why did we ever separate when we already had everything we ever needed in each other?

I bring the picture to my chest, hugging it to me, wishing I could go back in time and right my wrongs. Wishing I could change so much. But I can't, and that's the most heartbreaking thing of all.

My head drops, and tears fall down my face in despair. A sob chokes out of me, and I can do nothing but mourn the time that I've lost and will never get back.

I hear his footsteps before I see him. I can sense him the closer he gets. Our electricity grows stronger with every inch that diminishes between us. The side of the bed dips, and his warm hand presses against my back. In a moment, he has me pulled into his arms, our picture squished between us as we hold each other.

"I'm so sorry," I cry, feeling like this is all my fault. If I never had left, we would've still been together. If I would have just went with him on tour, or we would have just left for New York, our lives could've been so different. Instead, we've lost five years of our lives apart from each other. So much time lost that I'll never be able to get back.

"You have nothing to be sorry for," he mumbles against my neck.

I peel back from him, looking at him through blurry eyes. "I do. It's all my fault. I wish I never left. I should have stayed home. Or went to New York. It was the biggest mistake of my life." A part of me hates saying that because I experienced so much. I learned so much, and I met some great people.

But those experiences meant I lost out on the love of my life, and none of that is worth losing him over. We could have grown together; we didn't need to do that apart.

He frowns at me. "What happened to you?"

I shake my head. I'm afraid if I tell him how ruined I've been, the horrible things I've done and what I've been through, he'll think differently of me. I won't be his Luna anymore, and that thought is heartbreaking enough for me to keep my mouth shut.

I roll off him, curling back underneath the sheets. I pull them up to my neck, feeling so lost and confused, and even alone. Because I know Roman will tear these words from me piece by piece, and any love he still holds onto, any thread that still connects between our two hearts, will be frayed.

322

"Luna," he demands.

I don't answer him, burrowing further into the pillows that smell like him, worried that this will be my only chance. So afraid that the bond we hold will be fractured by just a few words. "I don't want to talk about it."

"Well, we need to talk about it." He pulls the sheets back, ripping it away to the end of the bed. My head lifts off the pillow, and I scowl at him, my brows dipping low over my eyes. "Don't look at me like that. We're going to lay all this shit on the table. Right here. Right now. I'm not waiting another second."

"Another second for what?" My hand reaches toward my naked neck, my fingers clutching my throat when it feels like it's closing in on me.

He leans forward, leaning toward my face. I can feel his breath against my lips, and his dark brown eyes stare into my gray ones. It almost feels too much, like I need to lean away from his stare. I haven't been looked at like this in so long, like the meaning of the world is held in my irises. Like one touch could heal him and break him at the same time.

Roman's look is absolutely everything.

"I'm not going to let you leave this room until you talk to me. Come on, Luna. Just fucking talk to me. It's *me*." He looks hurt by the fact that I'm keeping anything from him. This isn't how we were growing up. He knew every time my period started and stopped. He knew when I was having cramps. He knew when I was upset. He knew every inch of me. I knew almost every time he took a shit. We don't hide things, so the fact that I'm hiding something now isn't sitting well with him.

"I don't want you to think differently of me," I sigh, looking down at the sheets. For all I know, he might not even find me attractive anymore. I feel different, maybe I look different to him, too.

His hand goes to my face, running across my cheeks. His fingers go to my eyelids, dancing across my nose and down the side of my jaw. "You don't have to be perfect, Luna, but that doesn't mean you aren't a masterpiece."

I breathe out, my heart beating from my chest. "I don't know where you want me to start."

"The beginning. I want you to start at the very beginning."

I look up at his white popcorn ceiling, tears filling my eyes and spilling down my temples. Roman's hands are there instantly, wiping them away before they fall to his sheets. "I met friends. We traveled, went to a lot of different places. Sleeping outside—"

"You were homeless?" He butts in, his face turning into a fierce frown.

I shrug, not really feeling like we were homeless, more or less just travelers. A lot of people are just like us, living and wandering across the lands. "No, I wasn't homeless. We lived in Arizona for a while. Then we moved to California, and eventually I went to Maui, by myself."

"Where'd your friends go?"

I bite my tongue, the sharp pain helping me tamper down the scream that wants to break free. "They died. Some of them died."

He frowns at this, blinking at me as if my face will show their cause of death. Before he even has the chance to ask, I tell him.

"My friend, Shauna, she died in Arizona. We were hiking in the desert, and it was hot. We were out of water and we were all dehydrated." I don't tell him about the white horse, still not sure whether that was a figment of our imagination or if it was real. Either way, I take it as a moment where Roman was subconsciously there to help me. "She died, out in that desert. It was so hot, a-and we had to leave her there." I pull the sheet up to my eyes, wiping away my tears.

I can feel him next to me, wanting to comfort me, but also wanting to give me the space he thinks I need. I don't know what I need, but just having him close gives me a comfort I've been looking for since I left Wisconsin.

"My other friend, Neil, he killed himself." My words are muffled from the sheet over my face, my tears so heavy I can barely get the words out. Roman reaches out, tugging the sheet down so I can speak. "We traveled from San Diego to Santa Cruz with this couple. We went to this weird place in the middle of the woods. They were all on acid."

"Did you try it?" I don't look at his face, not wanting to see the disappointment in his eyes.

I nod, wincing as I feel a little guilty. "They're called Deadheads—"

"Deadheads? You went to party with fucking Deadheads? What the fuck, Luna?" His voice raises, and I shrivel into the mattress.

"I didn't know…" My eyes crack open, and I can see the shock and discomfort on his face. "What? Do you know them or something?"

He shakes his head, his eyes wide. "I know *of* them. They aren't all bad people, but some of them…" he grimaces. "What happened to your friend?"

"He got puddled…" I lick my lips, watching his jaw grind. He's never angry. I don't like the irritation radiating from him. He isn't going to like my story. "He pushed me out of the way. I was the one the Deadhead was trying to puddle."

He sits back, anger firing up in his eyes. "Fucking hell, Luna." He runs his hands up and down his face, his skin turning red from the friction. "You could've died. I never would've known." The last part of his sentence is said quietly, almost to himself.

My hand reaches out, my fingers curling around his wrist. "I'm right here."

He looks up at me, the rims of his eyes red, raw. "Keep going."

I shrug. "I left California after that. Trish stayed with Neil. She gave me money, told me to get away from Willie and go home."

"Who's Willie?"

He says the name like it's sour milk, his mouth twisted up in distaste.

My lips press together, not liking the look on his face.

"You're going to tell me anyway. Just keep going." His words come out so sure, with such certainty, all I can do is listen.

I take a deep breath, averting my eyes to his sheets. "Willie was a guy I was casually seeing, but I broke it off before we left for Santa Cruz." I keep out the part of him raping me in the woods. "Trish could tell there was something off about him, so she gave me her money, and I left."

"You were coming home?"

I gnaw on my lip, feeling the skin shred away. "I was."

"What happened?" He frowns.

I look up at him with this, gauging his expression. "I saw a magazine of you. Of your girlfriend talking about your stint to treatment."

He scowls at this, dropping his head between his shoulders and letting out a curse. "You fucking believed the stupid media?"

I shrug, feeling so broken-hearted over the entire thing. "I didn't know what to believe. I just knew once I read that, I couldn't come home. So, I left, off to Hawaii."

His head dips so he can look me straight in the eyes. "She wasn't my girlfriend. She never was. I'm guessing it was something like your friend, Willie."

He says his name like poison, and I stare at him. "I wanted to love someone else, Roman. I tried so damn hard to let him in. I wanted to fall in love, to see the truth."

"And what's the truth?"

"My heart is just as much mine as it is yours. There's this… barrier inside of me. It's like whatever let you in put up this invisible barrier miles high. I couldn't love someone else for the life of me. It doesn't matter who they were or what they said. My heart only beats for one person. My soul only aches for one person, and that's you." The words bleed out of me, spilling all over his clean sheets.

He swallows them up. His chest expands, and I watch a light brighten his eyes.

"Tell me what happened in Hawaii. What made you call me?"

My eyes close. "Do you still have that pick I gave you? The one I had engraved with our initials?" The bed shifts as he moves to the edge of the bed, and I can hear a drawer open and shut. The bed dips again, and my eyes flutter open.

In front of me is the pick. Worn and well-used, but I can still see the initials *R & L* engraved in the center. I slide it from his fingers, feeling the rough texture it's grown over the years. "I can't believe you still have this," I whisper.

"I've never played without it." He takes it back, his eyes lifting to my neck. "It looks like I can't say the same for you, though." His voice is sad, a little let down at that fact.

My hand lifts to where I've had his piece of gold sitting for so many years. I feel like a piece of me is missing, and that's because it is.

"I did, until yesterday."

"What happened?"

My nose burns and tears fall from the corners of my eyes. He doesn't wipe them away this time, waiting for me to answer. "Willie raped me."

His eyes widen, his neck turning a bright red. I watch as his fists bury in his sheets, clenching them between his fingers. "What?"

"I—"

"No, I mean, what? I thought you left him in California."

I nod. "He ended up coming to Hawaii. When he found me, he was… different. He was using."

I don't say anything else, not sure how much he wants to know. I don't want to relive this, but I know I need to tell someone. I need to tell Roman.

"Tell me," is all he says.

"H-he came to my house. I got away, b-but he attacked me on the beach. The next time I got away, I ran into the ocean. He t-tore my necklace off. I grabbed it and held it around his neck..." My breathing picks up, and I press my hand against my chest, feeling nauseated and so fucking sad. *He took my necklace.*

Willie took many pieces of me when he sunk to the bottom of the ocean.

"I put it around his neck and pulled until he d-drowned. I killed him," I whisper.

"You killed him," he says. Not a question. A statement.

I nod, my jaw trembling in fear. What if he hates me for what I've done?

He puts his finger up, sliding off the bed. "I'll be right back."

My eyes widen, panic making me sweat. "Where are you going?"

He doesn't answer, slamming the door shut behind him. A moment later, I hear a crash down the hall. It's loud, as if it happened just outside the door.

I jump, my entire body flinching as I curl deeper into the sheets. I pull them up to my neck, not sure whether I should go check on him or not.

The door creaks open, and I look up, seeing Roman walking in. His face is toward the ground, a distraught look in his eyes. His hand rubs the back of his neck, the other one is clenching. Fisting and releasing. Over and over again, I watch his corded arms twitch and flex.

He glances up, staring at me. There's so much emotion in his eyes, but the most prominent one of all is absolute ruination. He looks destroyed.

Walking up to the bed, the fronts of his thighs press against the comforter. "I wish you never left." His voice comes out choked, the words strangled in his throat. "I wish none of this ever happened to you. I wish I could go back, take all the hurt and pain that you've endured, that you must be feeling at this very moment." He leans down, his hand trailing over my naked neck, where I can see in his eyes the desire to see the necklace reappear on my skin. "I'd do anything in this world to erase the burdens you hold, but I can't. All I can do is carry them with you, help that weight lessen off your shoulders. Will you let me do that, Luna? Will you let me help you carry your pain?"

A sob bubbles in my chest. I can feel it climb, building as it rises. By the time it breaks through my throat, tears are flooding down my cheeks and my entire body is trembling. "Please, Roman. Please help me." There's nothing else I want in this world than for Roman to stand by my side. The fact that he wants me, after everything I've said, makes my chest burn with truth.

He really is my soulmate.

I can feel it in each touch. The electricity has only grown over time. There's a pain in me when we aren't touching, when we aren't near one another. The moment we touch, the pain dissipates. It fades off, and I feel whole again. The shattered pieces of my soul are slowly healing, they're starting to come back together again.

It's all because of Roman.

He crawls onto the bed, lifting me from beneath the sheets and settling me on his lap. My legs hang over the side of his waist, my arms curl around his neck. His fingers bury into my hair, his head dropping to my naked neck. He kisses where my necklace once lay, and more tears fall. I lean forward, my nose dropping to his brown locks.

His lips sink into my skin, warm and plump and so damn loving. "I'll buy you another. I'll buy you all the ballerina necklaces in the world."

I frown. "I don't want another necklace. They won't be the same."

His head lifts, his red-rimmed eyes connecting with mine. "What can I do then? What do you want?"

My fingers go to his sharp jaw, dancing along his stubbled cheek. Such a man, now. So much different than he used to be. But so much the same. My Roman is still inside this body. My heart still feels at home when I'm with him. We're grown, but we're exactly where we need to be. "I only need you. I only want you."

His gaze drops to my lips, and it only takes him a second. A flicker of indecision on his face before he leans forward, trapping my lips between his. My tears start all over again, falling onto his face and running between our lips. He leans back, licking my salty kisses from his mouth then comes back toward me, taking my lips again in a greedy kiss.

It's like coming home.

My chest hiccups with emotion, and I can't do anything besides cry into his mouth. My insides burn, it feels like I'm floating and finally being grounded all at once. There's nothing better than the tingling in my fingers, than my heart pumping so heavily, it feels like it's expanding throughout my entire ribcage. My body warms, and all the hesitations in my life clear.

The only thing I know, is that I'm exactly where I'm supposed to be.

"Roman…" I mumble against his lips.

He peels away from my lips, looking up at me. "What is it?" There's a worry in his eyes, his brown irises flickering with concern.

My palm runs along his stubble. "I love you. I love you so fucking much."

His chest stops, his jaw grinding as emotion takes over. His nostrils flare, and I watch as he rolls the words over his tongue for a moment, thinking of what to say.

The waiting stabs my chest.

"I love you, Luna. I told you years ago that I'd love you forever. I'll tell you now that I'll love you forever. Every inch, every piece, every breath. I don't care what you've done. I don't care what you do. My soul is your soul. Your soul is mine. Our love is our love, and distance, time, and mistakes aren't going to change that. True love doesn't fracture with time, because the moment the love comes together again, it's only stronger. That's us, Luna. Our love can withhold anything. I knew it when I was seven, I'll know it when I'm eighty. I fucking love you, Luna. Now and always."

"Now and always," I say through my tears. With a breath, I climb back on the bed and curl under the sheets. "Will you tell me about your time? What you did while I was away? Do you play anymore? How are the guys?"

He flicks his pick back and forth over his fingers. Like his fingers are the strings on his guitar. "We broke up almost three years ago, actually. The guys are good, though. Lonnie lives out in San Diego at our old condo. Flynn and Clyde are back in Wisconsin. Haven't talked to them for a few months."

"Why did you break up?"

He shakes his head. "Didn't you hear?"

I bite my lip. "I did my best to stay away from the media. I-I didn't know what I'd find. Plus, it's kind of hard to come by a TV when you live on the beach."

He frowns, scratching at his jaw. "I, uh, I was in a pretty bad place in the end. I was using, and shit just got really bad. I actually broke my guitar on stage. That was pretty much my lowest point." He looks embarrassed, like he should be ashamed for his actions.

"Why were you in a bad place?" I ask, my chest growing heavier by the moment.

He looks at me, sadness and grief in his eyes. "Is that even a question? Isn't it obvious? My mind, my heart, everything was fucking ruined because I didn't have you. I didn't know where you were. I had no idea if you were even okay or alive. I-I wrote you so many fucking emails, Luna. Why didn't you respond to any of them? Did you not see them? Not once?"

I shake my head, confused. "No, I didn't get any emails." Realization hits me. "I forgot the password for my loolooluna email, and I had to make a new one." He looks a little sad by that fact, but also a little relieved. "Why? Did you send a lot of emails?"

He cringes. "You don't want to know. There were a lot of bad nights that I was waiting for your reply. Probably for the best that you can't read them."

I think back to how dark I got at some points, wondering how deep his darkness became. If his hurt ran as deeply as mine did. By the sounds of it, the pain in my soul was similar to his. Our aches ran to our bones, and this is only the beginning of our healing.

"So, if the band broke up, what do you do now?"

A pride lights up his face at this, one that I haven't seen for many years. "I work at FDNY as a firefighter."

My eyes widen, and I almost want to laugh. "You're a firefighter now? Never saw that one coming."

He shrugs. "When I was in treatment, that was the only thing that seemed interesting at the time. Helping others, I guess."

I nod, imagining him in his uniform, saving kittens from trees and helping old ladies from burning buildings.

He turns toward me, a seriousness washing over his face. "What about you, Luna? What do you want to do now?"

I think about it. What I really want to do. The hardest part is that I actually know what I want. It's what I've always wanted, I just faked my disinterest with a smile, but a part of me has been hurting for years, missing what I love.

"I want to dance."

A smile breaks out on his face, big and vicious. "You have no idea what that does to me."

I smile, but a frown ticks at my lips too quickly. "I don't know what I'd ever do, though. Julliard would never take me back. I probably suck at dancing now, anyway."

He shakes his head. "I highly fucking doubt that."

I shrug. "I don't know. Maybe I should settle for something small. Like go to a community college and be a dance teacher or something."

His palms go to my cheeks, turning my face so I'm looking him directly in the eye. "Luna does not fucking settle. Why the hell would you ever think to settle on anything? That's not you, Luna. Don't lower yourself for no one. For fucking nothing. If you want to dance, you go dance. If you think you want to get into Julliard, you walk down there, and you demand a damn audition."

The thought brings butterflies into my stomach. I so badly want that, but the fear of being shut down, of being rejected… I don't know how I'd be able to recover. The thought of leaving something behind that was my passion, regretting it, trying to salvage it, and losing my chance, is excruciating.

I'd bleed out on the front steps.

"I'll have to think about it."

"You think about it, but I know you, Luna. You're going to dance again. I know it."

I settle into the bed, and Roman lies next to me. His head is propped on his hand as he looks down at me. We talk about everything. Every detail of our time apart. Every step we took, every breath we took. There wasn't a moment of time we didn't talk about.

We made up for lost time.

We talked until night came, darkness shrouding the room again. We only stopped for Roman to order some pizza to be delivered. We ate in bed, the pizza box between us, our fingers full of grease as Roman caught me up on our families. He hasn't seen my parents in years, but our parents still talk frequently, and he says they're doing well.

That made me cry.

I'm going to call them tomorrow. I'm going to apologize and tell them I'm home. That I'm never going to do that to them ever again.

I smile until my jaw hurts. Then we curl under the sheets, and Roman holds me. He curls his arm around my entire body. I snuggle against his front, loving the hardness, the manliness that he has become. I fall asleep in his arms, the scent of Roman surrounding me, and his love repairing me.

CHAPTER TWENTY-SEVEN

Luna

I wake up to the sound of a phone ringing. Roman rolls over, his arm leaving my side as he picks up the home phone sitting on his nightstand.

"Hello?" His raspy voice is so intoxicating. My heart settles, and I curl closer to him on his mattress, snuggling against his side. My head goes to his chest, and I listen as his voice vibrates straight into my ear.

"Now? What's the status?" He grows serious, sitting up slightly in bed. My face tilts toward his, and I watch as he brings a hand up, wiping the sleep from his eyes.

"Yeah. I'm on my way." He hangs up, dropping his head back to the pillow and letting out a groan. Turning his head toward mine, he combs my dark hair from my face, his hand curling around my cheek. "I wanted to stay home today with you, but there's an emergency. I have to go."

"What's going on?" I frown.

"Some carbon monoxide detected in some apartments over by Central Park. I don't know how long I will be. Going to vacate everyone from the building." He grimaces. "Will you be okay here? I don't want to leave you here alone, but I can't take you with me."

I sit up, combing my hair over my shoulder. "No. No, I'll be fine. I might take a walk today around the city. Explore a little bit. I also have to call my mom. I'll be fine. I'll just… see you when I get back, I guess?" I smile, this adulting we're doing feeling a little weird. Back in high school we had rules, a small town, nothing to really do besides hang out with each other.

Now we have lives, expectations, and obligations that we need to take care of.

"I wanted to take you around the city and explore with you," he grumbles, sliding out of bed and walking to his dresser. He opens his cherrywood drawers, grabbing a pair of boxers and a white shirt.

"I'll save the fun things for you." I don't want to tell him, because I don't know if I'll go through with it. But I'd like to make my way down to Julliard. I don't know if I'll be able to step inside, or even talk to anyone, but being able to look at the place of my dreams in the face will be a big enough step for me, I think.

"I'll be back as soon as I can. I'll leave a key on the counter." He walks up to me, his clothes in hand as he bends down, pressing a kiss to my lips. I deepen it, slipping my tongue in his mouth. I feel so broken after Hawaii, but every moment with Roman is giving me back a piece of myself that I've lost. He's healing me, just by being in his presence.

He peels away from me way too soon, stepping back with a grimace. "I've really got to…"

"Go, go." I wave him off, and he dresses as quick as he can, pulling a pair of jeans on and yanking his t-shirt over his head. He gives me one more glance before he rushes out the front door.

I fall back onto my pillow, looking at the ceiling. So much has happened over the course of the last few days. My entire life has taken a one-eighty. The darkness that has been seeping into my bones for the past five years has lifted and brightened with just Roman's presence. It makes me hate myself a little more, to be honest.

It makes my decision to leave in the first place that much more foolish. Why did I ruin something when it was so perfect? Was my immaturity and need to become independent that important? Was it even necessary? Why couldn't I just let things be as they were?

Leaving Roman was the biggest mistake of my life. I just hope for what it's worth, we can earn back the time we've lost.

Now for my next step.

I roll over in bed, taking the phone off the receiver. I stare at the buttons, taking a deep breath as I punch in the numbers I know by heart. The number that's been ingrained in me since I was seven years old. My finger twirls around the spiral cord, watching it suction against my skin as I listen to the loud ringing.

"Roman?" My mom's voice comes over the phone, surprised. Happy.

"Hi, Mom." Tears spring to my eyes, the sheets below me fill with tear-shaped droplets.

Her sharp intake of breath, followed by a small cry, "Luna?" she cries. "Oh my gosh! Charlie, Luna's on the phone!"

I hear shuffling as I try to quiet my cries. A moment later, I hear another phone pick up.

"Luna? Is that you, baby?"

"Hi, Daddy," I cry, a smile splitting across my face.

"Luna? Where are you? Are you with Roman?"

I nod my head. "No. I mean, yes, but he's at work right now. I am in New York, though."

My mom starts crying hysterically, and I can hear my dad calming her down from the other end of the phone. It breaks my heart, tears me in half. I did this. I did this to my parents.

"When… when did you get there?" Dad asks, tears in his voice.

"Yesterday. Roman got me a ticket." I wipe my face with my sheets, feeling overwhelmed with too many emotions.

"I don't understand. Goldie says you guys haven't spoken in years. How did you get ahold of him?"

There's no way I can possibly tell them what happened in Hawaii. They would fall to pieces. They would never forgive themselves, even though not an inch of it is their fault. They mean too much to me. I will not break their hearts.

"I was just ready to come home. I called Nora… I'm sorry I didn't call sooner."

"Home…" my mom's voice trails off.

A pinch in my chest stings, and I rub away the pain. I know home is Wisconsin. It will always be my home. But they also have to know, home is wherever Roman Hall is.

"Roman…"

"We know, Luna. We know," my dad says, and it only makes another flood of tears trail down my cheeks. I tear the phone away from my ear, burying my face in the crook of my arm.

They know. They've always known.

Everyone has.

"I'm so glad you're back with him. I'm so happy, Luna. You don't know how happy this makes me," my mom cries.

I want to crawl through the phone and hug my mom. I want to wrap them both in my arms and hold them tight.

"I'm so sorry—I'm so sorry for these last few years. You guys didn't deserve that from me. I wish… I wish I could take it all back."

My dad hushes me through the phone. "The only thing that matters is that you're back now. It'll give us an excuse to come to New York."

"I'd love that. I can't wait to see you." I smile into the phone.

"So, tell me. What's next for you, Luna?" my mom asks.

I bite my lip, debating whether or not I should tell them. But I know more than anything, they were some of my biggest supporters growing up, and nothing will make them happier. "I think I'm going to go down to Julliard."

My mom starts up a whole new round of crying. I can hear her pull the phone away from her ear, her sobs so emotional and so damn sad.

"Do you think they'll take you? After all these years?" my dad asks, much more collected this time.

I shrug, twirling my hair around my finger. "I don't know. But I'd like to try. If they don't… well, I guess that's my own mistake I'll have to live with. I'll find something else. But I want to at least try."

"Have you danced? All this time, have you danced at all?" my mom asks.

I bite my lip, this part making me nervous. No, I haven't danced. Not ballet. Though, I know I'm still flexible, I don't know if I have it in me to be a professional anymore. "I haven't."

"Let me look around for some studios you can practice in. I'll find you a place where you can get a new leotard, too. Will you be there for a while? I can call you back soon." Excitement builds in her tone, and I smile, thinking back to all those years ago. She was always excited when it came to my dancing. She always knew I had a skill, something better than many other people had. I was far more advanced than the dancers my age. I've always been that way. And she loved experiencing that with me.

"I can stick around if you want to look and call me back." I pull the sheets back, stretching my legs as I slide my feet to the ground.

"Okay, but wait! I don't want you to go yet. Can we talk for a bit? I missed your voice."

I slide to the ground, my butt hitting the floor and my back hitting the side of the bed. I want to talk to them, too, but I don't want to tell them about my journey. There were many good moments, but right now, the bad has tainted the good.

I only want the good.

I think my mom notices this. "We don't need to hear about your travels, Luna. Talk about anything. Tell me about Roman. It's been so long since we've seen him. How is he doing?" That brings tears to my eyes. Roman was just as much of a child to my parents as I was. And my parents were just as much parents to him as his own parents were. We're one large family, really.

I tell them about Roman. I tell them about the bits I've seen of New York City, and how beautiful and chaotic it looks. I tell them about his apartment, how messy it was when I walked in. I tell them about how we talked into the middle of the night, catching up on anything and everything.

I talk to them until my voice is hoarse. And then we talk some more.

"Thank you." I hand the cabbie some money, shutting the door behind me. I look up at the giant building before me, a little nervous, a little excited. Not sure if I should really go in there, but now is my chance, and if I walk away, I don't know if I'll ever be back.

I took a shower at Roman's, and by the time I was getting out, my mom was already calling me again with all the details I needed for my day. She gave me the addresses to a few studios and places that had dance uniforms. She made me promise I'd call her when I got home to tell her how my day went.

Once I was ready, I grabbed the key from the kitchen table and the small stack of money Roman left me, and I headed out.

Now I'm here.

At Julliard. My dream.

With a deep breath, I walk up the steps that are so long they could fit a school bus, and into the school. My eyes want to water, but I blink them away, biting my lip as I walk up to the front desk. My sandals echo in the vast area, and I suddenly wish I would've gone shopping with this money to get something nice to wear before coming here.

"How can I help you?" the woman behind the front desk asks.

"Can I… can I sit down and talk to someone?"

She looks confused, her eyebrows furrowing.

"I'm sorry. My name is Luna Lewis. I used to dance a few years ago, and my dance instructor was Leona Ivanov. She used to work here—"

"I know who Leona Ivanov is." She laughs awkwardly.

I blink at her. "Okay. Well, I was going to get a scholarship here, and I kind of screwed that up, but I was wondering if I could talk to someone about maybe auditioning, or how I can try to get admittance here?"

She blinks back at me this time. A little unsure on how to proceed. Her red fingernail taps against the desk.

"Is there anyone I can talk to?" I bite my lip, worried she's about to turn me away. Call security or something.

Did I really blow my chance?

She must see the panicked look on my face, the tears in my eyes. She stands from her chair, giving me a small smile. "I'll be right back."

"Thank you." I blink away my tears, stepping back and watching her walk away. She heads down the hall, out of sight. I turn around, looking at the tall ceilings. The glass walls that show the city. The expensive interior, the high-end tiled floors. Everything is extravagant. Everything is beautiful.

I want this so bad.

"Ms. Lewis?" I turn around, seeing a woman walking up to me in a pressed pantsuit. Her hair is pulled back into a tight bun, her thin limbs long and delicate.

"Yes?" I ask, suddenly nervous.

"Come with me, please."

I follow her, her heels clapping on the tiled floor while my worn sandals slap against my feet. I really should've done more before coming here. Done my hair, even, instead of just washing it and brushing it with Roman's flimsy black comb.

At least I brushed my teeth.

We walk into a grand office, the windows behind her looking out onto the beautiful city of New York. She points to a seat in front of a desk. "Sit down, please."

I do as she asks, pulling the chair up to the edge of the desk. I cross my leg over the other, then uncross my legs, sliding my hands between my thighs. It's chilly in here, and goosebumps break out along my arms.

"Luna Lewis," she says, sitting down at her desk. She slides glasses on her nose, perching them on the edge and looking at me over the top of them. She has a file on her desk, and her thin fingers tap over the top of it. "My name is Ms. Ramy, I'm the Admissions Director and one of the teachers here at Julliard."

"Hi." I smile. "I know this might be weird, but I dance with—"

She puts up a hand, and my eyes go wide, stopping mid-sentence.

"I know exactly who you are, Luna."

My jaw goes slack. "You do?"

She smiles, albeit slightly stiff. "Yes, I do. I am very good friends with Leona. We have spoken about you for years. She told me many times about her star dancer from a small town in Wisconsin. How she would dance over every building in New York City. She said you would put the dancers here to shame. I didn't believe her, but then she showed me tapes of you."

Tapes? I had no idea she taped me.

She nods, as if she could read my thoughts. "Yes, and I was quite surprised to see she was right. You had a great talent, Luna. Something not many people are born with. But, when she called and told me you'd quit dancing, it broke not only her heart, but all of ours as well. We had hoped to have you here. But you never came, Luna, and it's been years. So, tell me, why are you here now?"

Words can't form. I had no idea I made such a big impact, that the domino effect of my life has led us here, to this point now.

I've blown it all.

I take a deep breath, spilling everything on the table. "I, um, I went through some stuff a few years back, and it took me a while, but I'm here now. This," I say, looking around, "is where I've always wanted to be. This has been my biggest dream, for as long as I could have them. I know I was in the wrong, and I don't even deserve a chance here at this point, but I still want one. Whatever it will take, I will do it. I want this, so badly." A tear springs to my eye, and I wipe it away. But the woman in front of me sees it, and her face softens, just a little.

She opens her file, and I see my name at the top. My scholarship. She flips through, skimming a few pages before slamming the file shut. Looking up at me once again, she levels me a look. "Like I said, Leona is a dear friend of mine."

I nod.

"And I know you have it in you to be here. Have you danced lately?"

I cringe, shaking my head.

She blows out a breath. A disappointed breath. "Unfortunately, you just missed our auditions for this year. You'll have to wait until next September. But maybe that's a good thing. You can practice, *get back into dancing*. You come back here in one year with a routine. You dance in front of our panel. We will not be generous. You come with everything you've got, and if you're good enough, then the scholarship is yours."

I bite my lip, then lick it. But it's no use, bowing my head toward my chest, I let out a silent sob, covering my hands with my face. My palms grow a pool of tears, and my chest fills with the most gratitude in the entire world.

This is it. This is really happening.

Once I gain my bearings, I lift my head, wiping my eyes. "Thank you. Thank you so much." I smile, tears streaming down my face. It's useless to attempt to wipe them away.

She smiles. "I'll see you in one year, Luna Lewis. Please don't disappoint me."

"I won't. I promise, I won't." I stand up, leaning over her desk to shake her hand. I walk out, when she calls my name.

She looks me up and down from head to toe. A small amount of irritation and disgust is in her eyes. "I expect you have been through a lot, but when you come back, I'm hoping your appearance will be much more... up to the standards for what we expect here?"

I run my hand through my hair, which has been air dried and lays in a mess down my back. Roman's bathroom was seriously lacking the necessities.

"Yes, I'm sorry. This isn't... I won't come back like this. I'm sorry."

She nods, taking me for my word.

I give her one more smile, and then I'm off. Excitement building in my chest. I feel like I'm going to explode.

I can't wait to tell Roman.

With two bags in hand, I walk back into Roman's apartment. The moment I open his wooden door, a waft of Roman hits me in the face. I smile, even though the apartment is empty. This place is a part of him, filled with bits and pieces of his life. I could stay in this apartment forever and be happy, surrounded by everything Roman.

After I left Julliard, I stopped to the next place on my mom's list. A small shop with dance uniforms, specifically ballet. I picked out a black leotard. Classy, delicate, feminine. The fabric is stretchy, light, and reminds me a lot of the leotard I had when I was little. That one was a baby pink, though. This one is black. Black as the night. It reminded me a lot of the night sky on the beach all those years ago. The moment I saw it, my finger clutching the soft fabric, I knew it was the one for me. This one has a tutu combined to it, a stark black lace that looks like ink. I bought a plain pink leotard too, for practice. The black one will be for my routine.

In one year.

At Julliard.

I also found my shoes. A light pink pointed shoe. I bought some ribbon to sew into them. It gives me the added stability as it wraps around my ankle. Trying them on at the store, my toes instantly felt sore from the pointed top. It's going to be hell getting back into it, but the constant heavy beat in my chest tells me this is the right choice.

What I'm doing is what I'm *meant* to do.

After I bought my ballet shoes, I went to a small studio between Roman's apartment and Julliard. The owner was friendly, and after I told her a shortened version of my story, she was more than happy to lend me some studio time to practice. I don't need classes; I don't need a teacher. I need a place to practice, and music to practice with. Everything else will fall into place.

I bring my bags to the living room, setting them on the couch. Heading back to the kitchen, I open the drawers, looking for a pair of scissors. The counters are littered with dishes, the garbage bin overflowing with trash that Roman tossed in there yesterday in a rush.

I open every drawer, before I find them in the last one, right next to the tin foil.

Really, Roman?

His kitchen is nice, yet small. White cabinets and a creamy laminate countertop. I can tell when Roman moved in, he threw dishes in any which cupboard was the closest to him. That's definitely something I will be remedying soon.

Like, really soon.

With the scissors in hand, I head back to the couch. It's dark green, soft, and the moment I sit down on it, I sink into the cushions. The fabric is like a blanket, and I run my fingers across it, making the color turn from a dark green to a light green.

I open the plastic bag on the couch, sliding out the miniature sewing kit that I bought at a convenience store, and I get to work on my shoes. It's a long process, and not something a lot of people do. But to ensure there aren't injuries to your feet, I always make sure my shoes are perfect. I break them, hearing the shoes crack as I crack the soles. Sewing the ribbon into the insides of the shoes, I make sure the length is right, snipping the ends and letting the excess flutter to the floor. Picking up a slipper, I start scoring the pointe of the shoe. I've learned the hard way the difficulty of dancing with new, slippery pointed shoes. If they're scored, there's more traction while you dance.

Once the other shoe is done, I slip out of my clothes and try on my black leotard. It's tight. Tighter than anything I've worn in a long time, but it's perfect, molding to my waist and ribs in a tight hug. Grabbing my slippers, I slide the first one onto my foot. My toes cram into the top, and I wince as I snuggle them inside. I wrap the soft ribbon around my ankle, creating a small bow at the back of my calf. I repeat the same with my other foot, my heart beating out of my chest once I'm finished.

Standing up, my eyes fill with tears as I see my reflection on the patio window. My tall, slender form looks perfect, the black leotard making me look taller and even more slender than I really am. The sleeves are long and tight as they hug my thin arms. The back is a deep U, revealing most of my pale back. The shoes are stiff; it'll take a bit of practice to loosen them to my feet, but my prep helped. With a deep breath, I curl my foot, balancing up on my toes. My feet scream, the nails on my toes begging for mercy. Tears spring to my eyes, and I hold my breath as I hold my stance.

My hands go up above my head, stretching to the sky. The points of my fingers touch, and I stretch, feeling muscles awaken that haven't been moved in a long time.

I hear the lock on the door click, and the door swings open. I fall back to the soles of my feet, turning around and coming face to face with Roman. He has yellow and black heavy uniform pants on with suspenders over his shoulders. His white shirt is wet, damp with sweat and streaked in black. His face is streaked, too, with soot, or ash, I'm not sure. His fingers wrap around his matching coat, heavy as it drags on the ground. His fingers tighten around the neck of his jacket, his knuckles turning white as he watches me. There's a tiredness on his face, pure exhaustion lining his forehead. But his eyes…

His eyes are alit with a fire. So much determination in his gaze as he looks at me. Shock, happiness, love, heat, everything combined into his milk chocolate irises.

"Hi," I whisper.

He stands where he is, his dirty shoes cemented in the entryway. He looks amazed, zoned in on my outfit. He barely has enough focus in him as he tosses his keys on the kitchen table. I wince, hoping he didn't scratch the rich wood.

"What's… are you… you're doing it again? You're going to dance?" Shock and hope light up his eyes. He still hasn't moved from his spot.

I nod. "I have an audition at Julliard."

His eyes flare, his jaw going slack. "When?"

"One year. I have one year to prepare." I bite my lip, nerves creating huge, hawk-like butterflies in my stomach. I press my hand against my stomach, my leotard doing nothing to quell the flapping wings.

He steps forward, his dirty boots going straight onto his cream carpet. "Baby…" His voice is hoarse, emotion clogging him. He looks me up and down, the memories in his eyes going one million miles a minute. I can see it with every blink. Me as a child, me as a teenager, me now. Always the same. My leotard, my shoes.

I curl my feet, going up on my toes. My hands go up, creating a pose above my head. My fingers lay delicately upon one another. Tears flood my eyes, his face turning blurry as I look at him. I smile, my voice full of emotion as I ask, "How do I look?"

He blinks at me, his nostrils flaring. And suddenly, I hear his coat drop to the ground, and he's in front of me, his body slamming against mine. His large hands go around my waist, clutching my hip bones as he lifts me off my feet. Like I'm a feather, I'm suspended in his arms, pressed above his head, just as we've done one million times before. A part of me is nervous, the ceiling not that tall in here. But I still do my pose, arching my back, pointing my toes, tears streaming down my cheeks.

"I love you, Luna, so fucking much," he says from below me, his voice a low rasp.

A sob breaks from my chest, and I curl into a ball. He lowers me, clutching me against him as he sits us on the couch. His hands circle my waist, going to my naked back. "I love you, too," I whisper.

My bare legs are scratchy against his rough-textured pants, the thickness making them bulky between my thighs. His body is sweaty, the shirt sticking to him. Even in the fall, the air is warm outside. "How did it go today?"

He shakes his head, a darkness passing his eyes. "It was fine."

I run my fingers along his face, passing underneath his darkened eyes, wiping away a greasy dark smudge. "Doesn't sound fine to me."

He looks up into my eyes with a vulnerability in his that I haven't seen since we were younger. "It's just hard, you know? Working in a job like this. I see a lot of shit. I never thought this would be my life."

I grab the hair falling over his ears, tucking them back, playing with the ends. "Why don't you start music again? Is that something you want to do?"

He shakes his head. "No. I'm done with music. I love what I do. It just… it takes a lot out of me." He looks up at me, a softness in his eyes. "Having you here makes it so much better."

I lean forward, capturing his lips with mine. I dive my tongue in, kissing him with all my love, all my gratitude. I love this man with all my heart, with my entire soul. He fills me, completes every inch of me.

He kisses me back, his hands going to the back of my head, curling in my long, dark hair. I settle into his lap, my body fitting perfectly against his. I rub against him, and he grunts, lifting his hips against mine.

Leaning back, I look him in his dark eyes, wanting him so badly. Wanting him to fill me, to fix me, to heal me.

I need him more than I need air.

My finger goes up, curling underneath the fabric on my shoulder, I lower it down my arm, showing him my naked skin. Showing him how much I want him.

His hand goes to the fabric, stopping my movements. My eyes snap up to his, and there's a hesitation lingering there, one that makes me frown.

"No, Luna." He pushes my fabric back up, sliding it back in its place.

My eyes fill with tears, my jaw trembling. "Why?" I knew I shouldn't have told him about Willie. I knew I shouldn't have told him how ruined I was.

"I can't. You aren't ready."

"I am." I lean forward, my hands pressing against his pecs. "I want this."

"Maybe you want it, but you aren't ready." His hands attempt to soothe me, running up and down my arms, but it does the opposite. I try to crawl off him, but his hands go to my waist, pinning me on his lap. "If you don't want me, let me go," I cry.

His hand goes to my jaw, and he pulls me close, bringing me against his lips. He doesn't kiss me, just breathes. "There are scars in your eyes. Scars so deep I can see all the way to your soul, Luna. You try to hide them in your gray eyes, with your kisses and your smiles, but I see them. You're in pain, Luna. Your soul is in pain. I can feel it, Luna. I feel your fucking pain." His hand presses against my chest, right over my heart. "You're bleeding on the inside, Luna. You can't hide it from me."

I sob, breaking my walls down and showing him my hurt, my regrets, the pain that he sees, that I've been foolish to hide. He sees it all. He always has. "Heal me, then. Heal me, Roman." I clutch his shirt, needing him. I want him. All of him, yet he won't give me the piece of him that will heal me completely.

"Sex isn't going to heal you, Luna. You think it will, but it won't." He smiles at me, his thumb wiping a tear from my cheek.

"What will heal me then? I just want you, but you won't even have me. Is it because you think I'm ruined?"

He laughs, "You aren't ruined, Luna. You're mine."

CHAPTER TWENTY-EIGHT
Roman

"Dude, are you sure about this?" Dylan, one of my friends from the station, asks as we hop out of the cab.

"I've never been more sure about anything in my life," I say, stepping out onto the curb. We walk toward the doors in front of us, and Dylan grabs the handle, pulling the glass panel open for the both of us.

He shakes his head at me. "It's just hard to believe you went from being chronically single, almost celibate, to…" he steps inside, the noise nonexistent, "this."

I look around, seeing the diamonds all around me. "I told you, you wouldn't understand," I murmur, walking up to the first case of diamonds.

"So, tell me." He places the tips of his fingers on the glass top, instantly inciting a heavy frown from one of the workers. He shifts to a stand instantly, attempting to wipe his prints off the glass. All that does is create a smear, and he cringes, taking a heavy step back. "Why so soon?"

I shake my head. "It isn't too soon. I've known Luna since I was a child. I'm surprised it's taken this long, to be honest."

"When can I meet her?" He looks over at me.

I laugh. "Never." Dylan is one of the single guys at FDNY. This guy is and always will be a bachelor. He's like the guys from the band when we just started, although I don't think Dylan will ever change.

A man in a pressed suit walks up to me, looking as slick and polished as ever. "How can I help you gentlemen?"

"I want to buy an engagement ring," I say, nerves pounding against my stomach.

The man grows a smile, dollar bills shaping his pupils. "Well, we've certainly got a good selection. Is there anything in particular you had in mind?"

Dylan laughs beside me, and I shoot him a scowl.

The man waits patiently, his arms folded in front of his waist, a small smile on his face. "I honestly don't have a clue what I'm looking for."

He gives me a stiff smile. "Well, maybe we can narrow it down with a price range?"

I shake my head. "No price range."

The dollar bills in his eyes grow.

Dylan grabs my arm, squeezing tight. "Are you shitting me? Think for a minute, Roman."

I pull my arm out of his. "Luna is the love of my life. Whether it costs one thousand dollars or ten thousand dollars, she'll still be the love of my life. I'll know when I see the ring, I don't need a price to decide that."

He stares at me, blinking slowly. Then he gives me a loud slap on the back. "Fuck, man. You're in love. Can't wait to meet her."

I stifle a chuckle. "You're not."

If I had it my way, I'd just keep her to myself at this point. I don't need any reasons for her to walk out the door again.

"Well, let me show you some different cuts, and we can go from there?"

I give the man a nod, and he takes us down the line of different cases, showing me different types of rings. White gold, regular gold, rose gold. Princess cut, round, pear, oval. So many fucking decisions.

Only one stands out.

"That one." I point to it right when I see it.

The man looks to where I'm pointing, smiling when he sees the exact ring I'm referring to.

"Ah, nice choice." He pulls the rack out, using the utmost delicacy in lifting the ring from the holder. He holds it out to me, and I take it, knowing without a doubt this is supposed to be on Luna's finger.

"I'll take it." The diamonds in the center glimmer in the brightly lit room. It's perfect. Delicate. Not too heavy, but not too small. Small white diamonds surround the larger pear-shaped diamond in the center. The part of it that gets me, though, is the rose gold band. Seeing it, I instantly thought of her leotard. It has a pinkish hue that resembles every bit of Luna. It's so her. My heart crashes against my chest as I hold it in my fingers. Every other ring in this store seized to exist the moment my eyes landed on this one. There is no other ring.

This is the ring.

He rings up the total, and I hear Dylan choke behind me. I don't even blink, handing over my credit card. Being a rock star for enough years, I'll never be without money. I don't even need a job, to be honest. But not having anything to do with my days wouldn't be good for me. I needed something. Being a firefighter was that thing.

But Luna just completes my happiness. Entirely.

It's been six months since Luna came to me. Six months of her sleeping next to me. Of her eating with me. I have never felt as good as I have over these last six months. With me working, and her practicing for her upcoming audition, we've both been busy, but by the end of the night, we're together.

We talk, we touch, we heal.

The brokenness in her eyes lessens by the day. What she's been through is soul-crushing. Not anything I would even want someone I despised to go through. The fact that it happened to Luna makes me enraged with a need to kill. Not a feeling I've ever felt in my life, but with Luna, the feeling comes naturally.

She wants me to heal her. In bed, she pleads for it, her fingers gripping me with a desperation I know aches through her limbs. She needs me. I need her, too, but I refuse to break her further, and being with her when she isn't healed, mentally or physically, isn't something I'm okay with.

She hates it, but when she's ready, she'll understand why I waited.

I wait for her. I'll always wait for her.

The man slides the ring into a small velvet box, and puts the box into a thick, expensive, plastic bag. He holds the handles out to me. "Congratulations."

I smile, anticipation lighting my heart on fire. "Thanks."

I have a plan for how I'm going to ask her. It's been something that's been on my mind ever since we were little. Now that we're older, I can make it possible. It's right. The entire thing is just so fucking incredibly right, I can feel it in my bones.

CHAPTER TWENTY-NINE

Luna

My back extends, arching as my arms float over my head. My toes press into the floor, and I alternate foot to foot, swallowing down my wince with every step. My leg shifts up, becoming vertical with my body. My hand curls around my ankle, and I spin, each muscle in my body screaming in protest, but I continue on, finishing the routine that I'm determined and bound to perfect. I will, even if it breaks me.

My leg drops to the ground, and I rush into a leap, my legs going into a split before I land on my toes, spinning around on one foot, toe pointed, while my other foot lays against my calf, the sole of my foot flush with my skin.

Once my routine ends, sweat dots my skin, my black hair around my forehead sticking to my temples. My muscles burn, and every step aches as I walk to the bench. I can feel the fabric of my leotard sticking to my back.

I'm in the studio alone, and I'm grateful for that, because for anyone to see me right now would be embarrassing. I feel like I'm new, which in a sense I am. Staying away from dance this long really put me behind. It makes hesitations float from the back of my mind to right in front of my eyes.

Can I still do this? Or was my break too long? Maybe I blew it for good.

I keep my hesitations to myself, not even telling Roman that I'm worried it's over for me. That I'm too old. That I lost my chance. The thought brings tears to my eyes, and I bat them away angrily with the back of my hand. I don't want to be like this. I don't want to fail. I want to prove to myself that I'm still as talented as I used to be. I wouldn't be gifted with this need, this ability to dance if it was all for nothing, right?

I slouch onto the bench, my spine pressing against the brick wall behind me. Bringing my foot up, I pull the soft ribbon of my slipper, and it collapses from my ankle, the ends fluttering to the ground. I let out a whimper as I slide my slipper off and gasp when I see my toes. Blood seeps from under my nails, mostly from beneath my big toe, it's cracked, split all the way down to my cuticle. I could tear my nail off easily if I wanted to, and I probably should, to make an infection less likely. But I don't want to go through the pain, and dancing with a wound like that on my toe would be torture.

I slide my other slipper off, seeing my other foot in a similar condition to the first one. My toes are bruised, cracked and bleeding. My entire body aches in places that have never ached before, but I also have a feeling of absolution. There's this feeling inside of me the moment I put on my leotard. Like this is exactly where I'm meant to be.

Being with Roman completes that.

Grabbing my slippers, I walk barefoot to the back of my dressing room, putting as much weight as I can on my heels. I slide into the bathroom, slipping out of my leotard and into my clothes. I slide on my jacket, zipping it up to the neck. I haven't been exposed to the cold weather since I left home. New York doesn't get as bad as Wisconsin, but this winter has been a long one, as if it knew I was coming back from a long, warm adventure.

Sliding my leotard and slippers into my bag, I head out, locking the door behind me. The sidewalk is slushy as I walk onto it, the most recent snowstorm not staying long with the fluctuating temps. It makes for a sloppy city, full of brown snow mixed with puddles of ice and water.

I raise my hand, and within minutes a yellow taxi pulls up to the curb. Snow sprays from behind the tires, and I step away from the edge so I don't get splashed. I slide into the taxi, giving him the address to Roman's apartment.

All I can think about, at this moment, is a nice bath. I need to soak my muscles in hot water. I need to ice them, too. But warm water curling around my skin is the only thing on my mind.

It doesn't take long for the taxi to pull up outside of Roman's apartment. I hand him some money from my purse and grab my bag, then hobble to the elevator. I lean against the railing, taking as much weight off my feet as I can.

I've been practicing religiously. I'm so dedicated to getting this scholarship, I'll do anything I can. If that means a bleeding and bruised body, well, I say it's worth it.

I pull the key out of my purse, unlocking the door and seeing the apartment empty. Roman is busy at work a lot. The population in New York makes for a lot of after-hours emergency phone calls. He doesn't really have a schedule either. If he gets a call, he has to go right away. Doesn't matter the day or the hour.

He seems tired a lot, the long, unstable schedule seeming to get the best of him. But there's also a confidence in him, like doing something that helps people brings him a satisfaction that playing music didn't.

Music will always be a part of him, I think. He still has his guitar, tucked away in his closet. I have yet to see him take it out, but I will get him to. Someday. I don't think he's ready yet, but it will happen. I'll make sure of it.

I drop my bag just inside the door and walk straight to the bathroom, stripping my clothes off on the way. Bending down, I put the stopper in the drain and turn the knob all the way to hot. I grab the two bottles from the side of the top, pouring a generous amount of bubbles and lavender into the water.

I wait until it's filled to the brim, and push the clear knob in, turning the water off. Dipping my toes in first, I hiss through my teeth when the soap seeps beneath my cuts, causing an intense burn on my foot. I bite on my lip, pressing my hand against the cool tile on the wall as I step the rest of the way in, sinking into the hot water until my butt hits the ground.

Then I breathe.

The water hits the top of my chest, lapping at my neck in small waves. I close my eyes, leaning the back of my head against the back of the tub. My muscles loosen by the second, crying out in relief from rest.

I don't know how much time has passed. I think I've even fallen asleep, but the front door unlocking has my eyes cracking open. A sheen of sweat covers my skin. I wipe the top of my lip, the footsteps coming toward me warming my skin even more.

Roman.

He's so much more than I ever imagined him to be. My heart has always beat with his. We've always been in sync, from the moment we met it's never been a question. But over time, our love, our need for each other has only grown stronger. Being an adult now, it's unlike anything I could ever imagine. Our love didn't fade from our time apart. His love has ingrained itself deeper within me. He can read my every emotion just as I can read his.

What we have is so much more than love. It's so much deeper. It's almost painful, how much we love each other. There isn't anything like it. I don't think anyone in the history of the universe has experienced our type of love. We're one in a million, him and I.

"Luna?" His voice rasps, his footsteps growing closer.

I lift my head up, leaning to the side as I grab a bar of soap. "In here."

The door creaks open, and there he stands. He looks so sure, so certain. My neck tilts up to look at him. He's tall, well over six feet. His hair has alternated over the years from long to short. Now it sits mid-length. A little long, a little messy, so Roman.

Since he's become a firefighter, there's a build in him that he's never had before. A definition in his chest and arms that's grown over the months. He's always been strong, able to lift me like I weigh nothing, but it's so much more now. Everything about him is just… So. Much. More.

"How was practice?" he asks, walking into the bathroom. He lowers the toilet lid, taking a seat on top of it.

I left my leg, showing him my sudsy foot. It's covered in bubbles, but my toes poke through, bruised, faded with bloody wounds.

He frowns, kneeling down on the ground so he can take a better look. He grabs my foot, his fingers digging into my skin as he pulls it closer to him. "Luna," he winces, "This looks terrible."

"It doesn't feel much better," I mumble.

His finger presses on the cracked toenail, the blackish purple turning a sickly shade of white. "This can fall right off." He turns his head toward me, worry and sadness on his face.

I shake my head. "I'm just going to tape it."

He sighs, settling my foot back into the water. Grabbing the bar of soap, he lathers it in his hand and starts running it along my leg. "I don't like that you're getting injured like this. You're pushing yourself too hard."

I lean up, my wet fingers going to the back of his hair. "It's only temporary.

I just need to get through the audition in a few months. Whether I get in or not, it won't be this bad afterward."

"You'll get in," he says with such certainty. Like there is nothing he's more sure of in this world.

"I don't know." I frown. "Sometimes I wonder if it's too late. If I'm getting too old for this." I don't know why I'm telling him now, after I've been keeping it inside, but it's like the moment he's around, all my insecurities, all my worries, just bleed out of me.

He rubs the soap down my shins, along the soles of my aching feet. He spends extra time there, massaging the curve of my foot, the pads of his fingers pressing roughly. I let out a small moan.

"Anyone would be a fucking idiot to not give you a scholarship. Not only are you talented as hell, but your dedication to proving it to them says so damn much. I don't think I could ever try this hard or work as hard as you have just to prove them, and yourself, wrong."

I shrug, watching his hands as he moves to my other foot. "I don't know. I guess I just don't have as much hope as I used to. Dancing used to be so easy, no pain, nothing at all. It was effortless. Now I feel like there is a difficulty in my dancing. There's a pain." I shake my head. "Maybe I'm being stupid."

He drops my foot, moving up to my thighs and massaging them, then moving his hands over my waist. "I don't think you're being stupid. I think you're being human."

"I don't like being human." I pout.

He chuckles. "Well, I think I've got some news that you might enjoy."

This perks me up. "What is it?"

His hand trails up my side, his fingers dancing along the outside of my breasts. My nipples tighten into peaks, barely noticeable through the soapy water. But Roman zones in on them, his tongue peeking out slightly to lick his lips.

"It's a surprise," he whispers, dragging his fingers along my breasts, pinching my nipple ever so slightly. I arch my back, the water lapping against the side of the tub with my movements.

"Please," I whimper, needing him. He holds out on me, keeping a distance sexually while all I want is him. He knows this, too. He knows how desperate I am to hold him against me. I need him. I need every bit of him, but he won't take that extra step. It's frightening, torturous, painful.

His hand slides down my stomach, swirling the soap along my body beneath the water. His finger dips into my belly button, pressing gently, then he rolls the soap back up, sliding between my breasts and up to my neck. "What do you say? Will you let me surprise you?"

"How can I agree to something when I don't know what it is?" I moan, inching toward his hand, needing any kind of relief from the burn building low in my belly.

"Because you trust me. Because you love me."

"If you love me, will you help me?"

His eyes slide to mine, the dark brown turning black with want. "What do you need, Luna?"

I sit up, the water splashing as I slide against the bottom of the tub, until I'm right next to him, me on one side of the porcelain and him on the other. The water splashes, and I lean forward, my lips only inches from his. Water drips from my hair and onto his arm, but he doesn't flinch. He doesn't move.

"I want you. Please. I'm ready." My hand falls over the tub, and I press against the zipper of his jeans, feeling the bulge growing between his legs. "I know you want me, too."

He stares at me, his breaths heavy but even. I watch his jaw tick, once, twice, three times. "Tell me yes to your surprise, and I'll help you."

"Yes," I say before he can even finish his sentence. It's been years since I've been with him, and I need him. Whatever part of him I can get, I'm greedy enough to take.

His hand goes above my breasts, his fingers large as they splay against my chest. He pushes me back, and I slide down, my back hitting the foot of the tub. It's cool against my skin, even though the water is still warm. His hand slips beneath the water, his fingers dragging along my leg. From my knee, he trails up, sliding his fingers along the inside of my thigh. My leg twitches, need and anticipation firing up my insides.

My hands go up, my fingers clutching the edges of the tub. It's slippery, and I'm barely able to hang on. As his hand rests against my sex, pulsing with a desperate need, my hands slide off the sides, splashing into the water. I press them against the tub beneath me, raising my hips as they seek his fingers.

Roman chuckles, his other hand sliding into the water against my lower stomach. He presses down, lowering my hips back down to the tub. "Be patient, Luna."

"How can I be patient when you've been holding out on me for so long? You know how badly I want you, and you continue to torture me," I whine.

I can feel his finger slide between my folds. Poking through the top, he presses against my slit before sliding down, sinking knuckle-deep into my sex. My hip bucks, and Roman's hand goes back down, pushing me down to stay still. "I torture you because when I have you, it's going to be all of you. I don't want a piece, or a fucking sliver, I want every bit of you, Luna." His fingers curl inside of me, making me see stars. He pulls out until only the tip of his finger is still inside of me, then slides back in. So slowly, so torturously.

I release a guttural moan. It tears through my throat, echoing off the small bathroom walls.

"I'm ready," I moan.

"You're not," he mumbles, continuing his torturous fingering. He adds a second finger, and I curl my toes. They ache from the movement, but the ache between my legs is so much more painful at this point. I lift my foot, pressing it against the faucet, spreading my legs wide for him. I look over at Roman, seeing his eyes darken further at my positioning.

"When I have you, Luna, I'm never going to let you go. I'm going to have every. Fucking. Inch." He plunges in with each word, lifting me higher and higher toward my orgasm. I can feel the tingling in my body, starting at my toes and working toward my head. I start to feel lightheaded, the heat of the water and Roman's ministrations making my sight begin to blur.

His two fingers slide against *that spot*. That spot that makes my body thump with every touch. I can't take it, and I reach forward, grabbing onto his forearm and digging my nails in. They score his skin, creating small pink lines.

"I'm going to…" I breathe, my voice escaping my chest.

"Come for me, Luna. Let go. Let go of everything." His words alone make me unravel. My entire body turns to lava, liquefying me. I come apart under his hand, melting into the water as a tortured moan ricochets from my chest. Tears spring to my eyes, pain and love mixing together and streaming down my cheeks. I can't take it, and I close my eyes, everything that is Roman healing me. His healing hurts, though, as he puts me back together. My scars run deep, and Roman knows this, piecing me together in exactly the way he knows how.

Roman is the *only* one who could piece me back together.

My eyes slide open, and I'm here again. I look down, seeing the leotard I bought for my audition at Julliard. The black one with the black tutu. My slippers are even on, the ribbons laced up my ankles.

My cliff.

It's mine, I realize. The one cliff I've been coming to since I was a child. The one that has repeatedly taken me through the same cycle. Every time. The outcome is always the same.

Why am I here?

I tilt my head up, seeing the clear sky. No clouds. No nighttime stars. Only the open sky, as blue as the water below me. No wind today, either. There's a silence in the air, in the sky, and below me. I hear the waves, but their lapping is calmer than usual. It's like everything is in a lull.

"Hello?" I ask, and I'm not sure why. It's not like anyone has ever responded to me. No one is ever here, it's like this place is abandoned. No one ever visits, except for me.

No one answers this time either.

I spin around, looking out into the distance. The water is dark, nearly black. So much mystery underneath those waves, so much unknown that I can't see.

There is no wind, and there is no sand. No soft grains hitting my skin, wrapping around my legs like desperate fingers.

What am I supposed to do?

I walk to the edge, the tip of my slippers curling around the edge of the cliff. I look down, feeling like I'm looking into a funhouse mirror as the waves crash against the side of the cliff. It's like it grows closer and further away at the same time, making my stomach turn with nausea. I step back, not liking that feeling at all.

With a breath, I turn around, hoping I can travel the other way. Once I turn, though, I come face to face with a gust of wind. It's filled with sand, shaped in the form of a body. The gust whips me off my feet, pushing me back and off the cliff with one huge, aggressive push.

I shoot up in bed, fear lodging a scream in the back of my throat. My hands go to my neck, heaving breaths punching out of me as my heart pounds in my ears.

The bed shifts, and Roman sits up beside me, instantly pulling me into his lap. "I was wondering if you still had those dreams."

I nod. «Always,» I breathe. The aggression in which I plummeted over the side of the cliff scared me. Shocked me. I feel a little whiplashed from it. A shiver breaks out along my spine, and Roman pulls me close, holding me tight.

Tears flood my eyes, tumbling down my cheeks in rapid rivers. "Why do you think I keep having this dream? It has to mean something, right? I just don't understand." I wipe my face with my sleeves, feeling confused. I don't get it. I don't get any of it. "What does it mean?" I cry.

He turns my face toward him, kissing along my river of tears, licking the saltiness from his lips afterward. "It's just a dream. That's all it is."

I feel like it's not, but I curl into him anyway, seeking his comfort. He lies back in the bed, keeping me on top of him. His arms suction around me, pinning me against his body. I curl into his neck, the scruff from his beard tickling the top of his nose.

I close my eyes, hoping my dream doesn't take me back to the cliff. I have a feeling it's not just a dream. I hope Roman's right. I hope that no matter what, he'll keep me safe. That he'll protect me from everything and anything.

I hope, I hope, I hope.

CHAPTER THIRTY

Luna

The moment the taxi drops us off at the airport, I turn to Roman. "Where are we going?"

He has a nervous but excited look on his face. "I told you, it's a surprise."

I think of all the places he may take me; of all the things we could do. A part of me wonders if we're going home. I bite my lip, a bit of excitement filling me.

It's been a few days since he told me about our trip. I packed last night, thinking we might go to a fancy hotel or something. Head further upstate and go to a bed and breakfast. This, I wasn't expecting. Not at all.

He opens the door, grabbing the bags with one hand and my hand with the other before pulling me out of the cab. "Come on, you took long enough to get out of bed this morning. I don't want to miss our flight." He tosses the cabbie some cash and pulls me along. I can barely catch up, his large steps making me trip over myself.

I huff, racing after him.

Check-in is relatively quick. It's early in the morning, the sun barely cresting over the tall buildings. The line is short, and it doesn't take long for us to get through security. I look around for any type of indication of where we're going.

My heart stops when we pass the sitting area for Hawaii. I'm not ready to go back there, and a part of me is worried I never will be. It's a beautiful place, with such beautiful people and beautiful scenery, but it's been tainted for me.

We walk past the area where Roman and I met again after all this time. The moment where our lives connected again. My eyes water as we walk past, and Roman gives my hand a squeeze. I look up at him, knowing he remembers too. The place where our hearts met for the second time in our lives. The moment I saw him, it was the moment in my life where everything settled into place.

Soon enough, he curves right, heading toward a seating area. In the center is a huge sign that says Washington.

My eyebrows furrow. "We're going to Washington?" I've never been. Never talked about going. Roman has no ties there, and I don't know anyone there, either.

He smiles, a small, secret quirk on his lips. "You'll see. Be patient, Luna." He sits down in an empty gray chair, the plastic thin and slippery.

I plop down next to him, sighing when my muscles thump in relief. "Or you could just tell me."

He laughs, curling an arm over my shoulder. "Nope." My eyes narrow, and I want to keep bugging him, but to be honest, I'm just too tired.

We sit silently. I lay my head on his shoulder, tired from waking up so early. My body is exhausted, too. I've put in the extra work this week in anticipation of taking time off for a few days. My toes ache, and my muscles scream for mercy. Roman has seemed just as exhausted, switching shifts and pulling extra hours so he could take this time off.

I doze on and off for a while, until a flight attendant calls for everyone to board. Roman and I get up, my knees a little shaky as we walk through the concourse. I'm nervous. It's the first time I've been on a plane with Roman. The first time we've traveled anywhere together.

"You ready?" He turns toward me, buckling his seatbelt and then buckling mine as well.

I curl my fingers around his, the warmth of his hand heating my entire body. I don't know if I'm ready. I don't know what he has in store for us, but as long as he's with me, I guess I'll be ready for anything. "Yeah, I am."

364

Wow.

Washington is unlike anything I've ever seen before.

Mountains, city, ocean, everything combined into one. It takes my breath away.

Once we got off the plane, Roman got us a cab to a hotel right in Seattle. We settled in, ate some food, and started touring the city. It's been amazing, to visit something from a tourist's standpoint. When I traveled before, it was without a stitch of money in my pocket. I couldn't enjoy the wonders of gift shops and eating in restaurants. It's been a long day, my feet ache, and so do my cheeks from the constant smile plastered on my face, but Roman said he had one more stop for us.

That stop has turned into a hike. A hike through the forest slightly north of Seattle. It's cool here, not muggy like the forest in Hawaii was. But it's beautiful, and even with me out of breath, I can't stop myself from looking around at the greens of the tall trees and the mountains in the distance, their white peaks still filled with snow from this past winter.

"Almost there," Roman says, walking up ahead of me. I watch his ass flex in his jeans, wishing he would quit keeping me from him and just let us be together. He knows me, though, maybe even better than I know myself. He must see a darkness, a brokenness in me that I no longer feel. Because I feel like I'm ready, yet he continues to hold back.

"Here we are," he says. I look up, seeing us at the end of the trail. We're on top of a mountain, and as I walk closer, I gasp.

My shoes dig into the sand, my eyes growing wide. How did I not realize this before?

I point at it, walking further back into the forest. "You…"

He points out to the ocean. "Where the mountains meet the sea, Luna. Finally, we're here."

Tears spring to my eyes, my dreams and my nightmares colliding into one. "I'm scared," I whisper. "Every time I've ever been here, I've died, Roman." My legs shake. No, my entire body shakes.

He holds out his hand. "One day, a long time ago, do you remember what I said?"

I shake my head, too many emotions jumbling up every memory. I can't pick one out, not a single memory from my life. Not right now.

"I said that one day I'd be a rock star and you'd be a ballerina, and we'd go to where the mountains meet the sea."

Tears fall down my cheeks. "You aren't a rock star, and I'm not a ballerina."

He shakes his head, "No, but I was, and you will be. Does it really matter, at the end of the day? Here we are, Luna. The place that's haunted you your entire life, and we're here."

I look around, seeing little differences here and there. The place in my dreams was a little more open, where this one quickly goes into a forest. But there's so many similarities, too. From the sharp edge of the cliff to the dark water in the distance. It's like he plucked the details from my dream and painted them into the world in front of me.

His hand reaches out again. "Take my hand, Luna. Let's face this. Together." After a moment of hesitation, I place my shaky hand in his. He wraps his fingers around mine, clutching me tightly. His fingers are warm. He pulls me up, and every step is painful. Rocks crunch beneath my shoes. I don't want to go to the top. I don't want to go to the edge. But here is Roman, making me face my fear.

He always makes me conquer everything. Always.

He brings me to the top, far enough from the edge where even if I fell, I wouldn't tumble over, but close enough that I can see the waves crashing against the rocks, the water turning white as they angrily slam against the jagged edges.

I let out a shaky breath.

"Do you know what it's like to love you, Luna?"

I turn toward him, my eyes dry from the cool air and wet at the same time. "Tell me."

"Loving you is like breathing too much air and being deprived of air at the same time. Loving you is watching the time going by and wishing it could stop, just so I could spend just an extra moment with you. Loving you is painful, because every ounce of torment you've ever been through in your life I can feel. I see you, Luna, but I also see through you. I see your scars, I see your pain." His hand brushes across my face, across my chilled cheekbones. "But I also see your beauty, and you're the most beautiful person I've ever seen in my entire life. Your gray eyes have been engrained into me. I could spend the rest of my life sitting next to you. Watching you breathe, watching you dance. I want for nothing; I need for nothing. Not when I have you."

He drops his hand, taking a step back from me. Reaching into his pocket, he pulls out a small white box, barely noticeable dwarfed in his hand, but I see it, and it makes me gasp. My hand goes up to my mouth as he drops to his knee. Looking up at me, he continues, "You are pain, Luna, and you are beauty. But more than anything else in the world, you are mine. And I want to spend the rest of the seconds and minutes and years that we have, together. I don't want another wasted moment. You've been mine before I knew what love was. Be mine now, and tomorrow, and for the rest of our lives." Taking a deep breath, his voice grows raspy. "Will you marry me, Luna?"

My legs give out and I fall to my knees, the bones slamming into the rocky ground. My chest can't catch enough air, even with my gasps. Tears fall down my cheeks, blowing away in the wind. I can barely breathe, even when Roman has just filled me up with all the air in the world.

He waits patiently, watching me as he cracks the box open.

All it does is make me sob harder. The most beautiful ring sits cushioned in the middle of the box. The diamonds glimmer off the cliff, the sun, the ocean, my fucking soul. I want to reach out and touch it, but another part of me doesn't even want to breathe on it.

"I will…" I breathe in a shaky breath, my words coming out choked and strangled. "I will marry you, Roman. Now and Always."

"Thank fuck." He leans forward, grabbing onto my cheeks, smashing his lips against mine. I kiss him, giving him my entire life, my heart, my soul. Every kiss from him gives me life, heals my bones, pieces together the shattered parts of me that only he can heal.

"I love you, Luna," he says. Leaning back from me, he slides the ring from the box and grabs my left hand, pushing the ring over my finger. It fits perfectly, snug beneath my knuckle. I tilt my hand back and forth, watching the diamonds glimmer in the sun.

"I love you, too, Roman. Now and always."

I walk into our hotel room, listening as Roman slides the chain of the lock on our door. I slide my coat from my arms, draping it over the small table in the corner of the room. I can feel his presence before he even touches me. His feet are silent as he crosses the room, and then his breath is on my neck. He grabs my hair, pulling it over my shoulder, and kisses the space between my neck and my shoulder, his lips light, brushing. I close my eyes, tipping my head to the side to give him better access.

His hand goes to the collar of my shirt, pulling it over my shoulder. It drapes down my bicep, showing off the top of my cleavage. I inhale, feeling his heat and love surround me. His hand trails down, hitting the hem of my shirt. His fingers slip beneath it, running across my bare stomach. My skin twitches, and his fingers splay out, covering my entire belly.

He pushes on my stomach, turning me around slowly. I face him, tilting my head back so I can look him in the eyes. There's no smile on his lips, no laughter, no hesitations. He's sure. He's here.

He clings to the bottom of my shirt, and I lift my arms. He pulls it up, over my head, and his fingers release as he drops the fabric to the ground. I lift my hand behind my back, ready to unclasp my bra. His hand goes up, grabbing onto my wrist. Barely a flinch of his head, only a slight shake. I drop my hand to my side, and his snakes around my back. With a flick, my bra loosens. His fingers go to the straps, sliding them down my arms, the tips of his fingers sliding down my skin as they go.

He grabs the bra as it falls off my wrist, tossing it aside.

His hands go under my arms, behind my back, pressing his palms against my skin. My chest hits his, and my hands go to his biceps, my fingers wrapping around the muscles.

His mouth comes to mine, hovering above my lips. Not kissing me, just breathing me in. The emotions are heavy, and I swallow them down. We barely spoke on our hike down the mountain or in the cab on the way home. Too happy, too caught up in our emotions. My heart feels so full, so much like it's about to crack.

Now the emotions are getting to me. I feel emotional. My love hurts. I love Roman too much. It consumes me, and I want nothing but to be swept up in his love. I need him, more than I need my own heart, I think. That thought alone terrifies me, but if I were to be honest, I've known it all along.

"I love you," he mouths against my lips.

"I love you," I whisper.

I bring my arms down to his waist, pulling his shirt up, bringing my hands along his warm back, pressing and digging my fingers into the hard muscles. He grabs his shirt at the waist, pulling it over his head in one quick swoop. Then he's against me again, our warmth mixing.

A tear leaks out of my eye, and he wipes it away. Bringing his other hand below my butt, circling around, he lifts me off the ground. He takes a few steps forward, until his knees hit the bed. He climbs on, laying me down below him. My hair splays out on the floral comforter and the reddish pillows below my head. His fingers go to the button of my jeans, and he pops it free, sliding my zipper down.

I lift my hips, and he curls his fingers beneath my jeans, pulling them down my thighs, sliding them off my legs so, so slowly. They slip off my feet, and he drops them over the edge of the bed. His head goes down to my toes, kissing the bruises and scrapes. He moves up slowly, kissing my ankle, my shin, my inner thighs, his lips brushing so lightly, just a kiss against my skin. Feather-light.

I can barely breathe, every time his lips touch my skin, he lights me on fire, stealing my breaths as he goes. He kisses me over my underwear, his fingers going beneath the fabric, and he slips them down my legs.

Then I'm bare for him.

"So beautiful," he rasps. It's low, full of all the emotions I'm feeling.

He goes back down, pressing his lips against my hip bones, my flat stomach, my ribs, my breasts. His other hand glides up my side, his fingers dancing along my skin softly. So lightly. He kisses my neck, my jaw, my cheek, my lips, barely passing by before he grabs my left hand, lifting it in front of us. He kisses my fingers, my palm, my knuckles. He kisses the ring, closing his eyes against it as he breathes, taking a big breath before looking at me. "I love you."

"I love you," I whisper.

He comes back down, grabbing his wallet before pushing his pants and boxers over his hips, kicking them off the bed. Grabbing a condom from his wallet, he's about to tear it open when I press my hand over his. "Let me."

I slide it from his fingers, ripping it open. He leans up, his erection long and hard against his abs. Larger than from when we were young. Manlier, with a small patch of clean hair that leads from his belly button down to his erection. I grab his hardness with my hand, pumping it, just as he taught me all those years ago.

He tilts his head toward the ceiling, letting out a hiss between his teeth. With the slippery condom in hand, I pinch the tip, sliding it over his length, rolling it on until it hits the base.

I wipe my hand on the comforter, then bring it up to his hair. It's messy, falling around his face. I push it back, curling my fingers in his long strands. Pulling his face down to mine, I kiss him, burying my lips against his.

He kisses me back, diving his tongue into my mouth. I slide my tongue along his, moaning into his mouth as his hand comes to my breast. He tweaks my nipple, and I arch my back. With his free hand, he lines up his erection, pushing the head between my folds. He slides his head back and forth, pressing against my clit over and over again. I moan, pushing my hips up toward his.

Finally, he sinks in. Pushing all the way to the hilt, I can feel nothing but heat, his twitching erection pulsing against my walls.

Then, he moves, so slowly. He slides in and out, and I can hear the slick wetness of our bodies as they grind against each other. He grunts, his lips hovering over mine. I lift my head, connecting my lips with his. They barely touch, the smallest caress against each other.

He breathes in as I breathe out, and he breathes out as I breathe in. We inhale each other as he moves, keeping his body as close to mine as possible. Our bodies grow slick, damp with sweat. I feel an electricity between us, a connection that's deeper than physical. My chest grows warm, feeling like his heart is beating against mine.

I feel like we're one as we move with each other. I can feel his love, I can hear his thoughts. Everything about him is every bit a part of me.

His hands slide down, gripping my hips as he rolls over, lying his back against the mattress and settling me on top on his lap. My hair tumbles over my shoulders, brushing his waist. His fingers thread through the strands, messing them up as he takes hold.

I move, grabbing onto his hands, lacing my fingers with his as I press up on my knees, grinding against him.

He grunts, his eyes burning into mine with need. I move faster, grinding against him as a tingling starts in my sex. I can feel the pressure building, a growing orgasm that will knock me on my back. His cock hits a spot in me with every bounce, every move he slides against me that has my eyes rolling in the back of my head.

His small grunts and my small moans fill the room, and I move faster, our skin starting to slap against one another. My breasts bounce, and his free hand goes up, palming the weight and pinching my nipple between his fingers.

My head tilts back, a whimper slipping from my lips. He fills me so completely. He's so big, hitting every inch of me. I can feel him in my stomach, I can feel him in my heart. There isn't a part of me that isn't affected by him.

His hands leave my breast and hair, gripping my waist. He starts to control my movements, creating the pace that he wants. I move faster, chasing the orgasm that is burning through my blood. I can feel my walls fluttering against him, the imminent orgasm clenching him inside of me.

He lets out a guttural groan, his cock twitching, growing impossibly larger inside of me. He slams my hips down on him, and I break free, my orgasm rushing through me.

He twitches, and I can feel him come, his cock pulsing and emptying inside the condom. My vision clouds with lust, and I close my eyes, my chest falling against his as my hips continue grinding, wanting this feeling to last forever. His fingers dig into my sides, creating bruises on my hips.

I can hear his heart beating in my ear, the vicious pounding fast and erratic. He pushes my hair from my face, brushing it over my shoulder as his fingers trail down my back. I close my eyes, loving his heat, his body, his comfort.

Slowly, he pulls out of me, pulling the condom off and tossing it off the bed. Rolling over, he holds me against him, curling my body flush to his. He kisses my neck, my back, and brings his hand to my jaw, pulling my lips to his. "I love you, Luna."

"I love you, Roman."

CHAPTER THIRTY-ONE

Luna
2001

"What's got you looking so nervous?"

I glance over my shoulder, seeing Roman walking up to me. He's got a bright smile on his face, his arms snaking around my waist. His hand presses against my stomach, as if he knows there are butterflies flapping around, nerves filling and spilling out of me.

"It's just been a long time," I whisper, looking out our balcony window. The sun is only in the beginning stages of falling behind the tall skyscrapers. There's a shiny, orange hue in the city. Yellow cabs down on the street look miniature as they zip down the street. I can hear the honking, the people rushing down the sidewalks, the constant chaos of New York City. The summer greens are starting to turn into fall oranges and reds.

Roman presses a kiss against my neck, his lips warm and comforting. I curl into him, turning around and wrapping my arms around his chest. "I'm excited, but I'm nervous," I murmur against his soft gray shirt.

The timbre of his voice vibrates against my ear, "Nothing to be worried about. It's just our family."

I sigh, knowing he's right. It's been months since we've gotten home from our Washington trip. Months since we got engaged. I run my fingers along my ring, the new addition to my body that I promised I'd never take off. It's beautiful, perfectly my style. Roman couldn't have picked out anything more suited for me. For us.

Tonight, I get to see our families for the first time since I was eighteen years old. My stomach twists and turns with every moment that goes by. Our engagement party has been put off long enough, everyone's schedule not aligning with the next person's. But this weekend is the weekend everyone was able to come out. This evening we're just having our families over for a small dinner here, and my stomach has been in knots all day.

It doesn't help that next week is my audition at Julliard. I've practiced long enough. I'm ready. Roman thinks I'm ready. I could perfect my routine with my eyes closed. There isn't a move that hasn't been done one million times by my body. My toes, feet, legs, arms, every limb has been put through hell during this last year. It's been hard, the hardest I've physically beat my bones and muscles. But the time has come, and in only a few days I'll know whether or not I'll be attending Julliard.

Roman's hands lift, circling my neck before curling around my chin. He tilts my head up, and I look into his eyes, seeing his warm brown eyes with specks of gold flickering back at me. "It'll all be okay," he says, as if he knows my worries are more than just about seeing our parents tonight.

I press on my tiptoes, reaching up and touching my lips to his. His fingers press into my cheeks, a possessiveness overtaking him as he takes control. My lips open, and I slide my lips against his, needing his comfort when I'm feeling so out of sorts.

Knock, knock, knock.

Roman pulls back, looking down at me with a smile. My eyes are wide, and I bite my lips, excitement and nerves hitting me again.

I shouldn't be nervous at all. The excitement over seeing my parents is going to tear me in two, but I haven't seen them, or Roman's parents, in so long. I can't help the flicker of nerves mixing in as well.

"Do you want to…?" he turns toward the door.

I press my hand against my stomach, taking a deep breath. "You get it."

He nods, walking toward the door. I hear as he unhooks the chains and opens the door, and then their voices float through the room, my mom's in particular. My breath catches in my chest. I stay in the living room, not sure I'd even be able to take a step without crumbling to the ground. I inhale a shaky breath, hearing my mom's voice again, "Where's Luna?"

Suddenly, she's there, walking around Roman and straight toward me. I let out a choked sob, my arms reaching out for her. She rushes toward me, wrapping me in her warmth and the smell that I can't explain as anything besides my mom—warmth, a hint of incense, and a little marijuana. I bury my head in her chest, crying into her shirt and drenching it with my tears.

"My Luna. I've missed you so much, baby," she murmurs against my hair. I feel a pair of arms wrap around my back, warm and strong, and I cry harder, sensing my dad before I even see him.

"Luna, Luna, Luna, you've grown so much." His voice is a rasp against my back. I separate from my mom, curling into his arms. He hugs me tight, his arms slightly shaky as he holds me.

"I missed you," I cry into his chest. "I'm so sorry."

"There's nothing to be sorry about, Luna. All that matters is we're here now. All of us." My mom runs her hand down my hair, and it's so comforting I want to curl into her arms and never leave.

"Hey, sis," I hear from behind me. I turn around, seeing Harper, so grown, in nice jeans and a sweater. Her long hair lays in a straight sheet down her back. Her makeup is flawless. She's a woman now, and for a moment, I almost don't recognize her.

"Harper," I cry. It's been so long. So, so, fucking long.

I hear another voice clearly behind me, and I wipe my face, turning out of my parents' arms and see Nora standing there, so old, so fucking beautiful. Her curly hair is to her shoulders, a pair of tight jeans covering her legs with a band tee on top. "Look at you," she says to me, shaking her head. "How in the hell did you get even more pretty?"

I cry-laugh, rushing into her arms and pulling her against me. Her thin arms hold me tight, and we rock back and forth. She's a little peanut in my arms, but then again she always has been.

I feel a gentle hand on my shoulder and look, seeing Goldie with a watery smile on her face. "Luna, how are you doing?"

I pull her into a hug, and Cypress comes up behind us, his smoky scent and tall figure wrapping us all into a group hug.

After a while, we all separate, and I look at my family. They're all so much the same, but so much different. Each of the parents have crow's feet around their eyes, aged over time but still perfect. My parents still dress like hippies, my mom in a flowing dress and my dad's hair a little too long. Roman's dad has on a black leather jacket matched with a pair of jeans, and Goldie is wearing her own leather jacket.

Our family, back together again.

We sit for hours, talking, remembering. We were planning to go out to eat, but we lose track of time and miss our reservations. We end up ordering in, Chinese food from my favorite spot down the street. We all sit on the floor, laughing and crying. We talk about plans for our upcoming wedding.

There's only one place where we feel we should get married.

At home, on our beach, between our houses with the glistening water lapping in front of us. There's nothing that sounds more perfect, and it makes me grow excited. I can't wait to go home, to see the cornfield across the street. To visit the park we used to go to everyday. To see how much has changed in our little town and see what's stayed the same after all this time.

Our night is perfect. We stay up until well after nightfall. It makes me sad, wishing I wouldn't have stayed away from my family for so long, the people who mean the most in the world to me. I missed so much time, so many memories lost. But we're all together again, and I promise to make up every moment.

CHAPTER THIRTY-TWO
Roman

I sit in the station, my heavy, black boot tapping against the floor as I watch the clock. Luna has her audition today. She'll be waiting for me, watching for me. She's taken so much time and energy to prepare for this. I can't wait for the moment she gets on that stage. When she finally has the opportunity to show off her fucking amazing talent. She's going to blow everyone away. She doesn't even know how good she is, always downplaying her moves and acting like she isn't the best there's ever been.

She is. She's the fucking best. I've spent hours upon hours throughout our lives watching videos of professional ballet dancers, and I know without a doubt that she's better than every single one of them. Hands down.

I glance at the clock again, groaning under my breath as I wait for my shift to be over. I took an overnight shift so that I could take the morning off and be at her audition. I haven't seen her all night, and I'm sure she's a damn wreck. I doubt she slept a wink, too nervous about making the wrong move, about stumbling, about not being perfect. She needs to know that she could never do no wrong. That she's perfect in every move she makes. Nothing else matters when she's on the stage.

Nothing.

I look at the clock, seeing it's seven forty-five. Only fifteen minutes left until my shift is over, but I'm hoping I can leave a few minutes early so I can be there on time. Luna's audition is the first one today. Nine o'clock. Traffic is hell in the city during the morning, but I'll fucking sprint there if I have to.

I watch the second hand tick by, ready to bust out of here at any second. I grab my things from the desk and stomp to my locker to hang my uniform up. Another slow night. One phone call for an elderly lady who smelled an odor in her apartment. Come to find out the neighbors were just smoking a bit too much weed below her, and the scent was making its way through the vents and upstairs. Other than that, it was quiet, not a call.

I shut my locker, ready to bust out of here a few minutes early.

Footsteps pound my way. Multiple footsteps. I turn around, seeing my chief rushing toward me with a ton of my crew behind him. "We've got to move."

My eyes widen, looking at the clock. "Right now?"

"Yes, now." He rushes to his locker, grabbing his hat and jacket. "Move."

"Sir, Luna's audition…" I can't miss it. I can't miss it. *I can't miss it.*

He shakes his head, an urgency in his tone. "We need you for this, man. I'm sorry."

I feel the panic radiating off him. Opening my locker, I take my things back out, sliding my coat onto my arms. "Do you know what it is?"

The other guys are outside, and I hear the firetruck sirens starting up, the alarms loud and urgent.

"Not much was said. Just that we need to go. Now." He doesn't spare me another glance, running out of the station and toward his truck.

I follow him, seeing Dylan already strapped up in the back.

He frowns when he sees me. "Luna?"

I shake my head. "I'm going to miss it."

He slaps my back, a worry in his eyes. "We'll get you back soon. Maybe you can make it to the end of her audition."

The firetruck jolts forward, the sirens loud in my ears as we fly down the road. My hair blows in the wind, and an instant sweat breaks out from the heavy clothes, even in the cool fall air. I bring a hand up, wiping my forehead. "Yeah, maybe."

"Sorry, man." His voice can barely be heard over the blaring in my ears.

"Yeah, me too," I mumble to myself.

CHAPTER THIRTY-THREE

Luna

I t's dark.

I peak around the edge of the stage, seeing the judges sitting behind their booth. So intimidating.

The stage is grand.

So many seats, all black and encased in a rich fabric. Four different sections surround the stage, all of them filled with rows upon rows upon rows. It's dark throughout the auditorium, the only light cast upon the stage. The dark gray, smooth floor that's waiting for me.

There are a few other people out there, a few of the other people that are auditioning today. My eyes scan every seat, every row, every section.

Where is he?

I look up at the clock above me, seeing it's a few minutes before nine. I know he was going to try and sneak out a few minutes early. He didn't want to miss a moment of my performance.

I take a shaky breath, running my hands down my black leotard. The black tutu is beautiful, shifting with every step I take. My hair is so tightly slicked behind my head, my temples hurt, but not a hair is out of place.

I'm perfect. I'm ready to go. But how can I go without Roman? This dance is just as much for him as it is for me. We're in this together, we have been since day one. I don't know if I can go out on that stage without him. I don't.

I feel a hand on my shoulder and spin on my heels, hoping for one thing but coming face to face with another.

My ballet instructor.

My eyes widen, my jaw going slack. "Leona," I gasp, "What are you doing here?"

She grabs my arm, giving it a squeeze with a bright smile on her face. "I couldn't have my favorite student go on without watching her, now could I?" Her hands trail down to mine. She squeezes my fingers. "How do you feel?"

"Like I'm going to be sick," I mumble, pressing my hand to my stomach.

She looks me up and down, critiquing and appraising me at once. "Look at how much you've grown. Still the perfect ballerina." She clucks her tongue, shaking her head. "I'm glad you got back into it, Luna, you were made for this."

I glance over my shoulder, my eyes flitting over the seats again. Still no Roman. "I don't know… Roman isn't here yet."

Her eyes soften. "Still with that boy?"

I lift my hand toward her. "Engaged, actually."

She runs her finger over the diamond softly, watching it shimmer in the dark light. "Mmm, I would have guessed nothing less. You guys had something special, I will give you that."

My stomach twists into a knot. "He told me he'd be here. I want to wait until he gets here."

Her eyes narrow. "You aren't waiting for anyone. This is your time, Luna. You either take this chance, or you let it go."

"I don't want to let this go, I just—"

She shakes her head, grabbing my hands again. "Listen, I've known since the first day you walked into my small studio that this is what you're meant to do. If Roman is late, he's late. I can see in the way you're standing that you've practiced to death on this routine. Your spine is straight, your toes are already pointed…" she sighs, "Luna, take a chance. Go for it. This is your destiny."

I gnaw on my lip, knowing she's right. I'm meant to dance. I'm meant for every second of this. If Roman is late, then he's late. But I can't wait any longer. I have to do this.

He'd want me to do this.

I nod. "Okay. I'm ready."

She glances up at the clock. "Good, because you're late. Get out there." She turns, ready to walk out to the auditorium. "Wait, what song are you playing?"

I smile at her. "Did you have to ask? You should already know."

She grins, giving me a single nod before leaving the back of the stage. I watch as she walks down the side steps, taking a seat right beside the panel. With one last glance and one last check at the door, I press up on my toes as the first notes of *Canon in D* begin. I lift my head, snapping my spine straight, and make my way out to the stage.

The lights dim as I walk out, and I dance. I dance like every note has a clear path to my heart. My toes ache, my eyes water, but I stay strong. I dance like this is the best dance, the only dance, the *last dance* I'll ever do. I feel tall, like the tallest person in the world as I trail across the stage. Every move, every step is perfect. Not once do I falter, or slouch. The music runs through my blood, playing me for a puppet. The music plays, and plays, and plays.

I feel alive.

I can't stop the smile that breaks over my face from dancing on this stage. I've waited my entire life to be here, to perform, to do what I do best. This is where I'm meant to be.

My toes barely touch the ground as I dance from foot to foot. I spin, my fingers wrapping around my ballet slipper as it lays flush against my side. I keep my chin up as I leap, my spine held so straight, so perfectly aligned it aches. I leap into a split, feeling like I float across the stage as the notes from the music lift me higher than I've ever been before.

I've never danced this well. *Ever.*

My spine arches as I bend back, the crescendo of the music moving my body with each note that flows through my veins. I don't step a foot out of place during the entire routine.

I am perfect.

My body hums by the time the last note hits, and tears are streaming down my face. I end in a leap, my back to the judges. Taking a large breath, I can't stop the tears from streaming down my face this time. I'm sure my makeup is smearing, rivers of black trailing down my pale cheeks.

I turn around slowly, breathing through my sob. I watch the five sets of eyes, Leona's included, all staring at me.

No sounds. No clapping.

Nothing.

I bow, and then I hear the chairs screech. Glancing up, I see them all standing. Wiping their eyes.

And then they *clap.*

My hands go to my mouth to muffle my sobs. A smile breaks out behind my hands, even though I know I'm supposed to keep a professional face on stage.

"Well done," one of them says.

Standing there, I look out, my hands falling to my sides when I still see no Roman.

Where is he?

I glance over my shoulder, hoping to see him backstage, but he isn't there either.

"Luna?" I turn around, seeing the panel staring at me.

"Yes?" I clear my throat, putting on a small smile.

"This might be a little premature," a man says, glasses perched on the tip of his nose, "but I wanted to welcome you to Julliard."

My eyes go wide, and I turn toward Leona. She's wiping tears from her face, and all she does is give me a slight nod.

My throat releases a small cry, my legs shaking as his words hit me.

I'm in.

"Thank you. Thank you so much," I cry.

They sit back down, giving me a small smile.

I can't contain my sobs, so I give them a wave and run off the stage.

"Oh my God," I cry, running toward the dressing room in the back. I grab my black t-shirt, burying my face in the soft fabric. "I'm in." My shoulders shake as emotions run through me. Euphoria, so much damn excitement, and shock. But more than anything, I feel a hint of disappointment fraying the edges.

Where is Roman?

I frown, tearing out of my clothes as fast as I can. I slip into a pair of jeans and my shirt, which grow damp with splotches of tears. I put everything into my bag, switching out my slippers for a pair of tennis shoes.

It's after nine now. He should be here. Unless he's sick and he couldn't make it. But he sounded fine last night before he went into work.

I wipe my tears, releasing my hair from my bun as I walk out. It's busy on the streets, crazier than normal as I hail a cab. The streets are crowded, people rushing up and down the sidewalks, walking across the streets like everyone is in a hurry.

What's going on?

A cab pulls to the curb, and I hop in, giving him the directions to our apartment.

"Do you know what's going on outside?"

He barely looks over his shoulder, giving me a small shake of his head.

I frown, sitting back in the worn gray seats as I watch chaos ensue around me.

Something is *wrong*.

I roll down the window as we drive, a wave of smoky air hitting me in the face. I cough on it, waving my hand in my face and roll the window back up.

"Wait, what is that?" The cabbie slams on his brakes as we hit dead stopped traffic. Cars are honking, people are standing in the middle of the streets.

"What's going on?" I ask him, attempting to look around all the different cars and people flooding the area.

I open the door, ignoring the cab driver as he shouts at me. I slip out onto the street, the air a little dense. My eyes widen as I walk toward the chaos, seeing a skyscraper with huge flames and smoke coming from the top of it. Large, billowing puffs of dark gray, nearly black, smoke fill the sky. People run around me, knocking into my shoulders as they attempt to get through the crowds.

My eyes are saucers as I stare at the madness in front of me. That isn't just one tower, I realize, that's two towers that are on fire. And those aren't just any towers.

That's the World Trade Center. I see firetrucks up ahead, and a cry leaves my throat, breaking through my mouth in a painful scream.

"No," I cry, walking toward the mess in front of me. People are running around in absolute terror, but it's like everything is in slow motion for me. There's no sound. It's as if the only sound I can hear are the burning flames as they scorch every inch of the building in front of me. They're on max volume. I can hear the pops, the crackling as the wood and metal burn to a crisp.

He can't be there, can he? He was supposed to be off. He was supposed to be with me, watching me dance. Cheering me on. Sitting in his seat with a proud look on his face.

Not in this burning building. Not like this. *Not like this.*

There's suddenly a stillness in the air. I can hear everything and nothing at the same time. I look up at the burning buildings, pieces of white ash landing in my black hair. Tears stream down my face, mixing with the ash that fills my lungs with every breath I take.

It's almost as if I can hear a crack. A crack that fills the entire world, splitting through the seams of my entire being. My stomach hollows out, and everything in front of me erupts.

One of the towers shatter, collapsing into itself as the top floor falls, falls, falls. It echoes throughout the city, maybe throughout the entire world.

Falls.

Falls.

Falls.

There's a rumble that pounds through the streets as the tower collapses, so loudly, so incredibly loudly I can barely breathe.

The ash, rubble, and the entire world in front of me turns into a black cloud. A wave of smoke fills up the sky, tumbling toward me at a rapid pace.

My bag with my ballet uniform falls from my fingers, pounding to the ground in a soundless heap. I feel like the world slows down, everyone screaming. People start running, terror and chaos filling the streets. People are running. *Away.* As fast and as far away from the smoky cloud as they possibly can. Bumping into me, some people even slamming against my shoulders in an attempt to get away.

I run toward it.

I take off into a sprint, feeling like my legs are moving in slow motion as I make my way toward the building.

I know he's in there.

I know it.

I can feel him, the electricity that I've always felt whenever he's near. My heart beating heavier, faster, lighter, easier, as it always has. As it always does. As it always will.

I run, sprinting as the black cloud gets closer, the top of the building settling to the ground, the noises in the city so loud, the screams of terror, it all runs my blood cold.

Then, it's as if everything in my life *stops.*

The feeling of Roman, of his heart, of his soul connected with mine… stops.

I feel the severing of it, as if someone lifted the cord between our bodies and snipped it away with scissors. One easy clip, one building crash, and that feeling I've had for years, is gone.

In only a second.

A scream rips through my throat. I can feel the bloody, terror-filled scream tearing apart my vocal cords.

Suddenly, I'm lifted off the ground, a man in the crowd wrapping his arms around my waist, lifting me into the air as he sprints. My body thumps against his body, hauled up into his arms as he runs. My body flops up and down with his urgency. I reach for Roman. I beg for the feeling of him to come back, but it never does. I can barely see, barely stand to breathe as the smoke envelops us, the cloud of ash and dust tearing apart the street and everyone in its wake.

Until I can't see anything, and I hear nothing but a whoosh of dust as it powers into my ears. I scream, but I can't get a word out as my body fills with gray sand. Gray as my eyes. I hear a door open, and I'm shoved to the ground. Looking around, I see a crowd of terrified people.

The entire group curls on the ground, crying, the floor littered with rubble and glass and so, so much ash.

The air is filled with terror. I can taste it just as much as I can taste the ash on my tongue. It burns me from the inside out. Everyone, everything is filled with a white coating of dust covering their skin, rivers of tears clearing the ash away as it travels to their chins.

They feel so much terror, so much fear.

I crawl to the glass window, my palms filling with pebbles and dust that I barely feel. I press my hand against the glass, which should feel cool, but it doesn't.

It's hot.

I close my eyes, hoping for any kind of feeling. Anything to tell me he's still here with me.

Anything at all.

Nothing.

CHAPTER THIRTY-FOUR

Roman

ONE HOUR AGO

"Holy shit." My eyes widen when I see the flames billowing out of the North Tower of the World Trade Center. The sky is turning black because there is so much smoke.

"Terrorist attack." My chief gets off the phone, looking over at us with a grim expression. "A plane was hijacked. Hit straight into the North Tower. There are people stuck in there. We have to get them out."

We all nod, grim expressions on our faces. This isn't how we planned to start our morning, but here we are. We all gear up, sliding our helmets on as the firetruck pulls up right next to the building.

The ground below me shakes, and I look up just as a plane strikes the South Tower. People go crazy, running for their lives and screaming at the top of their lungs. Flames billow from the plane, and my eyes water, thinking of all the lives just lost in a split second.

So many fucking lives.

"Move! We have to move!" Chief shouts.

We hop off the truck, running to the South Tower. The air grows heavy, filled with debris and so much smoke I can barely see. I squint my eyes, running through the smoke and into the side of the building. We can barely get in the door as people bust out, clear panic written all over their faces.

"Upstairs. We need to get upstairs," Dylan shouts.

I look around, seeing a stairwell. "There."

We rush toward it, our uniforms heavy as we race up the stairs. I'm hot instantly, panic, worry, fucking terror eating away at every single bone in my body. We exit onto a floor, and it looks like a warzone. Things tipped over, everything left haphazardly as people left in panic. It smells of smoke in here, the building starting to burn and reaching the lower floors. We rush through the offices, checking for any survivors.

I glance out the window, seeing someone out on the windowsill. My eyes widen, and I rush over to it, attempting to open the window. The woman looks at me, tears running down her cheeks. I can't open the window, though. Nothing will get it to budge.

"Move out of the way." I wave my hands.

She does as she's told, sliding to the side. Then, it's like slow motion as the toe of her heel slips on the ledge. She looks at me, a look of terror in her eyes before she loses her grip. There's a knowledge in her eyes, like she knows what is about to happen. All I can do is stare at her, watch in horror as she falls backward, her arms windmilling around her as she falls into the sky.

I look away, a choked sob breaking from my chest.

"Holy shit." I wipe my wet eyes, a disassociation to my body and mind.

"We've got to move!" Dylan shouts, and I nod my head. Looking up and over at the North Tower. My eyes widen when I see someone standing on one of the highest floors, standing on the ledge of his window. He barely takes a second to think about it. He looks over his shoulder, fear and terror covering his features before looking below him.

And he jumps.

"Fuck!" I rush away from the window, moving to get other people out. We find people hiding under their desks, hidden away in bathrooms. We move as many people out as we can, telling them to take the stairwells on their way out of the building.

We move for so long, smoke filling the air and covering my lungs. My uniform weighs me down, and it feels claustrophobic, like I've been working for hours, even though I know it hasn't even been an hour.

We rush up the stairs, until the ground is hot and the air is stifling, and we can barely breathe.

I can hear their screams from the other side of a closed door. Pained, treacherous screams that come from the pits of their stomachs.

People holler for help, screaming and pleading for any type of assistance. My stomach bottoms out, tumbling to the ground below me.

"We need to help them," I shout.

Dylan shakes his head. "It's a death wish, Roman. We have to get out of here."

I listen to people screaming, terror and pain filling their voices. Pleading for help, pleading in pain, crying for their loved ones.

Help.

Help.

Help.

Pounding so heavily against the door, like every bit of strength is going into their fists.

I take a step up the stairs, and Dylan's hand wraps around my wrist. I glare over my shoulder at him. "I'm not going to walk out of here knowing these people died, Dylan. Fucking help me."

Pure terror makes his eyes water, and he nods. The rest of the guys rush up the stairs, into the heat, into the fire, the door opens, and a roar of fire billows toward us.

And then it's silence. Like my ears become muted, and I can feel the ground start to shake below me. The ceiling shakes even worse above me. We all freeze, staring at each other. And in one group decision, we grab those that we can, rushing down the stairs.

The cracking grows louder, into a violent roar that fills up every inch of air and space around me.

Life stops.

The entire world… *stops.*

Luna appears before me. Her face, soft and feminine, smiling at me. Loving me. Her gray eyes staring at me in comfort. She's younger, just a teenager. No worry or darkness in her eyes. Her soul touches mine, a glow emanating from her hand as she presses it against my chest. I bring my hand up, pressing it over her pale skin. She's warm against me, and even in this heat, her warmth brings me so much comfort. So much safety.

Then her hand separates from my chest, and she turns around, walking off into the distance. Her hair floats around her back, slapping at her waist as she walks. She looks over her shoulder, a soft smile on her face.

It's okay.

"I love you, Roman," she whispers, and I can somehow hear it over the roar of the world around me.

"I love you, Luna," I say back.

Then, there's only darkness.

CHAPTER THIRTY-FIVE

Luna

I stare at the TV, feeling nothing.

Seeing nothing.

Hearing nothing.

Nothing.

My mind is empty, my heart is empty.

My soul? Completely gone.

The phone behind me rings again, but I don't go to pick it up. I picked it up once, knowing it was my mom. She said they're on their way. Driving, they say. No planes. No airports. Everything is shut down. No way to get here. Nothing to do.

Just wait.

Wait.

Wait.

Wait.

I stare at the TV, watching as volunteers pick through rubble, like it's a game almost. Who can find the first dead body.

No one can. There isn't much to find, besides char, char, and more char.

The reporters on the TV cry, because there is no other emotion to have. Their red-rimmed eyes are filled with tears as they watch the horror only become more horrifying by the day. The death toll rises, the missing remain missing, the dead remain dead.

What used to be a beautiful city is now the city of ashes. Burnt to the ground in a horrible tragedy that will surely live on for the rest of time. It's all anyone talks about. There is no TV anymore. It's only news stations reporting our disaster.

Our little group at the shop was brought to the hospital, and after an all clear I was brought home. By who? I don't know. What time or day? No clue. I don't know much of anything, besides the fact that I'm here and showered. I don't know when I last ate. I don't know how long it's been since I've slept.

I don't even know how many days it's been.

All I know is that he's gone. Nothing, not even our love, will bring him back this time.

I feel it in the depths of my soul.

Roman is gone.

Swept away like he was never here in the first place.

Except he was, because the imprint on my soul is so much deeper than anything else in the world could ever be.

Roman is everything, and now he's nothing.

I blink, and blink, and blink, staring at the TV for I'm not sure how long. Watching the same stories on repeat.

War.

Tragedy.

Death.

So. Much. Death.

Thousands.

I wish I could reach into my chest and rip out my heart, tossing it into the rubble with everything else. What do I need it for now?

What is the point?

Knock, knock.

I ignore it, much like I ignore everything else. People come by, checking up on us. Everyone checks up on everyone, suddenly close-knit even though I barely spoke to anyone before. I don't want to talk.

I don't want to breathe.

Knock, knock.

"Luna!" My mom's terrified voice rings from the other side of the door, and my entire body deflates. With relief, with grief.

So much grief.

"Luna! It's Mom!" She screams, pounding on the door as if she could knock it down with her bare hands. She couldn't, but then again, maybe she could.

I get up from the couch, my body feeling stiff, numb, not my own as I walk to the door and unlock the hinge. Before I can set my hand on the handle, it's shoved open, and there she is, pulling me into her warmth. A gathering of people barrels into the door, sweeping me into their arms and checking me head to toe.

I'm fine.

I'm fine.

I'm so not fine.

I haven't cried since that little shop. Since the moment I couldn't feel him anymore, my tears dried up. It's like no tears exist in my body anymore. Not one.

I can't tell who's around me, but I can tell either way. I can smell my parents' familiar scents. I can sense Roman's parents, huddling around me, crying in grief.

So much grief.

I can feel the grief in the tips of my fingers, all the way to my toes. The sound of constantly being underwater. The sensation of constantly living in slow motion. It's like I'm living out of my body, watching myself go through the motions. Not able to stop or dictate anything. I just watch myself, hovering over my defeated form. I stare at myself withering away.

They watch the news. They talk. They attempt to get me to eat. So many things happen, but all I do is stare at the screen. Wishing this was all a dream.

But knowing it's not.

It's not until my mom bends down, forcing my gaze to hers. She stares at me, tears in her eyes. "Honey, I think it's time you come home."

Home.

Where is home?

Isn't home wherever Roman Hall is?

Maybe home is nowhere at all.

I nod my head anyway. "Let's go home."

CHAPTER THIRTY-SIX

Luna

My heart sits in my throat as I stare at the empty casket in front of me. Everyone cries. Everyone wears black. Everyone weeps and moans and gives me their condolences.

Everyone is *sorry for my loss*.

I don't look away from the oak-colored casket, with flowers upon flowers loaded on the center.

It's empty, does anyone know that?

"How are you doing?" My mother comes up behind me, this being the first I've ever seen her wear black in her entire life. She wraps her arms around my waist, and oddly, all I want to do is curl away from her embrace.

I don't want touch. I don't want anything if it doesn't have to do with Roman.

I shrug, feeling empty.

"If you need a break, you just let me know and we'll get out of here for a bit."

I nod, blinking at the casket.

People give me space, a wide berth around the wooden box. As if we're in our own little bubble. No one dares come within this space, I guess except for my mom.

September has turned into November. Our small apartment has been packed up in New York, and I'm once again living in my childhood bedroom at my parents' house.

Julliard is on pause.

After hearing about what happened, they gave me a leave of absence and told me that I could take my time, although the sad tone in their voices over the phone as they told me this made me think they knew exactly what the end outcome would be.

I'm never stepping foot back in New York. Never again.

It took a month for them to dig Roman's body out of the rubble, and what they did find of him and his crew was absolutely horrific. Roman's parents had to go identify the body, and the darkness in his mom's eyes since she got back from that viewing have been so haunting; I've barely been able to look her in the eye.

People walk past Roman's casket, bawling their eyes out as if they were his best friend. It makes me angry, seeing their balled-up tissues pressed to their faces. Their tearstained cheeks and their bloodshot eyes. Is their sorrow even real?

Maybe they feel real sorrow, and it's me that has the problem.

I still can't cry. My eyes are almost too dry, burning and scratching with every blink I take. My hands feel numb, my toes and fingers constantly in a state of cold. I can't sleep, my dreams a nightly occurrence of my cliff and fire, like they combined together in a never-ending nightmare. Every night, I go to sleep knowing where I'm heading, and I wake up in a horrified sweat.

Yet so incredibly exhausted.

My body weeps for sleep, but my mind continues to stay in this state of numbness that no amount of thawing will get me out from.

"Luna." I turn around, seeing Lonnie, Clyde, and Flynn standing behind me. They're all in their black suits, their hands tucked into their pockets and their shoulders slouched forward. A weariness and hopelessness lays in their eyes, and I so badly wish I had it in me to go comfort each one of them, let them know how much Roman loved them.

But I can't.

"Hi," I whisper, turning back toward the casket.

I hear footsteps, and a hand lays on my shoulder. I close my eyes in a flinch as Lonnie speaks in my ear, "I'm so sorry, Luna. Roman was unlike anyone else in this world. He loved you so much. I've never seen anything like it in my life. Your love was fucking true. It was pure. So damn real." His voice chokes up, and he clears his throat. "I've known him my entire life, and he changed when he met you. I know him, and he's going to be waiting at those fucking gates in the clouds, just waiting for the day you walk through to him."

My eyes burn, but no tears come. I imagine him, waiting. Waiting for years. Watching me live. Watching me grow old. All the while he stands there, his elbows on the clouds as he stands there all alone.

"Luna, I wanted to give you this." Clyde hands me a beat-up notebook, worn around the edges. The spine is broken, bent, and well-used. "This was our song book, but Roman used it mostly. I thought you'd like to have it." He smiles at me, a pool of liquid wobbling at the bottom of his lids. I look away, taking the notebook and smooshing it against my chest. Burrowing it against my heart that doesn't know how to beat anymore.

My black dress is soft against my skin, a light, flowing piece that ends at my knees. It feels like death on my skin, though. Just another reminder of what I've lost.

And I've lost everything.

"Thanks," I mumble, suddenly eager for his words. His handwriting. I turn around, walking away as I search for my mom.

"Where are you going?" Lonnie asks.

I look at the casket, knowing I have a while before they bring the empty box to the cemetery. Whatever remained of him was cremated. His parents gave me the urn, telling me they know he'd want to be with me.

It's back in my room, shoved underneath my bed. I don't know what to do. I barely know how to function.

"Roman isn't in that box," is all I say to the guys before I turn around and walk away, in search for my mom.

I see her by the front door talking to Goldie. Clutching the notebook against my chest, I walk up to her. She gets a concerned look on her face when she sees me. I haven't left the casket since we got here.

"Sweetie, what's wrong?"

"I'm going home for a while."

Her eyes widen. "What about the burial?"

My heart sinks. I don't want to go, but from the look in her eyes, she expects me there.

"I'll meet you there," I plead.

She stares at me, her eyes flitting across my face. Making sure I'm okay. Trying to read what I'm not telling her.

There is so much, Mom. So much.

"Do you need a ride?" she asks, looking over her shoulder for my dad. I lift my hand, bringing it to her arm. She flinches, looking back at me.

"I could use the fresh air."

Her face softens, a sad look covering her features. "Go ahead, we'll meet you at the cemetery in an hour."

I attempt to give her a smile, but I don't think one lifts my face.

Instead, I walk out, my flats soundless as I walk through the parking lot. So many cars, different sizes, colors, makes, models, prices. Our small town is busy this weekend. The famous rock star that lost his life during 9/11 isn't going to go unnoticed. Everyone heard. Hearts were broken all across the world.

Our sleepy town turned into a tourist attraction, and people flooded the doors of the church with such sorrow on their faces like they've lived here their entire lives.

They haven't. The truth is that no one knows him. No one except for me.

I walk through town, past my old dance studio. It's no longer a dance studio, but a bakery. I glance away without staring too long, my heart aching in the deepest areas of my chest. I smoosh the notebook further into my breasts, wishing this permanent pain would lessen over time, but I don't think that'll be the case. Over the days, the pain has only grown stronger.

There's a crisp breeze in the air, the weather inconsistent this time of year. We usually get a snowfall that melts right away. Then it snows again, and repeat. The chill in the air makes me feel like snow is on its way. The trees are stuffed with the most colorful leaves, from brown, to red, to orange. Some have fallen, their crunchiness tumbling across the streets with a light scratch.

I turn left, passing the park. It's empty, the swings blowing in the wind. There's a slight creak from the metal hinges. I glance away, my eyes burning with emotion. Every step I take is painful, my joints and muscles filled with an overwhelming amount of exhaustion. I brush the back of my hand against my face, and when I pull my hand back there's a streak of mascara on my skin.

My shoes crunch the leaves that have gathered to the sides of the streets, and my hands grip the notebook, my fingers pushing in between the pages.

What did you write to me, Roman?

It feels like he's close to me, with just this simple notebook. Something that he's touched. Written in. Something that he's hunched over, with pain in his heart and mind.

The cornfield is knocked down for the winter, and I can see over the hill, far out into the distance.

I make it to our houses, walking in between our yards and down the grass. My shoes kick the leaves, big piles gathered in our yards. What used to be well-manicured has turned into a mess these last few weeks. None of us have the ability or mindset to do something as simple as raking the leaves from the yard.

I head down to the lake, the stillness of the cold air shocking it into place. Barely any waves crest the shore. Maybe the lake is in mourning, too. Maybe it knows the greatness that has left this world, and it has no energy to shake the waves to shore. Maybe it's numb, like me.

I head onto the dock behind Roman's house, the boards loose and creaky, but I still walk down the length, all the way to the edge. Crossing my legs, I sit down on the cool wood, the breeze chilly out here as it brushes my hair away from my face.

I press the notebook against my lap, running my fingers across the hard cover. There are so many scribbles in it, so many scratches and doodles. My fingers run across the guys' names, stopping as I hit Roman's. It's his handwriting. A little messy, slightly illegible. Like he doesn't have enough time to slow down for just a moment to pick up his pen until he gets to the next letter. No, everything is mashed together. He pushed the pen too hard, too, as his letters are indented into the cover. I trace each letter, his scrawl so familiar it fills my chest with pain.

My fingers curl behind the cover, and I lift it, my throat closing up as I see the guys' songs. Some of their popular ones, the ones that still play on the top hits on the radio. My nose burns, and I use the sleeve of my dress to wipe the run.

I fold the stiff pages, crinkling from being unused for so long, and my eyes start to water the further I get into the book.

The boys lied to me. At least a little.

Maybe this started as a music book.

But it's not how it ended.

The first few pages are filled with music. But the music turns into poems. Poems turn into letters. Some pages are just filled with my name.

I miss you, Luna. Come home to me.

I wipe my eyes, the first tears since that day rolling down my cheek.

I can feel you out there, Luna. Can you feel me? I'm in so much pain.

I know, baby. Me too.

I don't know how to keep going without you. Where are you?

I'm here.

Luna,

I love you. I never should have left for California. Without you, none of this means anything. How can I tell you this, though, when I don't even know where you are? I want to cross every state and city until I find you and beg for you back. Would you take me back? My heart aches every fucking day that I don't get to see you. That I don't get to hold you. Our love story can't be over, right?

Tell me our love story isn't over yet.

Roman

I sob, my fingers turning white around the notebook as I read his words. I see the pain in the way he scribbled the letters, a little harshly, the letters smeared across the page.

My eyes swallow every word, every syllable that's written on the pages. My fingers brush the pen marks, wishing they would pull away with ink. Wishing his words were fresh, that he would still be here with me. Only he's not, and the paper is dry, crackly, and stiff. There is nothing fresh about his words.

They are long gone.

My fingers move slower as I get to the back of the book, and my tears roll faster as I get to the last page. I close my eyes, taking a deep breath as I read the last letter he ever wrote.

Luna,

There are so many things I wish I could say to you. Wherever you are right now, I hope you're okay. I hope you're exploring the world, finding whatever it is you're looking for. Find it, Luna, and then come back to me.

I'll wait for you. I wait, watching the clock tick by, hoping for a glimpse of you in the crowds as I sing my music. Hoping I'll see your dark hair swaying to the beat of the music. Wishing it would be your pale fingers lifted in the air as I sing my broken-hearted songs to the world.

The moment I find you, Luna, I'm never letting you go.

I'm going to look into your gray eyes for the rest of my life. We're going to watch the stars every night, counting and naming each constellation. We're going to watch the moon glow, lighting up the night as we sink into the darkness together.

I'm going to wrap your feet in the ribbon of your slippers, perfecting them just as you taught me to all those years ago. I'm going to watch you dance. I'm going to watch you conquer the stage, making every eye in the crowd shed so many tears they'll sweep us away. I'm going to watch you twirl and leap into the air. Fuck, Luna, you get so tall on stage. The beauty in your dance is exquisite. Like nothing I've ever seen before. I dream of you dancing. Every single night, it's you, with your pointed feet, and your beautiful spine as you make the most delicate moves I've ever seen.

I'll keep dreaming about you, until it's time for us to meet again. Because I know, Luna, that we will meet again.

Until then, I hope you think of me. Think of me as you travel and know that I'm thinking of you. And when you're feeling lonely, go to where I always promised I'd bring you. Go to where the water crashes against the dark walls of the cliff. To the place where the sand sweeps you off your feet. Where the salty air brushes the hair from your shoulders. Meet me there, Luna, and I'll be there waiting.

Meet me where I always promised I'd take you.

Meet me where the mountains meet the sea.

Yours. Always yours. Now and always.

Roman Hall

The notebook crumbles and smashes against my chest as I sob into the papers. The grief, the loss that I feel in every inch of my body makes me feel like I'm being pulled apart piece by piece. There isn't a shred of anything good left in me. I feel in ruins. Wrecked. Completely obliterated.

My face meets the cool wood of the dock as I roll over, until I'm crunched in a ball on the faded wood, the light color darkening beneath my face from my tears. Reaching into my bra, I pull out Roman's pick, the one I gave him so many years ago. I clutch it in my palm, wanting it to grant me all the wishes in the world, but knowing it'll do none of them.

I cry and sob, my screams echoing across the lake, across the dark waters of the cool afternoon. I cry until my arms are freezing, and a hand lays upon my shoulder. I can barely see through the tears as I look up at the sky, seeing my dad's sad face glancing down at me.

His face is one of pure torment, like my pain causes him pain. He bends down, picking me up off the deck. My hand snaps out, grabbing onto Roman's notebook and hitching it under my arm. I curl into my dad's arms, so sad. *So, so fucking sad.*

"I miss him so much, Daddy," I sob.

He presses his cheek into my hair, his own tears hitting my forehead. "We all miss him, Luna, but I can't imagine for a second what you must be going through."

"It feels like I'm dying," I cry.

He squeezes me tighter to him, like he can pull the pain from my body if he wishes hard enough. "I'll be with you every step of the way."

I burrow my face into his chest, wishing he could take it all away. Just for a second. Each breath is pained. So much pain.

"Let's go say goodbye to him, okay?" he mumbles into my hair.

I nod my head, wanting to tell him that there's no one to say goodbye to, because he's not there, but not having the energy at this point.

Meet me where I always promised I'd take you.

Meet me where the mountains meet the sea.

Closing my eyes, I take a breath, knowing exactly where I need to go.

CHAPTER THIRTY-SEVEN

Luna

I step out of the cab, the cool wind blowing in my face.

"Thank you," I tell the cabbie, handing him the folded-up bills in my hand.

He nods gratefully, and I grab my backpack, shutting the door behind me. I let out a breath, seeing a hint of my breath puff from my mouth. I look up at the mountains, shrugging the straps of my backpack over my shoulder.

The snow caps look so white. Only slightly whiter than my skin as they sit on top of the mountains.

I'm here.

Slightly north of Seattle, I only have one destination in mind.

Our spot.

I arrived in Seattle last night. It's been a week since Roman's funeral. I told my parents my plans. I told Roman's parents. With tears in their eyes, they all nodded. They understand. Even though I think a part of them doesn't understand.

I have to do this.

It's about a mile walk from the small city to the path, and from there it's about a thirty-minute hike up the cliff. The place where Roman proposed. I remember it as if it were just yesterday. How happy he was, the anticipation on his face.

The gentleness in his words. I should've known then. I know everything about him, but I was so sidetracked by the happiness on his face that I couldn't think of anything else. His happiness made me happy. We were two souls that were brought together again, and the only thing on our minds was being together. Enjoying every moment.

I walk through the small town, looking at the happy people. The couples, the families, the groups of friends. I pull the pick out of my pocket, holding the worn plastic between my fingers. Flipping it back and forth. I glance down at the faded letters, the *R & L* still engraved in the center.

I miss him.

"Whoa!" I get slammed back, a heavy, leather arm hitting my chest. I look up, seeing a group of men standing before me. Large, scary-looking biker men with leather vests on. My eyes widen, realizing I was about to walk straight into oncoming traffic. Cars whiz by, not a care in the world as they fly down the streets.

I didn't realize, didn't even hear them roaring by.

I glance at the blond man. "Thank you," I say, a little scared to be in his presence. He's tall, trim, but I can tell he's capable of doing things I can't even imagine.

We don't have guys like this in Wisconsin.

I glance behind me, seeing the guys walking back toward the bar. I see a line of motorcycles lined up outside, all shiny and black.

I swallow, slightly nervous to even be in their presence.

"You okay?" The man asks me. I take a look at his friendly face, his kind smile. Although, he looks a little concerned, maybe slightly on edge. He looks to be about my age, maybe a few years older. His blond hair is pulled into a ponytail at the base of his head. He's tall, too. Taller than Roman.

I nod.

He points at my face. "You sure? You're cryin'."

I bring my hand up to my face, wiping away the tears that I didn't even notice were there. "Oh, yeah. I'm okay." Embarrassment hits my cheeks, and I turn away from him. I'm sure I look like a wreck.

"What's your name?" he asks. Well, it kind of sounds like an order coming from his tongue.

"Luna," I whisper, gripping the pick between my fingers until my fingers go cold.

He glances down at it, concern lining his forehead. "You sure you're all right, Luna? Need me to take you somewhere?"

I shake my head. "I'm just going on a walk." Which, maybe I shouldn't have told him, since I don't know if he's a serial killer or not.

He puts up a finger, walking toward his bike. I stand where I am, on the corner of the cold street with my backpack on my back.

With my fiancé's ashes inside.

He comes back with a pen between his fingers. Without even asking, he grabs my hand, yanking it toward him. Not even a slight hesitation about how I feel about it. He writes on the inside of my wrist, the dark pen slashing across my pale skin. "Here's my phone number. If you're ever in any trouble, give me a call. Even if you aren't in trouble, give me a call." He frowns at his words, like he's unsure why he said them.

I glance down at the phone number and the scratchy scrawl next to it. "Lynx," I mumble to myself.

He nods. "That's me. I hope to see you around, Luna."

I nod, watching him turn around and walk back to his friends. He gives me a small wave, and I give him one back.

Turning back around, I hit the crosswalk button this time, waiting for the miniature person to glow green on the other side of the street.

Once it does, I head across, making my way toward the hidden path.

It takes a while, and my cheeks feel raw, and my fingers are numb, Roman's pick hot against my palm. But finally, I get to the top. The gravel crunching beneath my shoes as I walk. No other sounds. It's silent, as if the world around me is giving me the peace and quiet I need.

I set the backpack down once I get to the clearing, seeing the ocean dance rapidly before me. In the fall air, the water looks darker. The waves harsher. Unzipping my jacket, I set it on the ground and pull out the heavy urn. The black and gold swirl together in beautiful designs. It's heavy in my arms, and maybe that's because Roman took my heart with him, too.

Meet me where the mountains meet the sea.

A tear falls down my cheeks, blowing in the wind as I walk toward the edge. My jaw trembles, my lips quaking as I open the lid.

I love you, Roman.

The white tips of the wave bob and weave in the water. My hair blows back, swaying in the wind as I tip the urn. The chalky sand slides from the black inside, falling into the air, swirling into the wind. Every bit of Roman hits the sky, floating in a beautiful dusting as he falls toward the ocean. Bits of him blow toward me, the wind too strong to carry him over the edge, he hits my skin, wrapping around my ankles and wrists.

I feel him.

I close my eyes, my soul warming as I feel him with me. Tears fall down my face, blowing off my cheeks and into the world. I bend over, setting the urn down. Standing back up, my heart thumps, calming, racing, feeling at peace as Roman blows to the place he always promised me.

Meet me where the mountains meet the sea.

I'm here.

A cry breaks from my throat, bursting into the air and echoing into the ocean. The sand leaves my body, the rest of Roman blowing off into the wind.

Meet me where the mountains meet the sea.

He's here. He's with me.

I close my eyes, clutching the pick in my hands and raise my arms into the air. I listen to the wind whistle, and I swear, I can hear Roman's low timbre whispering within the wind.

And I *fall.*

EPILOGUE

Luna

My eyes open.

Glancing down, I see I'm wearing my pink leotard and white tutu. *Canon in D* plays softly through the speakers, and looking up, I can't see where the sound is coming from. I'm on a stage, though, from what I can tell.

Turning around, I see a stage full of people.

Every seat filled with anticipated faces, happy, free, with gentle smiles covering their lips.

I do the only thing I know how to do. *I dance.*

I let the music fill me up, bursting from my limbs and my bones as I float across the stage. It overtakes me, swallowing me and lifting me into the air, stretching me from one side to the other. My pointed shoes are perfectly laced. Better than I've ever done. I know there's only one person who could have laced them this perfectly.

Tears flood my eyes.

I go up on my toes, stretching my legs and bending my body to every strong note and tune. Tears flood down my cheeks as fast as my body whips across the stage. I dance like I've never danced before. I move as if I'm filled with magic, leaping higher, spinning faster, bending easier.

I just *dance*.

By the time the music comes to a close, I'm smiling, happiness beaming across my face. I've never felt more alive, more free in my dance.

The crowd cheers, the entire stadium of bodies clapping their hands and cheering as loud as they can. They're all standing, and I can barely make out one person in the crowd. It's dark, the only light shining over me.

I walk to the edge of the stage, giving a little bow just as a light beams into the crowd, front and center. I step closer, my toes hanging off the sides, and squint my eyes in an attempt to see who it is.

He claps, his hands lowering. A broad smile overtakes his face, tears in his eyes as he watches me.

Tears fall down my face, my hands going to my mouth as I realize who it is.

"Roman."

THE

end

My heart goes out to all the first responders, citizens, victims, and families who have been affected by 9/11.

AUTHOR'S NOTE

Years ago, one of my best friends told me she was going out to Hawaii to work on a farm and live for free. I was shocked, but happy for whatever she wanted to do. She's been through her own struggles and heartbreak.

I didn't speak with her much on her travels, but I saw pictures of her in Arizona with a guy. They were traveling, hiking, exploring. Living the dream. She looked happy, and she was making the most *beautiful* dream catchers. I wanted every single one of them, even though she was across the country.

Me and my family eventually had a road trip out to California. Well, at that time my friend was already there. She was living on a beach in San Diego. I remember visiting her, driving with my husband and child down to the beach to pick her up. She was tan, with tattered beach clothes and a carefree look on her face.

Our visit was short-lived, and my friend eventually made her way to Hawaii. Life for her didn't turn out how she'd hoped, and after a tragic phone call to me one day, I was on my way to pick her up from the airport.

She came home a dark person, but she eventually healed. She persevered, and I couldn't be more happy or proud of her.

I always knew I'd want to tell her story in one way or another, and I ended up combining two story lines I've had in my mind into one. When I told my friend about my thoughts, she told me the real stories of her adventures.

She spoke of the wild horses, the hot desert air, the dried-up canals in Arizona. She told me about a time when she became so dehydrated that she started hallucinating. Close to death, I'd imagine.

She told me about meeting up with the Deadheads and going to a Rainbow Circle in California. How cool and nice they were, but how they lived in their own world and have puddled people. She saw a guy she used to know who was puddled. He was gone mentally. Forever, they said.

She told me about her time in Hawaii, and how the avocados were as large as her head, and the centipedes were huge, and how she would go to the other side of the world and party with the locals, but they actually hated tourists.

I'm grateful I was given the opportunity to tell this beautiful story. I hope you all enjoy it and can see the beauty within tragedy.

ACKNOWLEDGEMENTS

I don't really know where to start with this.

I wanted to thank H. Because I love you more than I can ever imagine. You are my best friend and the pieces of your stories that you gave me to complete this book were necessary, and I couldn't have written this book without you.

I wanted to thank my ARC readers. It's nerve wrecking to put my baby into your hands first, and it means a lot to me that you take time to read and review for me. Every. Single. Time.

Rumi. You are everything. Thank you for always diving into my books and trusting my words. You give me your opinions and always make me feel more comfortable with my work.

Kenzi. Thank you for all that you do. I'm so glad to be working with you, and you are literally one of the sweetest people I've ever met. I'm so happy I met you.

Savannah. You are literally the best PA in the world, but more than that, I consider you such a good friend. I know I'm a pain sometimes, but you stick with me, and I'm so grateful to you.

Cat. You are such a huge part of my team. Thank you for helping me. Your formatting is impeccable. You bring my stories to an entirely different level. Thank you, babe.

Rachel. You have helped me since the beginning days of being an author, and you mean so damn much to me. Thank you for always reading my books – even if they aren't your typical genre. You are my go-to for just about everything. I love you.

Brittany. One of my early readers. You've been reading my books and loving my stories since the beginning. I love you.

To all my readers, I love you. Thank you for taking a chance on me. This book isn't my usual, but that you give me a chance means that world to me. I hope you enjoyed Roman and Luna as much as I did.

To my fellow authors. You make me a better writer, you give me encouragement when I need it, and you are always there when times get tough.

We are a strong community, and I respect and love every one of you.
To the people who have had the opportunity to meet their soul mate. Don't let go. Love is so special and so pure. Sometimes it isn't seamless, but that doesn't mean you should give up on it. Take it and hold on tight, because the truest of loves will be there in the end. Forever.

BOOKS BY A.R. BRECK

Grove High Series

Reapers and Roses

Thorn in the Dark

The Grove Series

The Mute and the Menace

Lost in the Silence

The Seven MC Series

Chaotic Wrath

Reckless Envy

Standalones

BLISS

ABOUT THE AUTHOR

A.R. Breck lives in Minnesota with her husband, two children and two dogs. She enjoys reading, writing and sharing her stories with the world. When she isn't working, A.R. Breck loves to watch horror movies, road trip around the country and read forbidden romance novels.

Follow me
Instagram: @ar.breck
Facebook: @ar.breck
Goodreads: @ar.breck
Email: ar.breck@yahoo.com

Printed in Great Britain
by Amazon